To the memory of my brother
Francis Woodward

The author would like to thank the Royal Literary Fund for their support during the writing of this novel.

The rooms were – small rooms, each was occupied by only one enormous object: in the tiny bedroom the bed was the enormous object; in the tiny bathroom it was the bath; in the drawing-room it was the bluish alcove; in the dining room it was the table–cum–sideboard; in the maid's room the object was her maid; in her husband's room the object was, of course, her husband.

Andrei Bely, Petersburg

Part One

I

28 Polperro Gardens
Wood Green
London
N.22

March 30th 1974
Wednesday

Dear Janus

I am very sorry that I have not been able to see you, or even write to you before this. I have been rather ill – since Sunday afternoon, in fact. I've had a very bad cold combined with asthma and have hardly been able to breathe. After a visit to the doctor's on Tuesday morning I was given a great variety of pills etc and am now a little better. (Lobo is crawling over me.) (I'll have to stop for a moment as she now wants to go out.) Of course, not being at work, I am imprisoned here in this box impersonating a room (I hope I'm going to get paid from work as I'm skint). Still, I am hoping that I shall be able to come and see you on Friday. If I don't, I hope that you will write to me as soon after you receive this letter as possible. I shall look forward to it!

Of course, what with so many demons flying around forcing gentlemen such as us to take too many drinks and whoop too loud and too often and even more strange and ludicrous actions! And even the changing of names as the mad women of Tierrapaulita do (to change themselves) does not one bit of good – and the changing of Billbaorosta or Januscjeckarama to: violas one day or violets the next or even after a while cirfrusias, cifrernas,

3

tirrenas, mabrofordotas, frabicias, fabiolas, quitanias, pasquinas, shoposas, zozimas, zangoras and that's the end of the alphabet! (apart from the missing tenaquilas and pogaliras). So think not of changing, my friend, (name or anything) and be damned to devils! For happy are those who whoopeth too loud and delirious are those who ludicrous are!

Now I have heard it said that the natives in the Northern part of Windhover Hill (so far unexplored) speak of a most monstrous Red Lion, that lives in those parts, and its roars can be heard echoing about the eucalyptus and Banyan trees in the valley of the source of the Limpopo. To my mind it is in the national interest that an expedition to discover the Red Lion must be mounted but that it should be properly funded. Many pleas to the Royal Geographical society have been fruitless so far and others snatch away the mountains of the Shangri-las but to the valley of the Red Lion a path must soon be made, and it is we that shall make it.

I hope very much so that dear Scipplecat is well and happy and I hope that you will convey my best regards to the aforesaid furry creature. Lobo also sends her best wishes.

Now look after yourself JJ and take care till I see you again. I'm afraid coughing and spluttering I must bring this letter to its terrible and inevitable end.

Try not to drink too much till I see you.

You must save some money so that we can go a-boozing. (Lobo is sitting on my head, my nose is full of whiskers)

I think the drink is getting the better of this letter

PAX Vobiscum

Lobo says goodbye for now

also adios from myself

Bill

Janus didn't usually leave his letters from Bill lying around, but this one had been left on the kitchen table, out of its envelope, half-unfolded, beside the glass cider tankard that held a posy of wilting daffodils, in a way that suggested, to Colette at least, that she was being invited, along with anyone else in the house, to read it.

And so she had read it, alone in the kitchen, waiting for Aldous to return after a morning at school to get ready for the funeral that afternoon. It was written in a painstakingly rendered Gothic script using a broad, italic nib and illustrated with exquisite marginal drawings. It was like a drunkard's version of the Book of Kells. The 'D' of 'Dear Janus' had been drawn as a D-shaped pub, with a little chimney, creeping ivy and an inn-sign hanging (she even recognised the decapitated Elizabethan on the sign as *The Quiet Woman*). The remainder of the word had been supplemented by a punning human ear, painted in such pure, Renaissance detail it could have been lifted from a Botticelli portrait. All around the margins of the letter were pen and ink drawings of almost-empty bottles and glasses, some tipped over and spilling the last of their contents, but again drawn beautifully. By the end of the letter the calligraphy, so crisp and rigid at the beginning, had broken down into a scruffy, barely legible scrawl, though Bill's signature was accompanied by what looked like a woodcut, in blood-red ink, of a clenched fist.

Colette tried to imagine the time it must have taken to produce a letter like this, picturing her son-in-law sitting at the little writing desk she'd seen in his and Juliette's bedroom, that was a small forest of pens and brushes, bottles of ink, little wrinkled tubes of watercolour, boxes of nibs. It must have taken him several evenings. An act of devotion. Colette found the sheer effort Bill had put into this letter to her son rather touching. At least someone in the world loved him.

By the time Aldous had come home, fresh and fluffy from cycling, Colette had long finished reading the letter, but she pretended to be reading it for the first time as he came in, to make it easier for her to show it to him.

But Aldous only gave the letter a cursory glance, reading the first few lines, and admiring Bill's graphic skills, giving a half-hearted, rather hopeless laugh at the D-shaped pub, before handing the letter back to his wife.

'What a load of rubbish,' he sighed, strolling towards the sink to fill a small saucepan with water. Colette felt briefly annoyed by her husband's indifference. He might not like the way his son had been behaving recently, the drunken tantrums, the wanton neglect of his talents as a pianist, but he could at least be interested in him. For the sake of the funeral they were to attend that day, however, she decided to be on his side.

'At least he won't be around to spoil things today,' she said, folding the letter, wondering if she should replace it on the table as though it had never been touched, then realising her son could hardly expect her to have ignored it for a whole day, 'thank Christ he went to work.'

'I wouldn't put it past him to turn up out of the blue,' said Aldous, lighting a ring beneath the pan he'd just filled, 'you know how he gets if he thinks there's a chance of free drink.'

They both recalled Christine's wedding, a couple of years before – the trampled-on wedding cake, the shattered bouquets, the drenched, sobbing bridesmaids.

'He won't,' said Colette, 'he doesn't even know the funeral's today.'

Aldous gave his wife a withering look, meaning to say you could never be sure what Janus knew and what he didn't.

'So it will be just you and me representing the Jones family,' Colette said, 'I hope there aren't lots of our nephews and nieces there, it'll make our children look so mean . . .'

The funeral of Mary, the wife of Colette's favourite brother, Janus Brian, was not thought worthy of James breaking his second term as an anthropology student at the University of Lincoln, nor of Juliette losing a day's pay at Eve St John's Toy Emporium, nor even of Julian, their youngest, missing out on double geography and P.E. at St Francis Xavier's. Of all their children Janus would have been the one most likely to have taken a day off work, had he known about it.

Aldous took a small package of newspaper from his jacket pocket, untwisted it, and tipped the contents into a mug. He hadn't had a chance to use it at school, the instant coffee powder he always packed at the last minute before leaving the house for work, tearing off a corner of the *Telegraph* and spooning on some Maxwell House, folding the paper over in a neat, airtight package, the clever origami of which always delighted his wife when she saw it. He emptied the bubbling saucepan into the mug. They hadn't had a kettle for years. The little, lidless, gaudily enamelled pots that came to a boil with a gradually strengthening wail of despair, always seemed to boil dry, thus melting the cheap alloys of their bases. So they only used pans now.

'Do you think I should wear a black tie?' said Aldous, sipping cautiously the black, sugarless coffee.

Colette sat down in her chair by the old cast iron boiler and opened a bottle of Gold Label barley wine with the bottle-opening end of a tin opener.

'Have you got a black tie?'

'No.'

'Then the question was academic, was it?'

'I suppose I could buy one on the way. You know what Janus Brian's like. How fussy he is about formalities like that . . .'

That their eldest son, and Colette's closest brother shared the same name, had never once been a source of confusion in their lives. At least, not once they'd started using her brother's middle name in addition to his first, to help distinguish him. Now he was always referred to by these two names – Janus Brian – even when there was no doubt about to whom the name Janus referred, even, sometimes, to his face – *Hello Janus Brian, how are you?* And Janus Brian didn't seem to mind. It was, after all, a permanent reminder of the compliment his sister had paid him in naming her first-born after him.

'I don't think he'd mind about a thing like that,' said Colette, 'I'm not wearing any black.'

'Women can get away with it,' said Aldous, 'men are different. They read things into ties, especially men like Janus Brian.'

Colette poured the Gold Label into a glass, where it fizzed half-heartedly, her second of the day. Colette had taken to this tipple recently, initially as a sedative, to reinforce the ever-weakening effect of her sleeping pills. She would drink two or three glasses in the evening, then take four or five Nembutals (the recommended dose was two), which would despatch her to a deep, dreamless sleep for eight hours. The problem was that awakening was a long, slow painful struggle. She woke as if from a pit of glue, always with a pounding headache and sensations of nausea, the only cure for which, she soon found, was a morning glass of barley wine. One of those and she was near instantly awake and fresh. A sedative in the evening, a pick-me-up in the morning. Barley wine was her wonder-drink.

Aldous looked at himself in the little mirror that was fixed to the wall by the back door. His tie was pale blue. His shirt a dark grey, fraying at the collar. A jacket of light tweed. His teaching clothes. He hadn't thought about it before, but it now struck him that he couldn't possibly go to a funeral in his teaching clothes. Standards of dress among the pupils at the school Aldous had taught at for nearly three decades had declined rapidly in the last few years, a wave of slightly bashful permissiveness had allowed hair to creep over collars, ties to be worn loosely, top buttons to be left undone, and shoes of the ridiculously elevated kind to be worn, the effect being to give Aldous a distorted sense of his own sartorial smartness. Against the haystack slovenliness of his pupils he had appeared dapperly elegant, but here, in the mirror, he could see how inappropriate his clothes would be for a funeral. He needed a decent tie, at least.

'I think I will get a new tie,' he said to Colette, who was dressed in the pink pullover with white trimmings she had knitted years ago for Juliette, to which she'd pinned one of her mother's old fake ruby brooches. She had dark blue trousers, green sandals, 'I'll call at Houseman's on the way.'

Houseman's was a gentleman's outfitters on the Parade. In the days when Aldous and Colette had had some money Aldous had bought all his clothes from there, though as money had become increasingly scarce, his visits had become less frequent, until he only ever went there now for underwear, making do with jackets, shirts and trousers from the Oxfam shop that had recently opened near The Red Lion.

'If you must,' said Colette, 'though it'll be a waste of time and money.'

Though secretly she was glad of the distraction and delay a detour to Houseman's would take, since she was dreading the funeral. Or at least, she was dreading the actual interment, the lowering of the coffin into the grave. Janus Brian had chosen a spot for his wife in Ladore Lane Cemetery just across the path from where their mother and their sister Meg were buried. Colette found visiting these graves a painful experience at the best of times, that their deaths, both from natural causes (old age and a heart attack), had come so close together (Nana first, then Meg) had been a source of anguish in Colette's life. To be there for another funeral, to witness the lowering of a coffin when it had troubled her so much before (so deep, so dreadfully deep) might, she feared, prove too much for her to bear. On the other hand, she was looking forward to the little gathering that was to take place at Janus Brian's house afterwards, a meeting of sisters and brothers, brothers and sons, wives and daughters. It was so rare for them all to be gathered in a single place, especially with Janus Brian, who had become very reclusive in recent years. Though he lived only a mile away from Colette, visits to his house in Leicester Avenue, a cul-de-sac of pebbledashed semis, were often coldly received, and rarely reciprocated. In fact, he only ever visited Colette to announce one thing – the imminence of his own death.

'Nothing funny about it dear. This is it,' he said once when Colette opened the front door to see him standing on the step in his work clothes (a dark suit with a narrow black tie), 'my number's up. Will you get off the floor?' Colette had got down on her knees in mock worship at her brother's feet.

It had happened several times, usually as a result of reading some health article or other, that Janus Brian would discover symptoms in himself of a fatal disease. Now she couldn't even remember what it had been. An innocent pimple, wart, or pedunculated polyp. A benign confusion of cells. A temporary thinning of the blood. As with most hypochondriacs, however, Janus Brian remained annoyingly free of real illness.

Then, only last week, he'd called at the house in his dark suit and Colette had poured ironic gratitude on his presence, unrolling an invisible red carpet, forming a solo guard of honour, kissing him on both cheeks like a Russian at a superpower summit, before she noticed how Janus Brian's countenance had fallen. His face was a game of Kerplunk and someone had just extracted the crucial straw sending all the marbles tumbling. Colette thought that perhaps death really was coming for him now, after a dozen false alarms. But it was not his own death that Janus Brian had come to announce – it was that of his wife.

Colette had always felt responsible, in some way, for the marriage of Janus Brian and Mary Moore. The Waugh children – Lesley, Agatha, Meg and Colette – had all married within a few years of each other, in a post-war nuptial frenzy. Colette didn't want to see her favourite brother left out, sensing that he desired husbandhood while feigning indifference to women. She fixed him up with numerous blind dates, always keeping an ear to the ground for marriage-hungry spinsters, inviting Janus along for evenings in the pub with eager single women. Janus was not spectacularly good looking; tall, bespectacled, balding, thin-lipped and with too much chin, in some people's eyes he was rather plain, if not ugly. But there was an air of dishevelled elegance about him, a look of casual distinction that some women found attractive. Over the years Colette had rooted out plenty of females willing to wed her brother, but for a man she supposed mostly uninterested in women, he proved surprisingly fussy in his preferences.

'She was a charming young girl, dear,' he would say the following morning, 'really charming, but, you know, I felt that she had rather a tall forehead, and it seemed to come forward slightly, and then go in again,' he described the shape with his hand, 'do you know what I mean?' 'No. I thought she was beautiful.' 'She was, in her way. It was just that her forehead was the wrong shape.' Another time, she recalled, it was the eyes that put Janus off. 'They were *grave* eyes,' he said, selecting the adjective carefully and with much thought. 'What do you mean?' 'I don't know how else to put it. She just had . . . *grave* eyes.' Then there was a girl he described as having a 'wet mouth'. 'It's when someone makes slippery, sticky noises with their mouth while they talk. It drives you mad. I could never marry a girl with a wet mouth.'

How many would-be wives had Colette procured over the years? Ten? A dozen? And then he goes and picks the most unlikeliest of mates from under her nose; Mary Moore, sister of Reg Moore, Janus Brian's oldest friend, and one time admirer of Colette.

'Janus never wanted that sort of wife,' Aldous had said, many years later, 'He always wanted a glamour-puss for a wife. A dolly-bird. A long-legged, high-bosomed blonde.' It had not occurred to Colette that her brother was much of a connoisseur of female beauty – pernickety over minor anatomical details like the height of the forehead, yes, but not the sort of man to be drawn to the brazen sirens that filled his sizeable archive of Silver Screen and Movie Goer.

'How do you know?' said Colette, indignant that Aldous should claim to know her brother better than her.

'Can't you see how he fancies himself? He thinks he's some sort of suave film star. A Cary Grant . . .' Colette burst into a sniggering laugh at the idea, '. . . or an Errol Flynn. He's always been like that. A narcissist.'

Mary was not a beautiful woman. She was small and stout with dark, curly hair always cut at a sensible, practical length. Her eyes were those of a mouse – small, black and attentive while her little mouth was crowded with what looked like milk teeth, only just showing above the gums, too much of which were exposed when she laughed.

Then there was the oddness of her movements, the way she would suddenly clench her nose, as though stifling a sneeze, or a laugh. The strange, wine-taster's lip-poutings she gave, or the whole-face grimaces, produced for no reason, that came from nowhere.

Also, she was sterile.

Colette often wondered what sort of father her brother would have been, what sort of sons he would have had, what daughters. She liked to think he would have been a good father to his own children, because he was very awkward with his nephews and nieces. She remembered allowing him to hold his namesake Janus when he was a few days old, and Janus Brian had held the baby away from him, as though it might be covered in sharp spines, or that it might explode.

Once, when James was a little boy, Colette was washing his feet, which she did, as she'd always done, by sitting her son in a chair and kneeling down with a plastic washing up bowl full of soapy water. Janus Brian was in the house and witnessed the scene – mother kneeling before her son, washing his feet.

'What are you doing, worshipping that kid?' he muttered with a half laugh.

Children never came to Janus Brian and Mary. Somehow, it seemed to Colette, childlessness shaped their lives, gave it its character, its distinctiveness. How could they bear it, she wondered, to know that that was it? That their marriage was just that – two people – and would never be anything else, robbed of the phases growing children give to a family. How could they contemplate old age, tottering together along a lonely path into darkness, with no one to leave their house to but strangers?

When they finally abandoned, after years of tentative efforts, any idea of having children, Janus and Mary somehow raised a drawbridge against their possibility. Janus settled into his career as a draughtsman, producing blueprints for power stations. The concern with precision and accuracy that this job entailed seemed to spill over into his domestic life. Their house became a domain of meticulous order with always freshly hoovered floors, unstained upholstery, dusted ornaments that never moved, intricate and expensive crystalware that could sit safely at the edge of a table. Nothing in Janus Brian's house was ever broken. Their crockery was of complete and unchipped sets that were changed only when the pattern began to fade.

And then there was his garden, a steeply sloping series of terraces rising from a lush patio, passing through alpines, colourfully laden gazebos, little scalloped lawns, eventually flattening out to a kitchen garden where vegetables grew in straight lines. He and Mary had put everything into their garden. It was not a garden designed with children in mind. Janus and Mary's house and garden seemed to Colette to have become a celebration of childlessness.

She had only ever had the briefest glimpses of the interior of their marriage, and it always felt chilly to her.

Often when she visited, Janus and Mary would be in their sitting room watching the television with a neutral, bland complacency in their postures as they slumped in reclining armchairs and leather sofas.

Is that all you ever do, she sometimes felt like saying, *sit there and watch TV?*

But instead she said 'You've got a colour television. I didn't know you had one of those. Why didn't you tell me?'

Her brother turned to her, drawing his face away from the screen with difficulty, before saying 'Dear, when you buy a colour television, you don't go running down the street shouting "I've got a colour television! I've got a colour television".'

Mary giggled and said 'Why not?' underlining her remark with a facial tic from her considerable repertoire. This was the nose-draw, where she stretched the philtrum of her upper lip, as if to loosen a dried bogey in her nostril.

Colette was fond of Mary, however. She found her witty and friendly. Unpretentious. Unsnobbish. These things set her apart from the other inhabitants of that well-to-do cul-de-sac, along with the fact that she was membership secretary for her local branch of the Labour Party, which didn't seem to prevent her from being a popular participant in many coffee mornings. She was good at getting along with people. So Colette was upset when Janus Brian told her of her death.

'She was watching the telly,' he said, trying so hard to speak calmly in the hall at Fernlight Avenue. He seemed, as always, reluctant to penetrate further into Colette's house than its hallway. 'Sat in the armchair with a mug of coffee and a saucer of digestives. Then she said "Oh dear", and put her head on her shoulder and closed her eyes and that was it. I thought she was just dozing off, not something she usually does, but then she let the coffee go, scalding hot all over her lap, and when she didn't flinch I realized she'd gone. I wondered how I could ever have thought she was just asleep. There's a special face we save for when we're dead, Dear, and that's the face she had . . .'

So Aldous and Colette drove to Houseman's for a black tie, and Colette took the opportunity of stocking up on cigarettes at Hudson's, the tobacco-reeking newsagents two shops down. Then a straightforward drive along Green Lanes to St Nicola's church, where there was already a sizeable crowd gathering. In his haste, Aldous had forgotten to actually don his tie, and so spent an awkward few moments crouched down in the depths of the Hillman's footwells knotting the black silk around his neck, and then at the service found he was the only person so dressed. Even Lesley, Colette's other brother and Aldous's oldest friend, had not thought it necessary to wear any black. In fact, he was wearing the sort of teaching clothes (the lifelong occupation from which he'd now retired) that Aldous had felt so uncomfortable in earlier. His wife, Madeleine, was dressed in a bottle-green two piece with a matching hat and veil.

Colette was surprised by the turnout, and by the number of people she didn't know. As far as she was aware, Janus Brian had only one friend, Reg Moore, but his wife must have been rather more sociable, because the church was teeming with women her age and who were, prior to the service, chatting to each other with the comfortable informality of long acquaintance.

Taking her place at the front of the church, alongside her brothers, and her sister Agatha, pleased to find herself standing next to Janus Brian, whose face was stiff with the effort of self-control, Colette caught her first glimpse of the coffin – four tall candles at each corner, a tasteful spray of lilies on its top, and though it contained a person who had only ever existed on the periphery of her life, Colette felt immediately the surge of unwanted tears behind her eyes. Memories of her mother's funeral, her sister's, which had taken place in the same church nearly ten years before, were made intensely real by the stench of varnish and incense, the hopelessness of flowers and prayers.

Colette had once been a regular churchgoer, the whole family spending Sunday morning among St Nicola's religious kitsch, it's half-hearted attempt to evoke the grandeur of the Gothic. Nowadays only Aldous continued this tradition, taking leisurely strolls there and back each Sunday morning, seeming to find in Holy Communion a much more ordered and comprehensible version of Sunday lunch than the one he usually experienced at home. Colette, however, now only visited St Nicola's for funerals, and her convent upbringing meant she could not escape a sense of guilt at her lapse, even more so when she flirted, as she sometimes did, with agnosticism, even outright atheism. Her sister Agatha had surprised her once by announcing, in the plain, casual tone so characteristic of her, that she was an agnostic. She seemed to find a satisfaction in the word, and smiled slyly, as if not expecting Colette to understand what it meant.

14

'So am I,' she had replied instantly, in a childish attempt to appear unshocked.

But entering a church was, for her, like walking into a theatre for a part she had been rehearsing all her life. The words came so easily, the *Our Father*, the *Hail Mary*. She knew them in Latin probably better than she knew them in English – *Ave Maria, gratia plena, Dominus tecum. Benedicta tu in mulieribus, et benedictus fructus ventris tui, Iesus* . . . The automatic genuflections, the bowing of the head, the whole choreography of the Catholic Mass was written into her memory so deeply she could never truly call herself an atheist without a fear of divine wrath, or the pursuit, at least, of the nuns who had terrorized her childhood.

So she, and her brothers and sister, stood, sat, knelt, sang and recited in unison throughout the service, and only at the De Profundis did she look up

Out of the depths I have cried unto thee, O Lord . . .

And felt the surge of tears again. The coffin now amid clouds wafted by respectful altar boys from their quietly rattling gilt censers, dripping with the holy water the priest had shaken over it with such vigour she had felt a few droplets reach her,

My soul waiteth for the Lord more than they that
watch for the morning

She found herself mouthing the words along with the elderly, rather bumbling German priest, who had given her sister-in-law a middle name she didn't possess, and could not, at that moment, have possibly declared herself an atheist. She stifled more tears, and heard behind her the wet noise of loose mucus being sniffed. She wanted to turn to see who else was crying. She sensed Janus Brian beside her, stoically firm, unyielding to emotion. He too, as far as she knew, liked to call himself an atheist. Far too scientifically and practically minded ever to be 'fooled' as he'd put it, by the mysteries of the faith.

Things got worse for Colette at the graveside. Still next to Janus Brian, their arms linked for mutual support, Colette didn't know where to focus her attention – the coffin in half-shadow beneath them? The greengrocer's fake grass draping the edge of the hole? The all-surrounding wall of mourners? In the end she had to close her eyes, and look at nothing but the after-images of light that drifted behind her eyelids. She felt herself drifting with them, a dangerous thing to do at a graveside. The priest's words were mostly lost in the breezy air, as meaningless as the bickering sparrows nearby. She wondered if she was going to faint. She had never fainted in her life, and yet she was always expecting to. She drifted further, and became conscious of her brother's arm restraining her. She was being gently tugged back from a brink.

Afterwards at Leicester Avenue (never could Janus Brian's house have contained so many people), Colette found a moment to thank her brother for not letting her fall.

'Oh,' said Janus Brian, 'I thought it was you that pulled me back.'

They laughed, and Colette would have liked to talk to her brother more, to find out how he was really feeling about the loss of his wife, to try and ascertain if they really had been in love for all those years alone together, to know what it was like to lose a spouse, and to have no children, but Janus Brian was the object of a long, commiserating queue which seemed to consist, mostly, of the primly dressed cohorts of Mary's suburban coffee mornings.

Instead she spent some time trying to recognize faces she hadn't seen for many years. It was difficult. She must have seen these nephews and nieces since they'd grown up, but somehow she still pictured them as children. The little boy she remembered spreading peanut butter over a record player was now a tall man with a beard, going bald on top. The red-faced girl she recalled tying her teddy bears to a chair with a skipping rope was now a serious looking woman with a drooping bust and bags under her eyes. Frequently she found herself addressing strangers with questions like 'Were you a friend of Mary's?' Only to have them reply 'No, I'm your nephew, Douglas, auntie Colette,' or something similar.

To her further astonishment, there was a new generation sprouting, still at the infant stage, but whose arrival had taken

Colette mostly unawares. If she thought back she could recall now and then little cards arriving at Fernlight Avenue announcing the birth of these children, which had hung around on the mantelpiece for a few months, sometimes with blurred, black and white photos of sleeping, squashed faces and the caption 'Hallo!', until they were lost in the thicket of bills and postcards that grew up around them. And now here they were, in the flesh, full of childish energy and language, addressing her, to her horror, as 'great-aunt'.

She found her sister Agatha and brother Lesley sitting silently on a sofa. Colette rarely saw these siblings now, since their emigration to opposite sides of High Wycombe, a Chiltern dormitory town famous for making chairs. Lesley had moved there because he'd always had a passion for the Chiltern landscape. Colette couldn't quite remember why Agatha had moved there, presumably following Lesley's example, though the two had never been particularly close. Agatha was the oldest, in her late sixties, happily widowed and retired. Lesley, second oldest, retired schoolmaster, had at one time been tutor and mentor of her husband, Aldous. Lesley had taken Aldous to his bosom when he'd been his teacher, encouraging him through art school in the years before the war, paying the fees himself. Lesley had treated him almost as a little brother, but their friendship had cooled once Aldous had turned himself into Lesley's little brother-in-law, by marrying Colette. He'd never been quite the same man since, Colette felt, at least not since his own marriage to Madeleine Singer shortly afterwards. Colette had taken an instant dislike to Madeleine, and always believed her brother had made the wrong choice in marrying her. She could see it in his eyes, in the haunted looks he gave her over the tea-table in their bookless house when they visited, of a man who has realised, just too late, that he has taken the wrong course through life. Colette viewed Madeleine as a philistine, a gossip and a snob who'd put an end to her brother's life of reading and high culture.

How she hated Madeleine. The perfect housewife. The perfect mother. How she hated hearing about their latest coach trip to 'Wordsworth Country' or 'Constable Country', her cultured brother dragged with the rest of the common herd through the plastic tearooms and trinket shops of the tourist trails. On his mantelpiece last time she'd visited she'd noticed a Brontë Calendar, a tiny reproduction of Branwell's portrait alongside a tear-off pad of days and months.

She hadn't said anything. She'd never said anything. She'd always bitten her tongue, telling herself that it wasn't worth getting upset about. In fact, she always seemed to find herself apologising to Lesley and Madeleine, usually for something her eldest son had done. The last time it had been Christine's wedding, the marriage of Lesley and Madeleine's oldest daughter to a bushy-faced teacher in Bournemouth. Janus had turned up drunk at the reception, having travelled down separately. He'd played the grand piano that had sat unused in a corner of the hall, but had produced nothing but trills and glissandos. He'd danced drunkenly with bridesmaids, lurching around so clumsily they would end up on the floor. He'd shaken up the bottles of champagne and had sent fizzy cascades into the shocked, walrus-moustached faces of the groom's older relatives. Colette and Aldous had made their escape quickly and had travelled back to London alone, leaving Janus to run amok in Bournemouth. A stupid thing for them to have done, but it had been Aldous's suggestion. 'If we go now Janus will probably be stuck down there for the weekend and we'll get some peace at home.'

They did get some peace. Janus was held in a Bournemouth police station for Saturday night and most of Sunday. Lesley had had to bail him out. The letters that came from High Wycombe shortly afterwards were carefully measured in their mixture of indignation and sympathy. *How dare you leave us to deal with Janus, but now we see what you have to put up with,* were their gist.

Colette was vaguely aware, as Madeleine walked over to her, holding an empty sherry glass in one hand and a jar of home-made blackberry jam in the other, that she hadn't yet apologized for that incident, to either Lesley or Madeleine. They hadn't met since, and Colette still had the letter of apology she composed and never posted, in her old needlework box, along with all the other unfinished, never-to-be-posted letters she had written over the years, most of which began '*Dear Madeleine, I won't beat about the bush, I think you are a cow . . .*'

'I'm so sorry, Madeleine, about Christine's wedding,' she said.

Madeleine affected great surprise.

'Sorry? Whatever for. It was a tremendous success.'

'Sorry about Janus and his antics that day.'

Madeleine closed her eyes and gently shook her head.

'Colette, if there is one thing that gives me a constant supply of energy and happiness as I grow older, it is the knowledge that my daughter that day married one of the finest men in Bournemouth. The memory of your son's self-debasement and humiliation has completely faded and died in the shadow of Christine's happiness, except of course, to give me concern for yourself and Aldous's poor plight in having to cope with him. Is he still as terrible as ever?'

'Aldous is fine,' said Colette.

'I meant Janus,' Madeleine laughed embarrassedly.

'Well, he still enjoys his drink, like we all do,' she looked down at Lesley, still sitting silently on the couch. He gave a polite, non-comprehending smile in return.

After an awkward pause Madeleine became aware of what she was holding. She held it out for Colette.

'Anyway, Colette, this is for you. The blackberries grow all along the alley at the end of the garden, so last summer I finally found the time to make some jam. I've got far more than we could ever use.'

Colette took the preserve.

'How nice,' she said.

The jam was one of those barbs that Madeleine was always firing at her, compliments, kindnesses, gifts, but each with an inward pointing hook that stuck and hung in the flesh until it festered. She had become very skilful at it. A neutral observer would never have known what blackberry jam meant to these two women – how Colette's garden was so overrun with blackberries they could have outdone Robertson's in the production of blackberry jam. How in the days when Lesley and Madeleine had been regular visitors to Fernlight Avenue Colette and Madeleine were always talking about the blackberries, Colette saying how she was going to make lots of jam that summer, Madeleine how she was looking forward to having some. But Colette never made their blackberries into jam. The children ate what they could off the bush, but there were too many even for them. The rest rotted on their stems. But now Madeleine was making the jam, and giving it to her. Madeleine may as well have stabbed Colette and written across her forehead *incapable wife and mother*, in blackberry jam.

But Colette took the jam thankfully, smilingly, knowing it would sit in the larder uneaten for months, even years, forgotten about among the relics of that cupboard, to be rediscovered one day, opened, and found do be an inch deep in fungus. Colette's family had never much taken to jam, or marmalade. She bought it occasionally, on a whim, thinking it to be a treat, and perhaps a quarter of the jar would get used, then it would go runny, and greasy with the butter that had carelessly got in, and then it would be forgotten about.

'Although I say it is unnecessary for you to apologize to me about Christine's wedding,' Madeleine went on, 'you might like to have a few words with Christine herself, I'm sure she'd appreciate it.'

'Christine's here?' said Colette, surprised.

'Over there,' said Madeleine, pointing across the room, where Colette could just glimpse between the crowds, a figure of a woman in deep purple, sitting on a coffee table, who looked nothing like the Christine she remembered from that summer in the late sixties when she had been a regular visitor to Fernlight Avenue, the summer during which her friendship with Janus had blossomed. Then she had been a girl – happy, pretty, willing to please. It felt as though that was the last time she had seen her, because at the wedding she was all veiled and tucked away in her silk. Now, having passed through the chrysalis stage of her wedding, it seemed, she had emerged as a mature woman, still pretty, in a soft, dreamy, dark sort of way, but serious, confident and rather sad.

Madeleine having retreated into the crowd, Colette made her way across the room in an awkward and slow zigzag towards Christine, preparing the long apologetic speech she had wanted to deliver for a long time, not just for the wedding, but for the awful way Janus had treated her before that, when their friendship had come to an end – hounding her with phone calls, writing her a long series of childish, haranguing letters, once abandoning her in the middle of London without any money.

But as she nears she feels a nervousness creep up on her. It was to do with Christine's beauty and confidence, two female qualities which always unsettled Colette, since she had always felt a distinct lack of both. She passed close by where Christine was sitting, noticing the man she was talking to, who had cropped hair and round wire glasses, in the Auschwitz-survivor style John Lennon had recently adopted. She then realized that this man was the same hirsute hippy Christine had married herself to in Bournemouth, only then he was mimicking John Lennon's long-hair phase. Feeling a sudden rush of panic as she neared the coffee table on which Christine was sitting, she felt unable to break into their conversation, and passed quickly by, as if having something important to attend to in the kitchen.

She would catch Christine later, she thought. She had always liked Christine, but had always feared she would grow into a woman like her mother. Having married that deranged-looking teacher had given Colette some hope, since she detected some disapproval in Madeleine, despite her long eulogy to her daughter's happiness.

The kitchen, too, was crowded with strangers. She made for the cool air of the garden, which was empty.

When the kids had been younger they'd loved visiting Janus Brian for his garden. He would always begin by giving them a formal tour, where they would stand patiently and a little nervously while their uncle named all the plants, usually in Latin, telling them when they'd been planted, when they were expected to flower, or fruit. Then, the tour over, the adults would retire indoors while the kids ran riot in the flower-beds and vegetable patches, destroying most of the plants whose names they'd already forgotten.

It was always with a loud sigh of relief that Janus Brian saw them off the premises in the evening.

The garden now was as perfect as she remembered it from those days, already colourful with spring flowers – daffodils and hyacinths sprouting on the rockeries, crocuses peeping through the little lawns. Colette climbed the crooked stone path that took her through the different levels of the garden, past the dainty oval lawn backed by ornamental firs and its rustic bench, through the wattle-made laburnum arch to another tiny lawn, then past a dwarf willow and the herb garden to the level area where there was a long lawn on one side, the vegetable patch on the other – canes and trellises, ranks of winter and spring vegetables, frames, a greenhouse, netting, a little shed. More food grew here than could possibly be consumed by wan, wispy Janus Brian. Odd that a man who grew such an abundance of wholesome food in his garden should always look so under-nourished.

Beyond the lawn and the vegetable patch, where the garden ended, was the garden's real treasure. Through the tall trees could be seen a railway cutting, and in it, the rails that carried the little silver trains of the Piccadilly Line above ground. They passed so frequently the kids had never had to wait long to watch them rattling past. Colette watched them now, through the trees, and tried to remember the childish thrill of trains. These trains weren't up to much, however, not to a woman who'd travelled on the Silver Streak and the Flying Scotsman, leaning dangerously out of the carriage windows to watch those magnificent locomotives as they'd taken the bends on their way to the north. They could hardly be called trains at all, and they always looked so weak and vulnerable above ground, these tube trains, like snails out of their shells.

'I thought I'd find you here.'

Colette jumped, then turned to see Janus Brian standing close behind her.

'Janus don't,' she said, a hand to her chest, 'you nearly gave me a . . .'

'Sorry. I just had to get out of that house. Mary's friends are driving me nuts. They keep saying how brave I am. If I was really brave I'd tell them all to shove off and leave me in peace.'

Colette laughed.

'I'm just remembering the times we used to come here when the children were young. With Nana, do you remember? The children loved it. Nana too. She was always very complimentary about your garden.'

Janus Brian, without altering the expression on his face, simply said, 'Nana was a dream, dear.'

'How can you say that, Janus Brian, about your own mother?'

It had upset her greatly when Janus Brian had first started

denying the existence of the past in this way. Whenever she had related some anecdote from their childhood, a fond memory she wanted to share – the time their floppy Airedale Barry fell into the river Lea or the time a drunk from The Flowerpot tried to turn the water in the pond on Clapton Common into wine, Janus Brian would wait politely for Colette to finish, and then say, always with that same dry tone of pity, 'Barry was a dream, dear. The water into wine was a dream. It was all a dream.'

Aldous knew how it upset her. She was often in tears as he drove her home along the winding suburban back roads.

'What did he mean – *Nana was a dream*?'

'I don't know. It's just his way of . . .'

'Way of what?'

'He doesn't like talking about the past.'

'Why doesn't he?'

'I don't know. Don't take any notice of him.'

'I don't like being told my whole life is a dream,' Colette held pink lavatory paper to her eyes, crimping it with tears, 'Nana wasn't a dream, she was real.'

'I know.'

'He'll say I'm a dream next. Is that what he thinks? Everything is a dream?'

'I don't know.'

Now, in her brother's garden, where she can almost see the ghost of her mother reaching up to sniff the lilacs, the delightful phantoms of her children tumbling in the flower beds, she feels a strong urge to question her brother.

'You don't really mean it, do you, when you say that? You don't really think Nana was a dream?'

'Do you remember those lines from that poem in *Alice in Wonderland*, how does it go –

> *Ever drifting down the stream,*
> *Lingering in the golden gleam,*
> *Life, what is it but a dream?*

'I never liked Carroll's serious poems. He could be very sentimental.'

'But true all the same. What is the past? Dreams and dust.

And not even much dust. Would you like some tomato sherry?'

For the first time Colette's attention is drawn to the objects in Janus Brian's hands. A wine bottle and a glass. He holds up the bottle for her inspection, it has a plain label bearing Janus Brian's cramped handwriting. *Tomato Sherry – 1972.*

'The coffee morning dragons have got through all the off-licence stuff, so I'm reduced to raiding my wine cellar. It's not proving too popular for some reason.'

He poured some into the empty sherry glass Colette had with her. She remembered now. Those little gifts she used to get at Christmas, or on departure from a visit – *Cucumber Wine, Cauliflower Champagne, Brussel Sprout Whisky.* That was where all the fruit and vegetables from this extensive kitchen garden went – into the fermentation bins of Janus Brian's home brewing kits. She took a sip of the tomato sherry and felt as though something had jumped out of the glass and punched her in the nose. Janus Brian's home-brew was always like that. Unbelievably potent, and sweet to the point of burning, though her tongue, these days seasoned by regular drinking of barley wines, was more able to cope with it, and she downed it quickly for a refill.

'You know, dear, all my life I have been scared of death, but since Mary died I have come to the conclusion that it is life that's the really frightening thing.'

They sat on a bench that looked as though it had been made by seven dwarves, and shared the bottle of sherry together. Janus went on, 'Religion is supposed to make us cope with death, but we need something to make life bearable . . .' He suddenly looked at the full glass in his hand, then drank thoughtfully. 'That's what I was thinking all the way through the service. Did you understand a word that priest was saying? He had a very strange accent . . .'

'He was German.'

'And I was thinking all the time that we should be praying for ourselves, not Mary. Mary's gone. It's the people left behind that are suffering . . .'

'She isn't gone, not really, stop saying that,' said Colette. She didn't like this line of thinking that her brother was so insistent on pushing, partly because she felt it was true. She was not there to mourn Mary, but to talk to Janus Brian, and as far as she could tell, Mary had been all but forgotten about already amongst the nattering mourners. Mary was the past, and she was rapidly being overwritten by the present.

'Oh I know you still believe in heaven and all that ghostly stuff. But I never have. Not even as a little boy. I could always see, even from infancy, that it didn't make sense. The same with Father Christmas, the tooth fairy. I always knew it was just a trick.'

Colette remembered the Christmas Eve when Janus Brian had rigged a little web of cotton across the fireplace, a mesh of barely visible black thread taped to the surround. He'd called it his Father Christmas trap. On Christmas morning, he took the fact that it hadn't been broken as conclusive proof that Father Christmas didn't exist.

'What *is* that you've got in your hand?'

Janus Brian uttered the last remark as though it was a question he'd been burning to ask.

'Oh, just some of Madeleine's jam. A little reminder of what a terrible mother I am,' she said.

In the house the absence of the pair went almost unnoticed. The coffee morning women in their dark frocks chatted mostly with each other. Aldous found himself trapped with someone from the local branch of the Labour Party where Mary had been a voluntary helper for many years, and had to endure a long panegyric to Mr Wilson '. . . he's no fool you know. He's a fellow of the Royal Society . . .' and after escaping several such encounters, found himself in a circle that included Lesley and Reg Moore, Janus Brian's oldest friend and Mary's brother.

'Bloody good stuff,' said Reg, hiccuping stupidly, 'Janus certainly knows how to make a good wine.'

As a regular visitor to the house, Reg knew where the wine was kept, and felt obliged to help himself for the sake of the guests whose glasses were beginning to run dry.

'It's not bad at all,' said Lesley, who disguised his avid consumption of the liquor as a connoisseur's interest in taste, continually twirling his glass, sniffing the bouquet, then downing it in one for another sample, 'fruity. Very fruity.'

'Got quite a kick as well, hasn't it?' said Reg.

Lesley shrugged and wagged his head, as if to say the 'kick' was not important.

'What do you think, Aldous? But Methodists don't drink alcohol, do they? Is that why you're on the orange juice?'

'You're not a Methodist are you, Rex?' said Lesley, downing another glass and looking at his old friend blearily.

'Of course I'm not a Methodist,' Aldous replied, charmed to hear the middle name no one but Lesley and Madeleine ever used.

'No, of course you're not,' said Lesley, relieved to have got it straight in his mind, 'you converted to marry my sister.'

'Ah, that was your first mistake,' said Reg, swaying. His lips were shiny, his speech beginning to slur, 'changing your religion for the sake of a woman . . . A man with any sense would have insisted the woman change to his religion, not the other way round. You should have told Colette she had to become a Methodist.'

'I don't think the Methodists are that fussy about who they marry. It's just the Catholics that make a fuss,' said Lesley, 'isn't that right, Rex?'

'I'm not sure.'

'I went to a Methodist wedding once,' said Reg, curling his nose, 'we had to toast the bride with raspberryade. Luckily I'd taken my hip flask.' He turned again to Aldous, 'I suppose old habits of abstemiousness die hard. Go on, have some of this . . .' he looked at the label of the bottle he was holding to remind himself, '*Gooseberry Sherry 1971*. A very good year, wasn't it Les? A bloody good year for gooseberries . . .' He reached out to fill Aldous's almost empty glass of orange juice, Aldous quickly pulled his glass out of reach.

'Come on,' said Reg, irritably, 'it's a funeral, for Christ's sake . . .'

Aldous, who'd never had much of a stomach for either alcohol or Reg, placed a hand over his glass.

'I can't drink in the afternoon,' he said, 'and anyway, I'm driving.'

'So am I,' said Reg, 'all the more reason. It's a well known fact that alcohol improves one's driving abilities. I drive much better when I'm drunk. I do everything better. It's what drink's for. Do you know there is not one society in the whole history of humankind that has not discovered some form of alcohol? It doesn't matter if they're running around with bones through their noses, they make sure they invent booze before they invent anything else. We do it instinctively, like spiders with their webs. Drunkenness is our natural state, sobriety is a modern invention.'

Just then a burst of jangling piano music filled the room. Colette had come in from the garden and had made straight for the upright piano, followed by Janus Brian.

'Colonel Bogey', 'Kitten on the Keys', 'Tico Tico'. The atmosphere of the gathering was lifted, there was even some dancing. When, with a lap full of ash from the cigarette that had burned away in her mouth, Colette finished her playing, she heard a warm, buzzing sort of voice close to her ear.

'I don't think that was the appropriate music for an occasion like this, do you? Are you specializing in ruining funerals now as well as weddings?'

Colette turned to see Madeleine walking away. It was almost as if she'd heard the words telepathically, since there seemed no evidence that Madeleine had actually spoken to her. Colette left the piano and spoke to Aldous who had left Reg and the others to join her.

'Did you hear what that cow said to me?' she said to Aldous. 'No.'

'The bitch. I'm going to tell her what I think of her. I'm going to give her a punch . . .'

'I'm going to punch Reg before too long, if he keeps going on about drink. Perhaps we should leave.'

Madeleine, she saw, was now trying to revive her daughter Christine, who, having consumed many sherries, had quietly and gently passed out and was lying flat on the sofa. Her John Lennon husband was fanning her with a magazine.

Colette giggled to herself.

'Yes. I feel like going now. I'm just going to get my bag.'

Her bag was in the kitchen, which was now empty, many of the mourners having drifted away. There was another handbag in the kitchen, resting on a small chair that was placed with its back to the wall, out of the way behind the door. Colette recognised it as Madeleine's. She quickly opened it to double check. It opened with the smooth turning of a gold catch, and gave a smell from its interior of new leather. She rummaged quickly among lipsticks and compacts, tweezers, nail-scissors, hairspray, hairbrush, headscarf, purse, until she found some corroboration. A pension book in the name of M. Waugh. Colette stifled another giggle. Madeleine was a pensioner. How funny. How wickedly funny. Now she needed quickly to think of something to do with this handbag, and her eye fell upon the jar of home made blackberry jam that she had left on the kitchen work top on coming in from the garden. Quickly she took it, opened it with some difficulty, straining at the lid with white knuckles until there was a pleasing snap and the lid came off. Then she took a dessert spoon from the drawer, spooned the entire contents of the jar into Madeleine's handbag, closed it, taking care that the jam didn't ooze through the gaps, and, noticing how much fuller and heavier it seemed, replaced it as she had found it, on the chair. Then she quickly binned the jar, washed up the spoon, and returned to the living room. Madeleine was still with Christine, who was moaning quietly on the couch.

'Coffee,' she heard Madeleine saying, 'I'll pop into the kitchen and make some coffee.'

'Let's go now,' Colette said to Aldous.

On the doorstep, which was at the top of a flight of steep stone steps, Colette became weepy. She cried on Janus Brian's shoulder.

'I'll always remember Mary,' she said.

'It is best to forget,' said Janus Brian, though he didn't sound certain.

'You're going to say she was a dream, is that it? Mary was just a dream?'

Janus seemed to consider this as if it hadn't occurred to him before. He was turning over the possibility.

'No, I don't think so. Mary was real.'

'And everything else?'

Janus Brian shrugged and smiled, and Aldous ended the conversation by calling to Colette from the car in the street below.

Janus accompanied his sister down the steep steps and saw her into the car, silently. The Hillman Superminx (maroon body and grey roof) was the longest lived of the wrecks Aldous had bought since the Morris Oxford had gone.

Just as Colette was closing her door Janus said quietly 'Remember Dismal Desmond?'

Colette had shut the door. Aldous had started up and was pulling away so that she had no time to reply other than to nod and wave as the Superminx rolled down the gentle, curving slope of Leicester Avenue.

'Did you hear that?'

'What?'

'He said "Remember Dismal Desmond".'

Aldous didn't understand.

They drove left along The Limes, under the bridge that carried the Piccadilly Line above ground, then through a curious district of narrow, winding avenues lined with prosperous semis, where the pavements were given shrubberies for verges and where ornamental cherries and maples adorned the corners.

'Dismal Desmond,' Colette went on, 'I've told you about him. He was this toy dog we used to have, on wheels. You could sit on him and wheel yourself about. I used to sit on him and Janus would push me. Quite fast, racing round the garden. But he was old even when we got him. I think he was probably Agatha's first. He was in a real state – both eyes gone, leaky stuffing, filthy pelt. That's why we called him Dismal Desmond, he looked so sad.'

Colette seemed elated as she talked. It was the first time for many years Janus had said anything about the past. She paused for a moment before adding, more cautiously, 'So he didn't mean it, did he, when he said the past was a dream?'

'I suppose not', said Aldous. 'He just didn't want to think about it, or talk about it.'

'And now by mentioning Dismal Desmond he's saying he wants to talk about it? Do you think?'

'Maybe.'

2

'*Dead flies cause the ointment of the apothecary to send forth a stinking savour, so doth a little folly him that is in reputation for wisdom and honour.*'

The Sunday after Mary's funeral, Aldous sat in St Nicola's church listening to Father Gerhart reading from Ecclesiastes.

'*. . . the lips of a fool will swallow up himself. The beginning of the words of his mouth is foolishness, and the end of his talk is mischievous madness.*'

A reading Aldous had presumed was inspired by the current political follies, though he couldn't tell if it was directed particularly at Edward Heath or Joe Gormley, leader of the miners' union, whose dispute had led to power cuts last winter and the collapse of the Heath government. It was very difficult to tell which way Father Gerhart leaned politically.

'*The labour of the foolish wearieth every one of them, because he knoweth not how to go to the city.*'

The candlelit winter evenings had been fun at first. The shops had quickly sold out of jigsaws and playing cards. People were rediscovering the old amusements now that the telly was off. One night the telly had even born witness to its own temporary execution – broadcasting live pictures of the power station employee pulling the lever that cut off the supply to Windhover Hill, and as the lever was pulled, so the house went dark, the telly giving a little electrical whimper as it died. People were saying it was a blessing in disguise, that the long lost art of conversation was being revived. Someone on TV was even saying they should do this all the time, strikes or no strikes, for one or two days a week. Might be a good idea, but Aldous remembered how odd the front room had seemed without television – no one sat in it – there was no reason . . .

'By much slothfulness the building decayeth; and through idleness of the hands the house droppeth through.'

Now there was a minority Labour Government. Mr Wilson had won the election in February with fewer votes than Heath. There was likely to be another election in October. Heath had campaigned with the slogan *Who Governs Britain?* A question the election hadn't satisfactorily answered. A shame teachers hadn't been put on the three-day week. There were ration books in petrol stations. People were being urged to scrimp and save, like during the war. *SOS* had been used as a reminder to '*Switch off Something*', though Janus had said it stood for *Silly Old Sods*.

'A feast is made for laughter and wine maketh merry: but money answereth all things.'

That had to be the object of Father Gerhart's sermon. Aldous had never really got to know Father Gerhart. Their old priest, Father Webb, a cultured, gregarious Irishman who had become a family friend after burying Nana, had moved to another parish somewhere in the North. Father Gerhart was older, grey-haired and bulky in both body and face, with loose, pulpy lips that added a slur to his strong German accent. Though Aldous dutifully shook hands with him at the door every Sunday on leaving the church, they had exchanged very few words.

Aldous rather liked Father Gerhart, however. He found those whispered vowels and slushy consonants very soothing. He liked the way he performed the ritual of the sacrament, so slowly and ponderously, like a nodding dog, almost tripping over his own vestments, murmuring his Latin over the crumbled host, bathing his hands in the dish held by those nervous altar boys – *Lavabo inter innocentes*. Aldous found the whole experience of Mass very relaxing – except, that is, for the recent innovation of shaking hands with the strangers sitting next to you. It had come as rather a shock the first time it happened. *Let us now exchange the sign of peace,* Father Gerhart had said, then Aldous found that the ancient creature to his right, a hunchbacked great grandmother wearing a coat of scarlet wool with a turquoise turban on her tiny head, was offering her shrivelled little hand for him to shake. It had been cold and scratchy, and despite the gay smile of the nonagenarian, Aldous had had doubts about going to church the next Sunday. On that occasion however, the old crone had transformed into a petite teenage girl with braces on her teeth and butterfly-shaped barrettes in her hair. The two experiences cancelled each other out, and Aldous now even enjoyed that brief moment of hand-to-hand intimacy with a stranger, young or old.

Today was Palm Sunday. At the door, palms were being distributed, long, delicately tapering leaves coming to a needle-sharp point, dried to a crisp yellow. Aldous took a handful, then shook hands with Father Gerhart.

'I think you were at the funeral service on Thursday,' the priest said.

'Oh. Yes,' Aldous had almost forgotten.

'A dear relative? A kind friend?'

'No, not really. She . . .' Aldous had to pause to consider how he was related to Mary. Had she been his sister-in-law? Surely that only applied to the wives of one's own brothers. What was the wife of one's brother-in-law? 'She was my wife's sister-in-law.'

'Ah, well. Your wife will be welcome with open arms here, Mr Jones . . .'

'Oh, she's very busy, what with everything. That's not really an excuse, I know. She's here in her heart, I can assure you. By the way,' Aldous felt a need to change the subject, 'I thoroughly enjoyed the reading today, very well chosen. Foolishness – very apt for our current political climate . . .'

Father Gerhart looked a little surprised, as though the thought hadn't struck him.

'I was thinking always that Easter is a time we remember the foolishness of those who took the life of our saviour – but you are right to see a more contemporary interpretation, that is always how the Bible should be read.'

And with that, Father Gerhart averted his eyes, seeming suddenly very shy as he prepared himself to greet the next member of his flock.

After lighting a candle in Mary's memory, Aldous passed through the door into the sunlight, and strolled along Dorset Street, with that peculiar sense of freedom he always experienced on coming out of church, feeling as though he had all the time in the world to get where he wanted, to do what he liked. In such moods he could have happily spent a day enjoying the compact and orderly spectacle of each little suburban house he passed, with their brave little front gardens, their bushes of speckled laurel (a universe contained in each leaf), and soon-to-flower rose bushes. He admired the cars, many of which had been cleaned that morning, as the soapy gutters testified, plucky little things as well, with their sparkling chrome and glass, their armour of glossily painted steel. Aldous felt he had all the time in the world to admire these brightly coloured Sunday morning sights, though in reality if he wasn't home within half an hour Colette, by now happy in a kitchen full of steam and bubbling saucepans, would start to worry. And as he meandered along Hoopers Lane, past The Goat and Compasses with its flock of nineteenth-century workmen's cottages, he felt the sense of doom that always gathered about him when he thought about returning home after a spell away, however brief.

He heard whistling behind him, and laughter, and chirpy calling, but ignored it. At this point the slight bend in Hoopers Lane meant the houses on the left were foreshortened by perspective into nothing more than a series of contrastingly coloured bands, a sight which always afforded Aldous a little private delight – that the inhabitants of Hoopers Lane should have unconsciously built a rainbow together. He paused to admire it, which allowed the whistlers behind him to catch up.

'Been to church have you?' It was his daughter and her husband walking side by side. They had come up from the bus stop by the church, having taken a detour so that Juliette could indulge her passion for sherbet lemons at *Sweet Inspiration* (Formerly Dorset Street Sweet Shop) on the way to Fernlight Avenue. Bill had a sketchbook tucked under his arm.

It had become something of a tradition for his daughter and son-in-law to come over to Fernlight Avenue for Sunday lunch (usually a roast chicken, sometimes, if Colette was feeling daring enough, a spaghetti bolognese). They were usually there by the time Aldous had got back from church, having dutifully trundled up Green Lanes on a 123 or a W4. They must have been running late.

'What are you holding?' said Juliette.

'Palms,' said Aldous, brandishing them before his daughter's face, 'it's Palm Sunday today. They were giving these out at the door . . .'

33

'I don't understand,' said Bill, 'how you can sit there with all those hypocrites who are pretending to be so good, when tomorrow they'll go into a factory and make bombs to drop on Vietnam.'

Aldous searched without success for a telling answer, not wanting to get into a theological discussion with Bill, whose energy for arguments seemed limitless.

Aldous was fond of his son-in-law, though he had been angry with Juliette when she decided to drop out of school before her O Levels to marry him. He believed she had a good brain, and was wasting it. She could have been and done anything she'd put her mind to, but she'd thrown it all away for the sake of a bearded Marxist butcher and a life in a poky flat in Polperro Gardens.

Juliette seemed happy working at Eve St John's on Green Lanes – an odd little establishment, comprised of two shops side by side, one selling electrical goods and ladies' hosiery (a rather alarming combination Aldous always felt), the other toys. Aldous had begun to wonder if Janus had set a pattern that the rest of his children would follow, throwing away academic brilliance for a career in menial employment. Janus had been a gasman, a telephonist, and now worked in a builders' merchants, bagging and weighing nails for the carpenters of North London. James had at least gone to university after two years of drifting from one dead-end job to another.

Bill, too, had decided not to make use of his lively and intelligent mind, opting instead for the undemanding world of semi-skilled labour. He had been a steeplejack when he'd first wooed Juliette, impressing her by knocking back salt-laden cocktails in the public bar of The Carpenters Arms, a rough, noisy pub in Wood Green where Juliette, who, at fifteen, had grown from a tousled tomboy into a considerable beauty, drank illegally with other underage friends. She had fallen, so Aldous understood, for his public bar sophistication, his oratory, the glamour of his political radicalism, his skill as an artist, his wit. Juliette had told her father how different Bill was from other men she knew. He looked much older than his years, being lushly bearded in the manner of a sage of the revolution – he wore corduroy jackets decorated with small enamelled badges of the trade unions to which he didn't belong – and Communist icons (a clenched fist, Lenin in profile). A pipe smoker, he always wore ties, which in these times of shabby informality made him seem quaintly anachronistic. He had an untutored but genuine artistic talent which found its most fruitful outlet in the reproductions he would make, in oils on blocks of wood, of Russian religious icons. In the long arguments between Juliette and her parents that presaged her wedding, Aldous began to understand how impressive Bill must have seemed to a girl whose previous boyfriends had been drippy sixth formers and pimply students. Here was a man who by day scaled the few industrial chimneys there were left in north London, who had raised the steel flue that carried away the fumes of incinerated limbs at the East Edmonton Hospital (a story he always liked to tell), while by evening with callused, chapped fingers he painted the delicate, mantis-like hands of Russian Orthodox iconography.

Shortly after their marriage, however, Bill had unexpectedly developed a fear of heights and had plumped instead for the ground-level life of supermarket butchery. He'd always been proud of his hands, which were a working man's hands, and an artist's hands. The torn nails, the wounded, stigmatised palms. These days he always had a set of cuts to show, some fresh (an arc across the ball of the thumb), some mature and scabbed (the cloven end of an index finger), some fading and ghostly (a V on the back of the wrist), some few permanent scars, little crescents of shiny pink scar tissue on the tanned surface of his skin.

The problem with Bill, however, was that he was a drinker, and had formed with Janus a drinking partnership that seemed hell bent on scaling ever higher peaks of debauchery and derangement. At the same time, Bill was one of the few people, perhaps the only person, who could control Janus when he was drunk. He had a reputation as a gentle giant, a Hercules of colossal strength gained from a working life of hauling bricks up ladders, so that he seemed to act, in the friendship that had developed between himself and Janus, as keeper to Janus's lunatic, his bodyguard, henchman, minder. One particularly troublesome night at Fernlight Avenue, when Janus had passed into the violent, penultimate phase of his drunkenness (the ultimate phase being sleep), after most of the family had tried and failed

35

in various ways to calm, restrain or wrestle him, Colette had pleaded with her son-in-law to use his strength to subdue Janus.

'Can't you just punch him in the head and knock him out?' she'd said.

'I can't do that,' replied Bill, almost shocked.

'Just a punch to the head, just so we can get him into bed.'

'You can't just punch someone in the head. I might break his jaw, or something. I might give him a brain haemorrhage. This isn't some Hollywood movie.'

Instead Bill preferred to use his eloquence, his drunkard's camaraderie, his rambling abilities as a storyteller to soothe fretful Janus. And when this failed he would sit on his chest for half an hour.

This Sunday Colette had made a spaghetti bolognese for lunch, a carefully crafted meal, long in preparation, but which went almost unnoticed beneath the vociferous discussions that were conducted during its consumption, and which continued afterwards, when Aldous had taken the plates and cutlery to the sink for washing up. James was home for the Easter holidays, and seemed particularly keen, after two terms at university, to display his newly acquired knowledge.

'Wages are like prices,' he said, answering a point Bill had made, 'goods that are in high demand cost more. It's the same with wages, they reflect the availability of skills.'

'Well, well, well,' said Bill, who was leaning with an elbow propped on the mantelpiece, threatening to inadvertently cause a small avalanche of bric-a-brac, 'I'd never have had you down as an acolyte of that raving fascist Ted Heath. But then even Heath can see you've got to have wage control. You've got to have an incomes policy. You can't treat wages like tins of baked beans, paying less if there are more. There has to be a moral dimension to wage allocation, you have to pay people according to their value as people . . .'

'But if everyone's equal,' said Colette from her armchair by the boiler into which she'd recently flopped, 'they all get the same pay, is that right? The doctor, the dustman, they both get paid the same?'

'Well answer me this,' said Bill, 'What would cause more

disruption to society, doctors going on strike or dustmen going on strike?'

James laughed knowingly, as if to let everyone know he'd heard this argument before.

Colette thought for a second before saying

'Doctors.'

'Why doctors?' said Bill, raising a finger.

'Because if dustmen went on strike, their work could be done by soldiers, or even by volunteers if things got desperate. But if doctors went on strike – well, it would be a disaster. You couldn't have soldiers doing brain surgery.'

'Do you realize,' said Bill, 'that 95 per cent of doctors' work could just as easily be done by nurses? Do you realize that if the dustmen went on strike, the army couldn't dispose of more than a quarter of the rubbish, and that within a few weeks we'd be overrun by epidemics of cholera, typhoid, diphtheria, influenza, polio . . . Thousands, maybe millions of people would die. A doctors' strike would result in just a handful of deaths . . .'

'Isn't that amazing?' said Colette, who looked genuinely convinced, 'So you think they should swap around? Pay the dustmen what we pay doctors now, and let doctors live on dustmen's wages.'

Bill nodded, laughing, 'Doctors are just parasites. We should be talking about the poor nurses who, like I said, can do most of the doctors' work, yet just because the doctor spent a few years at university, paid for by his rich parents, he thinks he deserves to get paid fifteen thousand a year, or whatever obscene salaries they earn.'

'So get rid of doctors altogether?'

'Yes. Just better train the nurses and we won't have any need of doctors.'

'That sounds a wonderful idea. Darling!' She called to Aldous behind her at the sink, 'I'm a communist!'

Janus was sitting at the table. The silver spotted crippled cat, Scipio, his mother's gift to him seven years ago, was sitting in his lap.

'You tell them comrade,' he said, raising his clenched fist.

'What I don't understand about communism,' said Aldous, drying his hands and re-entering the main part of the room, 'is what happens in this perfect society, where everything is free and equal, when some selfish person comes along and tries to take advantage?'

'Selfishness is a by-product of private ownership. If everyone has what they need, why should they want any more?' Bill said this with a grimace, as though pleading to be understood.

'People are always wanting more than they need,' said Aldous.

'Like the miners,' said Colette, laughing, 'thirty-five per cent!'

'That's right,' said James, 'none of us need more than the basics for survival – a warm cave and lots of wild boar to hunt, but we all want more . . .'

'I can't believe you just said that about the miners, mother,' said Juliette sharply, the sherbet lemon rattling like dice against her teeth as she spoke, 'have you any idea what it's like to work down a coal mine?'

'No. Have you?'

'People only want more because they want the same as what other people have,' said Bill, 'it's a caucus race, the poor are always trying to catch up with the selfish rich who just get richer and richer. If we are all equal, this cycle of envy will stop . . .'

'But it would just take one greedy person taking more than they need to start the cycle up again . . .' said Aldous.

'Yes, you still haven't answered dad's main question,' said James.

'I told you,' Bill spluttered, 'the situation wouldn't arise . . .'

Howls of derision from half the room, Bill shouted to be heard above it, '. . . but if it did then we'd shoot the buggers . . .'

The howls intensified.

'Just like we'll shoot Ted Heath and Prince Charles and all the rest of them – string them up and let them dangle from the balcony of Buckingham Palace – you can't have a perfect society without first cutting out the rotten wood . . .'

For once Bill's voice was almost lost amid the noise generated by his opponents, who, sensing a rare victory, continued to pour scorn on his argument long after it had died. Bill, having given up verbally, resorted to gestures, spraying his extended family with machine gun fire, and lobbing invisible hand grenades to every corner of the kitchen.

These post-prandial Sunday afternoons were usually passed, as if by some unspoken agreement, without the accompaniment of alcohol. A kind of alcoholic truce, a drinker's cease-fire, the one point in the week when everyone agreed to pass the time soberly. But this particular Sunday afternoon it was clear that Janus had been drinking. Aldous had noticed how, every half an hour or so, he would leave the room for no obvious reason, to return a few minutes later. Once he followed him and crept up the stairs while he was in his bedroom. He could hear the gasp and sigh of a beer can yielding its pressurized contents, the muscular clenching of Janus's neck as he swallowed. When he came out of the room he leant across to the lavatory and pulled its chain, to provide a motive for his going upstairs. The traditional abstinence of Sunday afternoons had encouraged Janus to drink secretly. At any other time he would have drunk openly, not to say blatantly, but today, it seemed, he felt a need to drink furtively.

Aldous foresaw a day of troubles that depressed him deeply. For Janus to begin drinking so early would mean a long afternoon and evening of steadily growing tension and hostility, to culminate in heaven knew what drunken mayhem at night. Now he wished Colette had laced his lunch with crushed Antabuse tablets, as she had done in the past. They'd never managed those pills properly, somehow. The idea was that they induced a state of nausea if one took them before drinking alcohol, so deterring heavy drinking. Janus refused to take them voluntarily, so a couple of times Colette had crushed them with a rolling pin and mixed them in with the gravy of his roast dinner, or the sauce of his bolognese. They'd been warned by the doctor that to allow someone to go out drinking, unaware that they'd taken the tablets, could be dangerous, they were to be treated rather as a form of voluntary deterrence. So Colette would tell Janus, after he'd finished his dinner, that she'd spiked the gravy, in the hope he would abandon any plans for drinking that evening. But she'd underestimated his drinkers' resolve. His first action, on learning of her trickery, was to swallow a pint of heavily salted water, and then to vomit into the toilet, bringing up most of the tablets with his dinner. Aldous said she shouldn't have told him, just fed him the drugs and let him take the consequences, or at least let him digest more of his meal before she told him. That was rarely possible, as his evening drinking often started the moment he'd finished his dinner. So they'd given up on the Antabuse idea pretty quickly. Colette wasn't even convinced that they worked anyway. And for a few weeks after that Janus refused, like some paranoid Roman emperor, to eat any food she'd prepared for him.

Having succumbed to a rare defeat against James, Bill had retired to the music room where he sat on the windowsill next to the piano, leaning back against the window frame, almost hidden by one of the tall, viridian green curtains, reading *Under the Volcano*, and smoking his pipe. He was shortly joined by Julian, who was passing through a brief passion for the game of chess. He'd carried his little set into the music room, anxious for a partner.

Bill was known to be a good chess player. He could beat everyone in the family, including James, although Janus would usually put up a good fight. So chess was more than one of Bill's Marxist affectations. He was genuinely good at the game, and Julian had never known him decline an offer to play.

They set up the board on the piano stool and Julian knelt on the floor, plopping the pieces into position, while Bill folded a corner of his novel down and closed it. Bill's copy of *Under the Volcano* was the Penguin Modern Classics edition with a Diego Rivera painting on the cover. It was creased and scuffed almost to the point of disintegration, the corners of the cover nipped with white, the spine a cluster of parallel scars where it had been folded back too far. The wear and tear of this book was due to the fact that Bill Brothers had been carrying it around in the paperback-sized pockets of his jackets and coats for more than a year, continually reading and rereading the novel.

'This is the best book in the English language,' he said to Julian, showing him the front of the book and tapping the picture with his finger.

'Janus always says *Nostromo* is the best book in the English language,' said Julian, recalling the evening when Janus had given him a long lecture on Joseph Conrad.

'Janus is merely parroting a man called Leavis who decided, one day, that *Nostromo* was the greatest novel in the English language, and for some reason everyone has decided to agree with him, just because he's the Mr Big at Cambridge. In fact, no one has actually read *Nostromo* . . .'

'Janus has,' said Julian, with a certain amount of pride in his voice, 'he's shown me bits of it where Conrad uses triple quotation marks . . .'

'Triple?'

'Yes, you know, like someone saying someone else's words . . .'

'And that, of course, means it's a great novel . . .'

'And Conrad wasn't even English. He ran away to sea didn't he?'

'He did. But was he a drinker? That is the question, Julian. It is a well-known fact that no one can write a great novel in a state of sobriety, and I'm pretty sure Conrad never touched a drop of the hard stuff, or even the soft stuff. Now if he had had a can of Special Brew always to hand, or at least a few Gold Labels on his desk, we might be able to read *Nostromo* . . .'

'Oh,' Julian laughed, 'yeah . . .'

They played chess. Bill rapidly overpowered Julian who'd agreed to be Bobby Fischer to Bill's Boris Spassky. Shortly after the game started, Janus came into the room, the three remaining cans of a four-pack swinging in their plastic nooses from his hand. He began playing the piano.

Julian was so absorbed in his game the conversations of Bill and Janus passed over his head unnoticed. He could sense that their talk was louder and ruder than it had been, and that Bill was now giving only half his attention to the game, which impressed Julian all the more. Julian would ponder for ten minutes over his move, only to have Bill negate it with a casual sideways move of a knight. He concealed his thought processes with a slow, distracted commentary, 'you're moving there are you, Julian, well, in that case . . . I shall have to . . . move . . . there'. Julian couldn't at first understand why Bill spent so much time moving and reinforcing his pawns, until it became apparent that his forces had been sundered into two uncoordinated halves by a v-shaped wedge of them. Then came a small armada sailing down the queen's side that swallowed his bishops. Julian's queen was stranded in dangerous territory on the king's side in the distant ranks towards Bill's rooks. But by this time Bill and Janus were into their second can of beer and Bill had drifted away from the game and towards the piano, where he exhorted Janus to play Mussorgsky's The Great Gate of Kiev, which Janus did with all the gusto and flamboyance he could manage.

'Muchas Loudas!' cried Bill. 'If you play this on the piano at The Lemon Tree it is bound to attract some New Zealand foxes. Play more muchas loudas Janussimus, it is good for me to think much of my fatherland, even though we are speaking of a pre-Revolutionary bourgeois composer . . .'

Julian left the game, his queen still stranded. He'd been waiting perhaps half an hour for Bill to make his move, and he left the room unnoticed by the others.

In the kitchen there was still a lively discussion going on, James, it seemed, having taken the place of Bill at the mantelpiece.

'But how do you know the oak tree really exists? If you see it or touch it, you are experiencing mental sensations. How do you know that these have any relationship to what is actually out there?' He gestured grandly towards the kitchen windows which were filled with a frothy display of apple and cherry blossom.

Aldous and Colette seemed unable, or were reluctant to grasp the argument.

'I still don't understand, James,' said Colette, 'how can the tree be there and not be there?'

Juliette beckoned to Julian again and whispered to him.

'Go and tell Bill to come in here.'

Julian went back to the music room. As he opened the door, what had previously been the sound of muffled levity was now pronounced and intricately noisy. Janus and Bill sitting side by side at the Bechstein's keyboard. Two long haired, heavily bearded men, it was as though Marx and Engels were playing a duet – puffily red faced, Bill trilling tunelessly in the upper registers while Janus provided a variety of accompaniments – raunchy boogie-woogie, Mozartian Alberti sequences, lavish Lisztian flourishes. They didn't notice Julian enter. His chess set was still on the floor.

Julian walked round the piano and pulled gently at Bill's sleeve. Bill, in the midst of a cacophonic piece of improvisation, and laughing blearily all the while, didn't notice until Julian had almost pulled him off the piano stool.

'Juliette wants to speak to you,' Julian said once he had his brother-in-law's attention. He noticed a little flurry of worry pass over Bill's face, which quickly dissipated.

'Does she? In that case I must now take my leave of the concert platform. Ladies and gentlemen,' he said, standing to address the wall, 'there will be a short intermission while Janussimus my vice-pianist will entertain you with tunes he heard while on an expedition to discover the source of that great river . . .' his speech petered out for want of a river name.

'I suppose your savages never worry about whether trees exist or not,' Aldous was saying as Bill came into the kitchen.

Aldous and Colette were still trying to adjust to this new James that had emerged since he'd gone to university, the James that was full of ideas, mostly half-formed, but propounded with an authority that they didn't like to challenge, that wore faded denims deckled with patches, that had grown its hair long with a girlish centre parting. This weekend he was wearing a faded yellow cheesecloth shirt and a denim waistcoat with silver buttons.

Though still only in his first year, James did his best to talk about anthropology with the air of a seasoned expert.

'On the contrary, there are many societies who believe the whole of the empirical world to be the dream of a mystical creature, like the rainbow snake of the Aborigines, or the . . . the giant moth-pangolin of the Dorbourgon . . .'

Aldous was half-laughing, half-wincing, as though he found the idea gloriously repulsive.

'They sound just up Janus Brian's street,' said Colette, 'It's such a shame you didn't come down a couple of days earlier, James, you could have come to Mary's funeral. I think you'd get on with Janus Brian these days – he'd love to hear about these Bourbons whoever they are.'

'I think Janus Brian just says the past is a dream,' said Aldous, as if to excuse his brother-in-law, 'I'm sure he thinks the present is real.'

'But then he did say "remember Dismal Desmond",' said Colette, 'So he's admitting the past is real. Life must be real, if I was making all this up, surely I'd make up a better life for myself.'

Quietly, while this discussion had progressed, Juliette and Bill were talking in an intense undertone.

'We should have been home an hour ago,' Juliette said.

'But I've been playing the piano with Janus . . .'

'Where did you get the drink from?'

'What drink?'

'Don't be pathetic . . .'

At this point Janus entered the room. A stranger wouldn't have known he'd been drinking, but everyone in the room could tell. There was something in his stance, his pace, as though gravity took to him more keenly, and because of this the atmosphere in the room changed as instantly as if a switch had been thrown, the air became more acute, sound became clearer, the colour of things deepened a shade, and there were long, uncomfortable pauses in the conversation where before it had flowed seamlessly.

'We agreed that you wouldn't go out tonight,' Juliette said in a quietly angry voice. The room was now focusing on this hushed conversation.

Bill tried to sit on his wife's knee, dislodging the handbag that had been there. There was an awkward shifting of weight.

'Don't be like that my little darling, I've just been conversing with my most esteemed brother-in-law.'

Juliette's face winced as she caught the sour, beery breath that came from Bill's mouth. Bill seemed to think she was amused.

Janus, who'd been standing next to Bill, squeezed past Juliette to another chair and sat down. He took a cigarette from his packet, lit it, and put the box in the breast pocket of his thin cotton shirt. The sharp oblong shape of it was distinct through the fabric.

'I've got square tits,' he said, laughing.

Juliette looked at him and scowled.

'What did you say?' she said loudly.

Janus, affronted by her effrontery, didn't know how to reply at first.

'What?' he said, eventually.

'What did you say about me?'

'He didn't say anything about you, my sweet,' said Bill, croon-ingly, soothingly, 'he was just making a joke about his cigarette packet, he said it made him look like he'd got square . . .' and here Bill reddened and laughed childishly, bashfully unable to continue.

'I thought he was talking about me,' said Juliette.

'Touchy aren't we,' said Janus.

'How could Janus say that about you, my sweet little angel, you've got lovely little . . .'

'Oh for Christ's sake Bill,' snapped Juliette, pushing back a hand that was moving towards her chest, and pushing her husband off her knee, 'let's go.'

'Bill and me have got business,' said Janus, blowing a smoke ring.

'No you haven't,' said Juliette, standing up, 'Bill is staying in tonight with me, that's what we agreed, isn't it?'

Bill shrugged apologetically.

'Where are my fags,' said Colette, 'Ah, here they are.'

'Those are mine,' said James, triumphantly, 'look, they've got my name on them.'

'Why've you written your name on my fags?'

'Those are yours, over there,' said James.

Eventually cigarette ownership was established and fags lit.

'Well I'm going,' said Juliette, 'are you coming with me?'

'It's not quite as simple as that, my angel, you see, there's the question of the source of the Limpopo.'

Janus gave a shriek of laughter.

'The pubs don't open till seven,' said Colette, wads of smoke coming from her nostrils.

'What about the Limpopo, mate?' Janus shouted.

'So I'm going home on my own, am I?'

'Why don't you come with us?'

'It's Sunday,' said Juliette, 'we always stay in on Sunday evenings. We've got work tomorrow . . .'

'I haven't got work tomorrow,' said Janus, even though he hadn't been the subject of Juliette's last sentence. Nevertheless, the statement caused a stir.

'What do you mean,' said Colette, 'it's not a Bank Holiday, is it?'

'No,' said Janus, 'I've been given the sack.'

Suddenly everything that had seemed odd and unusual about the afternoon – Janus and Bill's drinking, their removal to the music room, Janus's quietness, fell into place.

'What do you mean you've been given the sack?' said Colette, above a barely audible groan from her husband.

'I mean I went into work as usual yesterday morning and Mr Hawes said my services were no longer needed.' Janus giggled.

'He can't just do that,' said Colette, 'what was he playing at?'

Janus was frequently in and out of work. He'd been sacked from Swallows before, then reinstated when Mr Hawes realised how much he needed Janus's abilities at mental arithmetic. When he worked there was a rhythm to his drinking, a recognizable pattern, which meant the others would know where he was and when he was likely to be drunk. Out of work he would be around the house all day, sometimes drunk, sometimes not, with no way of telling where or when. This was the reason Janus's news cast such a pall on the afternoon.

'You weren't drinking at work again, were you?' said Colette.

Janus shrugged, not quite able to admit it.

'You idiot, Janus,' she said, then, less forcefully, 'well, you won't have any money for drinking, then.'

Janus reached into his back pocket and waved a handful of five pound notes.

'Hawes settled up out of the till – back pay, holiday pay – this should see me alright for a while . . .' He gave a sneaky, jeering laugh.

'Get the money off him, James,' Colette said to her other son, who was nearest Janus, with such urgency that James made for the money, before checking himself, 'Don't be ridiculous, mother,' he said.

Colette had sprung out of her chair, 'Bill, grab it,' she nodded urgently at the wad Janus was still waving. Underestimating her seriousness, Bill seemed bemused, but by this time Colette was herself making a lunge for the cash. Janus repocketed it slowly and deliberately.

In the commotion Colette knocked a cup off the table. A glass smashed.

'What are you doing, mother,' said Juliette, annoyed that her own crisis had been overshadowed by Janus's news.

'Trying to get that money off him. There's enough there to keep him drunk for weeks on end. And what about all the housekeeping he'll owe me for when he's on the dole? I'm entitled to most of it . . .'

'There's no point . . .'

'Now we know what you're really worried about,' said Janus, grinning, 'just worried about your own supplies of Gold Labels . . .'

'I'm not the one who ends up in a police cell every other week. You don't know how to handle money, or drink. So come on, hand it over.'

She held out her hand, palm up, a debtor demanding payment. The hand was held just a little below Janus's face, Colette leaning across the length of the table to reach. Juliette and Bill, on one side, watched amusedly. James, leaning against the wall on the other, observing with a half-smile on his face.

Janus bent his face towards Colette's palm, as if to plant a kiss on it. Instead, he dropped a white bolus of spittle from his lips which Colette unwittingly caught. She slapped him, rather weakly, across the side of his face with her soiled hand. Bill stood up to restrain Colette, who was attempting further strikes.

'Oh God,' said Juliette, in a disgusted way, 'let's just go, Bill.'

'Shut your face,' Janus suddenly snapped, his lips curling, 'Bill's coming to the pub with me.'

'If you're going to the pub,' said Juliette to her husband, 'I'm bolting the door. You can sleep in the front garden.'

Janus by this time had managed to drag Bill to the door. Bill was shrugging to his wife apologetically, as if to say the situation was beyond his control.

'We're not going to the pub,' shouted Janus, 'We're going to discover the source of the Limpopo!'

The last word was spoken with a rolling-eyed, growling voice, as Bill was pulled backwards through the door. Janus whooped loudly in the hall. Bill gave a loud 'Shhh!' Then the front door was slammed.

The kitchen was suddenly very quiet. Juliette stood up.

'I'm going to get the bus,' she said.

Aldous put a consoling arm around Colette's shoulder, who seemed on the verge of tears. There was a sense of shock in the room at her reaction to Janus's news. But she had quickly recovered herself.

'I just can't stand the thought of him loafing about the house all day, cadging money and fags off me, and then getting half-cut whenever he likes . . .'

'Why don't you chuck him out then,' said Juliette, with the impatient air of someone who's been through scenes like these countless times.

Colette glared at her daughter, 'Oh it's oh-so simple, isn't it? – just sling him out . . .'

'What was all that about the Limpopo?' said James, still laughing with incredulity at the exit of Janus and Bill. Juliette raised her eyes to heaven, then shook her head in controlled despair.

'Bill has been obsessed with Victorian explorers ever since that series on BBC2 – *The Great Explorers*. Stupidly I bought him the book for Christmas, now he and Janus have this silly fantasy about being Richard Burton or John Hanning Speke, or Mungo Park. It was funny at first, but like everything with Bill, he just takes it too far. One night him and Janus explored the end of Hugo and Veronica Price's back garden, saying they were searching for the source of some river, not the Limpopo – the Irrawaddy, I think it was. They took a box of Kleenex tissues with them and left a trail down the side of the garden so they could find their way back. Another night they climbed over the barbed wire beside the New River and followed the canal for miles, Bill came home caked in mud. If he does anything like that again he can sleep in the front garden, like I said.'

'The big kid,' said Colette, restored to a level of calmness by Juliette's anecdotes.

Juliette eventually left the house to catch her bus home, a look of stoical resolve on her face as she marched off down the road. James went out later to see some friends.

Aldous and Colette spent the evening alone together in the front room, Colette, a glass of barley wine by her side, reading *Dombey and Son*, Aldous doing some pencil sketches of the palms he'd been given that morning in church, and which he had placed in the lotus vase (of his own making), on top of the blank television. They formed a pleasing, unusual display, these tall, tapering leaves sprouting from the curled geometry of the vase. The lamp on the mantelpiece gave them a large shadow, which loomed on the wall behind them. Julian sat with his chessboard going through the moves of Capablanca v Eliskases.

It was how they spent many evenings when Janus was out. They were distracting themselves from what would be a long evening of waiting, of listening – for the footsteps on the path, for the key in the lock, trying to determine from these sounds the mood of their eldest son.

They went to bed around midnight, unfolding the bed settee on which Colette had spent the evening reading. They could have slept upstairs, in the large back bedroom, which they'd used intermittently since James had gone to university, but in truth they preferred sleeping downstairs in the front living room, they'd grown used to it in the years when there'd been nowhere else for them to sleep.

Colette swallowed six Nembutals, downed the dregs of her last Gold Label of the day, and settled down to sleep. Even with the drink and the pills it took her a long time to finally drift off. She heard noises outside, the front door open, some suppressed laughter. She instantly recognised James's voice. He must have brought a friend home. She heard them giggling in the kitchen. Aldous heard them too. With James home there was little to worry about. He could handle drunken Janus on his own. And so they went to sleep.

3

Nearly three weeks had passed since Mary's funeral. In that time there had been no communication from Janus Brian other than a black-bordered, slightly blurred photo of Mary that came in the post one morning, about a week after her burial. It showed her in a summery blue frock standing in the shade of an orange tree. She was smiling. On the back was written, in Janus Brian's economical but rather shaky hand – *The Gardens of the Alhambra, Granada, 1972*.

Colette had propped the photo against the clock on the kitchen mantelpiece, the first port of call of most of the letters that came to the house. Since there was little post in the days that followed, the photo enjoyed a prominent position for some time, and Colette frequently found herself, as if in a dream, transfixed by its presence – and would just stand there, staring at it.

She tried to imagine Janus and Mary's last-but-one holiday together. What did they do with their time, just the two of them, for that fortnight each year? A lot of it would have been spent watching golf, she supposed. That had been one of their passions, if passion was the right word. Their first visit to Spain had been to tour its golf courses, way back in the 1950s, when foreign travel, even to the Continent, had been a hazardous and rather daring enterprise – not something Janus Brian would have dreamt of before the war. But then the war had changed him in so many ways – three years in the Middle East escorting wage convoys, though never firing a shot in anger, had given him a confidence and self-assertiveness he'd never possessed before. Spain would have been a partial reliving of those desert years he always reminisced about so happily.

Where the passion for golf came from she never knew, but

every summer postcards would come from Spain, bearing a King Juan Carlos stamp on the back, while on the front not a scene of exotic mountains or magnificent palaces – but the eighteenth green at Valderrama, Jack Nicklaus teeing off on the first at Valladolid or Arnold Palmer sinking a long putt before the clubhouse at Bilbao.

She remembered Janus Brian saying once how the golf courses of Spain – being lush, green lawns often in the middle of arid deserts – always made him think of the Garden of Eden.

Colette began to feel rather haunted by the picture of Mary under the orange tree. At first she thought her brother would want to be left alone in his grief. But his last words to her – *Remember Dismal Desmond,* and now this photograph, and the pleading, beseeching stance it seemed to take on her mantelpiece (*Go on, go and visit your brother, see how he's coping without me* – it almost said), made her decide that it was time to pay Janus Brian a call.

Aldous had taken some persuading.

'He'll get in touch if he wants to see you,' he said, 'you know how he likes his privacy.'

'But he has been in touch, he sent the photograph of Mary.'

'That was just a formality. He likes to do everything correctly.'

'I still think we should call round . . .'

'Not just out of the blue,' said Aldous, 'shouldn't you write a letter first?'

The conversation had taken place in the garden of The Owl, a small, country cottage of a pub near Redlands Park, where Colette and Aldous sometimes went for an early evening drink. They drank there because of its garden, which meant they could take Julian with them, and sit under the sprawling canopy of a chestnut tree, sipping their drinks and listening to the juggernauts on Goat and Compasses Lane.

Discussions about visiting friends or relatives often followed this course. Colette would be in favour of a spontaneous visit, an idea which usually appalled Aldous. Colette would become insistent, Aldous doggedly resistant. Since Colette couldn't drive, however, Aldous usually got his way, and would only ever admit defeat if Colette went into a really desperate sulk, wailing in the passenger seat about her husband's unfairness, how he always stopped her seeing her brothers and sisters, distant or half-forgotten cousins, old friends – how it was his fault – because of his cold unsociability – that they had no real friends now. And Aldous would reluctantly change course and visit the friends or relatives they hadn't seen for years, and a usually deeply embarrassing evening would follow, where their hosts would politely try and make light of the disruption the visit had caused.

'Of course, if we had a telephone,' Colette would say on the way back, 'this need never have happened.'

But Aldous didn't like telephones.

He was persuaded, however, in the garden of The Owl, that a visit to Janus Brian might be appropriate. He was, after all, recently bereaved, and he lived alone with few friends. They had a duty to make sure he was coping, to see if he needed any help. And so, after finishing their drink, Aldous drove them to Leicester Avenue.

Leicester Avenue had, in the 1920s, been cut into a gently sloping hillside, which gave it the feel of a gradually deepening canyon, a small suburban gorge of rockeries and shrubs. The further into the canyon you penetrated, the higher the front doors hung above pavement level. Janus Brian's was reached by a mossy concrete staircase that zigzagged between honesty bushes and lavender bushes. To the side of the front garden was a driveway leading to a garage that was set back a little, but Colette found this cemented approach too steep to walk safely, especially in the dark as it now was, and she opted instead to climb the concrete steps to her brother's front door.

There was no reply to her ringing and knocking. She yoo-hooed through the letterbox and rapped on the windows. Julian lingered on the lower slopes of the front garden popping seed cases while Aldous nosed around the side of the house.

'The car's here,' he said, peeking into the garage, 'perhaps he's gone for a walk.'

'Janus Brian doesn't walk anywhere,' said Colette. She was peering through a gap in the living room curtains at her brother who was slumped in a chair in front of the still-glowing television. The colour television.

He was wearing his dark suit, but without a tie, and without shoes or socks. His lemon yellow shirt was open, revealing a vertical strip of bland, pallid, grey-haired flesh. She knocked on the window. Janus Brian didn't stir.

The question of whether or not Janus Brian was dead quickly entered the minds of Colette and her family, but even through that thin gap in the curtains to the dimly lit room beyond, it was evident that he was alive. His body had the motionless animation that all living bodies have. No living body can truly mimic the stillness of the dead. But it was also clear that Janus Brian was more than asleep. He was in a denser, more opaque form of unconsciousness.

It had not occurred to Colette that her brother was much of a drinker, even when she found out about his hobby of winemaking, or when he took the trouble to explain to her his methods for increasing the alcoholic yields of his home-brews. (It was very technical – all to do with sugar.) Surely, she thought, he didn't actually drink the stuff, except in an emergency, as at the funeral, when the sherry had run dry. It was just something to inflict on relatives at Christmas. It was a harmless pastime, a by-product of his gardening.

Janus Brian did finally stir, after much tapping at the window, and hallooing through the letterbox. Colette saw his eyes open and look at her, uncomprehendingly, for a long time. He closed them again. Colette rapped on the glass, enough to make Janus Brian sit up. Then he lifted himself shakily from his chair, immediately losing balance and falling forwards, luckily face-first into the plump leather couch. He picked himself up again from this, gave an odd, trembling salute of acknowledgement to his sister, who had watched the spectacle all the while as a dumb show, through the glass. She saw him leave the room, so hurried across the front of the house to the door, and peeped through the letterbox. Janus Brian in his hall, leaning at almost forty-five degrees, a shoulder propped against the wall, half-sliding, half-walking towards the front door, which he opened after much clumsy messing with bolts and latches.

And when he opened the door, Colette immediately caught a smell that she'd never noticed at her brother's house before – sweetness. It reminded her of the savour she would sometimes sniff if she opened the lid of a tin of Golden Syrup that had been forgotten about in the back of the cupboard. Still a radiant shock of gold beneath the lid, but the syrup would have crystallised, and the smell would be a rank, rancid parody of sweetness.

No words were exchanged when Janus Brian opened the door. He seemed too weak to utter any. Colette and Aldous silently and urgently took an arm each, since he looked perilously close to collapse, and guided him back into the living room. Julian idled in unnoticed, and gazed at the colour television.

Settled in his chair, and at close quarters, Colette and Aldous were able to appreciate Janus Brian's condition more fully. He looked very ill. His face was grey, his eyes yellow. Around his lips there was an orange, flaky crust. His hands were as white as something sculpted in alabaster, but the skin under his finger-nails was deep purple, as though he was wearing nail polish.

'I'm sorry that you should find me like this,' Janus Brian at last moaned, leaning back in his swivel armchair, a black leather seat pivoting on its feet by means of a ball and socket joint, a very precarious and disconcerting piece of furniture for a drunk, 'but it's the house – it's so empty. I'm stupid.' He clutched his head and the seat wobbled. Janus Brian began revolving unintentionally. Colette grabbed the arm of the chair to steady him. 'The first week was okay. I thought "this isn't so bad. Not as bad as you imagine it might be." But then by week two the house had changed. Everything had changed . . .'

'Don't worry,' said Colette, stroking her brother's bony shoulder, 'sit there and I'll make some coffee . . .'

Janus Brian weakly called after her as she made for the kitchen, revolving as he did so, 'I don't think there's any . . .'

There wasn't. There seemed to be no food of any kind, the cupboards being mostly empty save for condiments – HP Sauce, a tin of Coleman's Mustard and such like. The one thing there was, in vast quantities, was sugar. One cupboard contained nothing but, white paper packets of it stacked neatly like sandbags. One had burst on the floor, and a train of ants was at that moment busily carrying it away, grain by grain, to a nest under the door. There was more spilt sugar on the draining board. Sugar crunched beneath Colette's feet as she stepped across the lino. White sugar. Tate & Lyle. Refined.

And there were wine bottles everywhere, some standing, some on their side, some in pieces on the floor, all empty. She read their labels: Cucumber Cordiale 1972, Banana Wine 1972, Tomato Sherry 1971, Runner-Bean Wine 1970, Swede Wine 1969, Carrot Wine 1969, Raspberry Wine 1965, Asparagus Wine 1964, Melon Wine 1963.

'Sugar turns to alcohol,' Colette now recalled Janus Brian's explanation, 'if you increase the temperature and put extra sugar in, you get a higher specific gravity. If you increase it too much you kill the yeast, and the fermentation falls off. You don't often realize, do you dear, that alcohol is really just another form of sugar?'

Sugar adulterated. Ruined sugar, its molecules like crumbling battlements, admitting the spirit of drunkenness. Sugar that is full of dreams, of loss of balance. Topsy-turvy sugar. Tipsy sugar. Sweetness at the point of burning. Sweetness so sweet it plumbed the senses and set them awry. Sweetness beyond sweetness. Transcendent sweetness . . .

Janus Brian had, it seemed, been drinking his way through the vintages of his little, homespun vintner's. As his cellar depleted so he desperately had tried to brew some more. That was what all the spilt sugar was about. In the scullery she found several fat demijohns of brown liquid bubbling through airlocks. One of these was smashed and had leaked a broad puddle of immature wine across the floor, leaving a sticky residue.

How forethoughtful, thought Colette. There can't be many self-sufficient drunks in the world, autarkic alcoholics who never once have to burden the off-license but who simply press what-ever fruit, flowers or vegetables are growing in their gardens and transform the juices into alcohol. But home-brewing is a slow, painstaking process. It takes method, routine, care and above all patience. The slow chemistry of fermentation can only happen over weeks and months. Janus Brian was down to his last couple of bottles of kitchen garden wine, while the stuff he was brewing was by now barely more potent than lemonade.

She later learnt that the matter that was fermenting in the scullery was nothing more than tea wine. Incapable of reaping anything from the garden to use, Janus Brian had simply gone to the kitchen cupboard and taken the first thing that had come to hand – a packet of PG Tips tea bags. It surprised her really, that he'd even gone to those lengths. It wouldn't have surprised her if he'd just mixed some sugar, yeast and water together and had hoped for the best.

'I keep seeing her dear,' Janus Brian said as he continued to swivel, 'I keep hearing her. The floorboards upstairs will creak, and I'll think it's Mary getting dressed. I see her passing behind the crack of the door. I hear her in the kitchen opening cupboards . . .'

'You need time to get used to it. It will take a long time,' said Colette. It was natural, she said, that his mind should go on seeing her and hearing her, when that was what it had been doing constantly for nearly thirty years. 'It is like an echo,' she said, 'Mary will go on echoing around the house. But like any echo, eventually she will begin to fade.'

'But the echo's getting stronger, not fainter, dear,' said Janus Brian, 'at the start there was nothing, but now she's busy around the house all day.'

'Perhaps you should think about moving house, make a new start.'

'I couldn't.'

That night Colette stayed with her brother, sending her husband and son home alone. She washed clothes, hoovered and made the bed. The shops were closed, so she searched the cupboards again for food but found little – a box of candles, a can of shoe polish, a packet of spaghetti. In the fridge, to her surprise, she found a dish of fresh kidneys and a small block of cheese. She made a meal of grilled kidneys and spaghetti with cheese.

Janus Brian ate tentatively before being violently but unproductively sick in the downstairs loo.

After tidying up the rest of the house, and filling Janus Brian's dustbin to its brim with empty wine bottles, under protests from her brother who wanted to re-use them, she settled him down in the big double bed that filled the master bedroom. He asked her to stay with him for a while and talk, so she sat on the only chair, a little dressing table stool upholstered in white leather.

Janus lay in the bed, the sheets up to his chin. His body gave very little shape to the broad counterpane, so that he appeared as nothing more than an old, yellowish, wispy head, talking on the pillow. He was still wearing his glasses.

'You're very fat,' he said, in the manner of someone making a commonplace observation.

'Am I?' said Colette, shocked by her brother's bluntness.

'Yes. You didn't used to be fat, did you? You used to be very thin.'

Although a little hurt, Colette also felt curiously gratified by these remarks. They meant that Janus Brian had noticed her, had registered and accepted her physical presence in the world as something real.

'How much do you weigh?' he went on.

'I don't know. We don't have any scales.'

'There are some scales in the bathroom.'

'I'd rather not know at the moment, thanks.'

'I bet you weigh more than me.'

It was possible, despite his five extra inches of height.

'Do you still sniff those little tubes of glue?'

She felt real shock that Janus should know about the addiction that had almost destroyed her five years ago.

'How do you know about that?' she said, quietly.

'I saw you doing it once, when I called at your house. I'd discovered a blood clot in my wrist which turned out to be one of my wrist bones, but which at the time I thought was about to give me a fatal embolism, and I'd called round to break the tragic news to you. You answered the door with a wad of lavatory paper over your nose. I thought you had some sort of bad cold, but I couldn't get any sense out of you at all – you were away with the fairies. Eventually you took the pad off your nose and offered it to me. I took a sniff and nearly passed out straight away. Then I saw all the squashed up tubes by your armchair. What were they – rubber solution of some sort?'

'Romac,' said Colette, 'from puncture repair outfits.' She was still astounded by her brother's recollection of the event. She had no memory of it whatsoever.

'I mentioned it to Aldous once, when I happened to see him, and he sort of waved my question away as though it was nothing important, just one of your little fads . . .'

'Well,' said Colette, refocusing herself, 'in answer to your question – no, I don't sniff them anymore.'

'But why did you do it?'

'It's like drink,' said Colette, 'it has the same effect, only much faster . . .'

The next morning, shakily sober, Janus Brian drove his sister to the shops and they filled his boot with convenience food – tins of ravioli and spaghetti, frozen faggots, rissoles. Janus Brian bought six sliced loaves.

'They'll go stale, Janus Brian,' said Colette when she saw them.

Janus Brian looked at his little sister pityingly.

'They're for the freezer, dear.'

'You can't freeze bread, can you?' said Colette, amazed. She had no fridge, let alone a freezer.

'Of course you can freeze bread, dear. It'll keep for months, and when you defrost it, it tastes even fresher then when you bought it.'

Unloading the food at Janus Brian's house, Colette thought her brother looked almost back to his old self. All he needed was a shave and he would appear fully recovered.

He gave her a lift back to Fernlight Avenue.

'You will look after yourself, won't you?' said Colette, as she prepared to get out of the car.

Janus Brian gave her a reassuring nod, closing his eyes to add emphasis, though behind his glasses they were difficult to see.

'Shall I call round again?' Colette said, rather hopefully.

'Pop over next week,' he said, to her delight.

She leant over and gave him a kiss on his bristly jowl, before leaving the car.

A week later Aldous, Julian and Colette, after another early evening drink in the garden of The Owl, called again on Janus Brian, and found the events of the previous week repeated in almost every detail, except that Janus Brian's drunken sleep was deeper, and his overall condition worse. Flat out on the couch with dried vomit down his front, he had grown a shallow, white beard. The food Colette had so optimistically bought the week before remained mostly untouched. There were six sliced loaves in the freezer.

Any hope that Janus Brian's drinking had been a one-off act of desperation in response to the shock of sudden loneliness now vanished. Colette quickly realised that her brother would need more than weekly visits. For the following week she called on him nearly every day, and thereafter a routine quickly established itself. Every other day, or sometimes daily, Janus Brian, already dangerously sozzled but appearing sober, would drive over to Fernlight Avenue sometime in the mid-morning to collect Colette and she would spend a few hours keeping house for him – washing, cooking, tidying up and chatting. Sometimes he'd take her back, and sometimes, if he was too far gone, she'd take the bus. Conveniently the W2 went almost from door to door. She was usually home in time for Julian's return from school.

Once or twice a week she'd fit in an evening visit as well, sometimes accompanied by Aldous and Julian. They'd sit watching TV with him. Janus Brian loved TV, even though he scarcely seemed to comprehend what happened on the screen. It was while watching TV that Janus Brian became most animated, as though he actually drew energy from the machine. He liked action films, particularly those portraying World War Two. He liked American detective shows, especially *Kojak*. With the cop shows it was the style of the thing he seemed to enjoy, rather than the stories. He loved the way Kojak talked, the way he dressed, he loved his car, and the wisecracking sidekicks who trailed around after him. Whenever Kojak offered a choice phrase Janus Brian would repeat it and laugh.

'He's like Yul Brynner, isn't he, Aldous – you know Yul Brynner, don't you Colette? *Who loves ya baby?* Janus Brian produced a deep, growling New York accent, 'Look at those rings he's wearing – he makes Sherlock Holmes look a bit old-fashioned, doesn't he? That's a Buick, Colette – a Buick. When he wants to show it's a cop's car he puts a portable revolving light with a magnetic base on the roof and plugs it into the cigarette lighter.'

Julian, during these evenings (he preferred visiting his uncle to staying at home with his brother), sat silently on the couch doing his homework. Janus Brian seemed not to see him.

Despite her regular visits, Colette found she could do little to stop Janus Brian's drinking. Out of home-brew, and having been dissatisfied with unfermented tea wine, he had soon resorted to buying drink from the off-license. He had followed, at first, the habit of his long-standing hobby and had bought wines, mainly German, but had soon found them watery and weak in comparison to his powerful home-made brews, so had switched to the fortified varieties – sherries and ports. Over the following few weeks, however, Janus Brian realized, as all novice alcoholics do, that as a ratio of drunkenness to the pound, only the spirits offered reasonable value. He was soon on the gin. A bottle a day.

It is surprisingly easy, he said to Colette after confessing to the volume of his new mode of alcoholism, to drink a bottle of gin in a day. If one begins in the morning and continues throughout the day at an even pace one can maintain a kind of anaesthetised variety of drunkenness without ever tipping over the edge, quite, into oblivion. This was the state Janus Brian obtained, for the most part. The best Colette felt she could do was to prevent her brother's consumption of alcohol overtaking his body's ability to process it, and to make sure that he was taking in food as well as booze.

She found that the only food he would eat and keep down was fish. He developed a liking for the boil-in-the-bag varieties that had just come out. Colette had never seen them before, and thought them fascinating. A frozen, misted brick was dropped into a pan of boiling water. A few minutes later it emerged as a steaming, semi-transparent pocket which, when snipped at the corner, bled a creamy parsley sauce and an oblong of cod onto a plate.

On a diet of fish and gin, Colette began to hope that her brother would slowly pull through.

4

Colette and Aldous were in the bathroom at Fernlight Avenue – Colette in the blue-tinted foamy waters of the bath, Aldous in his trousers and vest at the sink, shaving.

Aldous was a cautious, rather nervous shaver. He had a sensitive skin that was easily nicked, and he bled every morning – little scarlet puddles on his face that in the lather looked like strawberries in snow. He endured the painful ritual because he could never bear the thought of being bearded.

Once, during a wartime razorblade shortage, he'd let his whiskers grow for three days, but the itchiness had nearly driven him mad. He'd resorted to fishing a blunt blade out of the rubbish and shaving painfully with that. And any beard he grew now would be white, and a white beard was out of the question. He would look like Father Christmas, as ridiculous as the beard of lather he wore each morning before the bathroom mirror.

The greying of Aldous's hair had begun when he was in his forties, and had been a slow process that seemed to have accelerated in recent years. It was still thick, combed straight back in a single, brimming wave that added an extra inch and a half to his height, but was now almost pure white. That the same had happened to his whiskers he could tell in the morning, when he saw them on his jowls. His beard grew slowly, and each morning there was a barely perceptible sheen of silver on his face, like dew on a lawn. It weighed him down, his hair – almost black when he was a young man, it now sat on his head like a puff of cumulus, reminding everyone who cared to look that this man hadn't, in the scheme of the average lifespan, long to live.

It was true. Another decade and Aldous would be an old man. He should, he knew, be looking forward to retirement.

Just two more years. A lump sum and a decent pension awaited him. Days free to do as he liked. Time to paint. For the first time since his days as a student, when he'd lived in lodgings with Lesley Waugh, he would be able to devote nearly all his time to painting, or listening to music, or reading, or whatever he liked. But the thought filled him with dread. Any thoughts about the future filled him with dread.

It was always the same problem. He could picture a happy future for him and his family, himself in comfortable retirement out in the garden painting the trees, his children happily married, grandchildren playing on the grass, Colette enjoying the odd glass of cider but nothing stronger, baking pies and making jam. And then he would ask himself the question – where would Janus fit into this picture? Aldous's thoughts about the future were always clouded by Janus. If Aldous pictured a future garden in which his family was happy, Janus would always emerge darkly from the bushes, a can of strong beer in his hands, whooping like an Apache, kicking over the flowers and card tables, screaming obscenities.

It was impossible to imagine Janus married, more impossible to imagine him a father. Almost laughable. Nor could he ever seriously imagine Janus having any sort of proper job, befitting a qualified musician. Occasionally the desperate hope would present itself, that Janus might settle down as a music teacher, but the thought was ridiculous. At times Aldous even wished that his son had never touched a piano, all it had done was give him a superiority complex, and had, via pub pianism, turned him into an aggressive and obnoxious drunk.

As Aldous shaved, observing the familiar faces he made to make the process easier (the sceptical philosopher, the affronted duchess, the smirking connoisseur), he could see his wife in the mirror, mottled slightly by the condensation on the glass. In the mountains of suds (how Colette loved bubble-bath, a bottle was gone in three or four sessions), she seemed like an angel reclining on a cloud, her breasts (plumper and rounder than he'd ever known them, even when she was pregnant) shining as though under a sheen of lacquer. Now and then he exchanged glances with her via the damp mirror, and smiled.

They were both revelling in the uniqueness of the morning.

They didn't normally use the bathroom together, but this morning was special.

For the last two or three years money, never in much abundance, had been especially scarce. At times Aldous feared falling behind with the mortgage, of losing the house. He fantasized that he would have to take their tent down from the loft and live somewhere in that. Everything he earned as a teacher seemed to vanish the moment it entered his bank account, as though that repository was made of some corrosive substance that dissolved money. Out of desperation he'd tried to make money from his paintings.

Not really knowing how to sell them, he'd entered them instead for the various competitions that it seemed fashionable now for certain companies to sponsor, and he'd had some success. First prize in a competition organised by Bukta, for a landscape painting that incorporated a tent. From memory Aldous had painted, during a few lunch hours, a portrait of their own Bukta tent as it stood in the farm at Llanygwynfa, where, up until 1970, they'd spent every summer for fifteen years. The prize was five hundred pounds and a small, two-person tent. Aldous wondered if they would ever use it.

Then there was a competition organised by the makers of Tia Maria for a painting that could be of any subject so long as it included the 'distinctive image' of a Tia Maria bottle. Aldous dredged up from the loft an old painting he'd done some time in the early Fifties, an interior of their old house in Edmonton, executed in the thick, impastoed style of the kitchen-sink school, of which Aldous was then an unacknowledged member. In the foreground, to the left there was the perfect space for a Tia Maria bottle, so, in the same style, he trowelled the image in, waited a while for the oils to dry, then sent it off. It won a thousand pounds and a five year supply of Tia Maria. Aldous was able to buy a car with the thousand pounds, and pay off some debts, but the supplementary prize caused him some anxiety. He hadn't really thought about it when he entered, now the idea of endless alcohol pumped into the house horrified him. A mountain of crates filling the music room, Janus permanently drunk on liquor, Colette also. What quantity of spirit would they send to meet the five year capacity of a family of drunks?

But it was not to be a one-off delivery. Instead, once every three months, a bottle of Tia Maria arrived by special delivery, and would do so for another four years. Never exactly the same day of the month, so chance dictated who answered the door and received the drink. If Janus got there first, the bottle was gone in a day and he would fall to a sickly state of drunkenness. Tia Maria, for some reason, affected Janus particularly badly, and nearly always caused him to utter a most tedious sequence of slow and nasty insults which gnawed at the consciousness of the listener until their selfhood seemed to pop, and they became someone else, equally aggressive.

Janus always maintained (quite wrongly, Aldous believed) that he never initiated the violence that erupted when he was drunk. His skill, he claimed, on those rare occasions when he would talk about it, was to incite other people to aggressive acts against him.

'It gives me a parallel into their minds,' he said once, holding his index fingers vertically and moving them against each other to signify two minds coming into contact, 'provoking people to violence is like undressing their minds,' he said, 'if you are violently out of control you are mentally naked.'

Aldous had scoffed loudly at the idea. He no longer trusted anything his son said, sober or drunk.

Aldous now dreaded the arrival of his prize, the menstrual ingress of alcohol, uninvited, into his house. It somehow ensured that even if his wife and son gave up the bottle completely, there would always be something to tempt them back.

Recently, however, Aldous had won a rather spectacular prize. The town council of a resort on the south coast had organized a competition to design windows for its new crematorium. There were two windows, one at each end, both eight feet tall, both with triangular arches at the top. Aldous had made designs based on an ascending flock of doves, circling round a sun, on one window, and a moon on the other. Semi-abstract, expressionistic, with the textural feel of fabric designs, Aldous's doves had won first prize, beating many hundreds of entrants, including the design departments of several colleges (including the Hornsey, Aldous's old college), and attracting a surprising amount of publicity.

The designs had appeared in the *Daily Telegraph* with a short paragraph about Aldous underneath. That was six months ago. Now the windows had been made and were installed. Aldous had taken a day off school and was to travel to the south coast resort for a special lunch with the mayor and other local dignitaries to be followed by the unveiling ceremony where Aldous would see his windows *in situ*, and would know at last how they would appear when transparent, how well they would catch the light, something that had troubled Aldous since he had made the designs. It is, after all, very difficult to imagine how something on paper will look on glass with the sun shining behind it.

Aldous and Colette wondered if this marked a turning point in their fortunes, because shortly after the article had appeared in the *Telegraph* a letter came from a monastery in Durham inviting Aldous to submit designs for a fountain to decorate a monastic quadrangle. Aldous had already made a design, a scaled down version of which he was currently sculpting in terracotta, which was really a three dimensional version of his windows, with ascending doves fluttering around a central fount of water which then crashed and spilt over them beautifully, or so he hoped. As with windows, it is hard to imagine what a fountain, on paper, will look like when water is pouring through it.

Money had not yet been discussed, although the oddly named commissioner of the piece, Brother Head, had warned that he had first to seek the approval of the bishop of Durham before they could talk about fees.

What future commissions might these projects open doors to! Aldous might become a celebrated designer of ecclesiastical windows, reglazing the vandalized churches of England with many-coloured glass, the cathedrals even. How charming it would be to become part of the thousand-year narrative of an English church.

That was a hope, at least. Colette was as excited about it. She was always exasperated by Aldous's unwillingness to exploit the lucrative side of art. Her fantasy was that they should tour the countryside, paying their way by painting pictures of any pretty pubs they happened upon, then selling them to the licensees. She half-imagined they could live like that indefinitely. But Aldous could not be cajoled into hawking his art, not because he had any qualms about the morality of the thing, he just lacked any ability whatsoever as a salesman. Now Colette hoped that her husband was beginning to be recognized for the extraordinary talent she believed him to be, so she made sure he shaved properly, closely, accurately.

And Aldous felt like singing as he dabbed and patted his uncut face dry, removed the earrings of soap that always grew on his lobes, the collar of foam that always grew round his neck and lowered a hand into the creamy, clotted water to pull the plug.

There was an unusual sound. A loud cascading of liquid, as though there was a waterfall in the room. Then Aldous felt something warm and wet pattering on his feet. Bending down he saw that the water was falling through the plughole into empty space. There was no pipe to take it away.

'Hey,' he said, then noticed the spread of milky water out from under the bath. Colette had just got out and had pulled the plug and the same thing was happening there. Water had been released into the unpiped open, to spread as it liked across the floor, through the floorboards, down onto the ceiling of the hall. Thinking quickly Aldous leapt over and replugged the bath, but not before a gallon or so of bathwater had escaped.

Underneath the sink Aldous found that the pipes had been cut out. Two shiny o's of freshly sliced copper. He found the same under the bath when he removed a panel. The bath was an old tub of enamelled iron with clawed feet. The waste pipe had been sawn off.

It took Aldous and Colette a while to understand what had happened. Colette dressed herself while Aldous hurried downstairs. In the hall he inspected the ceiling. A dark stain was growing in the plaster around the light fitting. He rummaged in the cupboard under the stairs for his hand drill, found a chair to stand on and began drilling holes in the ceiling.

'What are you doing?' said Colette as she came down the stairs.

'Relieving the pressure,' said Aldous, an irritable growl in his voice, 'The weight of water could bring the whole ceiling down if it's just left there − then there's the electrics to worry about − what the hell's been going on?'

The drill, with a little jolt, had made its first hole. A needle-thin stream of water fell.

'Get a pot or something will you darling?' said Aldous, repositioning his chair for another go with the drill, '. . . get several.'

Colette went into the kitchen and returned with an array of saucepans and bowls. For a few moments the two of them wordlessly concentrated on their task of draining the water from the ceiling – Aldous drilling little holes, Colette positioning pots and pans to catch the drops. After ten minutes or so there were half a dozen tiny waterfalls pouring out of the ceiling, and no sign of an end to the water trapped up there.

'I don't understand,' said Aldous, standing back to watch the strange spectacle of rain indoors, 'why would anyone want to saw the pipes out of the bathroom?'

'I don't know, but don't worry about it now, you've got to get to Waterloo, you don't want to miss the train.'

Aldous, as though having forgotten, rushed upstairs to finish dressing, leaving Colette to gaze into the little, deepening pools that were forming in the hall, seeing the milky traces of soap in the water, the scum of bubbles round the rim of each pan.

'I'll see you tonight then darling,' said Aldous, coming back down the stairs, making for the front door, almost kicking a pot over.

'I wish I was coming with you,' said Colette, kissing him.

'Janus Brian would never get over it,' Aldous laughed, conscious that his wife was showing a rare level of interest in his work. She never came to the door normally to see him off but would usually just sit in her chair, calling goodbye as he left the kitchen, but here she was at the front door straightening his tie and brushing the dandruff off his lapels. It wasn't just that he was setting off for the south coast to receive a prestigious prize. She had changed since Janus Brian had entered their lives. The regular visits she now made had instilled her with a new energy, and a sense of purpose, something she'd always felt an increasing lack of as the children grew older.

'This is going to be the start of something big,' she said, 'don't worry about the bathroom now, just think about your windows.'

Aldous was finding the worry in his face difficult to dislodge,

Colette could see that. After he'd kissed her he saved his last glance for the falling water in the hall, before turning his back on the house. The flood had provided a dissonant underside to their happy, late morning in the bathroom, a kind of inversion of it, its antithesis – unwanted, intrusive water that upstairs had been a desired luxury.

Anything unusual about the house, anything strange, odd, out of place, was usually the work of Janus. He came down, as always, after his father had left the house. He passed Colette in the hall, and didn't register the falling water at all, even though dribbles landed on him as he passed through. He washed at the sink in the kitchen, made himself a cup of tea. Scipio, who'd been asleep all morning on a chair, woke up, as he always did when Janus came down, and mewed seductively at his master's feet, curling in and out of his legs. Janus opened a tin of cat food, pulled the meat onto a saucer and put it on the floor for the cat. Feeding Scipio had been Janus's sole responsibility for all the years they'd had the cat.

Then Janus sat at the table with his tea. But he didn't drink his tea at first. He liked to wait until it had cooled down. Sometimes he would leave it cooling for half an hour, and then drink it all, nearly stone cold, in one go. While waiting he just sat there, one arm resting on the tabletop, the other in his lap, his legs crossed. His head was inclined forward, slightly, so that his long hair fell across it. With his thick beard his face was almost completely obscured by hair.

Since losing his job he'd spent most of his time like that – just sitting. He sat in the same place, in the same position, for hours on end – one elbow on the table, his other arm in his lap. If he left the table – to use the lavatory, to make tea, he would return to the chair as soon as possible and resume the position, with almost a palace sentry's sense of duty, almost as if the chair and the table had become body parts without which he couldn't survive for long. He talked very little. When the evening came he would eat the dinner Colette had cooked, then he would return to his room, and begin drinking. They would hear, from downstairs, the metallic retching of beer cans being opened. Four or five in quick succession. Then the muffled downpour of vomit falling into the lavatory. Then Janus would leave the house, primed for an evening's boozing in The Quiet Woman. Nearly every other night he went through this routine, returning noisily around midnight, usually too far gone to be any trouble. Drinking was the only thing that seemed to animate him now. Sober he was silent and inert, drunk he was alive, vociferous, energetic. What puzzled Colette most was where he was getting the money from. He'd been out of work for nearly two months. He handed over to her around half his National Assistance. That left him about five pounds a week to spend, which could pay for perhaps one night on the tiles, but not the four or five Janus was spending each week.

Colette thought she would leave it until the afternoon before asking her son about the bathroom. Janus Brian called for her exactly on time, pipping his horn perkily outside the house, and she walked through the small shower in the hall, to meet him.

She did worry sometimes when Janus Brian came for her in his car, even though he'd promised he'd never drink prior to picking her up, and would only take her home again in the afternoon if he hadn't had a drink in between. Colette could tell, by the quickening of his speech and the sweetening of his breath, he'd always had a drink before he'd set out. Probably just a swig of gin, a single mouthful, taken straight from the bottle, enough to prime him for life beyond the front door. But she didn't say anything. Instead she sat down in the passenger seat of her brother's Renault 7, still quite a new car, newer than any of the cars Aldous had ever owned and felt the soft, upholstered comfort of average luxury.

Janus Brian was unshaven, his tall head prickly with unkempt hair. As always, he did her seat belt for her, leaning across her to click the buckle into place.

'Don't think I'm mauling you dear,' he said, 'but it is better to be trapped than thrown out.'

Though only a mile separated Janus Brian's house from Colette's, there seemed an infinite variety of possible routes between the two. This was because their houses were on different spokes of London's radial street pattern. Journeys across the city from one suburb to another were awkward and eccentric and involved lots of detours and short cuts through the grids of residential avenues that lead nowhere in particular. This time Janus Brian turned left at the top of the road, down Hoopers Lane, passing The Goat and Compasses, then right up the busy Goat and Compasses Lane, an arterial road, one of the spokes that brought traffic into London from the north. A sequence of nearly identical straight roads turned off from here to the left, all running parallel, leading to Owl Lane. It was down to Janus's own whim which of these roads he chose. They were all named after places in Devon for some reason – Exeter Avenue, Honiton Road, Plymouth Drive. Janus Brian chose Wolfardisworthy Avenue, and put his foot down, a reckless burst of acceleration that had the bordering houses and parked cars flicking past with frightening velocity and which Colette endured in rigid silence. The needle passed sixty before Janus Brian took his foot off the pedal, then, turning right carefully into Owl Lane muttered, by way of explanation, 'Nice to have a spurt occasionally.'

Later, as they passed down Taunton Road to The Lemon Tree, he talked further.

'Would you mind, dear, if I talked about my bowel movements? I know you are not my doctor, but they have been bothering me lately. You see, I seem to have been passing live fish.'

'Have you?'

Janus Brian shrugged, as though it was beyond explanation.

'I mean, it is ridiculous. I know I eat a lot of fish, especially those boil-in-the-bag ones that you buy for me, but, you know, last night I was passing a motion on the toilet, not much came out, just a dribble, really, but when I looked in the bowl there was this brightly coloured – a sort of electric blue with yellow stripes – tropical fish in the pan swimming about. I don't know if I imagined it or what, I suppose I must have, but it's been happening for a few days now. Once I looked down and there was this little shoal of tiny red fish, absolutely beautiful, a sort of pinky red, like valentines, all turning at the same time, like a flock of birds. They swam round the U-bend as I looked, and were gone. I don't mind really, as long as they are nice colourful ones, but they do give me a bit of a start. The thing is, would you mind having a look for me, to see if you can see them as well? To prove to me that I must be hallucinating?'

Colette nodded in a tired sort of way. She was no longer surprised by her brother's faeces.

'Yesterday I had . . .' he paused briefly, as he always did before uttering any expletive or other unsavoury term, 'what I can only describe as an, inverted commas, "wet fart". Do you know what I mean?' He suddenly seemed pleased with his invented term, 'In fact that is what I seem to have nowadays instead of proper craps. But anyway, I had this wet fart yesterday, and afterwards I was absolutely sure there was a small goldfish in my pants. I could feel it wriggling there, gasping for breath. I had to pull my trousers down and have a look. There was nothing there, just a brown stain. Do you think I'm going mad?'

'Yes,' said Colette.

At the house Janus Brian paused on the doorstep, after opening the front door, and turned to the street below and shouted 'Bollocks!' as loudly as his weakened voice would allow. 'Sorry, but I sometimes feel this incredible urge. I'm beginning to hate the people in this road. When Mary was alive they were always popping in, but since she's gone and I've gone off the rails, they've shunned me completely.' There was no response from the street, not even the twitch of a curtain. 'There's a taxi-driver a few doors down who starts his taxi up every morning at about half past six and lets it run for half an hour to warm up. Bloody thing sounds like a tractor, keeping me awake. I don't see why I shouldn't retaliate once in a while.'

Colette did her usual tidying up, conscious, as always, that she worked far harder at her brother's house than she ever did at her own. At Fernlight Avenue it was Aldous who was usually lumbered, after a day's work, with hoovering, doing the washing-up and making the beds.

Janus Brian chatted, as he always did.

'Have you seen these new cigarettes they've just brought out? Reg brought me some over on Saturday. John Players Special.' He showed her a pack. They did look unusual, packaged in shiny, black boxes with the monogram JPS in gold. The pack Janus Brian handed her was empty. 'I'll have to get myself some when we go to the shops today. You can get these special plastic drum packs, a sort of cylinder, same colour, must hold about fifty.'

Janus Brian always had a taste for the luxuries his modest

but comfortable draughtsman's salary would allow. He probably earned less than Aldous but without any children all his earnings, and Mary's as well, went on themselves. This made Colette very angry when, as sometimes happened, Janus Brian would gently criticize Colette for the impoverished nature of her lifestyle; the fact that she had no fridge, telephone or washing machine, that Aldous's cars were always at least a decade old, that they had no furniture in their house that wasn't handed down from Nana, or from their dead sister Meg. Janus Brian had always enjoyed the newest styles and the latest gadgetry. His furniture was straight out of the Sunday supplements. He smoked Dunhills which he lit with a silver-plated Dunhill lighter, and he stubbed them out on an onyx ashtray with a spinning mechanism. He listened to Schubert and big band jazz on something called a hi-fi that he was always talking about in a jargon Colette couldn't follow, and which irritated her.

Colette's lack of a telephone particularly annoyed Janus Brian. He even offered to pay for the installation of a phone at Fernlight Avenue. He himself had what he called a *Trimphone,* a grey-green modernistic piece of plastic that warbled electronically instead of ringing.

'I've told you, Janus, Aldous won't have a phone. He just doesn't like the idea of it.'

'There you are, you see,' said Janus, 'you're always saying it's the kids that keep you living in the dark ages, but in fact it's your own choice. You choose to live like that.'

As Colette spruced up Janus Brian's house, particularly musty and dour after a weekend alone, she came upon something odd in the kitchen. In a small saucepan there was an open tin of Cherry Blossom shoe polish. The shoe polish seemed to have melted, coating the inside of the pan with a mushy, strong smelling tar.

'What's this mess?' she said.

Janus Brian seemed unconcerned.

'Sunday night. I'd run out of booze and I was going crazy for a drink. Nowhere to buy anything. Nothing open. Fucking Sundays. Pardon my French.'

'What's that got to do with shoe polish in your saucepan?'

'Oh,' he said, seeming to think that he'd already provided an explanation, 'I tried to extract the alcohol from it. Bloody waste of time. In theory it should be possible. I ended up with a teaspoonful of brown sludge that tasted like hell . . .'

'You mean you've been drinking shoe polish?'

'Refined shoe polish, if you don't mind. You see, if you boil it in a double boiler, catch the steam, in theory you should be able to separate the spirit . . .'

'Janus,' said Colette, 'What are we going to do with you?'

Colette smiled when she heard herself uttering that phrase. The last time she'd heard it, it had been applied to herself by Mrs Lawrence, a large and loud Jamaican woman she had befriended when Julian had started going to primary school. Their children Julian and Nicky were friends, and as the Lawrences lived nearby, in a flat above a hardware shop on Green Lanes just at the bottom of Fernlight Avenue, she and Mrs Lawrence caught the same buses when they took their sons to school (another awkward non-radial journey – two buses to go less than a mile!). It was around that time that Colette began sniffing bicycle glue and taking sleeping pills, a combination that meant, some mornings, she was just too far gone to take Julian to school. Then Aldous would have to take Julian down to the hardware shop and ask Mrs Lawrence if she could take him to school with Nicky. A favour-exchanging relationship soon developed between them, and sometimes Julian would go to Nicky's home after school and play with his toys for an hour or two, and likewise Nicky would sometimes come to Fernlight Avenue. It was when Mrs Lawrence came to collect Nicky one day that she witnessed Colette in one of her states, staggering, delirious, mumbling nonsensically, her hair awry, her glasses crooked. Mrs Lawrence had been brisk and humorous in her reaction

'What you going to do with her, Mr Jones,' she said to Aldous loudly, 'You going to sell her?'

She felt sad when the Lawrences moved, just as they were getting to know them. Mr Lawrence had landed a job in America and the whole family had uprooted and gone to Florida just in time to watch the *Saturn V*s taking off. Nicky had been such a sweet little boy. Colette remembered the time he'd been sick at one of Julian's birthday parties, a pink trough of puke on the floor, and two silver tears rolling down that little brown face.

Now it was Janus Brian's turn to be useless. And yet with him the question had a more urgent feel. What *were* they going to do with him? Something needed to be done, but what? Colette couldn't go on being his housekeeper for ever. Whenever she thought he was getting better, that he was beginning to pull himself together, she would find something like this, a little home-made shoe polish distillery, and everything would be back to square one. She suspected, though couldn't be sure, that his level of alcohol intake was steadily increasing.

Whenever she confronted her brother with the question of what plans he was making, he would always end up in a trough of suicidal self-pity.

'Bring some cyanide with you next time you come, will you dear? This poison,' he pointed to a gin bottle, 'is working too slowly.'

This is what he said after she found the shoe polish. He flopped in his Mastermind chair and wept faintly. Little tears again, sweet as Nicky Lawrence's, like silverfish scurrying down his face.

'Don't talk like that.'

'Well, what am I good for? I'm just waiting to join Mary. That's all I want.'

'Why don't you move,' she said, 'sell up and buy somewhere smaller. Somewhere without all these memories.'

'The only house I want is a wooden one,' he moaned, 'six feet under.'

Colette understood how central she had become to Janus Brian's life. She was his main support. She felt like the rampart of a dam. If she weakened, if she cracked, the waters came dribbling through, and soon there was the flood. She was holding back the lake of Janus Brian's despair.

Colette sighed, exasperated, suddenly wanting to slap her brother's bald pate. Then she found herself thinking about Aldous. While she was sitting in this stale house, he was somewhere on the south coast lunching with dignitaries. She wondered what he was doing at that precise moment. Being chauffeured to the crematorium, like a film star, watching the curtain fall from his monumental windows. No, she thought, looking at the clock on the mantelpiece, too early. He was probably still on the train.

'Come on, Janus,' Colette said, with sudden assertiveness, 'let me read you something.'

And Janus Brian brightened. He had come to adore being read to by his little sister. He himself had chosen *Bleak House*, suggesting the novel only half-seriously for the dark aptness of its title. Its main effect, it soon transpired, was soporific, and Janus Brian would often fall asleep after a few pages of the wranglings of Jarndyce and Jarndyce. At this rate Colette reckoned it would take about two and a half years to read *Bleak House*, and around half a century to read the complete works.

When Janus Brian slept, as he did that morning, Colette slept as well. Zonked out in his Mastermind chair, Janus Brian could sleep for two or three hours. Colette would go upstairs and have a long nap in her brother's double bed, losing herself in the luxury of space, what seemed an acre of mattress in comparison to the *put-u-up* bed-settee she and Aldous had become used to. It sometimes struck her that that was why she enjoyed her visits to Leicester Avenue so much. Whereas she lived in a crowded house made shadowy and awkward by its accumulated objects, Janus Brian lived in a house that had few objects and little history. What there was instead was space, open reaches of carpet, walls not shrunk with shelving and cupboards, rooms that with their absence of things seemed to her like ballrooms, arenas, stadia.

But it was not how she would have liked her house. After a few hours the absence of history became as intrusive, in its own way, as stacked books or mounds of outgrown clothes. And she could never sleep deeply in the double bed, troubled by the odd space she was occupying, her brother's wife's, whose absence from those pillows had emptied the house to an intolerable degree, for Janus Brian. After a shallow and restless sleep the thought struck her that day – supposing as she'd slept, Janus Brian, half-cut, had come up the stairs to find her in his bed. In his state of mind he might have taken her for a ghost. The thought made her sit upright suddenly. She was stupid to use her brother's bed. There were other beds in the house, though not as comfortable as this. And as she sat there, she had the distinct feeling that Janus Brian had visited her while she slept, she could sense it in the subtlest of spatial shifts – the door ajar by an extra half-inch, perhaps, or another millimetre of light between the curtains. She wasn't sure, but she felt a need to go and investigate her brother's whereabouts. She found him soon enough. He was in the bathroom, contemplating his naked self in the mirror.

Colette had become used to her brother's nakedness, though it had shocked her the first time, when he appeared in the kitchen one evening while she was making the dinner. He'd made no excuse or apology for his nudity, he simply drifted into the kitchen, poked about in some of the cupboards, and then drifted out. Aldous recalled the same event with some amusement. He'd been in the living room, and had noticed a faint breeze rustle the pages of his *Daily Telegraph*. He lowered it and saw a rear view of nude Janus Brian, tall, yellowish pink, skinny, heading for the kitchen. He raised his paper and continued reading. A few seconds later another breeze set the pages fluttering and he lowered it, to see nude Janus Brian passing in the opposite direction. Without clothes Janus Brian made no sound as he walked. He was a visual event only.

At first Colette thought her brother's nudity was a form of laziness, that he couldn't be bothered getting dressed, even to answer the front door, but Aldous realised that Janus Brian was obtaining a certain thrill in exposing himself, and he himself confessed to her, 'I'm afraid, my dear, that I am what is called a "narcissist".'

'Are you?'

'Yes. I am falling in love with my own image. I will stand before the wardrobe mirror for hours admiring myself. My body. I am sorry but I believe I am beautiful.'

Now Colette watched her brother through the ajar door of the bathroom. He was standing before the long mirror, naked except for a pair of black socks and his glasses. His back was to her, his front reflected in the mirror. He was just standing there, his arms hanging by his sides, full square before himself, unexcited, still, absorbed in self-contemplation. She tried to gauge the expression on his face. Her brother had always had one of the least expressive faces she had ever seen. It hardly seemed to move, even when he was talking, or laughing, or crying. It was no different then, naked before the mirror. His body looked unbearably feeble, like a baby's, quite pink and solid, but totally without any visible musculature. His body was all loose skin and tendons, it seemed, and little pouches of fat.

As she watched he lifted his hands to his chest, cupped his breasts and lifted them, then pushed them together to create a wizened cleavage, then let them fall back into their shapeless repose. He repeated this two or three times, after which his hands moved down his body towards his genitals. Colette failed to avert her eyes. She was amused by the fluffiness of the hair down there and the way everything seemed neatly folded and tucked away. He lifted his flaccid penis by its foreskin, let it fall back, doing this several times as though testing for signs of life in a dead kitten.

'When we were at school,' said Janus Brian, showing no other sign that he'd noticed Colette's presence, 'we used to compare cock sizes, me and Reg. Mine was always the bigger. Mind you, he was circumcised, so mine always had the additional bulk of the prepuce. I knew I had one of the biggest, if not *the* biggest cock in the class. But since those days I've never seen another man's cock, so it's hard for me to know where I rank in the league of penis length . . .' Janus Brian now turned away from the mirror and faced his sister, 'What about Aldous?' he continued, 'how do we compare? I mean on a purely dimensional level?'

'To be honest I never pay much attention to dimensions. I wouldn't say there was much difference.'

'That's a pity,' Janus sighed and turned back to the mirror. Then he said, 'Do you think another woman will ever gaze with fondness upon this sight again?'

Colette remembered the trouble she'd gone through to find him a wife, his seeming indifference to all the possible mates she'd procured, the unusualness of Mary Moore. She thought it highly unlikely, almost impossible.

'Maybe one day, Janus, when you've got over all this.'

Janus didn't seem to hear her. He turned back to his reflection.

'You know who I keep seeing in this mirror?' he said. Then, before Colette could reply, 'Our father. I've been thinking about him a lot lately.'

Colette was tempted to say *Dada was a dream, dear,* but she said 'Have you?'

'Yes. I keep seeing him in my face in a way that I've never noticed before. And then I realized it was because I can't remember him as being much younger than I am now. In fact I am now older than he was when he died. I am older than my father. Isn't that what they call a paradox?'

'Yes.'

'So now I look like my father as I remember him. But I must have looked like him all my life, it's just that I never knew him as a young man. And then I find myself thinking about his body. I never saw it. Did you?'

'No.'

Their father took a bath once a week in the zinc tub that was kept in the scullery and was brought into the living room before the fire. When their father was bathing no one was allowed in the living room.

It disquieted her to think of it now, her father behind the oak door of the living room, in the middle of all their living room things, their books, furniture and carpet, standing, as he must have done, utterly naked. Colette can remember her father on the beach at Broadstairs, sitting stiffly in a deckchair, fully clothed even to his trilby hat, reading *The Times* on a hot day.

'I keep wondering if he had my body. I inherited his mouth and his eyes and his hair. What about the rest of me?' Colette knew what he was going to say next, she could see the mischievousness in his face, 'I keep wondering if I've got a bigger cock than Dada.'

'Well, I couldn't say,' said Colette.

'If I had ever seen him naked, I don't think I would have been so scared of him. And I feel cheated by the fact that he died before he became very old. I was denied the opportunity of cradling his weakened body in my arms. We should be able to do that to our fathers.'

'You were very scared of him weren't you?'

'I was scared of something he was capable of being. I don't know if that was him or not.'

He meant the violence.

Dada was gifted with violence. He was an expert, a virtuoso, he could modulate violence to match exactly to the prevailing situation, he could express the subtlest nuance of anger with it. He could orchestrate and choreograph his violence with the skill of a Stravinsky or Diaghilev.

There is one variation of Dada's violence that Colette always remembered in relation to Janus Brian.

Janus Brian was scientific. As a youth he had dreams of being a scientist splitting atoms, or an engineer, building bridges. He loved the world of nuts and bolts, of test tubes and pipettes. As a boy his favourite toy was Meccano, with which he was always building elaborate contraptions. He once spent several weeks making, to his own design, a most beautiful racing car. Every day he would be at the table bolting together delicate metal plates with little nuts, bolts and washers. He saved up his pocket money for the parts, the most expensive being the friction motor that would propel it. Then the four large rubber-rimmed tyres. Janus Brian was continually modifying it, dismantling a section when he saw design faults, reassembling it until he had created a small and ingenious masterpiece of childhood engineering. Nearly two feet long, with a steering wheel that worked, it was a perfect model of a full size racing car such as those that raced at Brands Hatch.

One Sunday evening in the living room Janus was playing with the car he'd only just finished constructing, giving it its first test run. He would wind up the motor and let the car go, its flywheel rasping, so that it shot across the floor and crashed into something – the skirting board, the foot of the dresser, a chair. Dada was in the room, sitting in his armchair reading a newspaper. He showed no sign that he was at all bothered by Janus's playing until, for the second time, the car crashed into his foot. Amongst the people in the room there descended an awkward hush. Dada's next action was slow, deliberate and meanly purposeful. He leant over, put one foot on the front of the car, took the rear end of the car in his hand and, with a sudden, brief and violent wrenching, twisted the whole thing into a U-shape. Nuts and bolts snapped from their joints and plopped onto the floor. A wheel fell off and rolled across the carpet. Then, discarding the ruined toy, Dada settled back into his armchair and raised the white cliff of his newspaper.

How sorry Colette, then scarcely more than a baby, felt for her older brother. He didn't show any sign of emotion but just scuttled over, picked up the warped body of his car and the scattered debris, took it back to his bedroom. The only sign of how he felt was in the manner of his handling of the car, he seemed to nurse it, as though it was a wounded animal, a bird with a broken wing.

How savagely their father had acted upon that distraction. A mere distraction. Such brute ruthlessness. He seemed to Colette as merciless as if he'd just torn the head off a kitten. And so controlled. Dada never seemed to lose his temper, his violence always seemed considered and planned, even though it was often spontaneous. And he was equally capable of violence to his sons as to objects. Always his sons. He never raised his hand against a woman. In fact, he seemed to be instinctively scared of them.

That is what Janus Brian and Colette talked about, as Janus Brian stood naked before the mirror, Colette behind him. It is something she has often thought but has rarely spoken about. Dada was afraid of women.

He thrashed his sons with a belt for the least misdemeanour; dropping food on the floor, not speaking clearly, a breakage of something in the house. Janus Brian was so terrified of him that once, after having broken a cup, he spent a whole Saturday hiding in a wardrobe, waiting for his father to go out. He didn't even dare go to the lavatory in case his father heard him, so he went in the wardrobe. Colette still had the wardrobe. It was in Julian's room now and she could still, more than forty years later, see the stain in its wood, and detect the odour that still lingered there.

Only women could control Dada. Sometimes the intervention of his wife or one of his daughters would save Janus or Lesley from a beating. She remembered Agatha, who could only then have been a teenager, scolding her father for excessively beating Janus, and Dada grumpily submitting to the young girl's chastisement. It meant that a curious power structure existed in the household, where Dada was the instrument of discipline under the control of the females. The boys were the oppressed of the house, almost totally powerless, leading miserable lives.

'I think you should get some clothes on,' said Colette, in an attempt to distract Janus Brian from these thoughts about his father, which she could see were disturbing him.

'I was going to have a bath,' said Janus Brian, 'but then I noticed this mirror. Have you noticed how no two mirrors reflect you in exactly the same way? There are several mirrors in this house, and they all show a different me. This one is the best. It seems to show me as I was twenty years ago. The one in the living room shows me as a corpse.'

'I'll run the bath for you,' said Colette, turning on the taps. 'It looks like I'll be having my baths here in future as well.'

'Will you?'

'Someone's cut the pipes out of the bathroom – the sink *and* the bath. Aldous thinks we'll need a new bath, and we'll have to wait till he retires before we could afford one of those.'

Janus Brian adopted his 'stop talking like a mad woman' expression.

'What do you mean "someone's cut the pipes out of the bathroom"?'

'Exactly what I say. I had a bath this morning and flooded the hall. It baffles me completely – who would do such a thing, and why?'

'My dear,' said Janus Brian, 'isn't it obvious?'

'Not to me.'

'Were they copper?'

'I don't know.'

'I should think they were.'

'So what?'

Janus Brian explained, as if to a dim-witted child.

'Copper piping could fetch quite a few pounds at a scrap dealers.' The penny dropped.

'You think Janus has . . . no, surely he wouldn't do something like that.'

'Why not. Let's face it dear, from all that you've told me, he sounds like a raving alcoholic, and he's just lost his job. My dear, I know what it's like when you can't get hold of a drink. Look at what I did with the Cherry Blossom. Alcoholics turn to alchemy when they run out of money. I tried to turn boot polish into gin, your son has turned your bathroom pipes into Special Brew.'

When she returned from Leicester Avenue that afternoon Colette was slightly horrified to find that her son was sitting in exactly the same position by the table, as though he hadn't stirred a muscle in all that time. Only slightly, because it had happened before when Janus was on the dole, that he would fall into these silent, motionless, almost catatonic states, neither moving nor talking for hours on end.

She could also tell from the moment she entered the room that he'd been drinking. It wasn't just the ceramic mug at his elbow that a stranger would have assumed to contain tea, but which was brimful of beer. He was a different colour – redder, there was a very thin layer of sweat on his face and when he did speak his voice was fuller and louder than normal.

The sickliness of the situation struck her. That the kitchen had been untouched for four hours, so that the hurriedly displaced breakfast things of that morning were still where they'd been left, the only difference being in the falling-off of temperature, the entropic dullness of everything, and this despite the continued presence of a living thing, her son, in the room. That he should have sat there all day slowly consuming the beer he'd obtained through a deal with a scrap merchant after stealing the bathroom pipes.

In the hall the vessels were full, and some had overspilt, although the dripping seemed to have stopped.

'You could have changed them over,' she said, in her annoyed voice, 'instead of just sitting there.'

Janus gave no response.

His mother sighed, tipped a panful of bathwater down the sink, refilled it with fresh water from the tap, and boiled it.

Colette paused for the first time that morning while the water grew to a slow rage in the pan, and felt, as she sometimes felt after coming back from Janus Brian's house, that she was seeing her kitchen as it really was, and not as she imagined it. In its reality it horrified her. An uncoordinated mess of decorations, overspilling cupboards, shelves teetering on the edge of avalanche beneath the accumulation of bric-a-brac, most of it trivial. The porridge-coloured carpet had seemed a great find when Aldous brought it home from the public waste disposal site one day after having dumped some old furniture there. It had seemed nearly new, and fitted the kitchen floor almost perfectly, covering that old cracked and worn red lino that had been there for nearly twenty years. But the carpet proved almost impossible to keep clean. It had darkened to a dirty grey and was steadily accumulating scabby stains as each day's spillages hardened. They wouldn't budge. The ceiling seemed to mirror the floor's defilement, registering the condensed fumes and vapours of two decades of cookery, a parchment of spreading brown stains and pockmarks like a diseased hide. Then there were the walls, four of them, each a different colour, representing four unsuccessful attempts to decorate the entire kitchen in one scheme.

'Do you know anything about the bathroom?' she said, as if to herself. When Janus was like this it was easy to forget he was there.

Then Janus spoke.

'Do you know how to make a Möbius strip?'

Thinking it to be some sort of joke, of the 'how do you make a Maltese Cross' variety, she said 'No, I don't. How do you make a Möbius strip?'

'I've made one, look.'

And she saw that he had a loop of paper in his hand, and learnt that a Möbius strip was a thing, not a process.

'It's just a loop of paper,' she said.

'But it's only got one side, look,' and as she came over he picked up a pen and handed it to her. 'Try drawing a line along one side.'

She did so, carefully moving the paper under the pen as it scored a blue mark along the length of the strip. After a while, her pen met the beginning of the line it was drawing, joining up with itself. Colette was confused.

'You see,' said Janus, 'you haven't changed sides, and yet if you look, there is a line on both sides of the paper.'

It was true, but Colette was still more confused than astonished.

'The loop has a kink in it, the ends being sellotaped together after a half-turn. It is a two-sided object with only one side.'

'Is that what they call a paradox?'

'Paradox lost,' said Janus, browsing the book from which he'd learnt about the Möbius strip, 'paradox regained.'

'Is that what you've been doing all morning? Making this thing?'

'No. The rest of the morning I've been thinking about it.'

Colette went back to the kettle, filled a cup with boiling water and dropped a tea bag into it. Tea tasted so much better from the pot, but like everyone else, she was sacrificing quality for convenience. Pouring brewed tea from a pot through a strainer aerates it in such a way as to enhance the perfume of the leaves. Tea stewed in a mug is stagnant and, moreover, the paper of the tea bag always contaminates the flavour.

'So, can you explain what happened in the bathroom this morning?' Now that Janus was talking she decided to try again.

'No. What's happened in the bathroom?'

'Someone's cut all the pipes out.'

'Have they? I wondered why it was raining in the hall.'

'Don't try and be clever, Janus. Just admit it.'

'Admit what?'

'You did sell them, didn't you? Sold them so that you could buy some drink.'

'Ye-es,' said Janus, drawing out the word as though it was unbelievably obvious.

'But why?'

'Because I didn't have any money.' Janus laughed the answer, again as though it was obvious. As though whenever you find yourself without any money the obvious thing to do is cut the pipes out of the bathroom.

'Who did you sell them to?'

'A bloke.'

'What bloke?'

'Just a bloke I know who buys copper piping.'

Colette was speechless at Janus's blatantness. He went on, made a little nervous by her silence, 'If it's bothering you that much I'll get a job and pay for the pipes to be put back.'

'It's not that easy. Daddy says the way they've been hacked about we'll need a new bath and a new sink.'

'What's the problem. It's not like you have a bath every day.

Or even every week. You can get a bath round Janus Brian's when you start smelling too much.'

'That's not the point.'

'What is the point?'

'The point is that you've done something so awful, I'd doubt it even of you. Just to make a few quid to pour beer down your neck.'

Janus made a face, the tongue half-extended, the teeth showing, the head jiggling from side to side, that translated, roughly, as *I couldn't care less*.

'So how much did you get for them?'

'Not much.'

'How much?'

'A fiver.'

'Five pounds? And you've spent it all, I suppose?'

Janus reached into his trouser pocket, and after some fumbling brought out two ten-pence pieces and a penny.

'So where have you been getting the rest of the money?'

'What money?'

'You've been out drinking every other day, where've you been getting the money?'

Janus shrugged, as though he didn't actually know where the money came from.

'Just friends,' he said. 'I borrow a bit here and there. I play the piano, people buy me drinks.'

'In that case why did you need to sell the pipes?'

'There's only so much you can borrow. And they've got a juke box in The Quiet Woman now, if you play the piano people start shouting at you . . .'

It was almost an unconscious piece of deduction that led Colette upstairs to Janus's room. She knew that if he'd resorted to cutting the pipes out, he must have sold easier, more missable things than the pipes already. And then she'd remembered the bag she'd found one day in Janus's room, a canvas hold-all that seemed to contain all the moveable treasures of the house – James's Woebley air-pistol, her own Agfa camera with a built-in light meter, the binoculars, the Tri-Ang stationary locomotive that had been one of Julian's favourite toys, and many other long-forgotten objects – vases, antique heirlooms from her mother's house, her grandmother's house, the little cottage in Wales where Aldous's father was born. She'd had no idea at the time why Janus should be storing all this stuff in his room and was rather touched by the care he was evidently taking in looking after these objects.

Now she found the bag in a different corner of the room. It was empty.

She took the bag downstairs to the kitchen where Janus was still sitting. She flung it at him.

'What have you done with it all?' she screamed.

'All what?'

'Everything that was in that bag – my camera, the binoculars – all those things you had in there . . .'

'Have you been poking around in my room?'

'It's my house. Just answer me.'

'I don't know what you're talking about.'

'You've sold them, haven't you – the moving camera, that was in there – there was Nana's marquetry, her brass vase, that statue of Our Lady, those apostle spoons, I saw them all.'

Colette was furious at having not guessed Janus's intentions with those objects. To think she'd thought he was simply treasuring them when he'd done nothing less than burgle his own house. A swag bag.

'They were just a few things,' said Janus impatiently, 'nobody was going to miss them.'

Colette reached over and hit her son across the face. His hair and beard were so thick it was like thumping a pillow, yet Janus was evidently hurt. A long strand of spittle fell from his lower lip. It took a moment for him to react. With a jerk of the whole body he pushed the table away, hemmed in as he was by it, sending everything on it crashing to the floor. The table toppled over, and being a stout piece of utility beechwood its falling seemed to shake the whole house.

'You shouldn't have done that,' said Janus, holding his face and standing up.

'Shouldn't I?' said Colette, who'd gathered herself after the initial shock of the table falling over. She hit Janus across the face again with her other hand, so that she struck the side of his face he wasn't holding. She wanted him to know, to feel the depth of her anger. She could have gone on hitting his face for the rest of the afternoon, and she may have, had not Janus hit her back.

Colette had never been hit by anyone before. Even in the countless drunken tussles that broke out when Janus was drunk, he never actually struck his mother, although he had inadvertently knocked her over or caught her with a flailing elbow a few times. But he had never deliberately hit her. But now he had. A sharp blow from those piano-playing hands across the side of her face. Her glasses were knocked off. She saw a blinding light, then silence, then noise, and finally burning pain.

'Get out of the house,' Colette screamed when she'd recovered.

'Why should I?' said Janus. His voice had a tremble in it. Colette could sense he was shocked by what he'd done.

'Get out of the house now.'

'Why don't you get out of the house? You're the one causing all the trouble. You hit me first . . .'

'But you've sold all those things . . .'

'They were just things . . .'

'They were special things, how would you like it if I sold all your music?'

And she went into the music room that was a storeroom of all Janus's records, and music manuscripts. She went to the shelves and started scattering their contents – the old, fragile books were flung across the room, the Mozart sonatas, pieces by Brahms, Chopin, Liszt, all of which bore Janus's textual markings and notes. Then she went for the record player.

'No you don't,' said Janus, who seemed fully recovered from the initial shock of striking his mother, and took her by the shoulders, pulling her backwards. She fell on the floor, amid the scattered music. Then Janus took hold of the record player, he reached into it and gripped the pick-up arm. With a few twists and pulls it came away and Janus held it, as though in triumph in his fist. Feeble wires hung from its tip, like the roots of an unusual flower.

At that moment they heard the front door go, and Julian, in his school uniform and a briefcase in his hand, stood in the doorway.

'Is dinner ready?' he said.

'Julian,' his mother gasped from the floor, unable to get up because Janus had his foot on her chest, 'do something to stop him, he's destroying everything.'

Julian looked at his older brother who was taking no notice of him. Janus was looking down at Colette.

'Would you like me to stamp on your breasts?' he said.

'I'm going upstairs,' said Julian, 'tell me when dinner's ready.'

'Aren't you going to do something to save me?' screamed Colette as Julian receded, 'don't you want to save your mother's life – Julian, you little coward, come back, he's going to kill me . . .'

But Janus had finished. He took his foot off his mother, left the room, and then left the house, singing to himself.

By the time Aldous came home late that evening, Janus had been gone for several hours. In that time Colette had recovered herself, had tidied up the mess in the music room, had uprighted the table and cleared away the fallen things. The house appeared undamaged, apart from the record player, but Aldous rarely played records. He wouldn't notice the ripped-out pick-up arm.

She made Julian's dinner and he came down to eat it silently. She was still furious with him for not coming to her assistance. How could he have just left her lying on the floor with Janus running amok? But she didn't say anything.

Aldous came home at about eight o'clock, flushed and bright with the acclaim of the south coast.

'The windows looked wonderful,' he said, 'as the curtain fell the sun came out at just the right moment and sent a shaft of sunlight through the glass. The light came through the moving trees outside in such a way that the birds in the glass seemed to dance . . .' He paused for breath, full of his experiences, '. . . do you know, I got to the station and I was looking for a bus stop when this chauffeur in jackboots whisked me off in a limousine, straight to this huge reception at the town hall, where I was guest of honour at a table sitting next to the mayor and his wife, and waiters with bow ties were serving up dish after dish, I don't know what I ate. Beautiful stuff. Then to the crematorium, loads of press people interviewing me, asking me what other work I'd done. People kept handing me business cards saying they'd be in touch. Then the windows. I couldn't help feeling a bit proud of them. They did look good. Makes it a bit of a shame the only people who'll see them are people at funerals . . .'

The maiming of the bathroom hurt Colette. The damage was severe and they didn't even dare think how much it might cost to repair. There was no cash. Aldous's money for his windows had come and gone six months before the unveiling ceremony. So the bathroom fell into disuse. The family now washed at the large stone butler sink in the kitchen, almost as big as a bath itself while the bathroom became a desiccated, rarely visited space. Dust collected around the plug of the sink, and coated with grey the inner slopes of the bath. The bathroom gradually became a boxroom. Unused junk that couldn't quite be thrown away was stored there – a broken chair, an old bicycle that was too small now for Julian. Sometimes Colette used the bath as a bird hospital, where the injured blackbirds that she occasionally rescued from Scipio's claws could recuperate. Flightless, they would skip about on the porcelain for a few days, and then die. Some lasted a little longer, and one even made it back into the garden. She would cut a branch from one of the fruit trees and put it in the bath to make the sick birds feel at home. She would dig up worms from the garden, chop them with a knife into many living parts, and poke them with tweezers down the young birds' throats. The birds, raw with their injuries, would remain motionless at first, apart from a sort of trembling, but later, if things went well, they would perk up and then hop around, and even fill the bathroom with song, in a cheeky attempt to claim it as their own territory. But there was always the longer term problem of how to get them back into the skies. Their injuries nearly always meant they'd lost their flight feathers, and Colette was never sure if these grew back, or if they did, how long they would take. Without flight, a bird in the wild is nothing more than cat food. And there was only so long a wild bird could endure the captivity of the bathroom. So Colette's efforts nearly always ended with a little feathered corpse in the bath, which upset her more than finding them injured in the first place. The way they nearly always perked up, hopefully fluttering their useless wings, before giving in. Colette could never understand. She gave them everything they could want in the bathroom, she fed them on sops, nursery food, mashed-up Weetabix, milk, worms, a truly splendid diet, and they seemed all glossy and alive one day, but then the next they would be dead. When they had been so tenacious of life. It really puzzled her.

5

Julian had often thought about killing his brother. Sometimes he felt that if he had a gun he would shoot him. He liked to imagine the night when, armed with a real gun (not James's pellet-firing air pistol), he would steal into Janus's bedroom, picking his way through the litter on the floor to where his unconscious brother lay folded in blankets. Then three plump bullets sent into the soft mass on the bed.

What would he get? Even if he got life he could be out by the age of twenty-five. A sympathetic judge might let him off altogether. If he was told about how he'd found his older brother standing on his mother, destroying the record player, if he knew how often Julian had had to listen to the crash and tinkle of domestic violence, if he'd known how many nights he'd feared for his life (an exaggeration, perhaps, but a judge wouldn't know), or those of others in the house, he was sure the sternest judge would see sense and let him off, pat him on the shoulder and say, 'there there young lad, not to worry, I'd have killed my brother in the same circumstances . . .'

Julian had been hurt by Colette's accusations of cowardice. He always knew it would happen one day that she would call upon him to deal with Janus, that she would notice how her youngest was approaching adulthood, and so could no longer wallow in the luxury of uselessness. He was destined to become a resource, part of the armoury Colette drew upon, along with Mr Milliner next door, James when he was home, and as a last resort the police, to control Janus. But now was too soon. His mother didn't realize (just because he was big for his age) that Julian wasn't ready to tackle Janus. He needed a little more time, another inch or so of height, a few more layers of muscle.

His mother had taunted him when they were alone at breakfast the next day.

'I told Juliette what you did last night, and she said you were a coward too.'

Julian hadn't said anything but carried on reading his *Beano* at the kitchen table. He was attached to reading the *Beano* as a means of prolonging his childhood. His mother had placed an order for the comic at Hudson's on the Parade when he was six, and every week she collected the *Beano* for him, which had 'Jones' pencilled on its cover. Julian these days liked her to leave it for a while so that the *Beano*s mounted up, then she would bring home a batch of five or six for him to read at once. That he still poured over the *Beano* every week Colette found rather charming, but it annoyed her now.

'It's no good hiding behind Biffo the Bear doing the strong, silent routine, young man,' she said.

Julian hadn't taken her up on the point that Biffo the Bear had recently been replaced as the *Beano*'s cover story by Dennis the Menace.

'Any normal son would have done something to help their mother, instead of drifting off upstairs.'

Julian had sunk further into his comic.

A few years ago, when the *Beano*s had started to accumulate, Colette had nagged and nagged at him to throw them away, and he had. He remembered sitting on the edge of his bed with a stack of fifty or so *Beano*s with Biffo the Bear on the cover, building up the courage to dispose of them. Eventually, in one swift, brutal movement he binned them. It was a moment he spent continually regretting and he wondered now why he'd done it. Somehow his mother had conjured up an apocalyptic vision of accumulating *Beano*s, piling layer upon layer like sedimentary rock until there was no room left in the house, and he'd felt a sense of guilt at using up so much space.

And then the *Beano*s changed. A complete editorial rethink had removed Biffo from the cover and replaced him with Dennis the Menace, relegating the former cover star to a half page strip tucked away somewhere in the middle. At the same time the older, more skilled artists had retired, to be replaced by incompetent, cack-handed idiots who couldn't even draw in perspective. Lord Snooty had been lovingly drawn, Bunkerton Castle's neo-Gothic architecture rendered sensitively in pen and ink. The new artist revelled in the vulgar craftlessness of the post-decimal era, and even put long trousers on Roger the Dodger. The effect, for Julian, who still loved the *Beano* for the wit of the Bash Street Kids and The Three Bears, the latter of which was still beautifully drawn, was to render the 'Biffo' *Beanos* of immense historical importance. His first encounter with a 'Dennis' *Beano* had been a horrible shock, to compare with the end of steam as a piece of wanton cultural vandalism, and so he had begun collecting them again, in case they should change even further for the worse. And he mourned his old 'Biffo' *Beanos*, having only two or three in his current collection. It made him feel angry and cheated and he vowed never to throw anything away again

Julian had refused to be drawn by his mother's taunts. He said nothing, and the taunts ended when his father, who was still unaware of the trouble the day before, came into the room.

O for a gun, thought Julian, a real, true, faithful gun. How else might he do it? A swift, accurate stabbing, again while Janus slumbered in drink. What about garrotting him with a length of piano-wire taken out of the Bechstein? Every little vein proud on his brother's head, every little capillary, even the ones in his eyes, bursting. Would his mother call him a coward then? Would she call him a coward when he walked into the kitchen, his hands dripping with blood, 'Mother, there's something I think you should see in Janus's room . . .'

But Julian would never have the stomach for that. It was an indulgent fantasy with which he vented the anger that had built up over the years of witnessing, or hiding from, the violence. He had long given up hope that Janus would leave Fernlight Avenue and find a home of his own. Colette had gone through a phase of suggesting it to her son on a weekly basis, but she never seemed convinced herself that it was a good idea, saying there would be no one to play the Bechstein. When Juliette placed small ads for affordable flats under his nose he simply laughed in her face. What Julian really desired was a means of controlling Janus, rope to bind him with, drugs to dope him, some form of electronic tag that would show as a blip on a radar screen so that his whereabouts could always be known. If the blip could also show his level of intoxication, by gradually turning a deepening shade of green, say, that would at least provide some form of warning.

Julian was alone in the house, as he usually was on Friday and Saturday nights. Bill had been round earlier and had taken Janus out for a night at The Quiet Woman. Aldous and Colette, after they'd left, set off for The Red Lion. It had become a habit over the last few months, since Janus Brian had been on the scene, for Aldous and Colette to go to the pub together. Suddenly, it seemed, Julian had become old enough to look after himself.

'You'll be all right, won't you?'

'Yes.'

'You can come with us, if you want, but you'll have to sit in the car.'

'No thanks.'

He had accepted this particular offer once, but sitting in the car in a dark car park for a couple of hours on a cold night was not an enjoyable experience. Instead, he had come to rather look forward to his evening at home on his own. Suddenly he had a freedom he hadn't had before. To explore his own house.

When he was much younger he'd found the house at night, especially upstairs with its open doors leading into huge, unlit rooms, rather frightening, and had to ask someone to come with him when he wanted to go to the toilet, but these days, somewhat to his surprise, he didn't find the house frightening at all, despite the fact that it was just as dark and shadowy as it had always been, darker, if anything. Seven empty rooms. The occasional drip from the tank in the loft, the echoey plop of water into water, a breeze stirring the branches of the cherry tree which almost touched his window, the hysterical calling of the screech-owls who lived in the oak tree.

Now he realised the house was more frightening when it contained people. Alone he could watch any programmes he liked on television, and later could prowl around Janus's bedroom hunting for pornography, which he'd heard it rumoured was hidden somewhere in there. But Janus's bedroom was such a catastrophic mess, the floor invisible beneath a heap of litter, that his furtive searches always proved fruitless.

Eventually Julian would go to bed at around ten o'clock, a while before the pubs closed. That meant he was out of the way if there was any trouble when the drinkers returned home later, which there often was.

This particular evening he was in bed going through the card index system of the library he'd founded in his bedroom. His mother hadn't believed him when he said he was opening a library in his bedroom. She just thought he meant he was putting up some shelves for all the homeless books of the house, the ones stacked up in corners of rooms, or lying forgotten on floors, or in the loft. He had done that, but he had also catalogued them. And when his mother came into his room one day hunting for her old copy of *Summer Lightning*, he'd insisted she became a member before he would let her take it away. She'd reluctantly agreed (it was a pound membership fee), and he'd stamped a date in the book, and fined her when she forgot to return it.

Having appointed himself librarian of the house, Julian soon found himself swamped with books. Scattered throughout the house they could pass unnoticed, but condensed into a single room they soon overspilt the shelves, and had to be stacked in columns on the floor. There were some of his mother's father's books (mostly exotic tales of colonial exploration and conquest), and her mother's (yarns of anthropomorphic animals), and the remains of the library his father had amassed in the days of his lodging with Lesley (translations of classical poetry, *The Golden Treasury*, *The Lives of the Artists*, *The Geology of the Chilterns*, John Forster's *Life of Charles Dickens*). *Communism and the British Intellectual* was a title he liked to have on display, though he wasn't sure where it had come from. *The Weimar Republic*, *From Utrecht to Waterloo*. Those must have been leftovers from James's history A Level. There were a lot of Juliette's old books as well. *Sue Barton − Student Nurse*, *Pony For Sale*, *Fury − Son of the Wilds*, *The Story of Wimpy − A Wump*. Julian was undiscriminating in his fondness for books. So long as they were books was all that mattered. Many were old library books his family had failed to return. His family never quite understood libraries.

There was a tap-tap-tap at his window.

Being an upstairs bedroom, Julian's window was never knocked at, though when he heard accompanying noises – coughs and quiet chuckling, he went quickly over and opened the curtains. Bill Brothers' face was peering through the glass at him, his thick hair awry. When he saw Julian, Bill gave a small whoop of delight and asked him to open the window, which he did. Bill had to lean back to avoid the outswinging glass, holding precariously onto the mullion with one hand. He stamped with one foot upon the slates of the small, sloping kitchen extension roof beneath him and called to someone Julian couldn't see.

'This is a bloody good roof, speaking as a one-time steeple-jack, I can say – my professional opinion – is that this roof is one of the best bloody roofs in Windhover Hill,' then addressing Julian, 'Greetings, little brother-in-law, forgive this ungodly intrusion, my fellow travellers and I appear to have no key to these premises, so Janussimus here kindly showed us an alternative route, up the ladder and across this fine slate roof to your bedroom, whose light betokened that you were yet awake, and through whose window we thought we might gain entry to the aforementioned premises,' while saying this Bill hauled himself in through the window and half-stumbled in amongst all the books of Julian's room. Janus then appeared at the window, whooping ridiculously.

Julian got back into bed as Janus climbed through the window. Bill laughed a long giggly laugh that deeply reddened his face.

'We were searching for the source of the Limpopo,' he said, 'which we believe is in this vicinity.'

'I thought it was the Zambezi we were after.'

'Zambezi, Limpopo, Irrawaddy,' Bill shrugged, as though it didn't matter which. 'Mr Mungo Park, my fellow Fellow of the Royal Anthropological Institute,' Bill went on, laying a comradely arm across Janus's shoulders, 'world renowned expert on the sexual lives of the savages of Windhover Hill's unexplored regions . . .' Julian also laughed. He was glad that they were in such good humour, and that Bill had returned with Janus, because Janus rarely caused serious trouble while Bill was around. Books were spilling everywhere, the carefully arranged piles merging into one slithering mass.

There were more people to come. Next through the window was a man with long dark hair and a Frank Zappa moustache with its accompanying tuft of a beard. This man Julian recognised as Guy Sweetman, a long-time drinking partner of Bill's, whose wife, Angelica, had become an object of fascination for Janus, his 'Angel'. Julian had never seen Angelica, but he'd noticed poems about her written on Janus's bedroom wall, such as the following

To Angelica Sweetman

My sweet Angelica Sweetman,
It's you I want to meetman,
It's you I want to greetman
On any road or any streetman,
Let me kiss your little feetman,
Let me kiss your lips and teethman
Let me have you in my sheetsman
You've got me all on heatman
I can't drink and I can't eatman
So nurse me at your teatman
My sweet Angelica Sweetman.

which Janus had written in his mother's pink lipstick across his ceiling.

Then came Hugo Price, another long-time friend of Bill's, a dark haired Welshman with bushy sideburns and black sunglasses, he reminded Julian a little of the pop singer Engelbert Humperdinck.

'I thought we were all dead men,' he said quietly as he lowered himself into Julian's bedroom. As he did so, sliding in on his backside, his shirt rode up exposing a midriff matted with black hairs, as though this man's clothes concealed the body of a gorilla. Julian knew Hugo by sight again, he was married to a woman called Veronica, whom Janus and Bill had taken a teasing dislike to. They seemed to think she was a bit of a snob, affecting a life of middle-class affluence with her fondue sets and her hi-fi's, her prissy little dinner parties where bottles of cheap supermarket wine were decanted into earthenware carafes.

Other people followed Hugo Price into Julian's bedroom, but Julian didn't recognise them – a man with blond, curly hair, whom Bill introduced as 'Steve, celebrated actor of stage and screen' (it later transpired that Steve had had bit parts and work as an extra in several television cop shows, including *The Sweeney*, where he had played a leather-clad hit-man, and *Special Branch*, where he had played a corpse – 'much tougher role', he quipped). He was carrying a small bottle, almost empty, of whisky, and gave quiet, half-hearted whoops, a watered down version of Janus. Then, through the window, came a much older person, a man with a grey beard and triangular eyebrows, whom Julian had never seen before, and who seemed rather embarrassed to discover that there was a young boy in bed in this room.

'I think we may have been following a false tributary,' said Bill, 'I left a trail of cheese and onion crisps but they've been eaten by marabou storks.'

'There's a lot of books in here,' said the older man, who was called Graham, 'it's like a bookshop.'

Julian felt rather elated that these people should all be in his room, these exotic emissaries from the adult world, taking an interest in his books. He usually experienced a sensation of near total invisibility in their presence.

'What's this? *Pony For Sale?*' said the actor, picking up from a shelf one of Juliette's old books.

'What about this', said Hugo Price, picking up another book, '*Sue Barton – Student Nurse.*' He opened it and pretended to read, '"She looked into his eyes with passion and squeezed his stethoscope." Not sure this is appropriate reading matter for an impressionistic young comrade.'

'*The Story of Wimpy – A Wump*,' read Bill, going through the spines on a shelf, '*Anne of Green Gables. Sue Barton – Staff Nurse, Sue Barton – District Nurse, Sue Barton – Night Nurse*, Sue Barton . . .'

'Sue Barton Lesbian Nurse,' continued Steve, 'Sue Barton – Nymphomaniac Nurse . . .'

'*Civilization and its Discontents*,' read Bill, almost accidentally, rather dampening the growing wave of giggling, then, as an afterthought, 'Sue Barton – Psychiatric Nurse.'

Julian was starting to regret incorporating Juliette's juvenile library into his own, and determined afterwards to remove these books from their shelves. Though he had, in fact, read *Sue Barton – Student Nurse*, and had rather enjoyed it.

'Look at all these *Beanos*,' said Steve, fingering through a stack of comics, 'There must be hundreds here. Good old Biffo.'

The echoey, distant sound of a cascade told them that Janus was being sick in the lavatory, and with much near falling, slurred yodels and cries of triumph the company left Julian's room, and Julian got up to close the window into the dark.

Female voices could be heard downstairs – there was Juliette, sounding rather cross, and Veronica Price herself, a rare visitor to Fernlight Avenue, whom Julian had seen only once, at Juliette's wedding. She was a teacher, so he understood, and as such she rather frightened him, since she carried herself with considerable height and breadth, a towering figure amongst his sister's friends, so tall it almost seemed her face was out of sight. And there was Rita Michaelangeli, a smaller darker woman, possibly prettier, though it was difficult to tell as she always wore dark glasses, and had frizzy hair that concealed much of her face. Julian hung around on the landing listening to the voices downstairs. It seemed that the women, especially Juliette and Veronica, were cross with the men for climbing up the ladder and walking across the kitchen roof, when the back doors to the music room were open anyway, as they always were. Fernlight Avenue was never locked. 'Where is he?' he heard Juliette saying, then, told that he was upstairs with Janus, a kind of groan.

Laughter was pouring out of Janus's bedroom. Having had his own bedroom invaded Julian felt at liberty to wander in there and investigate the source of all the amusement. Bill was dominating the proceedings, as ever. It seemed that, at Janus's request, he had embarked upon a portrait of Janus and Angelica, a vast mural filling the entirety of the plain wall on the doorside of Janus's bedroom. Bill kept up an amusing Rolf Harris like commentary as he worked, while Janus posed, and James, Steve and Graham watched on in genuine, awe-struck amazement at their friend's abilities. Bill's skills. For, within just a few minutes, an image had emerged on Janus's bedroom wall, recognizable Janus and recognizable Angelica, the two figures naked but for fig leaves, Angelica with plump, voluptuous breasts and curvy hips. Bill's portrait was an imitation of Massaccio's depiction of Adam and Eve. Bill was laughing almost hysterically as he produced this portrait using a thick pencil he had to resharpen with a small pocket knife almost continually, and then, full of excitement, he rushed about the house looking for Aldous's paints, wanting to borrow them to complete his portrait.

'You've got to give it to him,' Graham said, when Bill had left the room, 'Even when he's pissed out of his skull he can get a good likeness. He's still got a steady hand.'

Steve the actor seemed utterly mesmerized by the image.

'That is very beautiful,' he said, approaching closely the pencilled, life-size image of Angelica, whose breasts, even though composed of just half a dozen strokes of a 4b pencil, seemed to have all the weight and volume of real breasts, so that he couldn't resist reaching out to touch them, 'That is very beautiful, and very clever.'

Bill had rummaged through three rooms in search of painting materials. By this time Colette and Aldous were back from The Red Lion, relieved, like Julian, to find the house full of people. On evenings like these they tended to encourage the guests to stay for as long as possible, or at least until Janus was too tired and too drunk to be a problem.

Interest was beginning to mount in the downstairs rooms as to what precisely was going on upstairs.

'What do you need paints for?' said Rita Michaelangeli.

'I am, like your noble namesake, executing a fresco for his holiness Pope Janus the second.'

Eventually, people began climbing the stairs to have a look as Bill, with a skill that dazzled everyone, began colouring his painting. It had the splashy, drippy, sketchy feel of the rushed portrait, though there was such sincerity in every mark and stroke, such accuracy in the proportions, and in the expressions on the faces, that it drew gasps of astonishment from everyone who entered the room. Though no one seemed to have thought of what Guy Sweetman, who was married to the naked Eve in Bill's portrait, would make of it.

Guy had been distantly tolerant, so it seemed, of Janus's infatuation with his wife, and had taken his drunken eulogies and anonymously posted love-letters as part of some sort of game, the extension of one of Janus's many pub-personae. But this evening, when he ambled into Janus's bedroom to see what all the laughter was about, he was less tolerant.

Guy Sweetman had been a schoolfriend of Bill Brothers, he was tall, slim and dark haired. He was handsome, and he knew it. He wore black velvet jackets, jeans belted with a big silver buckle, Cuban heeled suede shoes. He looked, as many young men seemed to these days, like Jesus Christ, and sometimes he would play up on this resemblance by affecting an all-knowing, miracle-working, parable-telling manner. When introducing himself to strangers he would say 'I *am* Guy', not 'Hi, I'm Guy', but simply 'I *am* Guy', placing this awesome emphasis on his name as a state of existence, no mere label, but an entity. He had, as far as anyone could tell, never worked for any length of time, apart from short stints of bar work or behind the till in Windhover Hill's one betting shop, and yet he never seemed to be without money. He subsisted on the borrowing of small change from his countless acquaintances, the calling in of favours, the affection and generosity he seemed to inspire in people. Bill always said how Guy could talk himself into and out of anything. He could charm the birds from the trees. A sweet-talker.

To Janus, however, Guy was a mere brute, a talentless, hirsute waster who tried to conceal the abject nullity of his person-ality with these contrivances, his Christ-persona, his half-hearted hippiedom (he once, after an absence from The Quiet Woman of more than a year, claimed to have hitch-hiked to India, though it was discovered through a friend of a friend that he had been merely living in a squat in Balham).

Janus's infatuation with Angelica had begun at a party at the house of Hugo and Veronica Price, where she had allowed Janus an evening of clumsy smooching and sympathetic listening. Janus's whole life, from then on, seemed to be devoted to repeating that experience with Angelica.

Guy put a hand on Bill's shoulder.

'What are you doing?' Guy said, his voice quiet, as ever.

Bill turned, his loaded brush dripping on the floor.

'I'm just daubing a quick Sistine Chapel style painting on my brother-in-law's i.e. Pope Janus II's bedroom wall,' he gave a laugh that would normally have placated Guy, a laugh that was meant to seem out of control, but wasn't.

'I'm not happy with it,' said Guy, gesturing towards the image of Angelica, 'I don't like it . . . you've painted my wife on the wall, man, she's starkers for Christ's sake.'

'I know,' Bill's voice had become imploring, realising, suddenly, that Guy was very cross. Janus watched, annoyed at how quickly Bill seemed to defer to Guy, as though he had some sort of power, as though he'd really been taken in by Guy's messianic persona, 'Shall I paint a bra on her, perhaps, you know, a Playtex cross your heart . . .'

'It's my woman, man,' he said, by way of explaining everything, 'come on, man, it's my woman.'

'It's my fucking wall,' said Janus.

'Yeah, well if it's your wall what's my wife doing on it?' said Guy, turning suddenly to face Janus.

The crowded room became silent. Angelica herself was not in the house. She had never been to Fernlight Avenue.

'It's my wall, I can have who I like on it.'

There didn't seem to be a strong argument against this statement. Guy instead concentrated on the principle at stake, 'But she's my woman, and I'm not having her in the nude on the bedroom wall of this piss artist. I don't care whose wall it is, the wall is not the point. The point is the woman depicted, she's mine, not yours, you're a sick-in-the-head bastard, and I'm telling you to get this off your wall now.'

'Hey, Guy,' Bill said, 'this is a – you know – for Christ's sake, man,' (Bill was trying to speak to him in his own language, that sad mixture of Americanese and Sixties flower power) 'this is a work of art, man, it's an image of beauty.'

Guy didn't seem convinced. He made further protestations, declared repeatedly that the image depicted was of 'his woman', and as such was his property. His behaviour dumbfounded the people in the room, who knew Guy to be a peaceable, easy-going sort of person, astonishingly vain, it was true, with a whiff of arrogance about him, but never one to make a scene like this.

When, finally, he made a lunge for the paints and brushes that were set up on the floor, with the intention, it seemed, of destroying the image himself, Janus physically intervened, and a tussle ensued, with the two men rolling silently about the floor and across Janus's bed, until separated by Bill and some of the others. Ruffled and red faced, Guy left the room, spitting quietly to himself, and that would have been an end of it, but for the fact that as Guy retreated, approaching the top of the stairs, Janus went quickly after him and gave him a strong push from behind that sent him crashing into the top of the stairs and down the stairwell, Guy just managing to remain upright as he plunged the depth of the staircase to the bottom. In the process he smashed his face into the wall at the top of the stairs and bloodied his nose. Bill and Steve rushed out onto the landing to restrain Janus, the women downstairs came out of the kitchen to see wounded Guy standing stupidly in the hall, his hand over his nose.

Rita Michaelangeli gave a little shriek at the blood that hung on Guy's beard. Veronica made stern, schoolteacherly noises that expressed a despairing opinion of men in general, and these men in particular.

'Has anyone punched Hugo?' she said, almost hopefully.

'I hope not,' said Rita, 'or anyone else. Blimey. All that blood.'

There was still disturbance upstairs, as though Janus was trying to make his way downstairs in pursuit of Guy.

'Don't let that bastard anywhere near me,' cried Guy through his blood, spitting red as he shouted up the stairs, the women were shocked, having never heard Guy shout before, 'If he comes anywhere near me or my wife again, he's a fucking dead man, do you hear me!'

Guy left through the front door, slamming it.

The noises upstairs continued. Julian came down. He was pounced on for information.

'What's going on up there Julian?' said Juliette.

'Janus is punching everyone.'

'Everyone?' said Juliette incredulously, as she made for the stairs.

'Don't go up there, Juliette,' said Veronica, 'it sounds dangerous.'

'What are they doing?'

To an unenlightened listener, the noises upstairs could have been made by a party of large men attempting to move a very heavy and awkwardly shaped piece of furniture. There was a general sense of weight shifting, objects being dropped, occasional grunts and cries of exertion.

'Bill!' Juliette called up the stairs.

'It's gone quiet now,' said Veronica.

Bill appeared at the top of the stairs. He looked shocked, and his jacket sleeve was ripped. He seemed just about to come down when a cry made him return to the front bedroom.

Then the cacophony of broken glass, something landing in the bushes of the front garden. Colette rushed to the window and looked out.

'There's a dressing table in the garden,' she said, 'I'll go and get Mr Milliner.'

'Mr Milliner?' said Veronica.

'The next door neighbour,' explained Juliette.

'But there are about four men up there, surely they can control Janus.'

'It doesn't sound like it, does it? Mr Milliner's a policeman, he knows all the holds . . .'

'Hugo!' Rita called up the stairs.

'Why worry about Hugo?' said Veronica, 'It'll do him good if he gets a punch in the gearbox. I'm sorry, Juliette, I shouldn't be so flippant. I've never known Janus like this, does he often get violent?'

'Only every other night,' said Juliette

'Really? But he's never like this in the pub.'

'No, he saves it all for when he gets home.'

A sound from upstairs that could have been a piano landing on someone's toe. Then Janus's yelp, 'But you're my favourite brother-in-law!'

Hugo appeared at the top of the stairs. He was without his dark glasses. He was carrying the velvet jacket he'd previously been wearing, carefully folded over one arm. He glanced behind him, then descended the stairs silently, almost as if in a trance. He acknowledged none of those in the hall as he reached them. His face was shiny with sweat and he was breathing heavily, as though having run for a bus.

'Hugo, what's been going on up there? Where are you going?'

'Out of this house,' said Hugo, fumbling with the catch on the front door.

'What's Janus doing?'

'An imitation of a mad dog,' said Hugo quietly, finally succeeding in opening the front door, unintentionally readmitting Colette. He left as she entered.

'That's right,' called Veronica after him, 'just piss off and leave us on our own with a madman . . .'

'Mr Milliner's out,' said Colette, 'on the night shift with the vice squad. I've telephoned the real police . . .'

'You expect me to walk home on my own?' Veronica went on calling after her husband, who'd long gone.

'I'll get him back,' said Rita, running out of the front door after Hugo.

'Me and Bill will walk you back,' said Juliette.

'If Bill's still alive. Do you think we should do something, Juliette?'

'Perhaps Bill will knock him out,' said Colette hopefully, 'I can't understand why it's taking him so long, he's usually so good at handling Janus. Where's Aldous? Has he vanished again?'

Aldous had developed an ability to dematerialize in times of stress, reappearing a while later, usually in his red armchair by the bookcase in the front room, the *Complete Works of Shakespeare* open in his lap.

A period of silence followed from the rooms above, before Bill appeared once again at the top of the stairs. This time the ripped jacket sleeve had been removed entirely, revealing the white shirt beneath. Bill had the appearance of someone who'd been leaning out of the window of a high-speed train. He puffily and rather cautiously descended the stairs.

'Are you hurt?' said Veronica.

'Not much,' said Bill.

'Where's Janus?'

'He's having a lie down.' Bill appeared ominously calm, 'Graham's reading to him.'

'Reading to him?' said Juliette.

'It was the only way we could get him to stop thrashing about. I tried everything else, he just wanted a story.'

'What's he reading?' said Colette, but the question was lost.

'Bill, you're bleeding,' said Juliette, noticing a red stain in his beard. Bill touched it with his finger, looked at the blood thoughtfully and shrugged. There was a knock at the door. A sliced-up image of a policeman was visible in the warped glass.

'That was quick,' said Colette opening the door. It transpired that neighbours had already called the police before Colette had got to the phone box.

The situation was explained to the policeman, a bearded man in late middle age. Julian, who'd been in the hall all the time, experienced the fascination he always felt when seeing a policeman at close quarters, and marvelled at how the house always seemed to shrink and decay slightly in their presence. Colette and her daughter had an urgency in their voices, like advocates pleading a case, fearful the policeman would wonder what all the fuss was about, since the house had been calm and silent since his arrival. But the fact that neighbours had first called the police, and that a dressing table was lying in a nest of broken glass in the front garden, along with the testimony of Colette and Juliette, seemed enough to convince him that Janus could be taken away for the night. 'For a breach of the peace?' the policeman suggested, as if not caring which law he was arrested under.

He went upstairs to see Janus on his own, having been directed to his bedroom. Listening at the foot of the stairs the others could hear Janus's voice talking with a cheery amiability to the policeman, as though to an old friend; they heard the deep, firm baritone of the policeman, equally amiable.

After a few moments the policeman came down the stairs.

'Your son seems quite calm . . .'

'No,' Colette interrupted him, 'it's one of his tricks, as soon as a policeman's on the scene he's as meek as a baby. Don't be fooled by him, as soon as you've gone and Bill's gone and everyone else he'll be back to how he was, and then it'll just be me and my husband to manage him – he could kill us, you saw what he did to the dressing table.'

The policeman looked a little troubled, then went back upstairs.

'I don't think your mum and dad should be left here with Janus like this,' said Veronica to Juliette, 'if the police don't take him away . . .'

The policeman returned.

'Your son will come voluntarily with me to the station for

the night. I'm not arresting him or charging him with anything. He's just getting himself properly dressed.'

The party waited in the hall for a while. Veronica went into the kitchen to get her things. The policeman whistled, asked Colette, by way of conversation, where her husband was, was told he was probably in the front room. The policeman popped his head round the door and saw Aldous sitting in his red armchair reading from a large, thick book.

'Good evening sir,' the policeman said.

Aldous looked up, smiled, then continued reading his book.

Then Janus descended the stairs. He looked as if he'd spent his evening doing nothing more than sitting in a chair. His face was pale, dry, his clothes clean and untorn. He had no blood on him. He was wearing a brown shirt. Colette thought he looked thinner than she'd ever seen him, and that his head was made absurdly huge by the thickness of his hair and beard.

He shook hands with the policeman, as though greeting an old comrade, then made several requests that delayed his departure.

'Can I just get my jacket?' He went upstairs to get his jacket.

'Can I say goodbye to my father?' He popped his head round the front room door and said goodbye. Aldous didn't look up.

'Can I just say goodbye to my cat?' He went upstairs and nuzzled his face into the silver fur of Scipio's tummy.

Such requests may have gone on indefinitely had not the policeman finally put his foot down and left with Janus, pulling him gently by the arm.

A weight lifted. Aldous emerged from the front room.

'Ah, you've resurfaced,' said Colette.

Juliette scolded Bill.

'You're not going out with Janus any more,' she said.

'I shouldn't think you'll want to, will you?' said Veronica.

Bill looked surprised.

'Janus is my friend . . .'

'Friends don't give you nosebleeds,' said Juliette.

'That was an accident.'

'An accident?'

'The back of his head hit my nose, that's all . . .'

'What about your jacket?'

'That was another accident.'

'I can't believe you're defending him, after what he's been like tonight . . .'

'People don't understand Janus, I'm the only one that does, and perhaps your mother as well. You don't understand him . . .'

'I understand him all right.' The two were alone in the hall now, the others having removed to the kitchen.

'No you don't, because you don't understand the artistic temperament.'

'Ha! Is that what you call it? You think getting blind drunk and throwing dressing tables through windows amounts to artistic temperament. So those people who hurl roofing slates at each other and put traffic cones on their heads outside The Carpenters Arms every Friday night are all artists are they?'

The conversation went on like this, quietly, in the hallway, for some time, until eventually they left, with Veronica. Before closing the door Juliette had a word with her mother.

'We've got to do something, he can't live with you here any more . . .'

'I'm sure things will settle down soon,' said Colette, closing the front door on her daughter before she could disagree.

6

Colette had wanted to tell someone about the things Janus had stolen. But she felt unable to. She didn't want to turn her family against him any more than they were already. Aldous would have been disgusted, guessing already, though without proof, that Janus had cut out the pipes. How would James feel if he'd known how his brother had sold his air pistol, his binoculars? How would Julian have felt about his steam engine? So she had kept quiet about the thefts, which meant that she grieved for them alone. Though she did find herself confiding in one person, Reg Moore, Janus Brian's brother-in-law and only friend.

'You don't realize how important things are until you lose them,' he'd said one evening at Fernlight Avenue. The phrase was a cliché, a truism, a banal platitude, and yet it had come to her as a fresh piece of wisdom – profound, resonant, enlightening, when Reg Moore had uttered it.

'I didn't realize how important Elizabeth was to me until she died.'

He had also lost a wife.

Colette and Reg had known each other since childhood. In fact, when Janus Brian had married Reg's sister Mary, Reg had assumed that this was to be part of a straight sister trade-off, and that he would marry Colette, and for a while Colette had allowed him to court her. But Colette had never seriously been interested in Reg, at least not once Aldous had arrived on the scene. Then there had followed a period of time in which she'd enjoyed the attentions of two men who, by a strange quirk, were of very similar appearance. Reg could easily have been the slightly younger brother of Aldous, both were tall men with dense coifs of black hair and deeply recessed eyes, although

Reg's, like his sister's, were dark and mouselike, always darting about inquisitively, which gave him a shifty, sly, slightly devious appearance. Aldous's eyes were grey and sleepy. 'Come to bed eyes' Colette's sister Meg had called them.

Even after Colette married Aldous Reg lingered around in the background, on the off-chance that Colette might suddenly realize her mistake, and elope with him. But in the end, shortly after the war, Reg himself married, darkly handsome Elizabeth, who bore him two darkly handsome sons. That was nearly thirty years ago now, and Colette had seen Reg perhaps half a dozen times in all those years, usually at the wedding or funeral of a mutual friend, and whenever they met, if Reg could get her alone, he would resume, as if the days of their courtship had only been the week before, his still clumsy and gauche attempts to win her heart, which only confirmed for Colette that she'd made the right choice all those years ago.

Now however, as housekeeper and nursemaid to Janus Brian, she was brought into regular contact with Reg. Elizabeth had died of cancer three years before Mary, and his two sons had moved far away from home. When he met Colette now he used her as a confidante in whom he could talk about his loneliness, about the emptiness of his house, the emptiness of his days, the difficulties of finding a new partner, particularly when he was limited to his own age group.

'Elizabeth and I didn't grow old, not for each other. Elizabeth to me was still a woman of twenty-three when she died. But now that I'm looking for a wife from the same age group I'm suddenly finding myself courting the very old. It's quite horrific. Sixty-year-old widows with purple rinses and surgical stockings, and I can't believe we're of the same generation. I'm drawn towards younger women, but no one under fifty is going to give me a second look, are they?'

Often Colette found herself cornered into having to compliment Reg like this.

'Of course they are, Reg, there's plenty of women who go for the older man . . .'

'But not when they look as old as I do, do you think?'

'You don't look old, Reg, not to me . . .'

And this was true, as far as she was concerned. Aldous and

Reg, having an almost sibling-like resemblance when young, had aged at equal rates. Their hair had admitted the encroachment of grey at exactly the same rate, their bodies had spread evenly, not into obesity, but into a comfortable, middle-aged paunchiness, and their skins were still both comparatively smooth, though Reg's was a little darker, as it always had been. Both he and Mary had always borne some trace of a forgotten Mediterranean genealogy.

If in the race of life Reg and Aldous were still neck and neck, in terms of their personalities their divergence continued apace. Her husband still took an innocent and simple delight in the mundanities of life, which enlarged his imagination and preserved his humour, whereas Reg's personality, after a lifetime of working in insurance, had shrunk. He'd become a chauvinist, a bigot and a pedant.

Where had it all come from, this bitterness of Reg's? Colette at first took it as a joke, something he said to humour her, but she soon realized that he was expressing something he sincerely felt when he railed against Janus Brian for listening to Schubert on a Sony hi-fi. 'What do you want to listen to music on that Japanese muck for?' he would say, smiling, 'Why can't you listen to it on an English hi-fi?' Then there would follow a long and, to Colette, immensely tedious discussion on the relative merits of Japanese and British music systems, where Janus Brian, if not exactly sticking up for the Japanese, would say that quality of music reproduction transcended patriotic considerations, and that if the Japanese made the best record players, he would buy them, while Reg's contention seemed to be that British, or 'English' record players were the best simply by virtue of their national provenance, all the time giving Colette sideways glances. 'All those nips are interested in is reproducing pop music for teenagers. You can't get the layered quality of a symphony orchestra out of one of those tin-pot things. We were making record players while they were still running around on horseback . . .'

'You can't run around on horseback,' interrupted Colette. Reg didn't seem to understand. His preference for everything English knew no limits. Even to literature, to landscape, even to television detectives.

'They're pathetic, those American detectives,' he would say, after Janus Brian had been enthusing about the latest episode of *Kojak, Colombo, Ironside* or *McCloud*, 'they take a whole hour-long programme to work out something Sherlock Holmes would have solved in five minutes. They wouldn't stand a chance against Father Brown, or Lord Peter Wimsey, or even Miss Marple . . .'

Had he always been like this, Colette found herself wondering, or was it something recent? A lifetime of actuarial considerations, of warning against risk, of permanently having in the back of one's mind thoughts of flood, subsidence, epidemics, war, revolution, of calculating the life expectancies of young men just setting out in the world of paid employment, perhaps all these had had a narrowing effect on Reg's mind. Whatever it was, she felt uncomfortable in Reg's presence.

He had taken to calling at Fernlight Avenue at odd times, ostensibly to discuss Janus Brian, and what to do about him, but the conversation would always quickly slip away from that subject towards Reg himself. He would tell Colette and Aldous of his loneliness and of his attempts to find a new partner. He'd joined a Singles Club but was depressed by the people he met. He'd been on various dates with a number of widows and spinsters, but they had all ended in disappointment.

'She sounds very nice,' Colette said, after Reg had described an unusually attractive sixty-year-old he'd met, 'will you be getting together, then?'

'She's not interested in sex,' said Reg, 'that's the trouble. What is it about women when they get old? They seem to lose their sex drive. It just goes. Or is it that they've never had it, but have just been pretending all their lives, and when they get past childbearing they no longer feel the need to keep up the pretence? Have you puzzled that one out yet, Aldous? What are they up to, these women?'

Aldous endured these visits mostly in polite silence. Reg was often mildly drunk when he called, and Colette slowly gathered that he was almost as much a drinker as Janus Brian. Often his speech was slightly slurred and his lower lip shinily wet. After a while he learnt what nights Aldous taught his evening classes and then called only on those, always leaving before Aldous was home. And it was during these evening visits without

Aldous and if Janus was out of the house, that she discovered Reg's unexpected abilities as a sympathetic listener.

'He's apologized several times,' Colette told him one evening, 'and he says he'll never do anything like that again, but I just keep thinking about the things he's sold. Those little things of my mother's. That picture she always used to have on her bedroom wall – a marquetry picture of an alpine scene, the mountains were made of different types of wood, and the water was made of walnut, because it looks ripply, and there was a single pine tree that was green. I can remember that picture from when I was a child, and I always used to wonder where the artist had got a piece of green wood, but later I realised it must have been stained green . . .'

'It was just a picture, Colette, that's all it was.'

'No, it was more than a picture, Reg. It was part of my mother. Ever since she died the things she left in the world have slowly disappeared. There's very little left now. I used to think objects stuck around for ever if you just left them, but now I realize it actually takes lots of energy and effort just to keep things as they are. If you do nothing things just drift out of existence.'

'But you can't stop the world from changing.'

Colette thought for a while.

'I sometimes say a prayer to St Anthony when I've lost something.'

'I thought you were an atheist.'

'I would be if it wasn't for St Anthony. He keeps a tiny flicker of faith alive in me. The amount of times he's found my cigarettes for me, or my matches . . . Now I keep thinking I should pray to him for those things Janus took. And then I think I should pray to him to find my mother, and then I think I should pray to him to find my childhood, because I've lost that just as much.'

'Why do we pray to St Anthony? Was he always losing things? Or was he always finding things?'

Colette enjoyed these conversations, though she seemed to find it hard to convince Reg that there was anything wrong with Janus, her son. She didn't tell him how he hit her. She hadn't told anyone about that, but she told him about the drinking and the disruptive behaviour.

'He's a man who likes his beer, that's all,' Reg said, in a gently coaxing voice, urging Colette to agree with him, 'there's nothing wrong with that. He just has one too many every once in a while . . .'

'No, it's not just once in a while . . .'

'You should think yourself lucky, Colette, to have a son who still cares about you. Look at mine, I don't see them or hear from them for months on end. And then you've got the benefit of his musicianship. How many people can listen to music like that, live, in their own house . . .' On this particular evening Janus was at home playing the piano, and the slightly muffled melodies of Schumann's Kreisleriana were a pleasing background to their conversation.

'Do you think Janus cares about me?'

'Of course he does, woman,' Reg was sitting with his hands resting on his widely separated knees, which gave him an authoritative air, 'you only have to look at him to see how he adores you . . .'

'Adores me?' Colette was allowing herself to be convinced.

'Of course he does. Probably why Aldous hates him so much.'

'Aldous doesn't hate him, he just hates his drinking . . .'

'Ah well there's your problem, you see. I said you should never have married a Methodist, and never trust a man who'll change his religion for the sake of a woman, didn't I say that to you the day before you got married?'

Colette didn't recall Reg ever saying any such thing. Reg went on.

'No Protestant can really understand what booze is all about. Alcohol is at the centre of the Catholic mass. Christ turned his own blood into wine for heaven's sake . . .'

'Don't Protestants believe that?'

'Of course they don't. They don't believe in anything. How could anyone take their faith seriously when it was founded by Henry VIII?'

'Aldous drinks,' said Colette defensively, 'though he never gets drunk . . .'

'Of course he does. One drink and anyone's drunk, the effects begin with the first mouthful. The problem with your son is he drinks that fizzy muck they put in cans. He should try some

real ale. Proper beer, like we used to drink before the war and
the Krauts bombed all the breweries. That's what he should be
drinking. Fizzy booze just sends you bonkers, but real ale
enhances all your senses and aptitudes. You think better, you
drive better, you make love better . . .'

Sometimes the conversations between Colette and Reg
became so engrossing for the pair of them that Reg would
lose track of the time, and Aldous would come home to hear
their laughter coming from the kitchen, noticing how it
quietened as he entered the room. Sometimes he would meet
Reg in the doorway as he left, or on the front garden path,
or would see his white Triumph Dolomite pulling away as
he came up the road. And he grew increasingly impatient of
Reg's visits and did his best to make him feel unwelcome,
not returning his pleasantries but for gruff grunts and grum-
bles. Reg wouldn't be put off, however, and continued his
almost nightly visits to Fernlight Avenue. Aldous finally lost
his patience when he found that Reg had taken Janus out for
a drink.

Janus had been sober for a fortnight, and such times were
to be treasured. Reg was keen to prove that Janus's aggression
was not to do with his drinking too much, but with the type
of beer he was drinking.

'I promise you, Colette, let me take him to The Farmers
Arms and I'll bring him back and he'll be as pleasant and
charming as he always is.'

And so Reg had taken him to The Farmers Arms, a glossy,
modern pub in New Southgate that sold real ale. The two of
them returned at two o'clock the following morning. Reg was
sober, bloody and frightened. Janus was bloody, bruised and
only semi-conscious.

From Reg's hysterical, confused ramblings they got a vague
and familiar picture of what had happened. Janus had begun
insulting the wives and girlfriends of various drinkers in The
Farmers Arms. Someone had taken Janus outside and battered
him with roofing tiles. Reg had had to take Janus to the local
casualty, where he had fallen asleep after raving and raging at
nurses and doctors.

'He's a damn madman. I'll never be able to set foot in that

pub again thanks to your son and it's the only real ale pub in Southgate,' Reg wailed.

Aldous snapped. He took Reg by the lapels and hurled him at the hall wall.

'Ouch,' said Reg, screwing his face up as the back of his head took a knock, repeating the word less emphatically when it seemed Aldous had ignored it.

'If you set foot in this house again,' said Aldous in a quiet growl, 'or interfere with my family again . . .'

New chins appeared around Reg's face as Aldous's grip created a concertina effect.

'I'm not . . .' Reg gurgled. Aldous tightened his grip, stifling the protest.

'I don't want you poking your fat nose around here again. Do you understand?'

Aldous gave Reg an underscoring shove before releasing his grip, and Reg hurriedly retreated through the front door and down the path.

'Don't worry,' said Reg, emboldened by distance, though pale and shaky, almost crying, 'You wouldn't get me back in this house if you paid me,' he coughed and then gave a big, self-controlling sigh, 'you're all bloody mad. You take a look, Aldous, and see what you've made here. It's a bloody madhouse.'

It wasn't the last time they were to meet, however. Colette's regular visits to Leicester Avenue made that inevitable, and shortly after The Farmers Arms incident she found herself phoning Reg from her brother's house.

Colette's visits to Janus Brian had become part of a regular routine, almost daily at one point. She now tried to visit only two or three times a week. If she left Janus Brian alone for more than three days, she found, it was likely that her brother would relapse into a state of depravity, naked and asleep in a nest of his own filth, the mattress swollen with faeces, the carpet slushy with urine, the bitter stench of vomit everywhere.

He was becoming a baby. He reminded her of when James was a child, and how he would, when cross, turn his food bowl upside down and tip its contents all over the table, or the floor, or his own head. Janus Brian was now tipping his food bowl over, the only difference being in the contents of the bowl. She hadn't had to deal with human faeces since her children had grown up, but Janus Brian, despite his meagre diet, still managed to produce regular amounts of pungent, watery matter.

And it was with an expectation of filth that Colette had approached the house alone one early summer morning after nearly five days absence, having herself been down with a stomach bug, yet the house, she discovered, was surprisingly tidy. The floor in the living room had a spruced-up feel, as though recently hoovered. The kitchen surfaces had been wiped, the food, what little there was, correctly stowed. As she wandered through the house calling for Janus Brian, she began to think something dreadful had happened. In her brother's inverted world tidiness and cleanliness must surely be signs of catastrophe, and when she reached the main bedroom, where Janus Brian usually slept in the big double bed he'd shared for nearly thirty years with Mary, she allowed herself a little scream, because hanging from the ceiling was a noose.

A pear-shaped loop of rope tied with a skilful approximation of that difficult hangman's slipknot, hanging from a hook that had once held a macramé plant holder. The mere shape of it Colette found hideous, just as the mere shape of a spider can be hideous. Repulsively macabre, yet thankfully empty. Empty, she hoped, meaning unused. Yet Janus Brian was not in the house. Surely, if he'd been found hanging, she would have been informed. Or had his body, hanging from the noose, somehow evaporated where it swung? The only person she could think of asking was Reg, and so she phoned him. He popped over a few minutes later.

'It was my fault, I think,' he said, as they walked upstairs, 'he did it on my advice.'

'But you said he's okay.'

She could smell that Reg had already been drinking.

'I don't mean he's done it, I mean he sought to do it. I was going to drive over and tell you, but what with the way things are . . . When are you going to get a phone?'

'Tell me what happened to Janus.'

Reg's usually perfect hair was unsettled, his lower lip was glistening.

'I wish you had a phone, Colette. Then I could talk to you. I'd love to have a chat with you over the phone one day, just you and me and the wires . . .'

'Aldous won't have a phone. He thinks they are intrusive.'

'Yes, he's built a little castle there at Fernlight Avenue, hasn't he,' said Reg as they walked into Janus Brian's bedroom, where the noose still hung, 'and he's got you behind a moat and draw-bridge locked in a tower with a big silver key . . .'

'No he hasn't.'

'Come on,' said Reg, suddenly impatient, taking hold of Colette by her shoulders.

'What are you doing?'

'For God's sake Colette, we'll be dead before long, all of us. The Russians have got a forest of missiles with our names on them. What the hell does it matter?'

Suddenly Reg's hot face was right up against hers, and she could see that his shiny, wet lips were bunched up and making to kiss her own. She pushed him away. He pushed back. They struggled lamely, then fell onto the bed. For just a second, perhaps less, it crossed Colette's mind that she might as well let Reg get on with it, instead of struggling against him. There was a time after all, in those innocent years before the war, when she could have found herself married to him. So similar to Aldous – in stature, hairstyle, complexion, even in certain aspects of personality (a vagueness, a boyish charm) and yet now, on the bed, Reg breathless on top of her, groping like a teenager at the buttons of her coat, the smell of stale beer in his mouth, he came across as a mere shadow of her husband, his weaker, darker self, and she found him repulsive. Apart from that, lying on her back, she had an intolerable viewpoint – Reg's face gormless with lust and, behind it, the noose, unused, hanging from the ceiling. She pushed him off and slapped him hard across the face, and Reg rolled backwards, gasping.

Too bashful, drunk and stupid to make any further advance Reg lay on his back and spoke between gurgling noises.

'I drive better when I'm drunk. It sharpens my reactions, it raises my alertness. It enhances my judgement of speed and distance . . .'

'I'm not a car, Reg.'

'That is my point. It is my mistake to think that I could operate you in the same way, if you see what I mean . . .'

'Just tell me what happened to Janus.'

Reg sighed, and then sat up, with some difficulty. His hair, ruffled, was ridiculous, sticking up in big spikes. His tie was over his shoulder, his shirt hanging out of his trousers.

'I'd been over here nearly every evening last week, and I just got fed up with his whingeing on and on about how miserable he was since Mary died. It got me annoyed, because he seemed to have forgotten that I've lost a wife as well. It was only four years ago Elizabeth died, and I felt pretty bad but I didn't hit the bottle like he has and mope around getting on everyone's nerves. It's been nearly a year now, for heaven's sake . . .' Reg, who'd been working himself up to a long rant, checked himself and spoke more calmly. 'So he kept saying he couldn't see any future and what was the point of everything. So I said to him, why don't you just do yourself in? Top yourself, I said, top yourself', (there was a gently urging tone to his voice), 'why don't you just do yourself in, I said.'

'What a thing to say to your best friend, Reg. How could you?'

Reg looked troubled, wiped his lower lip with the tip of his index finger, looked abstractedly at the dampness he had reaped.

'Do you think I've done a bad thing?'

'Yes.'

'Well I never thought he would do it. He's too cowardly.'

'But he's completely drunk most of the time, he could do anything.'

'When he's drunk he couldn't tie his shoelaces, let alone a hangman's noose . . .'

'So you told him to go and hang himself?'

'Christ no,' said Reg, offended, 'I think hanging is one of the worst deaths imaginable. No, we discussed lots of alternatives. I said I could give him some pills that would do the trick. Elizabeth's medication. You know she was in great pain for the last few months. Terrible pain. She was given these superpowerful painkillers, like little red and black torpedoes. Elizabeth always had a big stockpile of them, and when she died there were a lot left over. Several bottles full. I've hung onto them.

I think of them as my escape route. I've enough there to send an army to sleep. They were Elizabeth's only real legacy. She left me nothing else, apart from two sons I never see, of course, and a useless orange dog that wants nothing but to be fed and taken out for walks all the time. Anyway, we left it at that, but the next thing was he phoned me to tell me he'd rigged up a noose in the bedroom and he was going to hang himself, so I said don't be a bloody fool, but he said no, he was going to hang himself, so I just got fed up and called the police and let them sort it out. And they took him off to a loony bin.'

'Not the Hatch?'

'No, it's a place I'd never heard of before, out in the countryside in the middle of nowhere. The name'll come to me in a minute.'

'So he never got as far as actually trying to hang himself.'

'No,' said Reg, dismissively, 'it was always just for show. Like I said, he's too cowardly. Though, to be honest, it wouldn't be that bad an idea, would it. I mean, what sort of life has he got now? He's completely miserable, he's no company, he's got nothing to look forward to. The only reason I called the police was I didn't want his blood on my hands, if it ever got out I'd persuaded him to top himself . . .'

Reg offered to take Colette to the asylum, whose name he'd remembered, Haverford, but Colette declined.

'Don't be like that. I told you, I drive better when I'm drunk. At least let me drive you home.' This she agreed to, and wished she hadn't, as it was a terrifying odyssey through narrow streets at sixty miles an hour, skidding round corners, and at one point, in Goat and Compasses Lane, coming off the road and veering onto the grass verge, narrowly missing a tree.

Haverford Psychiatric Hospital was tucked away behind a ridge of chalk that was thickly planted with barley, three miles to the north of London.

Leaving London to the north Colette always had the impression that the city was an island of stone and glass in a sea of endless wheat. As soon as the buildings ended the great fields of dull yellow began. A foreigner travelling this way would not have a great impression of the English countryside. Even before the war it had been a featureless landscape of cereals and hardy crops – cabbages and potatoes, and since the post-war loss of hedgerows and the emergence of superfields the size of several parishes, The Great North Road had become a highway through sad prairies almost as far as Scotland. There *was* a sadness about that landscape, relentlessly simplified, big and empty when once it had been small and complicated. It had seemed more concentrated in those days somehow, more dense, so that, mile for mile, journeys were that much richer. Now, where horses had once worked the fields there were combine harvesters which produced so much grain it had to be stored in concrete silos, domed towers that marked the landscape more prominently than the 'Hertfordshire spikes' of the local churches.

Or the water towers. In these flat riverless tracts water was a scarce resource, soaking straight through the chalky soil into underground aquifers that could only be retrieved by the sinking of deep bores, then to be stored high above the ground. Odd, these water towers, it occurred to Colette. On the journey to Haverford they passed three or four, a modern concrete one near Cockfosters that looked like a piece of monstrous basketwork, another one was a black iron box on four legs with a ladder leading up to it. At the top of Stag Hill there was a Victorian brick tower that looked as though it had been converted into a house. Then, as they rounded the crest beyond Potters Bar and the flatlands towards St Albans were revealed, she could see them everywhere, scattered about the shimmering wheatfields, water towers, brimming with all their elevated liquid.

When Colette first saw Haverford Hospital, she noticed that it also had a tower, shaped rather like a modern grain silo, though square, and topped with a pyramidal cap of slate.

'Why do these asylums always seem to have towers?' she said to her husband as they pulled into the car park.

'As a look-out for escapees, perhaps?' offered Aldous. It seemed to Colette a quite likely explanation.

They found Janus Brian in a day room with magnificent, tall windows that gave onto a view of rolling parkland and beyond to the beginnings of the midland plains. Colette was astonished by how well Janus Brian seemed. In his light blue, monogrammed (an interlinking JBW) pyjamas and calf-leather slippers he seemed to have lost ten years. Blood had returned to illuminate his skin, which shone now in a way it had never done before. His face had filled, he even seemed to have thicker, slightly darker hair. It was as though the half empty husk of the brother Colette had known had been refilled.

'Apparently I screamed for the first two days without gin,' Janus Brian told them, once he'd settled them into a pair of the red, PVC armchairs that furnished the day room, 'and then I got the shakes, and started seeing things.'

'What sort of things?' asked Colette

'Well,' Janus was finding it hard to explain, 'I never actually *saw* anything, not properly. It was always just outside my field of vision. For instance, looking at you, I can't quite see the chair immediately to my right, but I would be conscious that there was something perched on one of the arms, but if I looked directly, it would vanish.'

'But what sort of thing? A bird, you mean?'

'No, it wasn't a bird, dear. It was more like some sort of giant insect-like creature. Rather frightening. Like an enormous fly, or woodlouse, something like that. Lots of moving legs. But about the size of a cat. Perhaps it was a cat, there are cats here, you know. But sometimes I would be aware that the room was absolutely full of these blasted things, but whenever I looked for them they scuttled away and hid behind the chairs, or under the tables. Just my imagination, I realise now, but at the time they were sending me potty, and I kept screaming for nurses to take them away. But that only lasted a couple of days, and now, as you can see, I'm fully recovered, I haven't had a drop of alcohol for nearly a week and I don't feel the desire for any.'

Colette, who'd once spent three weeks in a psychiatric hospital, knew about the spirit of self-confidence such places can inspire, and how quickly it can evaporate in the outside world.

'The only craving I get now is for water,' he said, 'I love the stuff. I drink it by the jugful. The doctors tell me I'm dehydrated, all the years of boozing have sapped my body of all its reserves of water and I'm as dried up as an Egyptian mummy.'

Janus Brian had a plastic jug of water on the table beside him, with its white, hinged lid. He poured himself a glass as he spoke. 'You don't think of things like that, things so simple. A glass of water. Yet life is totally dependent on it. I read somewhere that an average glass of water will almost certainly contain a molecule that has passed through the body of Aristotle. It's always the little things, isn't it, it's always the things that you take for granted that turn out in the end to be of life and death importance. Here we are worrying about nuclear bombs and Communism versus Capitalism, when it's just a glass of water that matters.'

Aldous recognized the heightened spirit of Janus Brian's discourse. Colette had been like that in hospital. It had come as if to counterbalance the flat years of her depression, as though her person had been replaced by a bright, talkative alter ego, and it had left him with the feeling that so-called normality is a sort of masque, played out continually. In madness we don't so much lose our minds as forget our lines, and it was in hospitals like these that the insane began to relearn the pretence of normality, which was why their inmates seemed so preternaturally normal. They hadn't yet learnt the subtleties of their roles, and were overplaying them.

For Colette, Janus Brian's residence in Haverford meant an extended period of rest for her, the first since Mary died. It took his internment to make her realize just how dependent he had become on her, and so she hoped strongly that this might be the beginning of his full recovery, and that when he came out he could begin leading a fully independent life again. But her feelings were ambivalent. She knew she would feel disappointed if he came out of hospital and spurned any attempts to help him. And she couldn't deny that responsibility for her brother had had a beneficial effect on her, she hadn't felt so good for years.

It shocked her how quickly she missed her daily visits to Leicester Avenue. With her son at home it had become something of a retreat, or haven. Now she was stuck at Fernlight Avenue all day with Janus drifting about the house. She did her best to avoid him. He wasn't usually up before eleven, so she would wait till then before going out to do the shopping. She could spend a couple of hours wandering down to the Parade and back, pottering about in all the shops. When she got back Janus might have gone out. Where he went she never knew, but it wasn't to go drinking. He usually came back sober some time in the evening. He really had run out of money by now. Presumably he'd run out of things to sell, people to borrow from.

Once, to avoid Janus, she'd gone down to Tottenham High Road to see if she could retrieve any of the things Janus had stolen, feeling quite certain that he would have sold them to the various second-hand shops that were down there. It was a long, tiring and fruitless task. A difficult journey, two buses and a long walk, and she felt depressed by the scruffiness and overall seediness of the district that in her childhood had seemed so grand and elegant. She poked around in all the shops but could find no trace of her things, returning disappointedly to Fernlight Avenue.

She visited Janus Brian at Haverford weekly. She had never known him so talkative. He would talk about anything. His mind free-associated. His numerous appointments with a psychiatrist and therapy sessions with a group of other would-be suicides has caused him to think about the past, and his own childhood.

'Apparently I thought Dada would castrate me,' he said, half-amused.

'Did you?'

'That's what came up in the sessions. Did you know this is the main drying-out clinic for the whole of north London? All the old soaks come here. They take you off the booze for a couple of weeks, give you a few therapy sessions, then sling you out. Some of the old characters here come back again and again. All they have to do is attempt suicide, or appear to have attempted suicide. Handy thing to know about . . .'

'Yes,' said Colette. 'What else do they say in these therapy sessions?'

'They just keep asking us about our childhoods. For some reason they want us to share our earliest memories. I keep telling them the same one, I just can't get it out of my head, and it's not even a memory, it's that story Dada used to tell, about the Man Who Thought He Was Jesus, do you remember?'

The story had been one that Dada frequently retold, with great laughter. He had been in The Flowerpot, an Irish pub on the fringe of Clapton Common. The area hardly merited the name, as it was really just a triangular wedge of grass surrounded by tall Victorian houses, with a small pond in the middle. It was near to where Colette's family had lived, after leaving Howard Road and moving a little upmarket to Stamford Hill. Dada had become a regular at The Flowerpot, and from his descriptions of the event that evening she had a picture of its interior, crowded with Irishmen in flat-caps drinking Guinness and singing Irish Folk songs to the accompaniment of someone on the piano accordion, when into the pub burst a wild looking figure with matted hair and a long tangled beard who claimed he was Jesus Christ. He was ignored at first, but then he lifted his hands, palms outward, above the crowd, to show that they had been running with blood. 'I am the risen one,' he cried, 'I have pushed back the stone at Golgotha and I sit at the right hand of the Lord!'

Gradually he was engaged by the drinkers. Someone bought him a pint of stout and he drank while a circle gathered around him, who, drunk as they were, seemed rather convinced by the man's claims to be Jesus Christ. They kept asking him to perform a miracle. When he appeared to heal Frank O'Shea of his bad back, a state of great excitement ensued, and the man was requested again and again to perform further miracles. So a great hush fell on the pub, the accordionist stopped playing and the singing ceased, as the man prepared to announce his next miracle.

'For the benefit of all men on this night of great thirst I will perform for you a re-enactment of the miracle I performed at a wedding in the village of Cana in Galilee. I will turn the water in the pond on the common – into wine!'

The Flowerpot emptied, the drinkers, empty glasses in their hands, following the Man Who Thought He Was Jesus out of the doors and onto Clapton Common, across the unlit grass to the pond.

What happened then? Colette was never sure if Dada had been one of the crowd, or even whether he was there that night, and the story sometimes varied. The one she remembered was of the man walking straight out into the water until he was at the centre of the little pond, up to his waist in the muddy, murky liquid. Arms outstretched he proclaimed some words. What words? Miraculous incantations. A cheer went up and the drinkers closest to the edge of the pond dipped their empty glasses into the water and drank. Then, instantly, they spat out what was only filthy, stagnant pond-water. Incensed they turned on the Man Who Thought He Was Jesus. They splashed into the pond with him with the intention of ducking him under. The Man Who Thought He Was Jesus was sharp enough to make a hasty escape, was lost in the darkness and the spray of the water that was being kicked about. There the story dissolves into a myriad of variant endings. Sometimes he merely vanished into the night, other times he was chased around the common, or found hiding in Piggot's Church, prostrate across the altar, self-crucified.

'Do you think Dada was actually there that night?' said Colette, 'When you think about it it sounds a bit made-up.'

'He may have embellished it a little. I don't suppose there was a big crowd at the pond, but the event definitely happened. I remember other people talking about it, friends of Dada's, other kids' dads. I think it's probably basically true. But it has made me think about Dada and drink. It never occurred to me before, but Dada was out most evenings in that pub, as I recall. Do you think he had a drink problem?'

Colette thought. It was true, he did drink almost nightly at The Flowerpot. But she could never remember him drunk.

'He may not have appeared drunk,' said Janus Brian, 'but that doesn't mean he wasn't. I think maybe his drunkenness manifested in the violence he showed towards me and Lesley. I think maybe he was an alcoholic.'

It was rather a difficult idea for Colette to take in at first. She'd always thought of her father as a tower of moral rectitude, a Victorian patriarch, brutishly disciplinarian. Someone to be feared and respected. Her clearest memories were of his old age, however, when he'd mellowed a little. He still drank, bottles of stout by the fireside, reading travel books. A man who never went abroad, in his old age he'd developed a fascination with the great Victorian explorers, and loved to read Livingstone's accounts of his travels. Where had the violence gone? If it had been inspired by alcohol, surely it would have persisted in different forms even after his sons had left home.

'No,' said Colette, 'Dada was never out of control when he was thrashing you or Lesley. That was always the frightening thing, the way he administered those beatings so calmly, somehow. Almost clinically. If it had been drunken violence it would have been like my son's, wild and out of control, randomly striking out at whoever was near him.'

'But the more I think about it, the more I think there was a drastic mood change that came over him when he was violent. I don't know. I'm just starting to think that alcohol played a big part in Dada's life. And one of the fellows here was telling me about a theory that's come up, saying that alcoholism can be inherited. Which could explain a few things, if he's passed it on to me and to you, if you don't mind me saying, and to your son, and to Lesley . . .'

'Lesley's not an alcoholic.'

Janus Brian paused, seemingly greatly surprised that Colette didn't know.

'Surely you've heard about his escapades from Agatha? I thought she'd told everyone. She usually does, the gossip.'

He then went on to fill his sister in with stories about Lesley's drinking, about how he had taken, like his father, to going out alone each evening to seedy pubs in the shabbier parts of High Wycombe, and returning, unlike his father, in a state of near unconsciousness each night. Madeleine had confided, foolishly, in Agatha, despairingly telling her sordid tales of having to undress her husband, remove his soiled underpants, sponge the vomit from his clothes. Colette absorbed this information greedily.

'So it's passing down through the generations, this drinking gene,' Janus Brian went on, 'One of Agatha's lot, Douglas, I think, or is it Kevin, has turned out to be a raving alcoholic. He sounds rather like Janus, as a matter of fact.'

Janus Brian stayed in Haverford for nearly three weeks and when he came out he seemed greatly recovered. Colour had returned to his skin, he walked with more certainty, and had lost that perpetual drunkard's stagger. He had begun to eat properly. She hoped that this marked the beginning of his rehabilitation, she worried about how he might feel once he was back in the house. On the day of his release she went to Leicester

Avenue to prepare the house for his return, and was shocked to realize that the noose on which he'd tried to hang himself was still hanging in the bedroom. She took it down.

When Janus Brian arrived in the afternoon, delivered by Reg, he was full of plans.

'I've decided you're right, dear. I'm going to sell the house and move somewhere else. I'm going to the estate agent's tomorrow. This place is too full of memories. I need to make a fresh start. Wipe the slate clean. I could sell this place and buy somewhere smaller, and release a considerable amount of capital that's tied up in this house. Also, my dear, I realize I've been an awful burden on you this past year or so, I've been an awful bloody nuisance, so I'm going to move right away from the area. I need to be out of New Southgate, out of London altogether.'

'But where will you go?' asked Colette, rather taken aback by the boldness of Janus Brian's decisions.

Janus Brian looked at her as though the answer was obvious.

'High Wycombe,' he said.

Colette mouthed objections but couldn't say anything.

'Dear, I've had enough of being a pain in the neck for you. You've been so sweet this year, but now I thought it would be time to go and be a bloody nuisance to Lesley and Agatha.'

'But it's so far away, Janus, I'll never see you.'

'It's only an hour's drive away, dear. Be reasonable. Where else can I go, to be honest? I want to move right out of the area, but I don't want to move somewhere where I don't know a soul. High Wycombe's the only place outside London where I have any connections with family. House prices are much cheaper as well. It's the obvious answer. I don't know why I didn't think of it before, it's so obvious. High Wycombe!' He said the last words with a sort of absurd emphasis, raising his small fist and thumping the television gently, just as a prospector might have thumped a map of Idaho at the beginning of the gold rush.

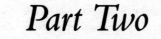

Part Two

7

28 Polperro Gardens
London

19th October 1974

Dear Janus

Report from the front (and back)

It is night now here, somewhere just outside Windhover Hill
in Sinai. Occasional bursts of gunfire can still be heard. The
fighting has been growing heavier the last few nights (usually
after closing time). The Egyptian Unit that I am with at the
moment has been taking heavy bombardment from the IRA from
the East Ridge. That was up until last night due to the troubles in Rome. Their morale is now very low. In Rome there
were more calls for the impeachment of the Pope! The
'Holywinegate Committee' headed by Cardinal Jack Dash is
still asking for the controversial scrolls. A venomous attack by
Cardinal Amin caused near havoc in the Sistine Chapel early
in the week, and 200 clergy walked out. The Pope at once flew
off to his summer palace in Peckham! All this has had a very
demoralising effect on the IRA contingent here. Solly Flanagan
(General Commanding) has retired to The Red Lion, five miles
from the front line and his two hundred men have put down their
pickaxes and started on the stout (which is running in short
supply!) ((NEWS FLASH) . . . The 'Holywater Men' in
Lourdes have decided to cut supplies to Windhover Hill, Uganda
and other sources supporting Mark Philips.) As November 5th

approaches it is feared there will be a major battle, unexploded Brocks 2p bangers have already been found outside and inside the cease-fire line. El Fata, The Salvation Army and the Black September Group have reinforced the Goat and Compasses approach road. Things seem to be getting worse!!! The UN, Nato, Warsaw Pact Dancers and 3rd Elf Brownie Group peace keeping force are having a hard job to stop the supplies of gin getting through and keeping Ted Heath's organ boys apart!

When o when can our thirst-quenching begin? Some men are like musical glasses, to play their best tunes they must always be kept wet!!!!

Woooooeeeeeaghhhghh! That's better.

Nitty Gritty section of letter now follows –

A long time in the distant past (the Jurassic, or was it the Ordivician period) one Janussimus did bash (thump) ((squash)) the man they call Guy on the nose and ears, causing the blood to flow – subsequent exclusion from The Quiet Woman followed, voluntarily.

Nitty nitty gritty bit now comes –

Guy is no longer on the what they call scene at The Quiet Woman – he has not partaken of a drink there for several weeks. The coast is therefore clear, the beaches uncluttered, the sands refined, the waves polished and the dunes swept, for the reinstatement of senator Billisimus and most imperial co-senator Janussimus to re-establish their consulship of The Quiet Woman in a matter of days. A coup is there for the taking – the power is lying on the streets just waiting for someone to pick it up (Lenin)

What say you to this Friday? Janussimus? Yourself.

What say you?

Signed by

Bill (me)

It was the first letter from Bill for several weeks, as elaborately decorated as before, with skilfully drawn visual puns (the phrase 'the coast is clear' and subsequent seashore metaphors were accompanied by a little pen-and-ink drawing of a coast with palm trees and waves). Janus didn't want to admit to himself that he was thrilled by this letter, but he was. His ban from The Quiet Woman had hurt him. Who the hell did Guy Sweetman think he was? In fact, he was a close friend of the landlord, John. Guy was closer to John than Bill was. It turned out that Guy could ban anyone he liked from The Quiet Woman just by having a word with John. Bill had told him not to come to The Quiet Woman for a while, but Janus at first hadn't taken it seriously. He'd gone there one Friday night, and the staff wouldn't serve him, not even that pretty little barmaid Kathy (she'd looked so embarrassed having to refuse him). Before he could even get a glimpse of who was in there John was round the counter and escorting him off the premises. Janus hadn't tried again. The sheer cheek of it. The effrontery. He who'd once single-handedly revived the pub's fortunes by playing honky-tonk jazz on The Quiet Woman's battered old upright now couldn't even get a drink. Janus had suggested he and Bill drink elsewhere, and Bill had agreed. But Janus had accumulated bans in most of the local pubs over the months and years. The Red Lion, The Carpenters Arms, The Goat and Compasses, The Owl. We should go further afield, Janus had suggested, try a different part of London where nobody knows us – and Bill had again agreed and in letters he had suggested The Rising Sun in Crouch End, The Stag and Hounds in Bruce Grove, The Britannia in Whetstone, but it never came to anything. '𝔍'll call for you – remember to save some money, we must find the source of the 𝕷impopo . . .' But Bill never did call. The promises came to nothing. Bill would write apologizingly: '𝔜our dear sweet sister insisted 𝔍 came to 𝕿he 𝕼uiet 𝔚oman on 𝔉riday – she likes to keep an eye on me . . .' Later came medical excuses: '𝕿he doctor says 𝔍've got to cut down on the booze – he says it's the booze that's causing the asthma – but he knows as well as you and 𝔍, that there're as many old drunks around as there're old doctors – come to think of it, most old drunks are old doctors . . .'

The truth was that Janus felt unable to go out drinking unless he was with Bill. And the imagined sprees in adjoining north London suburbs were a dream. They were not going to spend time and money on Christ knows how many buses it took to get to Whetstone or Bruce Grove. Bill was never going to get sloshed in some alien suburb of London with no hope of getting home at night. It was the pubs of Windhover Hill or nothing. And Bill was popular. He could charm his way into any pub. If he was with Bill there was a chance he could get into The Red Lion or The Owl. But now here was the news that Guy had left The Quiet Woman and that his ban might therefore be lifted. Bill had written his first letter in weeks, months. Such good news.

Janus went to see Bill at work. It was the only sure way he could think of contacting him. In all the time he'd known Bill he'd never seen him at work and he didn't recognize him at first. He was at the back of the Lo-Fare, a crowded, slightly shabby supermarket near Southgate tube, behind the butchery counter. He was wearing a white doctor's coat with a traditional butcher's striped apron, blood-splattered, tied across it. On his head was a white trilby hat, and his long hair was tucked up behind him in a bun.

'How could you work for a firm that makes you look so stupid?' Janus said, with a tone of deep disappointment in his voice.

'I'm only wearing this because we've had the health inspectors in today. Normally I can leave the hat off. Look, I've cut myself today.' He held up his left hand, the thumb heavily bandaged, as though this made up for the hat.

'I got your letter.'

'Letter?'

Had Bill forgotten the letter?

'Here.'

Janus produced the letter from his inside pocket, as though providing the proof in some intense legal dispute.

Bill took it and read it with interest. He *had* forgotten writing it. He must have been very drunk.

'May I draw your attention to paragraph four section three, where you propose a drinking session at The Quiet Woman?'

'Yes,' said Bill, thoughtfully, 'Guy has stopped going there, I'm not sure why . . .'

'That's what you said in the letter . . .'

Bill scanned the letter quickly several times. He was having difficulty deciphering his own script.

'Yes, that's right. The coast is clear. The coast is clear, the beaches uncluttered, the sands refined . . .' He broke down into exaggerated chuckles, 'I must have been so pissed when I wrote this.'

'So are we going tonight?' Janus was having trouble holding his patience.

Bill performed an elaborate mime. Somehow, purely with his hands, he managed to convey the information that Juliette was making it difficult for him to go drinking with Janus.

'My learned sister?'

'Her of the scholarly persuasion.'

Juliette had recently been attending evening classes. She was doing two A Levels, English and History, with a view to going to university. Her evenings were now spent in quiet study. Bill had to have the television down low while she worked on her essays in the bedroom. If they went to the pub they went together, once a week. Already Bill sensed the fledgling vocabulary in her conversation, those words that had crept in – *imagery, structure, narrative,* filling out week by week, day by day . . .

'But we need to discover the source of the Limpopo,' said Janus, somewhat pathetically. The sentence was difficult to say sober, coming, as it did, from the furthest reaches of their drunken theatricals, it writhed in the late afternoon air like an excised worm.

'I have a plan,' said Bill, consolingly, picking up an alarmingly bright and long knife, which he then sharpened against a steel.

'I'll try and slip out of The Quiet Woman tonight,' said Bill, the double entendre so commonplace it passed unnoticed, 'and call for you at Fernlight Avenue . . .'

'Why don't I meet you in The Quiet Woman?'

'I don't think . . . I mean, I can try and suggest that my beloved wife sees some of her student friends instead of coming to The Quiet Woman, or else spends an evening indoors to work on her latest dissertation or symposium or whatever she calls them . . . It would be best if you wait for me at Fernlight Avenue.'

The two were silent for a few awkward seconds.

'I've got some readies,' said Janus, offering Bill a glimpse of his dole money.

'I've just remembered, Mary Fox has got a job at The Owl. She started there last week. Why don't we go to The Owl?'

'I'm banned from The Owl.'

'But The Owl changed hands a few weeks ago. I think we should go to The Owl and pay a visit to Mary Fox. I've also heard Lucy Fox and Cassie Fox drink there now as well.'

It had been the appearance of Carl, an American from St Louis, Missouri, in The Quiet Woman one evening a couple of years before, that had started Janus and Bill's referring to sexy women as foxes. Carl, befriended by the pair for the duration of his brief stay in Britain, made a point of referring to desirable women as 'foxy', and since then Janus and Bill had used this term and developed it and elaborated it, so that now they conferred upon any fanciable woman the surname 'Fox', and indulged an anthropomorphic fancy when talking about them, a kind of code, favoured particularly by Bill, to disguise the meaning of what he was saying when talking within earshot of his wife, who, he believed, had no idea that when he talked about fox-hunting he meant prowling for dames.

'I want to go to The Quiet Woman,' said Janus with quiet emphasis, 'I want to see my friends again, it's been a long time . . .'

Bill looked uncomfortable.

'You realize that since Guy has stopped coming, Angelica Fox has not been coming either . . .'

He spoke carefully, as though fearful of igniting something.

'I don't care about Angelica. I just want to see my friends again . . .'

'Ok,' said Bill with his eyes closed, as though he'd reached a final decision. 'I'll call for you at about nine o'clock tonight. I promise, Janus, I will. You just stay sober and keep some money and I'll call for you.'

'Promise?'

'I promise.'

On the way home Janus bought a four-pack of Special Brew from the off-licence on the corner near The Goat and Compasses. In the kitchen at Fernlight Avenue he ate rapidly the dinner his mother had made, and then retired to the music room.

He played Schumann's Carnival from memory, then cracked open the first can, drank it in one go. He dallied for a while with his transcription of Beethoven's Quartet Opus 130. This project had engaged him, on and off, for several years, and was, he believed, the finest version for solo piano of that piece that had yet been written. The only other transcriptions Janus knew of were for two pianists, which even then failed to render the four-part complexity of Beethoven's music adequately. Janus worked on a couple of bars from the opening of the last movement (he'd originally intended to restore the Grosse Fugue to its rightful place here, but couldn't resist the flirty jig of Beethoven's substituted finale), before cracking open his second can, drinking it.

Then it was Fats Waller. Janus sang as he played. Art Tatum. Cole Porter. Gershwin. Dorothy Fields.

Janus opened another can, taking swigs intermittently but steadily. Errol Garner, Oscar Peterson. He was becoming a little tired by now. His back was beginning to hurt, his fingers began to feel numb. He left the music room and went into the kitchen, where Colette was sitting alone. Julian was upstairs. Aldous was in the front room, his territory on Friday nights, an area implicitly out of bounds for Janus.

Janus walked over to the sink, opened his mouth and vomited into it. He didn't hear his mother's cries of disgust. He turned on the taps to wash away the puke, and then looked at the clock on the mantelpiece. It had gone past nine. It was well past. It was getting on for ten. Still that bastard hadn't called. Had he really been playing the piano all that time? Why hadn't he called? Nine, he'd said. He should have called by now.

Janus left the house and walked up Fernlight Avenue towards the corner with Hoopers Lane, marked by a house with a spire and a tall, thin oak tree. In the front garden of the house there was a wishing well newly installed. Mrs Bird had gone to the trouble of bringing into her garden a full-size replica – brick and mortar base under a wooden canopy complete with winding gear, handle and bucket, but no well beneath. Like someone in the future having a replica of a bath in their front garden, or a lavatory.

There were other wells in Windhover Hill, though none were as new as this. Most of them were installed, it seemed, shortly after the building of the houses. A fad before the war, a boom in undug wells. Some houses even managed a fountain. He could hear them trickling in the dark as he walked past, along Hoopers Lane towards Windhover Hill Green.

Windhover Hill Green was mostly antique shops and pubs. There was The Marquis of Granby, where the nouveau riche of the district liked to park their Ford Capris and lean against their bonnets on summer evenings with pints of fizzy beer in their hands. The Volunteer was an old coaching inn over-looking the Green itself, its clientele mostly the old people of the area, who could remember, almost, the place when it really was a village. The Quiet Woman was a few yards down Chapel Road, past the station, in between a florist's and a pet shop.

Had a piano been playing, it might have stopped as Janus entered the pub. As it was, the newly installed jukebox carried on with its thumping melodies. Janus found Bill at the bar, drinking with Steve, the actor, and a woman Janus didn't know. Bill and Steve were well into their session, Bill was looking bleary and slightly hysterical, Steve's blond curls were fastened with sweat to his forehead. The woman, as small and alert as an antelope with eyebrows plucked almost to nothing, the empty spaces beneath filled with green eyeshadow, was looking at Steve in an admiring way, though saying nothing.

'You didn't call for me . . .'

Bill took Janus's arm and spoke reassuringly into his ear.

'I've only just managed to shake off your dear sister. I was just going to make my way over . . .'

A pint of lager arrived in Janus's hand, having been conveyed from the bar via Steve and then Bill.

Janus drank the beer quickly, draining the glass and handing it back to Bill.

The chain operated again in reverse, the glass returning to the bar for a refill.

'I want some nuts as well,' said Janus, with the sulkily defiant tone of a child testing the limits of its parents' generosity.

The beer and nuts were delivered.

'The others are over there,' said Bill pointing at a table some way away, 'I'll be over in a minute, I've just got to settle some business with Steve and his little fox . . . I'll be over in a minute.'

Janus found the others seated in a circle around a large table. There was Hugo Price and Veronica, Rita Michaelangeli, Terry, Graham, Scott, Lucy, Hazel, and some others he didn't know. No Angelica. Janus took a seat in this circle, the others shuffling their chairs to make room. There was an uneasy silence.

Janus then made a sudden exit to the toilet. When he returned to the table there were some empty chairs. Terry, Lucy and Hazel had made their escape. The others looked as though they'd been in the act of escaping as Janus returned, they looked sheepish, knowing now they were lumbered.

Janus took a pull on his beer then opened the first packet of dry roasted peanuts, and emptied the entire contents into his mouth. While he chewed on these he opened the second packet and added those to the half-chewed nuts already in his mouth. He opened a third packet, added them. By the fifth packet he could barely fit the nuts into his mouth, his cheeks bulging like a hamster's. Then, his mouth packed to capacity with half-chewed nut he said 'Bollocks!' as loudly as he could, spraying chewed peanuts widely before him. Wet pieces of nut landed in Hugo Price's treacly hair, in Veronica's frizzy afro, they stuck to the tinted lenses of Rita's glasses, they plopped into grey-bearded Graham's Double Diamond and Scott's pint of Watney's Red Barrel. Normally such a stunt would have met with whoops of laughter from those sprayed upon, but somehow Janus's drunkenness had outgrown the pub that had nurtured it, and he was now regarded here as an embarrassment. Thus Janus was in a dilemma. The quality which had won him popularity in the early days was now having an opposite effect.

For some time the others at the table carried on a conversation as if Janus wasn't there, and Janus's attention wandered. He noticed a couple sitting at a nearby table. A man with shaggy black hair and a winsome moustache sitting alongside his girlfriend or wife, a pristine little thing with cropped blonde hair and dangly earrings. They had been engaged in some intimate conversation of a gently competitive nature ('yes you did', 'no I didn't') that had now come to an end, and they were looking vaguely around them for want of anything else to say. The man caught Janus's eye for a moment, and so Janus said, quietly, 'Cunt.'

He said the word in a relishing sort of way, with an emphasis on the final consonant which he spat out, almost giving the word two syllables – cun-t. Quiet though it was, the couple picked up on this word instantly, and seeing that it was directed at them, assumed a kind of collectively sulky expression. Janus repeated and elaborated.

'Cunts. Fucking cunts. Fucking shitheads. Shitfaces. Fuckers.'

'Janus,' said Hugo, who'd noticed this vituperative digression, 'take it easy.'

'No, come on,' said the man, 'let's hear some more of what he's got to say.'

'Sorry,' said Hugo to the man, who seemed to take this apology rather indignantly.

'Doesn't bother me,' said the man, 'but if he says anything more he'll get this glass in his face.'

Janus let the incident pass. It had done its work. He had impressed himself upon this drearily happy couple, had stirred the man to an apelike hostility and had frightened the woman. He felt satisfied.

By this time, however, some other people had arrived at the table, and were sitting either side of Janus. Janus knew them vaguely as the 'heavy' friends of Guy that Bill had referred to. They were large, it was true, but they hardly looked threatening. One, in fact, looked rather like the television presenter David Attenborough. They were trying to engage Janus in some sort of conversation, of the ironically jovial type that heavies seem to specialize in, full of concealed threats and violent implications, 'that's a nice suit you're wearing, wouldn't like to see that spoilt. Play the piano don't you, be terrible if something happened to your hands.'

'Do you like penguins?' said Janus.

The Attenborough lookalike shrugged, as if to say he didn't get the implication, and he didn't care.

'I think it's terrible about the white rhinos,' Janus went on, 'and the giant pandas.'

'Yeah, well you'll be an endangered species soon,' said the other man, cottoning-on remarkably quickly – was it well known that his friend looked like David Attenborough, Janus wondered – 'if you get my meaning.'

'Why is spunk white and piss yellow?' said Janus.

The heavies offered no answer.

'So an Irishman can tell if he's coming or going.'

His old boss at Swallows, Mr Hawes had told him that one.

'Yeah, well you won't know if you're coming or going pretty soon,' said David Attenborough, 'if you keep causing my mates grief.'

'We're talking Mr pretty-boy Sweetman here are we, gentlemen?'

By this time Janus noticed that the table at which he sat was empty, apart from the three of them. Gradually, one by one, the others had departed, to the bar or to the toilets, never to return.

'Why don't you come outside with us,' said David Attenborough, taking hold of Janus's arm.

'What for?' said Janus.

'We've got something we'd like to show you,' said the other, taking hold of Janus's other arm, the two men then lifting Janus.

'What is it?'

'You'll see.'

They began walking Janus to the door. Janus felt suddenly weak. The two men were holding him so tightly his arms were hurting. He was escorted through the double doors of the pub and out onto the pavement. Here Janus's arms were held behind his back by the other man while David Attenborough prepared himself to deliver a sharp blow to Janus's midriff, savouring the moment like a bowler about to bowl. Visions of gorillas in leafy jungles, the grizzly bears of Yosemite, of mountain lions came into Janus's mind as he braced himself for the punch, but the process was interrupted by a voice.

'Len,' said Bill Brothers, who'd appeared behind David Attenborough's shoulder. Attenborough looked round.

'Oh. Hello Bill.'

'What's happening.'

'Oh, you know. Just going to teach this joker a lesson. He's been bothering people.'

'But that's Janus Jones.'

'Yeah, I know. Arrogant bastard. Needs his spleen stretching.'

'But you can't do that to Janus Jones, he's a special man. He's an important person.'

David Attenborough was rapidly losing his fire. He looked deeply bereft and cast Bill an expression that said something like 'Not even a little punch? Not even a smack in the chops?' And eventually Janus was released and the two heavies had to make do with scowls and nose to nose stare-outs, warning Janus to be 'careful in future' and to 'watch his step', before they reluctantly went back into the pub.

Janus and Bill stood beneath the sign of The Quiet Woman, a headless Elizabethan, which swung, with a squeaking sound, back and forth. Bright spotlights that lit the front of the pub made everything look blue.

'What's happening?' said Janus, 'I need to piss.'

He did so, copiously, casually, into the gutter, making no attempt to conceal himself. The incident with the heavies had reaffirmed yet again Janus's sensation that he was blessed, touched, indestructible.

By the time he had finished Bill was with Steve, the actor, though the girl that had been with them was no longer around.

The actor had a habit, when drunk, of snapping his fingers, both hands simultaneously, annoyingly out of synch with each other. He snapped his fingers now, as though anticipating delights.

Zipping himself up, Janus said, 'So where were you?'

'I'm here,' said Bill, 'we're both here.'

'Where's Angelica?'

Steve snapped his fingers and laughed.

'Not in there,' said Bill, 'I don't know where she is. She doesn't come to the pub with Guy these days.'

'Let's do something,' said Steve, 'let's go somewhere. I want to go somewhere.' Then he cackled.

'Why didn't you call for me?'

'I was going to,' said Bill, 'I was on my way. Look,' he looked at his watch, 'we can get to The Owl before closing. I know someone there who's a member of The Buckingham. He can get us in.'

'What's the fucking Buckingham?' said Janus.

'It's a club round the back of Southgate tube. You can drink there till three in the morning. The bloke's called Des, let's get to The Owl.'

To get to The Owl they walked along Parsons Lane, a broad avenue of ludicrously wealthy dwellings, where the rich elite of Windhover Hill lived. Their houses stood behind great striped lawns under canopies of majestic trees. Often the houses had names derived from these trees – *High Beeches, The Oaks, Whispering Willows*. The pavements of Parsons Lane were herringbone quarry tiles, the lamp-posts ornate wrought iron, there were grass verges and benches.

'The revolution,' said Bill as the three walked side by side along this road 'when it begins, will begin here. This very road will go down in history as the place where it all began, when the gates of bloody' (taking the name of the house they happened to be passing, a modernist affair of swish concrete, ceramic mosaics and glass domes) '*Lonely Birches* were stormed by the workers of The Quiet Woman . . .'

Steve laughed.

'. . . and we'll be patrolling these boulevards with cocked machine guns, strapped across our shoulders, Havana cigars in our mouths, the corpses of the capitalists swinging from the lamp-posts above us . . .'

'Cliff Richard lives in that one,' said Steve, 'or he used to anyway. He's a famous bloke.'

'A famous capitalist entertainer. His body shall swing from this lamp-post riddled with machine gun bullets,' said Bill. 'That one's owned by the bloke who owns Meccano,' said Bill. 'We could start by taking him hostage, we could use his empire to build munitions for the revolutionary militia . . .'

'Why don't we do it now?' said Janus, suddenly.

'Yeah,' said Steve, thinking Janus was joking, but Janus was walking along the path towards the owner of Meccano's house.

'Remember what Lenin said of the events of 1917,' called Janus, ' "Power was lying in the streets just waiting for someone to pick it up." That is the situation now. We could break in, start the revolution, come on . . .'

'Better come back, Janus,' said Bill, who'd stopped, suddenly rather concerned. The owner of Meccano's house was an imposing mock Georgian edifice with Doric columns supporting an entrance portico, tall windows, three flashy cars parked outside. Janus crunched his way across the gravel towards the front door, whooping as he did so.

The toy-magnate's house showed no response, and Janus, noticing that Steve and Bill were very slowly edging their way away from the house, returned to the pavement.

'Pathetic,' said Janus, as he caught up with them, 'Call yourselves revolutionaries? Lenin would have been ashamed of you.'

The rest of the journey along Parsons Lane was passed in a rather embarrassed silence, the brisk walk and the cold night air having sobered the trio slightly. Occasionally Janus gave drunken cries and whoops at passing Rolls-Royces, and at a small roadworks he jumped about on some stacked paving tiles.

Outside The Owl Janus had another piss, noisily visible, the cascade splattered on the pavement as passers-by tried not to observe.

'We'll see you inside,' said Steve, as he and Bill walked towards the door of the pub. Janus didn't reply but went on peeing, so much of it, clattering at his feet, forming rivulets and tributaries that trickled and snaked along the gentle gradient of what was now Goat and Compasses Lane. So much of it.

Entering the pub, however, he was soon aware that he'd been tricked. Bill and Steve were nowhere to be found. They must have passed straight through the pub and out of the other door. How they must have run to be out of sight so quick. Janus could see from the back door the view of Goat and Compasses Lane as it swept downhill past the entrance of Redlands Park, then up again, their only possible escape route, and they were nowhere in sight.

'Cunts,' said Janus to himself, and went back into the pub.

The bell had rung already for last orders, now it was being rung for closing time. He didn't bother trying to get a drink but left the pub vaguely in the direction he thought Bill and Steve must have gone, with even vaguer ideas of trying to find this Buckingham Club Bill had been talking about. But they couldn't get in without meeting this bloke in The Owl. Surely they hadn't had time to meet him and take him with them? Perhaps they were going to wait outside this club for him? Janus felt confused, slightly tortured. He felt like a stranger in a foreign country, suddenly. He sat for a while on the wall of a front garden, the houses here were back to normal size.

'Kill Bill,' he said to himself, 'Kill Bill, kill Bill, kill Bill. Such a pretentious creep. So false. Such a hypocrite. A toadying, slimy, pseudo–Marxist butcher bastard . . .'

'Hello,' said Mary.

'Hello,' said Janus, without looking up, but recognizing the voice.

'I saw you in The Owl. Ron lets me go early so I can get my bus. I have to walk up to the stop outside the tube, but I don't like it much. It gets a bit creepy. Where are you going now?'

'I don't know,' Janus groaned, wondering if he was going to be sick, holding his head in his hands.

Janus had known Mary since she was a small girl, being one of Juliette's childhood friends. She'd even come away on holiday to Wales once with them when Mary was about thirteen. That was the first time Janus really took any notice. He understood that she was beautiful, but he didn't find her beauty attractive, he wasn't sure why. She had pale skin and chocolaty hair, mauve lips and sweet, dark eyes. On her neck there were three large dark freckles, as though a lame vampire had tried to have a go at her, and failed. But she was too clean, too new. Unsullied. Not like Angelica, Janus's coeval, with her well-used, weatherworn face and thickened body, that coarse-grained skin of hers, the little wrinkles that appeared at the tops of her breasts when she was showing her cleavage. Angelica was a well-farmed landscape of woods and streams where you could walk all day over stiles and little footbridges getting covered in mud and burrs and thorns. Mary was a little desert by comparison, where one's own footprints are a sort of monument.

'Well,' Mary said, 'I'll see you.' And she began walking away. Janus then realized that she'd been hinting that she needed an escort along the dark, parkside upper reaches of Goat and Compasses Lane, and so he swayed to his feet and walked with her, uncomfortably fatherly.

To their right Redlands Park was dark behind its spiked railings. Janus suddenly thought that Bill and Steve must have gone into the park, that would explain their sudden disappearance. There was a gap in the railings they could have slipped through. Janus passed through the gap into the park. Mary followed reluctantly.

'Where are you going?'

'For a walk.'

Why was she following him? He should have clung to this young woman for all he was worth, she was his only friend in the world at that moment, and yet he was running away from her. And she was following.

To the left was the putting green, a blue lawn full of holes, to the right the pitch and putt, a sinister moonlit slope of fairways and roughs. 'Golf is a very stupid game,' said Janus. The avenue of ornamental cherries formed a tunnel of leafless, creaking branches which they passed through. Janus thought he would find Bill and Steve whooping it up on the swings and roundabouts of the children's playground, and so they went there, but it was empty, a motionless machine of glossily painted iron, glinting.

'I don't like it here, Janus, can we go back?'

Janus didn't reply. The park seemed to him a rather magical place after dark. All that space and not a soul in it. Huge sweeps of rolling pastures leading up from the playground almost to the horizon, above which a few rooftops peaked. On the other side were woods, a dense thicket of tall oaks and holly bushes that was all that was left of Windhover Hill Woods, which themselves were the last remnant of the Great Forest of Middlesex, which had once covered most of that extinct county.

Just visible in the other direction, near the lake, was Redlands Mansion, once the home of a Middlesex grandee, now a convalescent home for those recovering from traumatic surgery.

Sometimes you could see nurses wheeling them around the grounds, old men cocooned in blankets, taking some air, the stump of a limb protruding.

'The police sometimes exercise their dogs here after dark,' said Janus, as they sat on a roundabout.

'Not too fast, Janus,' Mary suddenly said, as Janus gave the roundabout a heave, sending it spinning at a nauseous rate. He left to have a go on the witch's hat, then a plummet down the polished slope of the slide, getting stuck halfway down. Then he sat on the rocking horse, a six seater contraption whose mechanism was concealed beneath the wooden body of the animal, whose face grinned madly as Janus worked the beast back and forth.

Mary's roundabout had slowed down by now, and she was rotating in a rather stately way, though Janus could hardly see her in the dark.

'Can we go back now?' she said, 'I'll miss my bus otherwise.'

She couldn't go on her own, not through the midnight black park with all its owls and bats. She was trapped here with him.

'This was all somebody's garden once,' said Janus as his horse slowed to a canter.

'I suppose it was,' said Mary.

'Beautiful, to have a garden that big. As big as a piece of countryside.'

'Yes.'

'I wish I had a garden as big as this.'

'So do I,' said Mary.

As they left the playground Mary asked if she could hold Janus's hand, saying she was worried she'd fall over as it was too dark to see the path.

'It is a very dark park,' said Janus as he felt Mary's hand slip into his. He didn't know what to do with this hand. Should he hold it, and if so, how tightly? It reminded him of the times he'd held a baby, when James and Juliette and Julian were born, the alarm he always felt at having a living thing suddenly squirming in his arms, the awful sense of future history, of someone's whole life packed up in the neat parcel of a baby. They shouldn't be so light, he always felt. He couldn't understand why babies didn't weigh the same as full-grown adults, in the same way that acorns should be as heavy as oak trees. Mary's hand was a little insistent portion of life trying to push its way into his. He tolerated her soft grip for a while as they walked together back along the path, passing the side of the lake, but after a while he loosened his hold, and Mary's hand, after hanging on for a little while, very slowly fell away.

The lake was of an impressive size for a suburban park, a graceful stretch of water with two densely wooded islands. For several weeks the council had been cleaning the lake, all the rising land between the lake and the mansions had been excavated into a series of terraced steps down which the lakewater, having been pumped to the top by a machine that worked night and day called a Mudcat, trickled down through a series of sluices and filters, cascading through a warren of U-turns and countless little waterfalls, until it returned, purified, to the lake. Janus and Mary could hear the rasping engine of the Mudcat from its anchorage out on the lake, and the drowsy answering gurgle of the filter trenches to the right.

The trenches were bounded by a low picket fence, easily crossed, and Janus then swiftly did so, Mary following reluctantly for fear of getting lost.

'I'm climbing Mount Kilimanjaro,' said Janus.

Once, when bored, Janus had decided to learn by heart the names of the principal mountains of every country in the world, and the knowledge had stayed with him.

'Now I'm on the summit of Pik Kommunizma. Now I'm on Popocatépetl. Voorstradt (highest peak in the Netherlands) . . .'

'I don't like it here, I'm scared,' said Mary, who couldn't keep up with Janus as he scaled peak after muddy peak, 'It smells.'

A rich odour of rotting pond life, of the sludge of countless fallen leaves, the sunken treasure of a hundred autumns, lurked in all the blind channels.

'Let's get back to the path,' Mary called, seeing Janus only as a vague silhouette on a muddy peak. Mary tried clambering after him, but she was unsure of her footing, the ground was steep and slippery, her feet were becoming heavy with mud. Janus, she could see, had his arms outstretched and was slowly rotating, as though addressing an all-encompassing multitude, then Mary took a stumble and sat in a puddle of purified water, and she cried.

When she next looked up Janus was gone.

8

Aldous had become afraid of his front door. Whenever there was a knock he dreaded what it might portend, and he would always hesitate before answering it. He thought sometimes that he should change the knocker because the current one was too heavy – a broad grin of chrome-plated steel that, no matter how lightly it was used (a little girl asking for her ball back) always gave a deafening report, as though a giant was nailing the house down with a silver nail. Sometimes he felt a desire to wrap the knocker in wool, or replace it with something made from softer materials. A doorknocker of felt and feathers would have done. Sometimes he thought of wiring up a doorbell to ring softly in the kitchen, or one of those musical chimes, a couple of tubular bells that would ding-dong gently in the hall. You could adjust the volume of those, so Aldous understood. No matter how urgent or frantic the caller, always it would be the same gentle ding-dong in the hall.

Often the caller was a steeplejack offering to dismantle the tall redundant chimneys that teetered on the top of the house, or a tree surgeon with a truck full of ladders and saws offering to lop, pollard, topple and completely remove the acacia tree in the front garden, which had grown to a considerable size. Aldous had watched this tree grow from tender sapling to its present form, larger in volume than the house, and yet he'd not noticed its growth at all. As with his children, the last thing he knew he had a baby in his arms, now his house was full of men and women who claimed to be his offspring. Likewise Aldous hadn't really noticed the acacia tree until the steeplejacks and lumberjacks and others with ladders had begun offering to cut it down. Where the hell had that tree come from? It was enormous, he had to admit. The roots were drying out the foundations, so they told him, desiccating the lower walls. A crack had appeared in the brickwork, zigzagging through the courses. On the pavement the stones had been upset, a little trap that could cost Aldous thousands of pounds in compensation should anyone injure themselves falling over them. That's what the passing arborealists said, but Aldous always shut the door on them, murmuring that when the time came to lop the acacia he would do it himself. But he never did anything about the tree. It had grown so immense, had spread itself so widely, filling every window at the front of the house, extending scabby limbs of pale bark across the pavement and out into the road, that he felt reluctant to interfere with it. The roots of a tree mirror in size and spread the above-ground network of branches. Then the roots of the acacia must have a grip on next door's foundations as well, and it was likely to have coiled its tubers around the sewerage, electrical conduits, gas mains, water pipes and telephone cables. Should Aldous saw some branches off, who knows what effects that might have on the subterranean self of the tree. It might cause the tree to tighten its grip on a gas main and thus rupture it. In truth he had an inkling that the tree was somehow holding the house up. Besides, he found the tree attractive. It was like having another garden in the sky. From the windows there was a view of a hanging tapestry of foliage that in the autumn became a collage of pale yellow sticker-dots stuck to the pavement.

It was a policeman's knock that came that Saturday morning. Aldous was alone in the house, for once. Colette had taken Julian to buy a new pair of shoes, and was to be out for most of the morning. Aldous had taken the opportunity to work on his fountain in the back bedroom. With James away at university Aldous had gradually reclaimed a small portion of the territory they'd donated to their children. In the bay window of that room he'd set up a small worktable (in fact the dining table from Meg's old house). There he kept his brushes in jars, his pens and their nibs in other jars, his pencils, boxes of charcoal, and his paints. There was a bottle of dried cow-parsley heads. He had a drawing board set at a pleasing slope on some old art books. He would retreat here to make paintings from the numerous sketchbooks he kept, or simply to draw the view of tangled trees and wedged-in gardens that filled the window. But this morning he was working on his fountain. He'd brought a pack of clay home from school and was assembling the model from the working drawings that he hoped had impressed the monks of Durham. Brother Head was still providing no definite answers to his letters. The bishop of Durham had prevaricated. He had committees and working parties to consult. Brother Head's letters were always cheerily optimistic, a tone which unintentionally conveyed a kind of indifference to Aldous's plight. No other commissions had come as a result of that piece in the *Telegraph*. This fountain was the only route he could take towards a future life of lucrative public art. Besides that, he could do with some money now, just for the amount of work he'd put into the design. Colette was always telling him, he had a right to some payment even if they never built the bloody fountain. Then another letter from the monastery would come: '*My, don't the months pass quickly . . .*'

Such worries melted away for Aldous when he worked, however. Drawing the radial structure of a cow-parsley head, or painting the buttressed architecture of a Hertfordshire church with its slender copper spire, required a level of engagement with the material world that made abstractions like money seem meaningless. This was how he felt as the doves took shape in his fingers. He had a baseboard fitted with a vertical copper pipe to represent the central pipe of the fountain, and he was assembling his doves, cut from rolled-out clay, shaped and textured with fingernails, a comb, a toothbrush, wire wool, anything Aldous had to hand, then moistened and fitted together in a clamouring spiral of ascending flight. When nearly dry he would cut the completed structure into sections that could be separated for firing and glazing in the school kiln, then reassembled again at home and made ready for despatch to Durham. Once they had the working model in their possession the monks could surely not refuse to offer the commission. Or at least some sort of payment.

The knock came when Aldous's fingers were deep in clay. The knock was so loud and emphatic it was as though a cleaver had sundered Aldous's work. Yet it could have been that little girl again, asking for her tennis ball back so that she could play fives against the garages. Aldous ignored it, tentatively put his fingers back into the clay. The knock came again. Five knocks – bang bang bang bang bang – that effectively chopped Aldous's sculpture into five wet pieces. He had no alternative but to investigate.

He opened the front door while wiping the clay from his hands with a rag.

The policeman was of the old school, not one of these cocky young chaps they seemed to send round nowadays, but a gentle, portly greybeard.

'Mr Aldous Jones?'

'Yes.'

'Father of Janus Jones.'

'Yes.' Aldous gave his affirmatives in a tone of weary anticipation

'Your son was involved in a serious incident last night.'

'Serious?'

'We believe he deliberately created an obstruction in Parsons Lane, using materials from a nearby roadworks. This obstruction caused an accident, resulting in injury to a motorcyclist . . .'

'Serious?'

'The motorcyclist is currently in hospital. He's not in danger, but he has a broken leg. And a broken wrist. Mr Jones has admitted to creating the obstruction. We have charged him with criminal damage and obstructing a public highway with intent to endanger life, both very serious offences if they result in injuries to members of the public. The magistrates have agreed. He will appear for sentencing next week.'

'Will he go to prison?' said Aldous, unable to disguise the hope in his voice. He failed so badly, in fact, that the policeman gave him a long, quizzical look.

'It's possible,' said the policeman, still regarding Aldous thoughtfully, 'it depends.'

Janus received a six-month prison sentence suspended for two years. Southgate Magistrates had viewed Janus's drunken activities very seriously. He'd managed to avoid prison, but the threat of incarceration was to hang over him for the two year duration of his sentence, if he committed any further offence, no matter how minor. The motorcyclist's testimony provided a full account of Janus's activity that evening, because Janus had spent twenty minutes in close conversation with him while waiting for the ambulance (which he'd called) to arrive. He'd told the motorcyclist how he was angry because his friends had deserted him. He had gone to Redlands Park with another friend, but had lost her in the dark. He had wandered around in the woods for some considerable time, possibly falling asleep at one point. At around four-thirty A.M. he was in Parsons Lane. He used the stacked paving stones he'd found at a roadworks to build an obstruction across the road, which was at the time deserted of traffic. The obstruction was, in effect, a low wall, about ten inches high, covering both carriageways. The motorcyclist, a milkman on his way to work, had crashed into this wall at around five-thirty A.M. When asked why he'd done it, the motorcyclist reported that Janus had said something incoherent about starting a revolution.

He had asked for twenty-five other offences to be taken into consideration.

The magistrate told him that he was lucky not to be appearing on a manslaughter charge.

The Sunday following Janus's court appearance, Aldous, Colette and Julian paid a visit to Lesley and Madeleine in High Wycombe. On the way Colette extracted from her youngest son a promise.

'You won't say anything about Janus to your aunt and uncle will you?'

Julian shook his head. He rarely spoke during these visits anyway. His mother needn't have worried.

'All in all it's probably a good thing,' she went on, 'It'll knock some sense into him maybe. The threat of going to prison is surely enough to make even someone like Janus toe the line. Don't you think?'

Father and son gave no response.

It had been at Madeleine's invitation that they were visiting. She seemed keen, having heard that Janus Brian was looking for a house in the area, to learn more about his plans.

'So he's really going to go through with it? He's really going to move all the way out here, to High Wycombe?' Madeleine spoke from the comfort of her modern rocking chair, which filled a gap in her living room between the ceramic mantelpiece and the colour television.

'Yes,' said Colette, 'He's made up his mind. I've tried talking him out of it a hundred times but he's very stubborn. I think it's a stupid idea . . .'

Lesley gave a resigned laugh but said nothing. Aldous lifted a cup from his saucer, drank and replaced it, the clink of porcelain sounding uncomfortably loud. Aldous always felt discomfort at Madeleine and Lesley's house. Everything there seemed to be breakable. He and Colette and Julian were sitting in a row on the couch, Lesley was in the armchair.

'Well I think it's marvellous,' Madeleine said, 'That he's decided to make a fresh start. It'll be just what he needs.'

Colette was silent. They hadn't visited Lesley and Madeleine for a long time, and may never have visited again had not Madeleine written to invite them. Madeleine now seemed to have the upper hand. Colette felt sure that her sister-in-law was reading the situation as follows – Colette has failed to bring Janus Brian through his crisis and so he has to resort to moving house to High Wycombe so that he can be under the more responsible care of his older brother and sister.

'Those vases,' Colette said, noticing a line of little ceramic pots lined up on top of the pelmet above the French windows, 'I like the way you've arranged them. We've done that in the back bedroom.' This was true, a line of ceramic pots on the pelmet of the back bedroom, the only difference being that Aldous had made their pots himself.

'Yes, dear,' said Lesley, 'we're copying you. Now tell me, Rex, about these windows you designed. I saw the piece in the *Telegraph*. Have you had any more commissions?'

'Not really,' Aldous replied.

'The bishop of Durham wants him to design a fountain,' said Colette, quickly. 'For a monastery.'

'How exciting, Rex, why didn't you tell me?'

'Well, it's still not settled . . .'

'And this commission came about as a result of the piece in the *Telegraph*?'

'Yes.'

'And have there been any more?'

'No.'

'Oh, there will be, I'm sure. It'll be just the start, Rex. Dear,' (meaning his wife), 'I think at last this man's talents will be recognized. One day we'll be going to see his work in the Tate.'

'That's unlikely,' said Aldous.

'I don't think so.'

'Unless I put them on the walls myself.'

A little round of laughter quickly died.

'I wonder if you could tell me,' Madeleine began after a short pause, 'I mean, I don't know anything about alcoholics. How does one deal with them? I've been to the library but I couldn't find much. I didn't really like to ask the librarian . . .'

'Why not?' said Colette.

'Well, I mean . . .'

'What do you mean?'

'It's a little bit delicate, isn't it?'

Colette shrugged but didn't speak. Seeing that she'd reached a dead end with Colette, Madeleine turned to Aldous, 'I just wonder what I should need to know. It's difficult isn't it?' She beamed that ingratiating smile at Aldous, and Aldous and his family grimaced inwardly.

'What makes you think we should be such experts?' Colette snapped.

'I just meant,' said Madeleine, with a hint of 'here we go again' irritation in her voice, 'that since you've been looking after Janus Brian for all this time (and I do commend your dedication) you must have a lot of experience by now of dealing with alcoholics . . .'

'*An* alcoholic,' said Colette, 'and for your information, we were just as much in the dark about it as you supposedly are, but I'll tell you this, it would be a waste of time nosing through libraries and doing your homework from books on the subject, because there is no book that could describe what it's like to have a chronic alcoholic on your hands, or that could describe what I've been through this past year or so.'

'Exactly my point, Colette. So why can't you tell me, from your point of view? All I'm asking for is a little help, a little guidance . . .' here she gestured towards Colette generously, as though handing her an invisible bouquet, 'from someone with experience.'

Colette sulked for a few seconds. Inwardly she was seething. It was not an unreasonable request from her sister-in-law, of course, but in its delivery every word was barbed and poisoned, every phrase contained the hidden message 'I am a better mother and wife than you are, have been, or ever will be.'

'The diarrhoea is the worst thing,' said Colette, after a pause, 'worse than the vomit. That's the first thing I've learned. The second is that Janus Brian tends to neglect his toenails. Every few months he starts to look like Nebuchadnezzar. You need to trim them for him once a fortnight. The third thing is not to be bothered by nakedness. Janus Brian likes to walk around in the nude. If he's very far gone he is likely to take hold of your breast. He will eat steamed fish, nothing else. Also, he needs to be talked to, for hours on end, sometimes. Or read to. I'm in the middle of reading him the complete works of Dickens, but so far we're still only on *Bleak House.* You will need to visit him every other day. If you leave it any longer he is likely to die. And he won't thank you for anything that you do for him. Not a word of thanks. Is that enough information for you? Do you think you can cope with that?'

'Well, I'm sure we'll do our best, but I'm also sure that there must be people, I mean, social services or something, that can help . . .'

Madeleine's sentence drifted into the room and faded away, leaving an edgy silence in its place, interrupted by Lesley.

'Perhaps when he's started breathing in the air of the Chilterns he'll start feeling better, you know there are some very good bus companies in the town that do little excursions into the countryside, Madeleine and I have been on several . . .'

'Janus Brian doesn't like the countryside,' Colette interrupted, 'and he's not coming here for the fresh air. He's coming here so that you and you,' she pointed in turn at Madeleine and Lesley, whose eyes were now closed, 'and Agatha can all take turns in looking after him, so that if he gets so sozzled, as I can guarantee he will, that he passes out in a pool of his own piss, there will be someone on hand to pick him out of it.

Though why he should think any of you should bother, when you clearly couldn't give tuppence, any of you, for the well-being of your younger brother, and you,' Colette pointed at Madeleine whose eyes were also closed by now, 'you with your library books, making out you're all concerned and caring when we all know full well that you'll visit him once when he's moved in and then never see him again . . .' Colette could have gone further but she'd run out of steam, and concluded her tirade with a dismissive hand gesture.

'Well, I think that's a little unfair, Colette,' said Madeleine, rocking back in her chair, 'We only want to do our best for Janus Brian, I'm sure once we get into the swing of it, and we gain some experience of coping with an alcoholic . . .'

'For God's sake!' Colette snapped, 'will you stop saying *alcoholic* as though you've only just learnt the word?'

'What do you mean?'

'I mean will you for once drop this pretence, this sham, when everyone knows you've turned my brother into a nervous wreck?'

'I think it's a bit rich blaming me for Janus Brian's . . .'

'I don't mean Janus Brian, I mean this man here, Lesley, who's sitting here acting the role of contented husband, when we all know what's really going on.'

'Do we?' Madeleine seemed genuinely puzzled. Lesley turned to the little row of books on the cabinet by his chair, a concession, Colette thought, after years of booklessness, and fingered through a crumbling, leather-bound volume of poetry.

'It would be a good thing,' said Colette, 'if he took his trousers off and chased you round the bedroom, once in a while.'

After a shocked pause, Madeleine gave a high-pitched series of chuckles.

'My dear,' she said, 'you really have excelled yourself this time. The banality of your remarks are matched only by their vulgarity.'

'Well it's true isn't it? *He* won't say anything because you've got him tamed like a poodle,' she nodded at Lesley, who was reading poetry intently through his bifocals, 'but we all know how he's suffering . . .'

'Suffering?' Madeleine laughed, 'Your family know all about

suffering, of course, how one must suffer to have a son like Janus . . .'

'Janus is doing very well, thank you,' said Colette, passing over the fact of his newly acquired criminal conviction.

'Is he? You will let me know when his next concert is won't you – where will it be, the Royal Albert Hall? The Royal Festival . . .'

'You . . .'

'How about,' said Lesley with suddenness, snapping his poetry book shut, 'we all go out for a drink?'

'Good idea,' said Colette, reaching for her handbag and spilling the teacup that was cradled in her lap. Cold tea spilt onto her trousers, she didn't seem to notice, 'the atmosphere has got rather stuffy in here.'

'It certainly has,' said Madeleine, waving away the blue fog of cigarette smoke that Colette had produced that afternoon, then she said to Lesley, 'I don't think I'll come with you.'

'Right-ho dear,' said Lesley, all eager suddenly. It was well known that Madeleine never went in pubs.

Wearing a countryman's cap and a long woollen coat with a tweed scarf, Lesley walked Aldous, Colette and Julian through the crisp, autumnal streets of High Wycombe to a pub he knew.

'Have you been drinking already, dear?' he said to Colette as they walked side by side.

'Only four Gold Labels in the car on the way here.'

Lesley and Madeleine lived in Cedar Way, a road which did not contain, nor was on the way to any cedars. It was a genteel thoroughfare, and looked as though it had been designed by the same architects who engineered the spread of the north London suburbs in the 1930s, for it had the same appearance of rustic comfort as Leicester Avenue or The Limes, or any of the roads of New Southgate and Cockfosters. The houses were set back behind long front gardens and were pebbledashed and bay-windowed, some with token half-timbering in their front gables. Lesley and Madeleine's house was a paragon of its kind, a front lawn in stripes, a border of well-pruned roses, a rockery of rare alpines, and a pond where a solitary plaster gnome, brightly painted and varnished, sat fishing. Their front door had a sunrise in stained glass, radial spokes of light over a landscape of ploughed fields. There was more stained glass in the bathroom, and in a little side window up the stairs, of seagulls in flight. All the houses in Cedar Way had stained glass.

There were views of hills in all directions, topped by stately beechwoods which were yellowing with the season.

The pub Lesley had in mind was twenty minutes walk, and was in a district of the town Colette and Aldous didn't know. He called it his local, and from his descriptions Aldous and Colette were expecting some quaint mock country tavern, but The Bricklayers Arms, a tatty looking building of flaking paintwork and blacked-out windows, was quite different. It stood on a busy corner of the A40, passed continually by juggernauts and other traffic. The door to the saloon opened onto an intense noise and odour, a dimly lit interior crowded with people. The floor was scrappy lino, there was a threadbare pool table, a jukebox. A sort of cheer went up as Lesley entered, as though he was a visiting celebrity. The clientele of The Bricklayers Arms was almost exclusively black, they wore brown leather jackets or frilly shirts, gold chains, their hair topiarised into extravagant globular hairstyles Colette understood were called Afros.

'Fine fellows,' Lesley said to Colette, having to shout above the chanting rhythms of the loud music as they sat down on stools around a circular table in the corner of the pub. Aldous was reaching for his wallet to buy a round of drinks when a friendly Negro beamed into his face and asked him what he wanted.

'Most of the chaps in here were my pupils a few years ago. Astonishing, isn't it? When they were at school they spent most of their time trying to make my life hell. I sometimes thought I must be the most hated man in High Wycombe. Do you know, I even, at one time, found myself agreeing with that man Powell, and thinking they should all be sent back to wherever the hell they came from,' here Lesley afforded himself a long, chortling laugh, 'but now we're all out of school they treat me like some sort of hero, and instead of throwing paper darts at the back of my head, they buy me drinks. I've been coming here for over a year and I've never once had to buy my own drink. It has restored my faith in humanity. Oh yes indeed. Fine chaps these . . .'

There was almost a queue forming to supply Lesley with

drinks. The table quickly filled with brimming pints of dark, headless beer. Negroes shook Lesley's hand, patted him on the back, hugged him. Boys brought their girlfriends over, tall lean women resplendent with tacky jewellery and great spheres of hair about their heads, and introduced them.

'Gracie,' a boy grinned, 'this is the cunt who used to teach me Shakespeare. You remember me don't you? Back of the class, always getting detention.'

The boy couldn't have been out of school for more than a couple of years, and yet to him such a great leap had been taken. Aldous knew it as well. Old boys who seem truly astonished, once they leave school, to find that their teachers continue to exist. They react almost as if they've seen a dead man walking, utter amazement, astonishment. Finding a former teacher drinking in their pub must have doubled or trebled that astonishment, hence Lesley's local fame.

'Absolutely. You were a little sod,' Lesley laughed, and the boy laughed as well, donating another pint to the crop that had formed on the table.

Colette had never seen anyone sink a pint quite like Lesley. It just seemed to fall into his mouth. It made her think of a line from the nursery rhyme about the old lady who swallowed a fly – *she just opened her throat, and swallowed a goat.* Lesley seemed to drink exclusively with his throat, hardly using his mouth except as a mere portal. A pint was gone in a single visit to his lips.

'Real ale,' Lesley burped, 'this is the only pub in the whole of High Wycombe to serve real ale. That's why I come here. Gorgeous stuff. What do you think, Rex? Isn't it beautiful? Not like any of that Double Diamond or Watney's Red Barrel muck.'

'Yes,' said Aldous, who thought his pint of Old Roger vile, like treacle mixed with aspirins.

'Hand-pumped,' said Lesley, lifting a second pint to his mouth. That too was gone in a matter of seconds. Colette looked aghast as the glass was drained. 'No bubbles,' he went on, wiping his lips on his sleeve, reaching for his third.

'Lesley,' said Colette, imploringly.

After sinking his third pint in as many minutes, Lesley paused to catch his breath.

'I feel sorry for my little brother,' he said, 'what a way to end up.' And then he laughed. 'Does he really think Madeleine, Agatha and I are going to be popping round every day to see how he is?'

'You are a bastard, aren't you,' said Colette affectionately, 'You've always hated Janus Brian.'

'We've never been on the same wavelength, that's all. You must remember he's much younger than me. He was still a snivelling kid by the time I first became a teacher. I suppose we never had a chance to get to know each other.'

'You've always looked down on him, haven't you,' said Colette. 'Why is that? You've always thought him beneath you, and not just in terms of age.'

'That's not quite fair, my dear,' said Lesley, 'though I'm sure Janus Brian will say it was so. You and he were always the tear-aways of the family. You spent your childhoods making fun of Agatha and me, less so Meg.'

This was true, Colette thought. She and Janus Brian, against the studious, prudish elders of the family.

'I think,' Lesley continued, 'that that must be part of the master plan at work here. Janus Brian is coming back for revenge, isn't he,' Lesley spoke good humouredly, 'he is coming to High Wycombe to make our lives a misery. Well I can assure you that if he's expecting me to go round and rinse the wee-wees out of his bedclothes every other day, he can think again. Madeleine likewise. And I doubt Agatha will have much time for him.' Lesley embarked on his fourth pint, this time taking it more slowly, pausing between pulls. 'In fact, I am totally baffled as to why he's coming to High Wycombe at all. He knows we don't particularly care for him, he doesn't like coun-tryside, as you said, so what's he playing at?'

Colette couldn't supply an explanation.

'Here is my other theory,' Lesley went on, emptying another glass, 'My dear little sister Colette has put him up to it as a way of getting him off her hands and dumping him on ours, so that if he pegs out we'll be to blame rather than her. This makes up, as she sees it, for what she perceives as my inade-quacies regarding the care of our dear, late mother. Am I right?'

'I'm glad to see you still feel guilty about it,' said Colette, who had forgiven Lesley. When their mother had died, Colette had been on holiday in Wales and had left Lesley in charge of the funeral arrangements. To save money he'd had her buried in a common grave with strangers buried on top of her. Colette had had to take a job as a bus conductress to pay for her reburial in a private grave. The whole episode had precipitated Colette's own breakdown, which she looked back on as the darkest period of her life. But still she had forgiven him. 'I have had no influence on Janus Brian's decision,' she said, 'it is something he has decided all by himself. I would stop him if I could, but I can't. You know what he's like. Obstinate. Worse than you.'

The noise was such that these conversations were shouted across the small table with all the force Lesley and Colette could muster, sometimes shouting, like Humpty Dumpty to his messenger, right into each other's ears. Colette was starting to get a headache and Aldous felt uneasy with Julian in the pub, even though it was only early evening, and he seemed quite happy sipping cokes and shandies. He surveyed the interior of the bar. Incredible to think there are so many black people in a town like High Wycombe, he thought to himself, in the heart of the leafy Chilterns. There were probably more black people in this one pub than there were in the whole of Windhover Hill, though not among the new populations of neighbouring suburbs like Wood Green, and the reaches of Tottenham and Stamford Hill where Aldous and Colette had grown up and which had once been devoid almost totally of black faces. Now these areas thrived with an imported culture, fascinating and frightening. Suddenly there were black people in generational layers, the older ones bringing along with them a barely comprehensible Caribbean patois, the younger speaking with the local inflections of north London.

Colette always felt comfortable amongst any diaspora – the Jews of Stamford Hill, the West Indians she worked with on the buses. They were somehow apart from the petty class distinctions and accumulated snobberies of Anglo-Saxon culture, and she could relax and be at ease among them. In the decor of The Bricklayers Arms there were the remains of that Anglo-Saxon culture, an array of stuffed deer heads on one wall, small and saintly, hardly bigger than cats' faces, and on the windows, covered from the outside, frosted lettering spelling out the pub's name, reassuringly old. But these were merely traces of the pub's past as a hostelry for white working-class men. Now they were overlaid by new and, to Colette strange and incomprehensible imagery – posters of all-black pop groups, a national flag ('Jamaica', someone told her), in the corner a small performing stage was set up, with silver microphones on stands, scuffed, black amplifiers. An elderly Negro came and sat next to her, he had a thin, neatly trimmed moustache and a waxily dark face, as though made of stained raffia, then lacquered. A cigarette was tucked behind his ear. He spoke in a deep growl.

'You smoke?'

Colette offered him one of her Players.

The man laughed, the interior of his mouth white and pink, shining like a lamp. He brought the cigarette out from behind his ear.

'I mean you smoke these.'

'Oh no,' said Colette disapprovingly, 'I could never smoke roll ups. Unfiltered, too strong for me.'

The man laughed again, a high, whimpering, choking sort of laugh.

'Unfiltered,' he said to himself, looking at the cigarette and laughing, 'this is unfiltered weed, man.' He holds out the cigarette to her, a crumpled, overbulky thing twisted to a point at each end. Cottoning-on, Colette feels shocked, but before she can react, Lesley is talking to her again.

'Do you know, of these coloured chaps, I've persuaded a good half a dozen or more to become regulars at St John the Evangelist's? And a good many more are members of their own Protestant churches, very religious people. When I first came in here, I thought I might be put in a pot and eaten by one of the lost tribes of High Wycombe, but they turn out to be most civilized. Do you mind if I take my trousers off?' Suddenly he stood up, unfastened his trousers and let them fall to his ankles. Baggy white pants were beneath. Lesley whooped, gave a salute and a grotesque forward thrust of the hips, then pulled his trousers up again. There was a loudly approving cheer from the regulars and some applause. No one seemed surprised, Lesley sat down as if nothing had happened.

'Perhaps we should be getting back,' said Aldous, who had only half drunk his pint of Old Roger, and was trying to avoid the attentions of some drunken girls who were pawing at him.

'Absolutely,' said Lesley, who had by now consumed more than a gallon of strong ale, 'Sing up!' He then began singing in a loud, operatic voice, his best Sunday-morning-in-church voice, though louder, a hymn, *Guide Me O Thou Great Redeemer.*

> *'Open thou the crystal fountain*
> *Whence the healing streams do flow;*
> *Let the fiery cloudy pillar*
> *Lead me all my journey through . . .'*

Locals joined in, approaching with pints, as Lesley continued.

> *'Bread of Heaven,*
> *Bread of Heaven,*
> *Feed me till I want no more . . .'*

Lesley leant back in his chair so far that he fell backwards onto the floor, arms outstretched, still singing, his mouth gaping with song. The locals poured Old Roger down Lesley's open throat, laughing as they did so, '*Feed me till I want no more*'. They rejoined as Lesley ecstatically gargled and spumed on the cascading beer. The manner in which this event occurred suggested to Aldous and Colette that it was a regular occurrence on Lesley's visits to The Bricklayers. The reason for his popularity here was his willingness, their former English master, to debase himself so abjectly on the floor of their pub.

Thereafter Lesley was barely conscious, and had to be more or less carried home by Aldous and Colette, taking a shoulder each, which was difficult, as Lesley was taller than either of them, his feet trailed along the ground, and it was mostly up hill back to Cedar Way. Lesley continued to burble and sing quietly.

When Madeleine opened the door she looked horrified.

'What have you done to the poor man? I knew this would happen if he went out with you.'

Colette became angry with Madeleine for keeping up the

pretence that Lesley wasn't an alcoholic, that this sort of thing didn't happen every week at their house, Lesley rolling home utterly blotto in the small hours, just as Janus Brian had described. Madeleine insisted it had never happened before. A furious row ensued, Colette sitting on the settee, Madeleine in the armchair, Lesley in between on the carpet, lying on his back, singing hymns.

'Well I think you've got a jolly cheek, Colette,' said Madeleine, 'to sit on *my* couch in *my* house and tell me that my marriage is a sham, as you put it. But of course, you don't know, do you, the work I had to put into this relationship to make it work. You may idolize your older brother, but you don't see the side of him I see. He can be a hell of a lot of work, I can tell you that. If it wasn't for his work in the church I don't know what would have happened. As for sex, you seem to think you invented the thing. Where do you think our children came from, Green Shield Stamps? You have noticed we've got three haven't you? Alright, I admit he's got a drink problem, like all his bloody family, like his father and his brother, yes, and you, and your son. Well there isn't a single alcoholic on my side of the family so I'd say that pins the blame fairly fair and square on the Waughs. Every time we come into contact with your family there's trouble. Oh yes, you can smell it a mile off. As for Janus, well, I've never forgiven him for what he did to Christine, he nearly gave the poor girl a nervous breakdown. And I don't care what you say about art, yes, Rex does some lovely paintings, and Janus can play the piano very well, but that doesn't mean you can go around throwing your weight about and behaving disgracefully, (I don't mean you, Rex, of course), but if you think Lesley . . .'

Madeleine stopped in the middle of her tirade because she had been hit in the face by Colette, a broad slap across the right cheek, and she was about to launch a subsequent attack on the left cheek but Madeleine grabbed her hands, and there followed an undignified bout of wrestling.

'How dare you! How dare you!' Madeleine shrieked, incredulous, as Aldous moved in to separate the two women, but Colette was incensed, and the fighting went on for some time, over the recumbent body of Lesley, who by now was snoozing peacefully on the floor, Colette making perpetual lunges at Madeleine, who sheltered, when she could, behind Aldous, who eventually managed to wrestle his wife under some control, having to lock her arms behind her back.

'I do apologize,' said Aldous, as Colette snarled quietly in his arms, 'I think she may have had more to drink than I thought.'

Although Aldous shared many of Colette's opinions about Madeleine, he was far too polite ever to express them, and indeed, Madeleine seemed to think of him as some sort of ally, the put-upon husband suffering at the hands of the drug-addicted, alcoholic wife. Madeleine made Aldous feel tragic, a feeling he found disagreeable.

'Yes, well,' said Madeleine, trying as best she could to compose herself, 'at least we've got everything nicely out in the open. At least we all know where we stand. Goodbye, Colette, I don't suppose we'll be seeing much of each other again.'

'Not if I can help it,' Colette growled.

'I just feel sorry for your poor husband,' she was talking to Colette, still under Aldous's restraint, as though she was some partially deaf elder relative, 'And little Julian. What must he be making of all of this? Coming round to visit his uncle and aunt and then all this happening.'

Colette made a sudden attempt to free herself from Aldous's grip, but Aldous pulled her away.

'I'll take her out to the car,' he said, quietly.

He pulled his wife through the hall.

'Oh, so you're going to throw me out now, are you, my own husband acting as that cow's bouncer, is that the idea?'

'Don't be stupid.'

Aldous managed to take Colette out to the car, Madeleine following cautiously behind. She saw Julian in the front room, reading a book as he sat on the orange swirl of the carpet. She went over to him

'You'll still come and visit us, won't you Julian,' she said to him in a confidential tone, 'Without . . . you know,' she paused and nodded her head towards the hall, 'when things have blown over, you'll still come to see us in the years ahead, won't you?'

He nodded. Madeleine's words, and her manner, ate at him like some burrowing tick, getting into his skin, into his blood.

Afterwards, in the car back to London, Colette falling asleep loudly in the back, he felt dirty. He felt a need to bathe, but he knew he was returning to a house with no bath.

9

A buyer for Janus Brian's house had been found – a young accountant with a purple mouth and a squirrel-like wife.

It amused Janus Brian that this accountant worked for a firm in the same part of the city as he himself had done for nearly thirty years. He would commute by taking the same stroll every morning up the close and through the alleys and along the High Street to the tube, even changing at the same stop (King's Cross) for the same destination (Liverpool Street).

'Funny how things come around,' he said to Colette after telling her the news, 'but it brings it all back to me, how Mary and I bought this place all those years ago. How clever we thought we were, how brave, just like this young chap and his wife . . .'

Colette knew what he meant about bravery. She'd felt the same when they'd bought their first house just after the war, when renting was still the norm. In those days estate agents were a highly specialized and rather secretive breed, mostly elderly gentlemen inhabiting oak-panelled offices, writing things with fountain pens in enormous parchment ledgers. Buying a house was a slightly mysterious process rooted in the arcanities of ancestral endowments and the ancient traditions of property and land ownership. Today estate agents were young blokes on the make, spivs and wide boys who displayed their properties in shop windows like stacks of washing powder, and as such had helped swell the value of properties like Janus Brian's modest semi by, in his case, around sixteen hundred per cent.

There was one difference between Janus Brian and his young buyers however – they had children, a toddler with chubby legs and a little girl with white hair tied up with pink ribbons.

Colette still could not quite believe that her brother had

managed it. That he'd maintained his resolve, on coming out of the asylum, to sell his house and move to High Wycombe. Secretly she blamed Reg Moore. Without Reg he couldn't possibly have survived. He would have given up after his first gazumping. If Reg hadn't driven him out to the Chilterns for countless weekends searching through all the mazy estates for suitable properties, he would never have lasted. It had taken a long time. All through the autumn, the winter and into the following spring before a swish bungalow was found near Amersham Hill.

Colette had to concede that the whole business of moving was doing her brother some good. It had focused his mind and given him a sense of purpose. He was drinking less, thinking more clearly. He looked less yellow.

Memory, for Janus Brian, was like an illness. That was the only explanation Colette could find for his improved health. With all its associated memories the house, and the neighbourhood, were making him ill. Colette at first found this hard to accept, since she regarded memory in quite the opposite way, as something nourishing. But with Janus Brian it was corrosive, malignant. That must be why, she thought, he so often regarded the past as a dream. By regarding the past as a dream he was inoculated against its virulent effects. But it worried her. What if, once he'd moved to High Wycombe, he came to regard his whole life in London, right up to his departure, as a dream as well? What would that do to her? Would she just become a kind of thing in his dream?

Colette had refused to have anything to do with Janus Brian's move. She'd not once offered to help him, even when he'd read the solicitor's letters out to her, explaining the various glitches and snags that emerged. But then again, Janus Brian never directly asked her for any help. Although he would sometimes drop strong hints – *you know, I really need to get out to High Wycombe next this weekend, but Reg is away . . . Is he? How frustrating for you.*

Not until the moving day itself did she finally relent. Not even with the help of Reg and his two sons, who were visiting, could Janus Brian manage. Also, there was surplus furniture to be had.

In condensing his life from a three bedroom semi to a two bedroom bungalow, Janus Brian found he had much that couldn't fit into his new house – beds, chairs, settees, tables, wardrobes. Aldous took a selection back to Fernlight Avenue in a hired van in the morning, while Reg and his sons helped Janus Brian with the rest of his things. By the time Aldous was back at midday Janus Brian's house was almost empty, and the new family's removal van had arrived. A fleet of cars – Reg driving Janus in Janus's Renault 7, Reg's two sons following in their cars, to bring their father back to London – was waiting to set off when Aldous and Colette had one last look around the empty rooms of Leicester Avenue. Colette felt tears come into her eyes, even though she'd hardly known this house in the time her brother had lived there, but the emptiness of a house is always sad, she felt. In just a matter of a few days it would be unrecognizable as Janus Brian's old house, once that new family had moved in, with their plans for playrooms, their new furnishing and carpets. This house embodied the thirty-odd years of her brother's marriage, contained its essence somehow, and yet it was to be completely erased. Surely it should be allowed to remain for ever as a sort of memorial to her brother's life, there should be something permanent left behind, but no. Now she could see houses for what they really were, mere shells, to be discarded and re-used, and this made her cry.

Then Aldous noticed the lampshades. In every room the lampshades had been left *in situ*.

'What about the lampshades?' he asked Janus Brian, who was about to get into the car.

'I was going to leave them. There are lampshades in High Wycombe.'

While Janus Brian shakily oversaw the loading of the last few boxes onto the removal van, Aldous took down the lampshades.

'Stupid to leave them,' he said to Colette. There were few lampshades at Fernlight Avenue, and those were getting rather dilapidated. In some rooms the bulbs hung naked and dazzling, but here were excess shades, little cylinders of printed fabrics, bubble glass, budget chandeliers, tulip shades, Aldous took them all and put them in the boot of his Superminx.

At High Wycombe there followed an operation that was the

reverse of the morning's work, extracting the condensed life of Janus Brian from a removal van and allowing it to expand to fill the spaces of his new home.

It was the first time Aldous and Colette had seen Janus Brian's new home, and they were horrified. Sycamore Drive was a steeply climbing road branching off from the even steeper main road, curving slightly between rows of newish bungalows and then flattening out a little at the top, where it ended in a turning circle. Sycamore Drive was another cul-de-sac. In all it seemed little more than a slightly newer version of Leicester Avenue, with smaller buildings and without the benefits of being close to the capital. Janus Brian had moved from one dead-end to another.

Colette managed to conceal her disappointment from her brother, but she could not help feeling distraught at the idea that Janus Brian, in moving into a bungalow, one of four radiating from the turning circle at the top of the cul-de-sac, had merely replicated his life in New Southgate. She wanted to ask him, *why, why, why have you done it? Dead-ends are dead-ends, they are the root cause of all your problems, blind alleys, no through roads, that is what your childless life has always been. You need to break free, to live in a thoroughfare, somewhere with passing traffic, somewhere that leads somewhere else, don't you see? But no, you've dug a tunnel from your prison cell only to come up in another one.* But instead she helped Janus Brian settle into his bungalow, suggesting where the chairs went, where the telly should go. She made him tea, she made him dinner, while Aldous and Reg formed an uncomfortable, settee-shifting partnership, and her son sat on the floor reading John Wyndham's *The Chrysalids*. Eventually Reg left in one of his son's cars, and it was just her and Aldous and Julian against Janus Brian's loneliness. When the time came for them, too, to leave, she could see instantly the despair rise behind his horn-rimmed spectacles. *My God, What have I done?* He seemed to say. *Too late now. Your house has been sold. This is where you live now.* But with the frantic energy and drama of moving finished, there was nothing left now but the old, familiar prospect of endless solitude before him.

'Agatha said she'll be over tomorrow,' Colette said, as she prepared to leave. Julian was already in the car.

'Lovely,' Janus Brian grimaced.

'And I'm sure Lesley will be over soon, and Madeleine.'

'Hmmm.'

'And we'll come over next weekend, I promise.'

'I'll defrost some faggots for you.'

'He's being so brave,' Colette said, on the way home, a journey mostly in twilight, dark by the time they got home.

They were about to settle down to bed but Aldous was in the grip of an idea. He had all the lampshades out of the boot, the ones from Janus's house, and he was fixing them up, taking down the dusty, decrepit old shade from the front room, rigging up one of Janus Brian's crystalware fans in its place. A floral print in the music room, lit from within, searingly bright daisies. A globe of prisms on the landing, where there hadn't been a shade for many years.

'Look,' Aldous kept saying, flicking the light switches on and off, adjusting the shades so that great circles of light moved shakily from one spot to another. As Aldous consolidated and adjusted his inheritance of light, he had the childish triumph of a boy raiding an orchard.

'It does look better,' said Colette, somewhat reluctantly, 'they do make the house look much better.'

10

Visiting Janus Brian was now a major undertaking. The journey to High Wycombe was a long and complicated one involving a perilous quarter arc of the North Circular with all its feeder lanes and flyovers, and then a miserable crawl along Western Avenue, past the Hoover Factory at Perivale, the Aladdin Lamp Factory at Northolt, the golf ball factory at Uxbridge, with its giant golf ball perched on a giant tee, then the heavy traffic through the sprawling dormitory towns of Gerrard's Cross and Beaconsfield. After the first week they couldn't manage a visit any more than once a month, and were soon down to less than even that.

That first visit was encouraging, however. Janus Brian seemed to be coping rather well with his new life. With the money he was rolling in since the sale of his old house, he'd bought an organ, a mighty Wurlitzer of an instrument he'd seen when passing an antique dealers in town. It had come from one of High Wycombe's last great cinemas, now a bingo hall, and filled a corner of his spacious living room.

'I'm sometimes up all night playing the thing,' he said, 'it's got an extraordinary range, you can play Bach toccatas on massed kazoos, or have "Colonel Bogey" sung by heavenly choirs, it's fantastic.' The first few visits centred around the organ, Colette and Janus sitting side by side playing duet versions of 'I Do Love To Be Beside The Seaside', 'It's A Long Way To Tipperary', and 'Pack Up Your Troubles'. Colette would try all the different stops, hearing her versions of 'Moonlight Becomes You' in weepy strings, 'Tico Tico' on tom-toms and castanets, but the novelty of this massive, twinkling instrument did not last for very long, and as the summer passed into another autumn, Janus Brian became more and more despondent, until one weekend

174

when Colette called, he answered the door in his old state –
far gone, shaky, yellow.

From one cul-de-sac to another. He said he liked the peace and
quiet of dead-end roads, but it was the peace and quiet that was
now driving him mad. 'Peace and quiet is wonderful when you're
living with someone, but when you're alone you need noise,
movement, activity.' The neighbours were unfriendly, worse than
Leicester Avenue. His next door neighbours collared Colette as
she went to the car, a look of slight despair in their eyes.

'He plays music at full volume all night sometimes.'

She knew this was true. Janus Brian had said as much. He
was playing Schubert symphonies on a new hi-fi at all hours.
Janus Brian had a special affection for Schubert, and used to
tell Colette that if he were ever to haunt her after his death,
he would come as a melody from a Schubert symphony.

'It's not that we don't appreciate the music,' the neighbours
went on to point out, 'but there is a time and a place.'

'He won't listen to our complaints,' said the man, 'I did ask
him very politely one morning if he'd mind showing some
consideration, and his reply was a four letter word . . .'

'It was eight letters, actually,' corrected his wife.

The man took a moment to count in his head.

'That's right,' he said, 'his reply was an eight letter word.
What's more, he answered the door stark – you know, completely
naked. My wife standing beside me . . .'

'This is a very quiet neighbourhood,' said the woman, 'a very,
very quiet neighbourhood. You ask anyone around here what
it is they like about the neighbourhood and they'll all say it's
the quietness.'

'My brother is a frail man whose wife has just died,' Colette
said, 'perhaps you could help him instead of criticize him.'

The neighbours didn't ask her about Janus Brian again.
Whenever she visited, however, she was conscious of their
observing eyes.

Lesley had visited once, so Janus Brian told her. He came
on his own about a month after Janus Brian had moved in.

'Bloody stuck-up fool, expected me to make him a cup of
tea. I was lying in bed and he was tapping at the window, so

I had to pull myself up and answer the door, then he just strolled in, took a look at me, then at his watch, said something like "what time of day do you call this?" Said something about the fact I wasn't dressed, then just sat in the kitchen waiting for me to make some tea for him, holding a hanky over his nose because of the smell, he said. Then he left, telling me about some church he goes to or other, said I should come along. Bloody fool.'

Agatha had been over as well.

'Telling me about her lodger, telling me how rich he was. She said he drove a Ferrati! I just fell down laughing, I said what's that? A cross between a Bugati and a Ferrari? She got cross, of course. She is such a daft woman. Do you know what she said the other week? I was looking for my *Guinness Book of Records*, I wanted to look something up, I can't remember now, and I asked Agatha, I said Agatha, have you seen my *Guinness Book of Records*? And she looked blank for a moment and then said, "Is that classical or Jazz?" *Classical or Jazz!* Can you believe it?'

Soon he was pretending to be out if Agatha knocked, only that didn't work. If he didn't answer the door she'd think he was dead and have the police round kicking the front door in in no time. He had no alternative but to tell her to her face.

'I said, I'm sorry, Agatha, I know you're doing your best and you're only trying to help, but I must insist that you piss off and never darken my door again. It was the way she nagged. On and on and on. She'd go round the house hunting for gin bottles, and if she found any she'd pour them down the sink. She told me off about everything – the house, my clothes, my smell, everything. Do you know she used to walk over from Ickfield Park, all the way up that hill? Terrifying. Still, seems to have done the trick. I haven't heard from her since. Thank Christ.'

Such stories delighted Colette, the failures of her rival siblings, humourless Agatha, hypocritical Lesley. How could they ever hope to understand Janus Brian? But at the same time she felt the distress of sole responsibility for Janus Brian's state. Later he said he knew from the day he moved in he'd made a terrible mistake.

'I wanted to be haunted,' Janus Brian said, 'I wanted Mary's ghost to visit me, but she never came, not to this sterile little bungalow, her ghost would never come here. In Leicester Avenue her shadows gave me the creeps, but now I miss them. And I want there to be an upstairs. I miss the upstairs. My life has been robbed of a dimension. There is no verticality to it, everything is flat and on a level.'

He bought a clock. Of all things, a clock. But he said he didn't have a decent one, and he went out to buy one. It occupied pride of place on the living room mantelpiece, a naked nymph, about six inches high, rendered in a ghastly, imitation gold, holding aloft, as though it were a torch of liberty, a clock-face which pitched back and forth, its own pendulum. The horror of this timepiece rendered Colette almost speechless when she saw it. The gaudiness of the figurine, her golden bosoms so pathetically exposed, the sheer awkwardness of the design, with its clockface bobbing back and forth, almost impossible to read, a piece of pornographic kitsch unworthy of her brother's tastes. Did he really derive some thrill, however abstruse and rarefied, from the contemplation of this revolting statue, this faceless, bare-breasted nymphet of wasted time? Did he imagine her, even in his most drunken hours, coming to life and frolicking, all gold, about the carpet? Did he think that she might put down her weighty clock and creep into his bed, vivid and smooth, to press her tiny nippleless paps into his face? Whatever it was, Janus Brian seemed inordinately proud of his new clock.

As the winter progressed, visiting became more difficult. Colette herself became ill shortly before Christmas, bringing up, to her and Julian's terror, a bellyful of blood into the kitchen sink. Julian was so terrified he ran out of the room, returning a few moments later, pretending he hadn't seen it. The cause turned out to be a duodenal ulcer, and Colette was in hospital for several weeks, an experience which she enjoyed. Colette loved hospitals, she liked being among the ill, the deprived, the lost. In a National Health hospital everyone is levelled, as in a prison, to a common social strata, a sort of aggregate of all ages and classes, which meant that Colette could befriend Judy, a fifteen-year-old West Indian schoolgirl who talked nothing but pop music and boys, or Ruth, an academic with gallstones.

'They don't know what causes ulcers,' Colette told Aldous, 'No one has said anything about the drink causing them, although I know that's what you all think.'

'But they've told you to stop drinking?'

'They've said not to drink while I've got the ulcer, because it aggravates it and causes acidity. But once the ulcer's gone, there's no reason why you can't drink.'

Aldous looked disappointed. He was hoping for a stronger warning from the doctors, *take another drink and you'll die*, or something like that, but the doctors seemed positively encouraging of Colette's drinking, especially with Christmas approaching. *Don't worry*, they seemed to be saying, *we'll soon have you drinking again for Christmas, don't worry about that.*

It was a bleak time. Janus, since his arrest the year before, had been subdued. The threat of imprisonment had had a sobering effect on him, and if he drank now, he mostly managed to moderate it to a few cans imbibed in the solitude of his bedroom, but his overall mood was sullen and hostile. He no longer spent time with Bill Brothers, and rarely went out drinking. In effect there was no longer anywhere he could drink legitimately in Windhover Hill or surrounding areas. Aldous couldn't help thinking that Janus was waiting, with immense patience, for his two year suspended sentence to expire, so that he could resume his life of wild inebriation. Occasionally he would lose patience and go out on the town, returning noisily at an ungodly hour, having miraculously escaped the attentions of the police, though the threat of an encounter with them was a new and effective means of controlling Janus, for he knew Aldous only had to make one call to them and he would be in prison for six months, even from the most deranged depths of his drunkenness he could perceive the brutal simplicity of this.

Aldous and Julian visited Colette in hospital every other day. It was a winter of dense fogs. One night the roads were immovably clogged with stranded traffic, they had to leave the car somewhere near the North Circular and walk the rest of the way to the hospital.

Colette came out just before Christmas. Throughout January there was hard snow on the ground, and they didn't get to

High Wycombe until early February, having not visited for over two months. It was a novelty for them to see the Chilterns under snow. As they feared, Janus Brian had sunk into an even deeper despair than the one he'd experienced in New Southgate. In the two months of Colette's absence he'd barely seen another human being. He was drinking perhaps two or three bottles of gin a day and hardly eating anything. He had grown a ridiculous, white, fluffy beard that looked as though it had been made by a child out of cotton wool. His hair had bushed out into a spiky grey crown surrounding his bald pate, but most concerning of all was his thinness, his leanness. Janus Brian had always been a thin man, but this was not so much thinness as hollowness. It was as though someone had removed a layer of something from under his skin, which now hung loose around the vacuity. He had deflated, sunken, crumpled. His body had hardly any muscle and he walked with a shaky, almost crippled stance. Amazingly he still drove his car, and would pop to the shops once a week for frozen food and a week's supply of gin and fags, which nearly filled his whole boot.

'I don't understand Janus Brian,' Aldous said to Colette one day as they were driving back from another visit. 'If I was in the same situation I'd develop some sort of scheme to get me through it. He likes drinking, so why doesn't he go to a pub to drink?'

'I don't know. He doesn't like pubs.'

'But he could walk to the nearest pub. There's one at the bottom of his road. He could make that his aim each day. Then he could aim for the next nearest pub and make that his goal, and so on and so on. Eventually he would be walking out into the countryside to go to the pub. He should do something like that. He would meet people and get fit. That's what I would do if I was him. But he just sits there swigging gin until he blacks out.'

Blacked out was how they often found him. Eventually, towards the spring, Colette, after having picked her brother out of yet another swamp of his own filth, bathed him, shaved him, cut his toenails and dressed him, said 'Janus, you've got no choice, sell up and move back to London. You don't have to buy a house like the one in Leicester Avenue, you could buy a nice little flat near us. There's even one over the road that's going for sale.'

'No, dear . . .'

'But I just can't cope with the journey out here any more. It's just too much to ask of Aldous and Julian . . .'

'The kid doesn't have to come . . .'

'But I can't leave him at home with Janus for the weekend, it's not fair . . .'

Janus sighed.

'Shall we play the organ?'

'No.'

'*Kojak*'ll be on soon. I know it was a mistake to move out here,' he said, consoling his sister's weeping, 'but it's too late. I've done it. And I can't move back, it would be too retrograde. One has to go forwards, one mustn't go backwards in life . . .'

'You call this forwards?' snapped Colette. 'You're in a worse state now than you were in Leicester Avenue, it hasn't done you any good at all . . .'

'Let's give it some more time. I haven't even been here for a year yet. And you don't have to come out here every other week, I'm coping, honestly. I may not look as though I am but I am.'

'No you're not, you're drinking yourself to death.'

Janus Brian gave an apologetic laugh, then said nothing. After a while Colette, lowering her voice so that Julian in the other room couldn't hear, said, 'Janus, I want you to come on holiday with us this year, in the summer. We're going camping in Tewkesbury. We went there a couple of years ago, there's this lovely little campsite in the middle of the town, we could put you in a nice B & B for a couple of weeks, it's a lovely town.'

'Tewkesbury?'

'Yes, have you been there?'

'Near Gloucester, out that way isn't it?'

'Yes.'

'No, I don't think I have. I may have passed through. No, I'd be in the way, dear, very nice of you to offer.'

'You wouldn't be in the way. Julian wouldn't mind.'

'Wouldn't he?'

'No.'

'Well, I haven't had a holiday for a long time,' said Janus Brian thoughtfully, 'a very long time indeed.'

Part Three

I I

30th July 1976 – 7.15pm

– *He's shot him.*
– *There's the light.*
– *Where did he get that coffee from?*
– *Polystyrene.*
– *What's going on? I haven't got a clue.*
– *There are some faggots in the freezer.*
– *A faggot (laughs).*
– *Valse Oubliez. Follow the fingering.*
– *Every stiff that comes in the joint owes you.*
– *Aldous, do you remember that?*
– *Count Basie.*
– *Do you know what's going on?*
– *There are some faggots in the freezer.*
– *Do you know Kojak calls homosexuals faggots?*
– *You figured a cockamamie heist.*
– *The only heist round here's a parking meter.*
– *Those cars.*
– *He's got two sedans inside.*
– *A first class wheel-man.*
– *If you said there were some faggots in the freezer to an
   American he would think you were very queer. (Laughs)*
– *The lights keep going.*
– *Do you know you use a gallon of water every time you
   flush the loo?*
– *I can't drink coffee any more, it makes me fart.*
– *Tell me what he's doing, Colette, can you follow these
   things. What? No. (Coughs)*

– Yes. In the cupboard.

– Do the faggots need defrosting?

– Look at the stars.

*– He's one cute cookie, I've had a tail on him for two days
and I can't pick him up for jaywalking.*

*– A gallon of water to flush away what can't be more than
a cupful of urine.*

– I wish I knew what was happening.

– Someone's going to get shot.

– He's just done ninety days on Riker's Island.

– I think there's a bulb in the bathroom.

– Gambling, prostitution, razzle dazzle.

– What's going on?

Colette, Juliette and Julian were sitting in the garden at Fernlight
Avenue. It was noon on a Saturday at the beginning of August.

The heat was so intense that Colette had taken off her blouse
and was wearing nothing but a pair of navy blue slacks and a
black bra, lounging in the laminated wicker hoop chair that
had once furnished the music room with its graceful
modernism. She was made-up because she had been getting
ready to take Julian to the pictures. Her lipstick was vivid and
complete, her eye shadow subtly applied, so that its peacock
blue was not quite as shocking as it might have been. In addition to her make-up she was wearing a coronet of sunflowers
which she had constructed, picking the small heads from the
array that grew within reach of her chair.

'I'm still not sure why you've done it, Julian,' she called to
her son who was wandering aimlessly around the garden,
wearing the sulky expression he'd adopted since learning that
Janus Brian was coming on holiday to Tewkesbury with them
tomorrow, 'you've written it down, word for word, everything
that Janus Brian said last weekend.'

'Read some more,' said Juliette, who was sitting in the grass
beside her mother, 'I almost get the feeling I'm in High Wycombe.'

Colette had found the papers on the kitchen table. A whole
sheaf of intricately scrawled A4. She had assumed them to be
some schoolwork of Julian's. Then she supposed he was writing
a play. Then, on closely reading the pages, she recognized the

monologue as Janus Brian's, and she relived the previous weekend's visit to the bungalow. They had watched *Kojak*, Aldous had (very badly) attempted some of the pieces he'd found in the piano stool, Colette had made a supper of faggots and instant mashed potato, which Janus Brian hadn't eaten. Then she read through more. There were pages and pages of the stuff. Preserved monologues dated and going back to their first visits in the spring of 1974, more than two years ago. If she learnt anything, it was that Janus Brian's small talk hadn't changed in that time – snatches of reiterated TV, babble about music and food.

Julian hadn't seemed bothered when she found the papers and had brought them out into the garden, where he was talking with Juliette, who'd come round for a visit. In fact, he seemed amused, and wanted his mother to read them aloud.

'Are you going to make it all into a play, or something?' she asked him.

Julian shrugged, picked up a yellow plum that had fallen from the Warwickshire Drooper.

'It's what writers do,' said Juliette. 'Copy down what people are saying, then try to pass it off as their own invention.'

Juliette had been a full time student at Ponders End Polytechnic for a year, studying English and Sociology, and was eager to demonstrate an academic disdain for amateur writers.

That Julian was a writer was still a joke in the family, although he had been writing novels since primary school. The first had already been rejected by a London publisher. It worried Colette a little when Julian, at the age of ten, packed up his novel in a heavy brown envelope with shining layers of Sellotape and posted it off to Pan Books whom she knew would not publish it. She wondered how the inevitable rejection would affect him? If he really was going to be a writer shouldn't he leave it until later in life, when he was more confident of his abilities? Rejection at such an early age might put him off writing for life and, indeed, when the novel came back with a polite card from Pan Books saying they didn't print original novels being 'mainly a reprint house', she thought that might be an end to Julian's career, since he didn't seem keen to send it anywhere else. But instead he began another one.

She remembered reading his early attempts at fiction. He'd filled several school exercise books with pencilled stories which he would ask her to read to him, without pause, and then demand critical appraisal.

'Is it a good story mum?'

'Yes.'

'Is it very good?'

'Yes, it's really very good.'

'But is it really, really very good?'

'Yes, it's really, really very good.'

'Are you just saying that?'

'No.'

'Do you mean it?'

'Yes.'

'Is it good enough to be published?'

Here Colette would have to pause, caught in the dilemma between discouraging promise and raising unrealistic hopes.

'Well, it just needs a little bit of . . .'

'A little bit of what?'

'It just needs polishing.'

'What do you mean?'

'Well, just little things, like spelling and punctuation . . .'

'But apart from the spelling and the punctuation, do you think it could be published?'

'Yes, probably, if you polished it up in other ways . . .'

'What other ways?'

'Sometimes you use two short sentences when you could run them together into one longer sentence. Things like that.'

So hard to convey to an eleven-year-old what their prose lacked in comparison to P.G. Wodehouse or John Buchan, his rather obvious role models. Now that he was a young teenager, Julian had become secretive about his novels. He didn't show them to anyone.

The grass in the back garden was yellow. Where the bare earth showed through the lawn, as it did in several places, it was patterned with deep cracks each wide enough to take a thumb.

Above them the seven trunks of a neighbouring poplar towered. Its leaves looked shrivelled. Scipio lay curled in a patch of shade beneath the lilac, panting.

With a languid regularity, every few seconds a few drops of water would pour over the top of the fence, the overspill from next door's lawn sprinkler, and land with a patter on the sunflowers.

There was talk of banning lawn sprinklers. There had already been a ban on fountains. The government was worried about the water levels in the reservoirs. There had been no rain for nearly two months. People were advised to have showers instead of baths, or to bathe in no more than four inches of water. Someone had suggested people put bricks in their cisterns to cut down on water usage. The government had appointed a minister for drought.

'I do think you should consider going on a diet, mother,' said Juliette, who shared with Julian a mild sense of horror at the sight of their mother's torso. Her body seemed to consist of layers, each overhanging the other – neck, bust, stomach – giving the overall impression of a person disappearing beneath their own bulk.

'Aldous likes me like this,' said Colette, and was about to start talking about Rubens, when Juliette suddenly snapped.

'Well dad always likes you, whatever happens – it doesn't mean it's good for you . . .'

'Well he doesn't try and nag me into dieting. Is that all you came round for, to give me a lecture?'

They had been talking like this for some time – for the most part amiably, but every now and then flaring into moments of petulant discord, usually sparked by some criticism of Colette her daughter was unable to resist – of her drinking (she had a mug of Gold Label in the grass beside her chair), of her weight, of her shameless back-garden exhibitionism, even of her neglect of the garden itself, criticism which Colette was always eager to be hurt by.

Julian was bored. He'd promised his mother he would go to the pictures with her that day for an afternoon showing of *One Flew Over The Cuckoo's Nest* at the Wood Green Odeon. They'd both been eager to see the film but hadn't been able to, Julian because it was an X-certificate, and Colette because she had no one to go with (Aldous didn't want to see it, since he found madness, even cinematic depictions of it, repulsive). Julian was feeling embarrassed at the idea of going to the cinema with his mother, and wasn't convinced (as his mother seemed to be) that he could get in to see the film, but accepted that going with his mother was probably his best chance.

His strongest desire, at that moment, was to be alone in the garden and so have the opportunity of peeping through a knot hole in the new fence and watching his next door neighbour sunbathing topless, as she often did on days like this. As it was, on tiptoe, he could just see over the top of the fence to the fence beyond, and then the next fence, fence after fence all the way down the road with hollyhocks and fruit trees sprouting between, and twinkling cascades of lawn sprinklers nodding back and forth.

'No,' said Juliette, 'I came here to tell you something else.'

A burst of piano music came from the music room, whose French windows were open, though the room itself was barely visible through the screen of fruit trees. The music was furiously rhythmic, a melodious piece of industrial machinery.

'It's Prokofiev,' said Colette, noticing how Juliette was distracted by the music, 'Janus has been practising it for days. He says it's one of the hardest pieces he's tried.'

'Has he been boozing today?'

'No,' said Colette, as though shocked at the suggestion, 'He couldn't play like that if he'd been drinking . . .'

They debated for a moment if Janus's playing sounded drunken. Juliette insisted that it did, being loud and cacophonously atonal. Colette said that Juliette didn't understand the music, and that if she knew more about Prokofiev she would know how sober the playing was.

'Besides,' said Colette, 'you know how he hasn't been drinking since he got that suspended sentence.'

'I'm afraid that's not true, mother.'

'Apart from the odd lapse now and then . . .'

'It's been more than the odd lapse. He's been seeing Bill again. After Bill finishes work on Fridays they meet up, then on Saturdays, sometimes Sundays. The whole weekend. Bill tries to put him off, he tries to turn him out of the flat, but once he's had a couple of drinks his mood changes and he starts being all sentimental and saying how Janus is the best friend he's ever had, how we're all being cruel to him, that we don't understand him . . .'

Juliette hung her head for a moment, trying to control her thoughts. Julian pitched in from beneath the plum tree, 'Why don't you call the police out?'

'No,' said Colette, 'she couldn't do that. One call to the police and he'll be in prison.'

'I've resorted to a simpler solution,' said Juliette. 'I'm leaving Bill.'

'Leaving Bill?' said Colette, quietly, resettling the sunflower diadem that had slipped down, 'are you really? When?'

'Tomorrow. That's what I came here to tell you. I'm moving in with someone else.'

'Who? Some professor or other I suppose.'

'His name's Boris.'

'Boris?' Colette said the name as though she couldn't believe it was a real name, not a name that people actually had. She reacted as though her daughter had said she was moving in with someone called Rumpelstiltskin, or Pinnochio. 'I don't believe you know anyone called Boris.'

'Well I do.'

'And what's he a professor of? Vampires?'

'He's not a professor of anything. He works for the GPO.'

'So what's he studying?'

'I didn't meet him at college mother, he's nothing to do with the college. He's a regular at The Quiet Woman. We've known each other for a long time. He's an old friend . . .'

'I can't believe,' her mother said, allowing certain latent snobberies to surface, 'that after a year at a polytechnic . . . I mean, I could foresee that you and Bill would grow apart once you became a full-time student, that doesn't really come as a surprise to me – but with all the fascinating people you must be meeting, you're shacking up with some postman who boozes in The Quiet Woman . . .'

'He's not a postman, he's a telephone engineer. He's skilled. Anyway, I didn't come here to ask for your opinion on him, I just came here to tell you my new address, as from tomorrow.'

'We're going on holiday tomorrow . . .'

'I know, that's why I came over today.'

'And what does Bill think of all this?'

Juliette paused, then looked around her, as if to make sure no one else was listening. The continuing noise from the music room meant Janus was out of earshot.

'I haven't told him yet. I'm telling him tonight . . .'

'How will he take it, do you think?'

'I don't know. I just hope he doesn't get all pathetic and start begging – I'd almost prefer it if he got angry. It's such a mess. I won't have time to sort my things out. Then we're supposed to be going to a party tomorrow night – Veronica's birthday party. I'll have to miss that I think.'

She then took a piece of paper and handed it to Colette. On the paper was written her new address.

'You mustn't let Janus see this,' she said.

Colette meant it when she said her daughter's announcement hadn't surprised her. Juliette and Bill seemed to lead entirely different lives these days. They didn't come round together on Sunday afternoons any more, they were rarely together. Colette could hardly remember the last time she'd seen Bill. So the news didn't upset her. She was fond of Bill, but had always felt the marriage to be a mistake. Juliette was far too young. Now, through college, she was getting back onto the road she had so wantonly abandoned when she was sixteen. But to move in with a telephone engineer from The Quiet Woman. That was disappointing.

Their conference in the garden ended when Colette realised what time it was. She and Julian were going to be late for the cinema. Aldous had taken the car into a garage for servicing in preparation for tomorrow's journey and they were reliant on public transport.

'I'll catch the bus with you,' said Juliette, who was going back to Polperro Gardens.

Colette went into the house and got dressed. She put on an extravagantly floral shirt that made her look like a walking rhododendron bush, and bluebottle-coloured earrings. Julian found it a little grotesque that she should doll herself up to go out with him. As though she was his girlfriend.

With the tumultuous sounds of the final movement of Prokofiev's Seventh Piano Sonata filling the house, Juliette, Julian and Colette were making their way through the hall to the front door when the music stopped and Janus appeared from the music room. He had the stiffly unstable gait of the slightly drunk. His hair and beard looked rumpled. Janus had become so lushly hirsute in recent years he reminded Julian of the Beatle George Harrison as he appeared on the cover of *Abbey Road*. Though on this occasion Janus wasn't wearing any trousers.

'Where are you going?' he said.

'Out,' said Colette.

'Where?'

'Just to the shops.'

'Great!' Janus suddenly whooped and then winked, 'I've got to go to the shops as well. I need new shoes.' Janus was holding a coffee mug that contained a transparent liquid, either vodka or gin. 'I'll come with you.'

The trio's hearts sank.

'Just let me get some trousers and feed the Scipplecat.'

'We've got to go now.'

'I'll catch you up.' Janus tottered vaguely into the kitchen, clicking his tongue for Scipio.

Colette and her two children left the house quickly and walked down the road.

'He doesn't know which shops we're supposedly going to, he'll probably go to the Parade and lose us,' said Colette. It was a long walk down gently sloping Fernlight Avenue, and Julian continually looked back to see if his older brother was in pursuit and was pleased to see an empty street. Finally they turned the corner at the bottom of the road, and crossed over the busy Green Lanes to the bus stop.

'He won't think of coming down here,' said Colette, 'and with luck a bus will come in a minute.'

They waited with an assortment of people, a mother and child, an elderly couple, two bored-looking teenagers, but the bus was a long time coming, and before it came Janus appeared from the end of Fernlight Avenue, riding Julian's old bike, which even Julian found too small for him now, and which looked ridiculously little beneath Janus, whose feet whirring round on the pedals were almost a blur. His hair and beard flapping in the wind, he shot straight out into the heavy traffic of Green Lanes, narrowly missing a lorry, wobbling between cars which honked and veered as Janus wove a drunken path between them. Colette was relieved to see that he was wearing trousers. The people at the bus stop gasped and laughed as Janus mounted the pavement and swerved up to them. As the wind lifted his jacket, Colette could see that his inside pockets were bristling with the necks of bottles.

'Where are you going?' Janus said.

'Wood Green,' said Colette, 'and there's no point in you coming, you won't be able to get on the bus.'

'I can cycle,' said Janus, 'and I've got a meeting with Bill today . . .' he scooted off on another highly dangerous circuit around Green Lanes, returning to the bus stop. The ridiculousness of the spectacle, this tall, Jesus-bearded man on the small bicycle, his legs whirring, looping in and out of heavy traffic, couldn't help but cause Julian and Colette to laugh. People were looking at them as though they were somehow responsible. Mutterings of disapproval could be heard all around.

Juliette was feeling gloomy.

'I can't let him get together with Bill today. If him and Bill get drunk together – I don't know . . . I'll just leave him tonight and let him work out for himself what's happened.'

When the bus arrived Julian and Juliette and Colette climbed aboard and sat upstairs, praying that Janus would be left far behind. After a little while they heard a commotion downstairs. Janus had been hanging on to the back of the bus as it sped along, and the driver had stopped the bus and insisted that Janus let go. Janus had demanded that the conductor stow his bike under the stairs, the conductor refused, saying the bike wouldn't fit, which was true. Janus, in protest, held on to the back of the bus, and the conductor refused to let the bus go while Janus was holding on. Eventually the driver left his cab and came to the back to take charge of the situation, physically pulling Janus off the hand rail at the back of the platform and pushing him down onto the kerb, throwing his bike after him, to a small round of applause from the passengers.

Call the police, call the police, call the police, Julian repeated to himself, mentally urging Janus on into ever more outrageous actions. An encounter with the police and Janus would be in prison, which would mean, Julian supposed, the restoration of harmony to their house.

'Perhaps they'll call the police,' Julian said to his mother, hoping that his mother would be equally as enthusiastic. But she wasn't.

'Why do you keep saying that?'

'I want Janus to go to prison.'

'But why? Surely he's not that bad . . .'

She had this talent for forgetfulness, Colette, Julian thought. How amusing Janus was being. But what would he be like by the evening?

'Anyway, Janus could never survive in prison, could you imagine it? Those delicate hands, his educated voice – what are the bank robbers and muggers going to think of him? If you send him to prison you might as well kill him.'

When the conductor came up the stairs Colette went out of her way to apologize to him on her son's behalf, again to Julian's embarrassment, who believed if they'd kept quiet the conductor wouldn't have known of any connection between them.

'I know what it's like,' Colette said, 'I was once a conductress myself.' The conductor, an amusing, grey-haired Pakistani who kept up a constant witty banter with his passengers, held out his ticket machine to Colette, 'You want to take over for a while?' Colette giggled while Julian looked out of the window and saw to his horror that Janus was managing to keep up with the slow progress of the bus. Surely someone would call the police soon, a maniac on a bike swerving in and out of oncoming traffic, whooping and shrieking and whistling, even if only for his own safety.

The bus journey from Windhover Hill to Wood Green was through three miles of increasingly decayed suburbs. Beyond the Triangle the road crossed the New River, then the area became distinctly shabbier, the tall Victorian houses mostly converted into flats and bedsits. There were Greek bakeries, a driving test centre, bookmakers and off-licenses. Then the huge edifice of Swallow's Builders' Merchants, where Janus had once worked, to the left Our Lady's Convent, where Juliette had been schooled before ending it all so abruptly to marry Bill Brothers. The school had since closed down and was now being used as a warehouse. Almost opposite was Polperro Gardens, where they now lived, and at the next bus stop, the grimly jaunty façade of The Carpenters Arms, where they'd met. The stop after that was Wood Green Town Hall, the concrete and glass monolith where they'd married.

Janus had managed to keep up with the slow progress of the bus as far as the North Circular, whistling and whooping at his family on the upper deck, but by Wood Green he had fallen a long way behind.

At Polperro Gardens Juliette got off.

'If you see Janus don't tell him I've gone home, say I've gone down London with Bill, or something.'

'Don't worry, he'll be looking for us in the shops. If he rings, pretend you're not in.'

On the steps of Wood Green Odeon, beneath its fairy-lit portico, Julian paused.

'They won't let me in,' he said.

'Yes they will,' said Colette, reaching into her handbag and producing a hairbrush.

'Mum, what are you doing?'

'I'm brushing your hair.'

'What for?'

'It'll make you look older.'

'Not out here for God's sake.'

Colette went at Julian's hair vigorously, nearly knocking him over as she pulled at the tangled mass of curls. Julian's hair was less curly now than it was when he was born. As a baby it was as though his head was encrusted with gold sovereigns. Old ladies drooled over him in shops and begged for locks. Colette had one she kept in a stoppered, blue-tinted glass jar filled with wood alcohol. She'd snapped the top off the stopper so that it was unopenable, fearing that Janus might, in one of his more desperate states, drink it. But Julian's hair had darkened over the years and was now a very deep brown, almost black, and the curls had unfurled slightly, so that his locks hung in big, unruly loops that the teachers at his school were constantly complaining about. One teacher, a priest, even brought Julian home one lunchtime in a Renault 5 while Colette was sitting having a quiet fag and a beer, demanding that the boy be shorn before he returned to school. Julian hadn't been to the barber's for about three years, and so Colette got out a pair of blunt scissors and hacked away at his head until a sort of order was restored. But ultimately it was a losing battle. And Julian, anyway, was hoping to be expelled from St Francis Xavier's, and, too nervous of authority to challenge it directly, was channelling all his rebelliousness into his hair.

Otherwise Julian was on the cusp of adolescence, his skin was becoming greasy, his pores enlarging, a first crop of spots appearing. He was losing that miraculous body children have, that hairless, fatless marmoreal figure where every childish muscle is visible, like the little angels in Blake paintings, and instead had developed a clumsy ineptness of movement, as though always carrying something cumbersomely broad and heavy, which he was – his future adulthood. But he had always looked older than his years. Always the tallest in his class, even as a five-year-old. Now, as a young teenager, he could easily pass for an immature eighteen-year-old, if his hair was combed back, and he didn't come too close to the ticket booth.

The attendant didn't even give Julian as much as a second glance as they passed through to the upper circle of the huge cinema to watch *One Flew Over The Cuckoo's Nest.*

'What a bitch,' Colette kept saying of the tyrannical nurse Ratched as she determined to extinguish the sparks of life that Jack Nicholson's presence had brought into being, 'such a bitch, I can't believe it.'

Her expressions of disgust were so voluble that heads turned in the crowded cinema, and people hissed for her to be quiet. Colette seemed oblivious of these, even when the person sitting directly in front of her turned and gave her a long, disapproving look.

'Mum,' Julian whispered, 'will you be quiet?'

'I am being quiet.'

'No you're not.'

Then came a loud whistle from behind them. Janus was standing at the back, grinning broadly, leaning over the rear seats and the heads of those occupying them, his jacket hanging open revealing bottles.

'Thought I'd find you monkeys in here, hallelujah.'

He stumbled down the steps of the aisle and blundered through the legs of those seated on Julian and Colette's row to the vacant seat that was, unfortunately, beside Colette.

Janus talked without pause at full conversational volume. He took the mug out of his pocket and poured himself a mugful of neat gin, insisting on Colette having some. She acceded, and wiped clean the ice-cream carton she'd had since the interval; Janus filled it with gin.

'There you go my darling sweetheart mother,' said Janus, handling the brimming carton with care, passing it to Colette, who drank with a resigned acceptance, and was soon giggling alongside her son.

'What's this film about?' Janus yelled.

'A mad nurse,' said Colette.

The man in front turned around and addressed Colette.

'Would you mind taking your foot off my shoulder?'

Colette, who'd had her legs crossed, the foot resting on the back of the chair in front, said, 'Do you mind, I've got a bad knee.'

'Yeah well I've got a bad shoulder, get your foot down.'

'How dare you speak to me like that.'

Janus was keeping quiet.

A woman sitting alongside the man joined in.

'You're disgusting, the pair of you.'

'Look at them, they're drinking . . .'

The usherette came over and shone a torch on Colette. The usherette was a woman of about Colette's age, and seemed nervous.

'Would you mind keeping the noise down?'

'Absolutely,' said Colette, then reached out and took hold of the hand that was holding the torch, 'I do most sympathize with you, my dear. I was an usherette once . . .'

'Thank you . . .'

'In the Beaumont, Stamford Hill, an eight-hundred seater, full every night . . .'

'Yes, thank you . . .'

'Shhh!'

'It's a most unrewarding job, standing there in the dark, people jeering and jostling, and you have to watch the same film over and over again. Mind you . . .'

'Will you be quiet?' someone hissed.

'. . . I watched *The Ladykillers* it must have been a thousand times and I was in hysterics each time, so much I couldn't do my job. But for you to have to watch a film like this every day three or four times a day, it must make you want to kill yourself.'

'Yes, it is a horrible job, thank you . . .'

The usherette managed to drag herself away.

An idea struck Julian, once Janus and Colette had resumed their raucousness. He slipped out of his seat unnoticed and went in search of a public telephone, with the idea of calling the police, who then might come and arrest Janus and put him in prison. As he was leaving the auditorium, however, in the opposite direction came a brigade of four bouncers in dinner jackets with bow ties, who marched swiftly through the darkness, almost sweeping Julian aside. How disappointing. He would be too late. In the lobby he found a telephone and dialled anyway, nine, nine, nine.

'There's some people making a noise in Wood Green Cinema.'

'That's hardly an emergency call. This line is for emergencies only. '

'But they won't be quiet.'

'Very well, we'll send someone, but this really shouldn't be an emergency call.'

As Julian put the phone down Janus emerged from the darkness beyond the double doors with a large escort at each shoulder, followed shortly by Colette, also with two escorts. While Janus was ejected firmly by his escorts, Colette was treated with an embarrassed sort of deference, her bouncers didn't know quite what to make of her. She recoiled if they tried to hold her, and so were reduced to an ushering role as Colette made loud protests, demanding to see the manager who, it turned out, was one of the bouncers.

'And this boy,' she said, spotting Julian who had withdrawn to a corner of the lobby, 'what do you think this sort of scene has made on an impressionable young boy like this, he's only fourteen for Christ's sake, seeing his mother thrown out of a cinema as though she was a common drunk. I've worked in cinemas before now, in the days when cinemas were real cinemas, picture palaces we called them, call this old fleapit a palace? It's a disgrace. You're a disgrace . . .'

'Fourteen you say?' said the smarmily polite manager, 'and yet this film is an X-certificate . . .'

Colette affected not to hear.

'Come, Julian, we won't grace this trashy little establishment with our presence any longer,' and took hold of Julian's hand, which made him appear even younger than his years, and flounced out of the cinema.

Outside, re-entering the broad afternoon daylight, the grinding noise of the heavy traffic and the fat, overspilling queues of shoppers filling the nearby bus stops, they found Janus at the bottom of the steps talking to a West Indian in a flat-cap who was laughing toothsomely at the anecdotes of recent adventures Janus was relating.

Meeting up with these two at the bottom of the steps, Colette burst into shrieks of laughter which she shared with Janus, who whooped.

'There's Bill,' said Janus suddenly.

'Bill?' said the West Indian. In a hoarse, chuckling sort of voice, 'No. Where?'

'He's over there,' Janus was pointing across and down the street towards the main shopping area. 'I've been looking for him all day.' He put his fingers in his mouth and produced a piercing whistle that had all the nearby heads turning in his direction. Neither Colette nor Julian could see Bill, though Janus walked swiftly off in the direction he'd whistled. The West Indian, his hands in the pockets of his white, flared trousers, sauntered after him.

A police car drew up outside the cinema and a tired-looking policeman emerged.

'Shall we go?' said Julian.

'Yes,' said Colette, still laughing, 'let's get something to eat.'

Three doors up from the cinema was a Wimpy Bar, crowded, for some reason at that time of the late afternoon, with drunks.

Colette and Julian sat at a table facing each other, a large plastic tomato between them, it's green spout scabby with dried ketchup.

'Mum,' said Julian, 'Can we go to Tewkesbury on our own tomorrow? Just you, me and dad?'

'What do you mean? Janus Brian's coming with us. I've explained to you . . .'

'But it's not too late to change things – and Janus Brian doesn't really want to come. He'd forgotten about it when we saw him last week. Don't you remember?'

It was true. It had taken an afternoon of patient explaining and re-explaining before Janus Brian could be made to remember. Even then, when they thought the matter was settled, he would suddenly turn away from the television and say – 'Dear, can you tell me again – what are we doing next week?'

'Julian – Janus Brian has been looking forward to this holiday for months. What are you suggesting, that I just don't bother calling for him tomorrow? He would be devastated. It would kill him.'

A man who was sitting directly behind Colette, who'd turned round the moment Colette had sat back to back with him, had been following this conversation with a leering sort of interest.

'It would kill me,' he said, 'to not holiday with you . . .'

He was dark-haired and ageing, his face loose and empty with drink. He continued to make barely comprehensible noises, rough growls and vague but loud exclamations, sometimes accompanied by clumsy hand gestures.

'You've got to try and make some allowances for your uncle. You've got to try and be nice to him . . .'

'Be nice to me,' said the man. He seemed to be of Eastern European origin, and spoke English with a richly pronounced rolling of vowels.

'Do you mind?' said Colette over her shoulder.

'Why not?' said the man, 'I have a thousand sheep.'

'In that case,' said Julian, 'can I stay at home? I don't want to come with you.'

'Come on holiday with me,' said the man, who, up until now, had been unable to see Colette's face properly, but now, finally turning fully in his seat, he put a hand on the crown of Colette's head, patted, then stroked her hair. 'I can take you to the Black Sea. Come with me to Odessa. I will take you to Transylvania. You like?'

'I don't think so. We're going to Tewkesbury.'

'And so they make wine there?'

'No.'

'Where I live, the rivers flow with wine. You ask my wife. I took her there last year. Margaret!' He addressed the female sitting at his side, a small and dour woman in spectacles who was scowling fixedly into her coffee.

'I don't think you should be talking to a strange woman like this if you are married.'

'What, you're not strange, are you. Tell me, what have you been doing. What have you been doing today?'

'We've been to the pictures,' said Colette, who slowly had grown to enjoy the slurred attentions of this man.

'The pictures? *Last Tango In Paris*, eh?'

'No, *One Flew Over The Cuckoo's Nest*.'

'You should see *Last Tango In Paris*, it's my favourite film. Come, I'll take you to see it now. Give me your hand. A beautiful woman . . .' He took Colette's hand, planted kisses on the back of it, red lips pouting from beneath a boot-brush-thick moustache, 'I shall take you out . . .'

'No, I'm not a beautiful woman,' said Colette laughing, withdrawing her hand.

'What, you're not a woman?'

'Yes, I'm a woman.'

'Let me see if you are a woman, eh?' he reached for the buttons on Colette's floral shirt, tried undoing them.

Colette gave a shriek of laughter, took hold of the man's hand and pushed it away.

'Let me see if you are a woman,' he repeated, laughing, 'let me see, let me see.'

'Julian,' Colette said, smiling, 'would you mind hitting this man for me?'

'Why don't *you* hit him?' said Julian, rather crossly.

'Aha, your husband, eh?' said the man, as if noticing Julian for the first time.

'Yes.'

'No.'

'We can settle this thing man to man eh?' he continued, glaring at Julian, 'with honour. You and me, outside of here . . .'

'He wants you to fight a duel over me,' Colette laughed.

'Swords,' the man said, making swishing movements with his hands, 'you and me, for the honour of this woman . . .'

By this time the man was leaning so far over the seat back he was almost sitting next to Colette. But then his wife, who'd barely stirred in all this time, leant across and, with controlled anger, whispered something in her husband's ear. This seemed utterly to deflate the man, who shrank to about half his original size, and was then led tamely from the restaurant by his wife.

'What a strange man,' said Colette, who'd watched his departure closely, following his progress through the doors, then, along the High Road, supported by his small wife, and out of sight. Julian could see how his mother looked flushed and bright-eyed, glowing with the attention she'd received. 'He was just drunk, I suppose.'

Julian wanted to bring his mother back to the subject.

'Do you mind if I stay at home for the holidays?'

'Yes I do. And I think you'd mind. Do you really want to spend the summer in the company of your brother?'

'Why don't you give me some money so I can go on holiday on my own?'

Colette laughed.

'At fourteen? It would be against the law. I'm sorry, Julian, but you're stuck with us. Between a drunken brother and a drunken uncle I know you don't have a great choice, and you'll hate me for ever and ever, but I have to put Janus Brian first. He'll be dead soon and then you can dance on his grave, but until then I want to make what life he has left as enjoyable as possible . . .'

Colette hesitated. Her son was looking devastated. She thought for a moment he was going to cry.

'Of course,' she went on, trying to repair some damage, 'I don't really want him to come. I'd much rather it was just you me and daddy . . .'

'No,' said Julian, 'you want him to come. You're actually looking forward to it. You like the company of drunks – you've proved that this afternoon. You'd be happier if the whole world was drunk.'

Colette laughed, thinking Julian's remark rather charming, and not quite knowing how to take it.

12

Janus put a hand to his face. It hurt. He fingered the strange, rough texture that adhered to its left side, followed it from his eyebrow all the way down to his jaw. Dried blood. He recognised the sensation.

Janus discovered that he was nestled in a rose garden. Thickly tangled rose stems studded with thorns were all around him. If he moved, they dug into his skin. It was a kind of trap into which he had somehow fallen. Or perhaps he had been pushed. Janus had no memory of how he came to be among roses. He wondered if he had been asleep for a hundred years.

It was hot. Looking up through writhing stems and the lush crimson heads of roses he could see bright blue sky. Then thirst struck him. The drought was in his mouth. His whole body was a desert.

He rolled to the side, crushing stems, feeling thorns against his legs. He could feel the pain but wasn't hurt, and discovered the roses he'd rolled out of were the ones that grew in the front garden of Bill and Juliette's house. He found himself facing their front door. At least, it was the front door to the house in which they occupied an upper floor. One ring of the doorbell would produce the landlady, Miss Steel, who lived downstairs. Bill and Juliette required two rings.

It was a little Victorian front door set in a recessed porch like a small cave, tiled attractively in terracotta arabesques to the sides, black and white diamonds on the floor. Janus stepped into the porch and pressed the bell twice. There was no reply. He rang the bell once. No landlady came. What day was it? Sunday. Miss Steel probably went to church on Sundays. What about Juliette and Bill? They didn't come round to Fernlight

Avenue any more. They stayed in bed on Sunday mornings. He rang the bell twice again. No answer.

Still Janus felt no pain. He felt he could easily have punched a hole through the frosted glass panel of the front door and turned the handle. He wouldn't have felt anything. But he didn't want to. He wanted to go home and lie down. So he began walking.

He tried to remember what had happened the day before. He could remember playing the piano in the afternoon, then following his mother and the others to Wood Green on Julian's bike. What had happened to that bike? Janus paused and looked back at the squashed rose bed to make sure the bike wasn't in there. He could have cycled home. But the bike wasn't there.

It took Janus nearly a whole day to walk home. He had no money for a bus, and the new pay-as-you-enter buses wouldn't admit the unmonied.

He took giant strides along Green Lanes, the events of the day before slowly trickling back into his mind . . . *So we'll go no more a-boozing* . . .

He'd followed the others to Wood Green. Then he'd gone into the cinema and found his mum and Julian watching a film. Couldn't remember what film. Then what? Getting thrown out of the cinema. Then seeing Bill walking along the High Road, only it wasn't Bill but his doppelganger. Then he went to Polperro Gardens. That was it. Polperro Gardens to call on Bill. He gave two rings of the bell, but only Juliette answered. Bill wasn't there, she said. Where was he then? She said she didn't know. You must know where he is, he's your husband for Christ's sake. She tried to shut the door, Janus put his foot in. You can't stop me from seeing my best friend, Janus had said. He's not your best friend, his little sister had replied. And Bill doesn't drink now, that's what she said. That's what the doc told him. *So we'll go no more a-boozing.* Or Bill could be dead. If Janus takes Bill out for a drink it could kill him. Kill Bill. She was telling lies. Of course he can still drink. Janus had seen him in pubs from which he himself was banned. He'd seen him reeling out of The Quiet Woman, or quaffing ale among the Tyrols and flock wallpaper with that barmaid in The Volunteer with the orange plaits and the ginger-beer coloured pubic hair (so he'd heard). He was in The Coach and Horses drinking with washed-up footballers, failed actors, gone-to-seed glamourpusses whose heyday was a bit-part in *Upstairs Downstairs*. Bill's liver is on the edge, said Juliette. Bill is jaundiced and his blood full of urea, Bill doesn't socialize now, just stays at home with a mug of Horlicks and his feet up in front of *Nationwide*.

'I'll call the police,' Juliette had said.

That was as far as Janus could remember.

Janus had written Bill a letter. It began '*Dearest Bill, so the sun has finally set on the golden age of our friendship . . .*' but didn't go on, and Janus never sent it. In their epistolary exchanges Janus always felt outdone.

Bill Brothers was a fucking fascist.

Janus passed Swallows, the North Circular, the Cock, the Bus Depot, the Library, the Triangle. He was thrown out of a Greek Cypriot Cafe (Kafe Aphrodite), whose aroma of coffee and cheroots had soothed him. The grey-whiskered, poker-playing proprietor had tolerated his penniless presence for an hour before finally asking him to leave. He had amused the clientele by spouting Euripides in the ancient version of their language.

My barque is freighted full with sorrow, there is no room to stow aught further. All hail!

My house and portals of my home, how glad am I to emerge to the light to see thee. Ha! What is this? I see my children before the house in the garb of death, with chaplets on their heads, my wife amid a throng of men, and my father weeping o'er some mischance.

He wandered for hours among the cedars of Brimstone Park, watched mandarin ducks nibble at the soggy nubs of Wonderloaf that were silting-up a corner of the ornamental lake, and visited the museum that occupied the ground floor of the stately Tudor home at the centre of the park.

He drifted through a room full of stuffed animals with waxy tongues and realistic eyes. Another room of local history. A penny-farthing. An ancient, wooden ice cream stall. A relief map, under glass, of Windhover Hill and environs before their suburbanization, a swathe of rumpled greenery, teeny-weeny trees sculpted in green sponge, the lanes marked in white, labels here and there marking the sites of present-day landmarks. The Goat and Compasses was said to be the oldest pub in the district, in existence long before the railway came, and The Red Lion, as well, was there at a corner of Green Lanes. On the map you could see how Windhover Hill was really a hill, a distinct though shallow prominence on the edge of the basin of the river Lea, geologically it was one of the first foothills of the Chilterns, though formed not of chalk but syrupy London clay.

There were some old postcards displayed on the walls. Scenes of an almost unthinkable rusticity, taken around the turn of the century, not long after the railways came. 'Mr Withens' smallholding, Windhover Hill Woods'. There was Mr Withens with his prize pig. An enormous, pink, tusked brute that looked only one generation away from a hippo. Janus laughed. There was a picture of a prize bull, a rosette on its horn, that once trod the soil of farmland near Fernlight Avenue, its proud, handlebar-moustachioed owner standing dangerously alongside. There were many other pictures of this sort. 'The stables at Windhover Hill Farm', showing a row of mucky-looking work-horses, another of horses harnessed to a plough, turning the soil of Grange Farm. 'Young girls in Hoopers Lane Orchard for apple picking'. This was a picture that struck Janus especially. Those beautiful young virgins in their smocks and floppy hats, sitting in dappled light beneath heavily fruited boughs, laughing. Girls then, dead by now, but those orchards must have practically bordered the garden at Fernlight Avenue, and extended all the way along Hoopers Lane almost as far as The Goat and Compasses.

Eventually Janus found his way back to Fernlight Avenue. He couldn't find his key so knocked but, as at Polperro Gardens, there was no reply. Is there no one in, in the whole world? thought Janus. He had to walk through the side alley, climb, with difficulty, over the tall gate at the back, and walk round to the music room's French windows. These were fastened, on the inside, by string, which snapped after one good tug. The house was empty. On the kitchen table there was a note.

Be good. We'll see you in three weeks. There is plenty of food in the cupboards, but you will need to buy some cat food.

Love Mummy

There was a five pound note set beneath a vase on the table. Of course, he had been told many times that mum, dad and Julian were off on holiday today. He'd forgotten. The reason he'd forgotten was that they had never told him where they were going, so the holiday hadn't seemed like a real event to him. Colette claimed that she didn't know where they were going herself, but would leave it until the last minute to decide. Janus felt the sudden thrill of having the world to himself.

So we'll go no more a-boozing. Janus remembered much wandering yesterday. Much roving from pub to pub, from park to park and back to Polperro Gardens. In one pub he had seen Rita Michaelangeli and Hugo Price. Or was it a pub? Was it a restaurant? Whatever, they were alone, sitting at a table, looking at each other with lovey-dovey eyes. How long had they been having an affair, Janus wondered. It seemed to have been going on for years. On and off. Everyone knew about it, except for Veronica, Hugo's wife.

Veronica Price. Her name stuck in his mind. There was something important about Veronica Price. Something to do with this weekend. Then he remembered. It was Veronica's birthday. She was having a party. Was it tonight? Odd to have a party on a Sunday night. Perhaps it was to be more of one of those genteel soirées with decanted wine and canapes that she was so fond of having. Whatever it was, Bill would be there.

Hugo and Veronica lived in Hoopers Lane, not far from The Goat and Compasses. Janus bought some Special Brews with his mum's five pound note and drank them quickly. Then he went to Veronica and Hugo's house at twilight.

Their front garden was asphalted, the sort of deep, black asphalt that is sprinkled with little chips of white stone. Their garden had been converted into a car park, though neither Hugo nor Veronica drove. The curtains were closed. Party noises, heavily muffled, were audible. Janus knocked and Veronica answered. A tall woman, the back-lighting of the house made visible the outline of her skull through the fine mesh of her tight, frizzy perm. Her eyes, as always, were set within greasy troughs of eye-shadow and mascara. She wore a black velvet choke to which the neck of her pleated dress seemed to hang. The dress was a Romanesque garment, bright red, pleated all the way to the ground, like a fluted column. Beneath it, clearly visible in outline, was a black brassiere of sturdy construction. Veronica's hostility towards Janus probably stemmed from the time, at another party, when he'd taken hold of her plump bosoms and jiggled them about. It must have been years ago, but the memory of their weight in his hands had stayed with Janus ever since, rekindled by the sight of her bra he now had. In certain lights Veronica had a mysterious, towering beauty.

She'd been laughing as she answered the door but when she saw that it was Janus her laughter stopped instantly and she closed the door a little, so that there was only room for her face, which said 'No. You weren't invited.'

'Charming,' said Janus.

Seeing she was about to close the door he blurted 'Is Bill in there?'

Veronica hesitated, as though not sure how to reply. She glanced back into the house, from which was coming tremendous laughter, oblivious of Janus's presence.

'I'm not sure . . .'

'You're not sure?'

Rita Michaelangeli's small dark head appeared beside Veronica, peeking out, childlike, from beneath Veronica's armpit.

'Who is it?' she said in a giggly, excited voice, then, seeing Janus, said 'Oh,' and withdrew.

'Anyway, whether Bill's here or not,' said Veronica, reasserting herself, 'I can't have you in my house Janus, not after the last time . . .'

'What last time?'

Did she mean the bosom-jiggling incident, but that was years ago, surely . . .

'You know perfectly well Janus, now go away.'

She began again to close the door.

'I'm surprised you invited *her.*'

'Who, Rita?'

'Yes.'

'Why?'

'But I suppose you've made it up with Hugo, otherwise she wouldn't be here. Very forgiving of you . . . very tolerant.'

Veronica gave one of her slightly disgusted, wrinkle-nosed, tight-mouthed don't-you-dare-try-and-pull-that-one-on-me faces and closed the door.

Janus walked back to the pavement and then along Hoopers Lane towards the railway bridge. How long should he give it? How long before the fuse he'd lit sparked its way up to the dynamite. How long before Veronica, dismissive of his hint at first, allowed it to grow and grow until she could contain it no longer. Poor old Veronica. She thought she'd landed the catch of the year with Hugo Price, beery old clapped out second-class honours graduate trading on his school playground repu-tation, which was fading fast. Turned out to be a ravenous womaniser bedding his pert little female students with monot-onous regularity. Discovered affairs led to ferocious rows and temporary separations, Hugo and Veronica were always teetering on the brink of divorce. Veronica was capable of a seething, almost delirious jealousy at any suggestion her husband was being unfaithful. She would find the morsel of doubt he'd offered her impossible to resist.

The railway ran behind the houses of Hoopers Lane. Hugo and Veronica's garden backed onto the dense undergrowth of the cutting. All he had to do was hop over the bridge and down onto the cutting, a short walk along the tracks and then a scramble through the mulberries and under the sycamore clumps and over the low fence into Hugo and Veronica's garden. The party would, on this balmy night, have spilt out onto the lawn long ago, there he could mingle in the dark with the party guests unnoticed.

A simple plan, yet every stage of its execution was fraught with difficulties. The bridge wall itself was higher than it looked, as was the drop into the cutting on the other side. Janus twisted his ankle on landing, then stumbled through an invisible mess of suburban detritus – bottles and beer cans, tangles of wire, rubble. He cut his knee. A train hurtled past. The railway here was a suburban commuter branch line that connected the merchants of the City of London with the countryside of Hertfordshire, and yet down there at track level, in amid all the brambles and clinker, these trivial little local trains seemed immense and powerful machines that sundered the dark with their blazing carriage windows. At this time of night there were few trains about, and Janus was surprised to see one at all. Thinking it likely that it was the last train of the night, Janus walked confidently along the tracks in between the rails, from sleeper to sleeper, small amid the vast engineering of a suburban railway line. Then the ascent through the cutting's undergrowth, a terrible struggle through thorny scrub to attain the Price's garden.

When finally he crossed their rickety wooden fence he found himself at the silent, far end of a hundred feet of garden, in something like an orchard. A wilderness of decaying apple trees bounded by a rustic bower straggled with passion-flowers, then a broad almost dead lawn with benches of white wrought iron, in the centre a small circular pond with a fountain in the middle, the operation of which was now banned by the emergency legislation brought in by the Minister for Drought. There was also a swing in the garden, a fixture left by the previous occupants and allowed to remain by childless Hugo and Veronica who had once, it seemed, hoped for a family.

Janus's entrance to the party went unnoticed due to the fact that Rita Michaelangeli was threatening to commit suicide having climbed out onto the roof from an attic window. There was a commotion in the garden below her, where some party guests tried to reason with Rita while others, too drunk to realize what was happening, blundered about stupidly on the dimly lit lawn, paddled in the stagnant pool, played on the creaking swing.

'Get a blanket,' someone was shouting, 'something to catch her in.'

'Lets all take our trousers off and tie them together to make a trouser-trampoline,' slurred a drunk, unbuckling his belt.

'She couldn't kill herself from there, it's not high enough.'

'What if she landed on her head?'

'Probably just end up a vegetable.'

Oddly, Rita had taken up onto the roof with her two bunches

of celery, and she was slowly, methodically, breaking off stick after stick and hurling them down on the spectators, but especially on Hugo Price, who was on the patio and in a dilemma. Veronica was shrieking at him. Her pleated dress was torn, exposing the left cup of her bra. In some previous struggle this bra had slipped out of position, and her breast was shakily overspilling, half her nipple was exposed, peeping cheekily above the lacy trim. Had no one thought to tell her?

'She's saying it's her or me,' a drunk that Janus vaguely knew said to him, 'so if he goes with Veronica he's got a death on his hands, if he leaves her he's probably risking a kitchen knife in the groin, at the very least. Between you and me I think a full castration job is on the cards.'

Another tussle erupted between Hugo and Veronica. Hugo received a swipe in the face from Veronica's hand, who then shrieked up at the rooftops for Rita to throw herself off. Yet Rita, dressed in a flowery, flowing, diaphanous dress that fluttered in the light nocturnal breeze, seemed almost in a trance, her treacly cascade of hair fluttering, she continued to lob celery stalks down into the garden rather like, Janus thought, a mourner tossing flowers into a grave.

From the shadows just beyond the reach of the kitchen lights Janus observed all this, finding himself almost yearning for Rita's fall, not because he particularly disliked Rita, in fact he was quite fond of her, she'd more than once bestowed upon him plucky little kisses and bosomy embraces, but just for the witnessing of something spectacular, a young woman plunging to her death, landing head first on patio concrete. What would happen? Blood and nervous, post-mortem convulsions? Screams from those nearby? Panic. Silence. So Janus watched, his heart lifting, edging Rita closer to the guttering, let her take just one step, let her fall, let her fall . . .

Bill was down there with Hugo and Veronica, trying to act as peacemaker, not succeeding very well. Veronica seemed to be holding him responsible for the whole mess, perhaps mixing him up with Janus, and she clawed at his beard, pulling away tufts.

Kill Bill, Janus thought. Veronica, get your best knife, your kitchen devil, put it through his mean little heart, get one of your fondue forks and take out his eyes, one by one, like pickled silverskins. Chop him up and put him in your Moulinex. Liquidate him. Pour him into glasses and chill him in the fridge, then drink him with a salt-rimmed glass and a slice of lemon. Just for the spectacle. Just for the event.

But Bill was retreating. He had come away from Hugo and Veronica and was tottering down the garden and into the shadows toward Janus.

'Oh, hallo,' he said, seeing Janus murderous beneath apple trees.

'Hallo,' said Janus.

'Are you okay?'

'Yes.'

'I've just been trying to save Rita's life, but I've given up.'

'Not worth it, really.'

'No.'

Bill giggled quietly and put a hand on Janus's shoulder, then attempted to embrace both shoulders with the single arm. Janus flinched.

'Veronica Fox has found out about Hugo Rat's secret love life vis-à-vis Rita Fox.'

Bill yawned, then drank from his glass, Janus having moved a few paces back to release himself from his brother-in-law's embrace.

'I thought the doctor said you couldn't drink any more.'

'What does he know?' said Bill, shrugging. 'Anyway, he said cut down, not give up, or did he say give up? I don't bloody know any more. I don't care.'

'I thought you weren't going out any more, that you didn't go to the pub any more . . .'

Bill took a swig, made some incomprehensible gestures, 'Me? The world is my pub, Janus, you know that. Anyway, what am I going to do but drink, now that your dear, sweet angel sister has fled?'

'Fled where?'

'Fled off to make a nest somewhere else.'

'Since when?'

'Since yesterday, my old fruit. You should know, you were round our flat while she was getting her stuff together. An emotional turning point in my life disrupted somewhat by the uninvited intrusion of a drunken maniac. Packing her things last night for immediate departure. Don't remember do you? My pleas for her to stay fell upon deaf ground, not helped by intrusion of aforesaid drunken person, who thus rendered my pleas worthless, since she blames my partnership in crime with you for the loss of our marriage. Thus I was required to remove you from the flat. In one last desperate attempt to save my marriage, I hung one on your beak, as they say . . .'

Janus touched his face.

'I don't remember.'

Though he did. Being pushed backwards out of the front door. Resisting. Finally Bill's fist in his face. Not once. Not twice. Three times. The final punch had sent Janus into the flower beds.

'You weren't there this morning.'

'I've been looking for her all day. Went round your mum and dad's but they were just going off on holiday. I made a nuisance of myself with your mum. She is a divine woman, your mother. She let me cry on her shoulder for an hour. It meant they were late getting away . . .'

'Didn't you see me in the front garden?'

'No? At Fernlight Avenue?'

'Polperro Gardens. I was in the rose bushes asleep.'

'Didn't see you, but my mind was on other things, old chap.'

'So you just walked off and left me to rot . . .'

Bill's manner suddenly changed. His warmth went.

'Don't you understand what I've just said? The woman I love has just left me . . .'

'Yes, but she's only my sister. You yourself said you never loved her . . .'

'I said that to *you* . . .' Bill began, but couldn't explain further.

'The good news,' said Janus, 'is that we can devote all our energies to discovering the source of the Limpopo.'

'I don't want to discover the source of the fucking Limpopo.'

'Well you can get stuffed, then,' said Janus, his manner also changing to match Bill's. Then more assertively, 'Get stuffed!'

Without saying anything, after a moment's pause, Janus took a swing at Bill's head, a wild, flailing swipe in the dark that missed Bill's beard by a good six inches, but which carried Janus's body with it, spinning around in empty space until it flopped clumsily on the grass.

Bill laughed, but it was a jeering laugh, such as he'd never directed at Janus before, and it angered Janus further, who launched himself at Bill's legs, knocking him off balance and onto his bottom with a thud. Bill said 'ouch' loudly, then gripped Janus's head with his legs while Janus growled. Janus, if anything, was taller than Bill, but Bill hadn't lost the muscle he'd built up as a steeplejack, and which was still kept toned by the physicality of carrying sides of beef, chopping and sawing them into steaks. Janus was pathetically out of his depth in challenging Bill physically, he was almost literally tied up in knots.

Bill had Janus on his tummy, his arms locked behind his back, sitting on him, Janus's long hair was bunched in his fist, he tugged at the hair and so lifted Janus's face off the grass.

'I could break your neck now with one pull. Kill you, or leave you paralysed for life. What do you say to that? Look what you've brought me to. Violence. I've never been a violent person. In fact last night when I punched you in the face was the first time I'd punched anyone. And now you've given me a taste for it. I'd like to stamp on your silly face again and again, until it's a pulp. Juliette's gone off with Boris the Wires and it's all because of you you useless fucker . . .'

'Not Boris . . .' said Janus, once Bill had let go of his hair and thrown his face back into the grass.

Bill sobbed, and then lay down. Janus rubbed his scalp and lay down as well.

'I thought she might be here,' said Bill quietly. 'Otherwise I wouldn't have come. I'd have stayed at home and swallowed a bottle of tablets . . .'

'No,' said Janus, 'No, don't do that,' he said it with some alarm in his voice, 'Dying is a horrible thing. It's disgusting. Death is for idiots. People like us should never die . . .'

Bill smiled at Janus. The warmth returned.

'Boris the Bold,' said Bill, thoughtfully.

'Boris the Billy Goat,' said Janus, equally thoughtfully.

'Boris the Bastard.'

They laughed.

'Has Rita jumped yet?' said Janus, who had his back to the house. Bill lifted his head.

'Well she's not on the roof any more. She's either jumped or someone's talked her down.'

The garden had emptied. Rita's threatened suicide seemed to have put a dampener on things, and many people had left, and the rest had gone inside.

'I wonder if Hugo and Veronica will split up,' said Janus.

'I hope so,' said Bill.

'That'll be two in one day. A record.'

'What do you mean?'

'Nothing. Why don't we ransack the house for booze and go somewhere . . . ?'

'Good idea,' said Bill, sitting up, 'tell you what. I'll nip inside, procure a couple of bottles of vodka, perhaps some tomato juice, and meet you out here, in five minutes.'

Bill stood up and made for the house. Janus sprang up and pulled him back by the arm.

'No,' he said, 'you won't come back will you?'

'Of course I will . . .'

'No you won't, you'll run off like you did that time at The Owl, you bastard. You'll make your escape.'

Janus's face was wrinkled with an indignant frown.

'I promise I'll be back . . .'

'Cross your heart?'

'Cross my heart. I promise . . .'

'I don't believe you.'

'Well what do you want me to do?' Bill said, exasperated.

'Stay out here with me.'

'Okay.'

'We'll do something.'

'Okay. What'll we do?'

Janus thought for a while, looked around him, like a child looking for something to play with.

'I think,' he said, slowly and carefully, 'that we may be very near the source of the Limpopo.'

'Do you?' said Bill, soberly.

'I do. I think we are very close to making a truly remark-able discovery, our names will be displayed on one of those boards they have on posh clubs in Pall Mall, and old bastards with white moustaches will talk about us over their scotch and sodas . . .'

'Will they?'

'Yes, look, it's this way.'

'Aha,' said Bill, pointing to the little fish-pond with its inoperative fountain, 'this must be it.'

'Oh no. That's a mere tributary. That's nothing. The river itself is this way. Come on, follow me this way.'

And Janus walked to the end of the garden through the little orchard, to the low fence at the end. Bill followed. Now in complete darkness, beyond the reach of the lights, they moved carefully among the thorny scrub of the railway cutting. Janus was conscious of Bill's quietness. Things had changed. Normally he would have been all giggles and sniggers on such a venture, but now he was silent, apart from the occasional throat clearing cough, and some rather noisy breathing. Janus had never known Bill, sober or drunk, so serious.

'There it is,' said Janus, once they cleared a certain level of the cutting, coming upon a view of the railway tracks beneath them, 'By Jove Dickie, this is it, old bean. The source of the Limpopo, what we've been looking for all these years, we've finally made it.'

The rails glinted green in the light from a distant signal.

'Yes,' said Bill, and coughed, 'what ho.'

'Careful,' said Janus as they moved through the scrub towards the tracks. Bill was holding onto Janus for support and guidance. He gave a sudden, spluttery, untidy cough that almost exhausted him of breath. They were on the tracks now. Again that sense of space, of being dwarfed by engineering.

'We've made it,' said Janus.

Bill was gasping. He fumbled about in his pockets for an inhaler.

'I feel weird,' he said, pantingly, 'it's what the doc said about the booze . . .' He coughed again, then gasped for air, gaping like a fish, down on his knees, then all fours, drawing desperately for air which had suddenly become a remote, elusive thing, difficult to catch.

Janus, on the other track, watched, amused, amused even further by the warm glow that was highlighting the interior arch of the Goat and Compasses Lane bridge, from which Janus had earlier jumped. It looked like the faint glow of sunrise. A train was coming.

The light bled along the rails, giving them form, and the steel suddenly filled with sound, the twanging, mewing sound that always came with the faster trains, as though the steel rail was suddenly full of trumpeting angels.

Bill had found his inhaler, he was puffing at it, shaking it, puffing, it didn't seem to make any difference.

'Get up,' Janus said, loudly and a little irritably, as a father might speak to a child who'd fallen in the playground for the tenth time.

'I can't move,' said Bill, his voice a crackly whisper.

The bridge was now a bright archway of light and the rails were tweeting and lively with vibration. Bill found himself in a cradle of twittering metal.

'It's coming pretty fast,' said Janus.

'Which way?'

'Up there.'

Bill seemed to think he had plenty of time but the train was nearly at the bridge. Janus estimated he probably had about twenty seconds to get out of the way, and Bill was still on his hands and knees.

'Can you go up there and stop it, Janussimus, because I can't move.'

It was the ground that was singing now, a low, mighty croon that made the earth seem suddenly a malleable thing, full of springs, like a mattress, or quicksand.

Intense light at the bridge now, then the train itself came into view, like the sun returning after a total eclipse, a sudden, piercing shining forth that cast long shadows.

Janus was relishing the moment. Death made visible, an entity, a thing with shape and noise, approaching. Whatever happened next, whether he saved Bill, or Bill saved himself, or if either or both of them died, nothing would be the same again after this moment. Like witnessing a birth. Janus was enjoying the last moments of his old life. He stepped onto the track with Bill, in-between the rails that were now shining like double shafts of sunlight breaking the darkness.

'We've got about eight seconds, Brothers,' said Janus to Bill, at his feet like a dog.

The train gave a sound from its horn. They'd been seen. The sound came again, shrieking with urgency. Bill, as if roused by this sound, grabbed wildly at Janus's leg, knocking him off balance. They fell across the track, lit now in a blaze of leading lights, they heard in their ears the ringing of brakes biting into steel wheels, the wheels biting into the rails, and a screaming of such ferocity it was as though the metal itself was crying out, as though the earth was crying out . . .

Janus could not properly recall how he managed to remove both himself and Bill Brothers from the path of the train, nor how they managed to effect an escape through the brambles while the guard and the driver, having brought the train to an agonizing halt over the spot where they'd lain, had searched with torchlight all over the cutting, later joined by police and firemen. All Janus could properly remember was the wheezing of Bill Brothers close to his ears, the drawing in and out of air through restricted airways. Bill's breathing sounded like something grotesquely heavy being dragged through deep grass, and all the time Janus wondered why he bothered with such weight, why he couldn't just drop it, let it go, be free of it.

13

Aldous, Colette and Julian arrived at Janus Brian's bungalow just after noon on the first day of their summer holiday. Net curtains were lifted in neighbouring bungalows about the turning circle, as Colette, after repeatedly ringing an unanswered doorbell, let herself in. Janus Brian had, of course, been constantly reminded of the fact that Aldous and Colette would be calling for him that morning. Only the day before yesterday she'd spoken to him on the phone to make sure he would be ready, and he'd sounded perky and optimistic, said he was looking forward to going away, that he would be ready with his suitcase at 12 o'clock, understanding how Aldous and Colette didn't want to wait around, that they wanted to get to Tewkesbury in good time.

So she was surprised, for once, by the squalor in which they found him. Semi-conscious and semi-naked on the bed, he'd evidently urinated while lying down, merely aiming himself roughly over the side of the bed, because the carpet beneath was drenched with pee.

Colette slapped him about the face, showing a rare loss of patience with her brother. Aldous, too, was cross, and stomped about the bungalow, rooting out Janus Brian's stock of alcohol, while Janus Brian wailed huskily.

'I'm not going,' he said, 'I can't do it. Buzz off without me.'

'You're coming with us,' snarled Colette, 'you're coming with us if I have to tie this bed to the back of the car.'

She yanked her brother out of bed and he fell in a crumpled heap on the floor. She and Aldous dragged him, his feet trailing, to the bathroom, where he was stripped and dipped. The quietness of his voice did slightly worry Colette. It was almost as though he'd lost his voice completely, and although he was trying to shout, barely more than a whisper was coming out.

Aldous did his best to tidy the bungalow, while Julian drifted from room to room, sometimes reading from the paperback he'd brought with him, Arthur C. Clarke's *Childhood's End*, noting with interest the faecal deposits in the bedroom where, in the top drawer of the chest, he found two pornographic magazines, a *Penthouse* and a *Men Only*. Almost instinctively he stole one of these, the *Penthouse*, slipping it into his inside pocket, then pushing it down into the lining of his jacket.

Colette soaped her brother's face and shaved it, sponged his scalp and brushed his hair. There were no clean clothes in which to dress Janus Brian, they had to make do with the least soiled elements of his meagre wardrobe, with the promise of clean clothes in Tewkesbury.

Aldous found several bottles of Beefeater gin, mostly empty, though one was nearly full. As Colette finished her grooming of Janus Brian in the living room, he caught a glimpse of Aldous passing the door with his arms full of bottles.

'Christ,' he whispered, 'what's he doing. No, don't let him.'

'No more gin now, Janus,' said Colette, 'not today.'

'Stop him for fuck's sake,' he cried, faintly, as a clinking sound came from the kitchen, of several empty bottles falling into a bin. Somehow he mustered the energy to escape his rocking chair and make it into the hall, where he met Aldous returning from the kitchen. A brief tussle ensued which resulted in Janus Brian falling onto the floor, where he seemed to writhe mechanically, like a piece of expiring clockwork, his false teeth gnashing.

'You bastard,' he moaned, 'you big bastard, you big bastard . . .'

Aldous and Colette conversed above Janus Brian, ignoring completely his floor-level invective.

'Shall we let him have some?'

'I've kept the full bottle, I suppose we could.'

'It might settle him down.'

'Okay. I'll lock the rest away in the boot, let him have some now and then, once we've got underway.'

'Okay.'

Janus Brian, still muttering expletives, was lifted back into the swivel chair. A cup of gin was put into his hand and he drank it lustily, spilling much out of the corners of his mouth. The transformation was instant. His voice returned, some colour (a pale violet) came to his face and his eyes began to focus.

He reached feebly across to a drawer in the television table and extracted a wad of five and ten pound notes, flipped through them rapidly, muttering, 'that should do', and pocketed them loosely.

'He's just been testing us, that's all,' said Colette to Aldous, 'to see if we really wanted him to come.'

But his drunkenness was real. His filth and his lassitude were genuine. He could hardly stand, let alone walk. Aldous and Colette took an armpit each and carried Janus Brian to the car. Ridiculously light, he was easily lifted, and on his journey down the cement drive, though his feet went through the motions of walking, they didn't actually touch the ground.

Janus Brian sat in the back of the car moaning weakly, Colette beside him, Julian in front with his father who locked the bungalow, under the covert observation of half a dozen other bungalows.

And then it was north, across the grain of the Chilterns, to Princes Risborough, Aylesbury and across the plain, all the way Janus Brian moaning in the back seat, occasionally uttering tremblingly assertive demands for gin, reaching out, when he could, to take hold of Aldous's shoulder and shaking him. Aldous, ignoring him most of the time, now and then called over his shoulder for him to be quiet, saying he wouldn't have any more gin before Bicester.

An American bomber passed low over the road towards its unmapped roost and everywhere there were the wintry carcasses of elms that had fallen to the disease that had recently sheared a layer off the English landscape. Colette was astonished and saddened by their abundance, so many dead trees, so suddenly dead.

Nearing Bicester Janus Brian's demands for gin grew increasingly frantic until at one point he reached forward and took hold of the back of Aldous's head, tugging weakly at his hair, while Colette tried pulling Janus back, and the car swerved into the path of an oncoming juggernaut, and then out again. Aldous yielded and pulled into a lay-by beneath pylons and, while traffic hurtled past, poured a cup of neat gin from the bottle in the boot, fed it to Janus Brian, who then slept.

After Bicester they left the busy roads, following the route Aldous and his sons had taken when they cycled to Wales. Aldous found himself looking out for cyclists as though seeking comfort in the idea that the art of cycling over long distances had not entirely died. All through the little villages in the increasingly complex landscape – Middleton Stoney, Lower Heyford, Middle Barton, Church Enstone, not a single cyclist.

By the time they reached Chipping Norton it had felt like a very long journey to everyone but Janus Brian, who now expressed a wish to urinate. They parked in the High Street while Aldous and Colette, again taking a shoulder each, escorted Janus Brian to the public lavatory under the limestone town hall. He walked with the cautious deliberation of someone who expected every pace to be the first step on a staircase, lifting each foot higher than necessary.

After Chipping Norton Janus Brian calmed, and began to accept his situation. He agreed to Aldous's rationing of his gin, being allowed another cupful before they left the village, and agreeing to have no more before they reached Tewkesbury. He submitted himself to his sister's summer holiday.

The rich verdure of the Cotswolds, starved of rain, had died. Everywhere there was yellow, that made it seem these dairy lands had become arable. But it was grass that shone golden in the fields, not wheat, grass that should have been lushly green, feeding the cows and sheep. Even the trees were beginning to wilt, apart from the elms that had already died, starkly vivid against the other trees, oaks and ash trees began to sicken, their leaves hanging loosely, shrivelling. Some people in the news-papers were talking about a permanent shift in the climate, that we may see the introduction into Britain of a Mediterranean, or even of a sub-tropical weather pattern, that the greenness of England may soon become a thing of the past, the land might dry up completely and be good only for the growing of olive groves and cork-oaks.

Colette tried to imagine it as they descended the Cotswold scarp and proceeded through the Vale of Evesham (even more emaciated, it seemed, than the previous hills), peasants taking in the wine harvest, orchards of lemon and peach, or perhaps banana plantations growing around the country pubs, the tower of a perpendicular church peeking above the orange groves. Or perhaps just desert. The Cotswolds eroded to rocky stumps above a dustbowl, cacti and vultures, the bleached skeletons of horses recumbent on the plain . . .

When they arrived at Tewkesbury, Aldous and Julian pitched the tent at the municipal site overlooked by the venerable Norman tower of the Abbey, while Colette went into the town to seek accommodation for her brother, who slumbered in the car. The town's B & Bs turned out to be full. The best Colette could find was a room in a guest house that wouldn't be available until the following day. The house was a quaint old Georgian place on the High Street, all varnished panelling and ancient furnishings, run by a tubby little woman called Mrs Brown, who wore her hair as Colette had worn hers in the 1940s.

'Does your brother smoke?' she said, after showing Colette the room.

'No,' said Colette, wondering if she could persuade Janus Brian to abstain from the habit for a while, or how she might explain his stained fingers and his blackened teeth.

'Are you quite sure?' Mrs Brown went on. She must have detected some hesitation in Colette's voice, 'because I really can't have a smoker staying here, this house is a firetrap . . .'

'Is it?'

'Oh yes. The only exit is the front door. All this varnished wood, it's very flammable. It may as well be soaked in petrol.'

'Don't worry,' said Colette, handing over a deposit taken from the wad of cash Janus Brian had given her charge of, 'my brother is a model of clean living.'

Mrs Brown seemed pleased.

There was still the problem of where to accommodate Janus Brian that night, however. The only bed Colette could find in the whole town was in The Grapes, an overpriced, pretentious hotel on the main street, which traded on an obscure association with Dr Johnson (*at The Grapes they dined on beef and oysters* was a line from Boswell the hotel displayed on a small plaque by the entrance). The staff were cool and aloof, beyond the reach of Colette's charm, on whom they looked down with sour, disdainful eyes as she booked her brother in for the night.

'Are you sure you'll be okay?' Colette said as she settled Janus Brian into his room that night after an evening spent in the bar, under the mildly disapproving glances of both customers and staff.

'I suppose so,' said Janus Brian, taking off his stained tweed jacket, 'why the hell have you brought me here?'

'Shall I take this jacket for you?' said Colette, choosing to ignore her brother's remark, 'I can get it dry cleaned tomorrow morning.'

Janus Brian handed her the jacket, then took his trousers off.

'Where are we again?' he asked.

'The Grapes.'

'I mean what town?'

'Tewkesbury.'

Janus Brian muttered the name to himself several times, as though trying hard to memorize it.

Eventually Colette left her brother semi-conscious on top of the bed clothes, half naked, with a tumbler of gin on the bedside table. She skipped down the narrow corridor as quickly as she could, knocking loudly on all the doors as she passed them, a quick thump-thump, left and right, with the flat of her hand as she ran past.

When she went to collect him in the morning she was relieved to find him up and dressed and looking far better than he had done the day before.

He told her how he'd spent the night searching for water. He'd woken in the middle of the night with a raging thirst. 'My tongue was like a parrot's cage.' He'd had no idea where he actually was. It took him half an hour just to find the light switch. He'd tried getting a cup of tea from the teasmade, but all he could get was the World Service Shipping Forecast, which made him feel even more thirsty.

Eventually, remembering that he was in a hotel, though he had forgotten in which town, he went to the bathroom for some water but had locked himself out of his room in the process. He was dressed only in his underpants. He couldn't find the bathroom either. He went wandering all round the hotel in the middle of the night, up creaking spiral staircases, along the warren of twisting corridors that led nowhere. Eventually he found the hotel bar, but the drinks were all locked away behind a metal grille. He stood there with his tongue hanging out, his fingers curled through the grating, staring longingly at bottles of bitter lemon and cream soda.

'Then I found myself in a truly wonderful place, which was the dining room, and everything was laid out ready for break-fast. There was a reverential quality about the place, as though I'd happened upon a small chapel or other holy place – all these crystal tumblers and folded napkins like little angels, shiny knives and forks, everything sparkling in almost darkness, it suddenly all looked very mysterious and almost sacred. And I walked between the set tables, creeping, as it were, looking at the tables as I passed between them in a state of wonderment. And then I discovered, on a large serving table beneath some tea-towels, an array of tiny little china jugs of milk. There must have been twenty or thirty of them, each enough for one or two cups of tea. So I drank them. One by one I drank the lot. They were lovely and cold. I found a napkin and wrote a little message,

> Sorry, but I was so thirsty

and left it on the table amongst the empty jugs. They'd satis-fied my thirst, and I laughed to myself on the way back to my bedroom, to think of the happenings at breakfast when they found the empty jugs, and my note.'

Eventually he found a night-porter who, having no access to a spare key, had had to crawl along a sloping extension roof and in through a window into Janus Brian's room.

'Very nice chap he was. Very helpful. Not like the day staff.'

Even after only two days there was a visible improvement to Janus Brian's state. His first night in the bed and breakfast went well and he was glad to be out of The Grapes (he said he couldn't afford more than a single night) and he reported that he even managed to eat the precisely cooked egg that Mrs Brown had provided for his breakfast. His first breakfast for months and he'd kept it down. He even seemed to be enjoying himself.

They had found somewhere to eat – Sam's Café, a snazzy little luncheonette on the High Street, a few doors down from The Grapes. The swanky modishness of the interior – red melamine table-tops, wallpaper with a crimson zigzag motif, chromium jukebox in a corner, seemed at odds with the character of the proprietor, a small, portly, ageing gentlemen with a bald head and a grey, handlebar moustache. He took their orders on a little pad of paper.

Janus Brian seemed quite keen to eat. On the laminated menu there was listed, under 'Lite Bites', a buck rarebit and a welsh rarebit. These dishes were rarities now, and evoked, for the elders, memories of pre-war suppers lovingly prepared by long since dead mothers.

'Do you know, I quite fancy a buck rabbit,' said Janus, using that fond old contraction.

'One buck rarebit,' said the waiter as he wrote, relishing the full version of the phrase, rolling it on his tongue. He was of their generation, the waiter, and knew food as they knew food, as something safe and predictable, without any of the dangers and threats posed by lasagnes and bologneses.

Many lunchtimes, afternoons and evenings were spent at Sam's Café. Janus Brian ate buck rarebits, scrambled eggs, beans on toast. As the days passed his appetite grew. He managed a shepherd's pie, a plaice and chips, ham and cheese omelettes. Of larger meals he always left a substantial percentage uneaten, but at least he was trying, thought Colette, at least he was interested in food, at least he was thinking about it. After eating they would sometimes sit in the café for hours, while Julian wandered off on his own, and they would read papers, or write postcards. One afternoon Colette wrote several cards while they sat at a table next to the rarely played jukebox.

'There,' she said when she'd finished the third one, shuffling them together, 'that's those done. Janus, are you going to send a card to Lesley and Madeleine?'

'I shouldn't think so,' said Janus Brian without looking up from his tabloid newspaper.

'Oh go on,' pleaded Colette, 'they'd like to hear from you. What about Agatha? Why don't you send one to her?'

Janus Brian laughed.

'I should think they're glad to see the back of me. I wouldn't want to upset them by reminding them of my existence with a postcard. On the other hand, perhaps I would, but I can't be bothered.'

Colette shrugged.

'I love writing postcards. I always have. It is strange, isn't it? We so rarely express ourselves to people we know in writing, except when we're on holiday. If we are judged in the future solely by our correspondence, they will only ever know us as people who live in tents and eat fish and chips. Look, I've written one to Janus, one to James, and one to Juliette and Bill.'

'Juliette and Bill have split up,' said Aldous, turning the pages of his *Telegraph*.

Colette put a hand to her cheek.

'I keep forgetting. I'll have to rewrite it. I can't believe she's living with someone called Vladimir.'

'Boris,' said Aldous.

'Shall I read out the one to Janus?'

'Do, dear,' said Janus Brian abstractedly.

'Do you have to send one to Janus?' said Aldous, who was sitting beside his wife.

'What do you mean? Of course I do.

Dear Janus, we arrived safely on Sunday evening and have found a lovely spot in the camp site overlooked by the tower of the Abbey. We hear it chiming all night, a beautiful sound. Weather v. hot. Grass all dead, bit like a desert. Do you remember the town? We used to stop here sometimes on the way to Wales. You must come here one day. Love Aldous, Colette, Julian and Janus Brian'

Aldous had his head in his hands.

'For Christ's sake,' he moaned, 'what are you trying to do. Are you trying to ruin the holiday?'

'What do you mean?'

'Telling him to come here.'

'I'm not telling him to come here.'

'That last sentence . . .'

'I'm just suggesting he comes here one day. I'm not telling him to come here now. He's not going to come here right now. Don't be so stupid . . .'

'But you just had to go that little bit too far didn't you? Writing him a card, okay, write a card if you must. Be pleasant, okay, what else can you be on a postcard? But suggesting that he comes here, there was no need to put that in . . .'

'Oh stop being so childish. And don't sulk. I'll write him another card. Okay? Happy now?'

Janus Brian raised his eyes from his newspaper, the front page of which was the single, enormous word *PHEW!*, and a picture of Blackpool Beach, carpeted with sunbathers.

'Come now, Aldous,' Janus Brian said, 'I can't think the prospect of a visit from my nephew can be all that dreadful . . .'

Aldous cast him a scowl that told him to mind his own business. Janus Brian returned to his newspaper.

Clouds were rare visitors to the skies above Tewkesbury, though some mornings would reveal exquisitely clear cumulus, heaps of vapour full of shadows, wonderfully three-dimensional. Julian watched one passing over the battlemented tower of the Abbey, where it seemed to pause, taking the exact shape, for a moment, of a human brain. He yearned for it to unload itself, to rain down on the parched flora of Gloucestershire. But the clouds were retentive, steadfastly so, hanging tantalisingly vast in the sky, enough liquid in some to keep a town like Tewkesbury in bathwater for a year. Where did they go, those morning clouds? By noon the skies were always empty. Where did they rain? Nowhere in England the papers said. Records were being set. The hottest day in history, the longest drought in history, ladybirds burgeoning, lizards multiplying, there were dust storms over Bedfordshire, bushfires in the Pennines.

The camp site itself, however, was lushly green. The camp warden had found a loophole in the hosepipe ban, which meant the site could be classified as farm land. He could water his lawns with impunity, and so the camp site nurtured the only green grass left in England.

'Like the garden of Eden,' Janus Brian remarked, 'Or a Spanish golf course.'

Things went well for the first week of the holiday. They settled into a gentle routine of sauntering around the town, savouring its pubs, cafés and tea shops, perhaps an undemanding drive somewhere in the afternoon, a relaxing evening at the tent, after which Colette and Janus Brian would stroll up the lane from the camp site past the Abbey to Janus Brian's B & B. By the end of the first week, however, there was a problem when Colette dropped Janus off. Mrs Brown was waiting for them, a look of concern on her small, stiff face. Her voice shook when she spoke.

'I cannot have Mr Waugh staying here any more,' she said.

'Why not?'

She beckoned the two into her antiquated sitting room and produced a bedsheet for them to inspect. Two cigarette burns, like a pair of brown eyes, stared at them from the whiteness.

'I made it very clear from the beginning that I didn't allow smoking in this establishment. It is clear that Mr Waugh has been smoking in bed, I cannot allow it.'

She went into a long description of a fire at a building further along the terrace, exactly the same as hers, when a negligent smoker incinerated a houseful of guests.

'Janus Brian, you didn't tell me you'd taken up smoking again,' Colette said for good effect, but it was too late.

'Homeless again,' Janus Brian said despondently as they stood on the pavement outside Mrs Brown's, 'I'm not going back to The Grapes. Definitely not.'

After some discussion back at the tent Colette came up with what she thought was a good solution to which the others agreed, and went back to speak to Mrs Brown.

'This may sound rather odd,' she said, 'but could my husband take Mr Waugh's room? I can absolutely guarantee he's a non-smoker.' A bemused Mrs Brown agreed.

Thereafter, for the rest of the holiday, Aldous stayed at Mrs Brown's, while Janus Brian slept at the tent. It was an arrangement that worked surprisingly well. Aldous, in fact, seemed rather too keen to make his exit every evening, returning the next morning properly washed and breakfasted, bright and cheerful with a newspaper under his arm. He was enjoying a holiday of comparative luxury at the B & B, paid for by Janus Brian who, for his part, seemed relieved to be away from the restrictive, formal atmosphere of Mrs Pyrophobe's, as he called her. He seemed comfortable on the foam rubber of the tent, or on the cotton and folding steel of the camping chairs.

Julian was bored. Agonizingly bored. The holiday had adapted itself to the pace of Janus Brian's life, which was slow and parochial. If Janus Brian had had his way, the entire holiday would have been spent in the saloon of The Black Bear, the waterside pub he'd adopted as his own. Julian had to continually pressure his parents into allowing something else to happen, to drive somewhere, a circumnavigation of Bredon Hill and its ring of ancient churches, north to see the misericords at Ripple, or west towards the Forest of Dean, or east across the plains full of orchards towards the Cotswold scarp, and into the unfolding richness of the Cotswolds themselves.

Janus Brian was a reluctant passenger on these journeys, he had no interest in the landscape or the countryside at all and was, for the most part, utterly disinterested in church architecture. If ever inclined to comment on these subjects it was only to remark how poorly England compared to Spain. As a man who knew intimately the dramatic sweeps of the Iberian golf courses, he would remark how feeble the Cotswolds seemed in comparison to the Sierra Nevada, or what a poor manifestation of stone was Tewkesbury Abbey in comparison to the grandeur of the Alhambra.

Janus Brian's interest in his surroundings perked up whenever pylons came into view, or an electrical substation, gas-works, sewage farm, or, if they were very lucky, a power station. Once, following the meandering Wye Gorge, happening upon the view of Tintern Abbey that had moved Wordsworth so, shattered stumps of sumptuous gothic beneath towering forests teetering on cliffs, Janus Brian missed the whole spectacle, drawn to the fixtures of an electrical switching yard just visible in the opposite direction. He saw the landscape solely in terms of its utilities, which he'd spent his working life depicting in working drawings, diagrams and blueprints. This process seemed to have instilled in him a heightened sense of their value, and he would often lecture the others in the car, alerting them to what he believed they were taking for granted.

'We forget how important electricity is to our society. Or gas, where would we be without gas? And piped water? What about piped water?'

'I liked the world before electricity,' said Colette, 'gas lighting. It was much cosier. Coal fires. I wouldn't mind getting my water from a well, or cranking a village pump . . .'

'You forget,' said Janus Brian, showing a rare passion for something that wasn't alcohol, 'hauling buckets of filthy coal up from the cellar, having to nip out and buy tuppeny gas mantles, earth closets. You call that cosy? That's living like peasants . . .'

Mostly their drives turned into urgent searches for pubs. Colette only drank at Whitbread pubs, because they served Gold Labels, so these searches were often tense and frustrating. In the wizened, yellow desert that England had become, pubs were like dark, shaded oases, and the family would spend hours in them. So what would start off promisingly for Julian as a day of exploration, would often congeal into a long noon and afternoon spent in the malty, shadowy environs of a pub. Julian's boredom would intensify.

He spent much of the time alone at the tent, declining the offer of a drink in a pub with the elders. He watched the habits and routines of families made transparent by the flimsiness of their habitations.

A family of four were opposite, a streetwise Birmingham woman with prolapsed stomach muscles and a face that carried a scar (a violet zigzag that indented her lower lip and continued down to her chin) of some previous catastrophe (a car crash?), her husband, also with prolapsed stomach muscles, but from binge-drinking rather than childbearing, and their two teenage children. The woman spent a good portion of every day sunbathing in front of her tent, tummy-down, the undone straps of her bikini top trailing either side like the loose ribbons of an opened present, revealing that moment where ordinary skin fills out to become the breast. Julian was watchful for any accidental disclosure, though the woman was annoyingly skilful in maintaining the concealment of her breasts, even when once, surprised by her husband dolloping a morsel of ice cream into the small of her back, and she quickly lifted herself up, she managed the manoeuvre without revealing herself.

In all his furtive hours of watching this family, Julian never once had any indication that they returned his curiosity. They carried on their lives as though Julian and his parents and Janus Brian and their tent were invisible. Yet they were barely thirty feet away.

The daughter was roughly Julian's age, perhaps a little older. Flouncy brown hair hung about her face in big licks and curls, but her eyes were small and a little mean-looking. Her mouth was thin and set. The boy was somewhat younger, fair-haired and dressed always in the ridiculous fashions of the day – calf-length voluminous trousers, not unlike the plus-fours Aldous sometimes wore in his youth, hooped socks and platform shoes.

The little flecks of tartan that trimmed some of the girl's clothes marked her as a Bay City Rollers fan. Both of them seemed to be, in fact, and for this reason Julian disliked them, though he kept an attentive eye on the girl in case at any time she should inadvertently reveal herself. For most of the time, however, she wore T-shirts over her bikini tops, which concealed her small breasts and rendered them uninteresting. Sometimes she wore bikini bottoms, and Julian tried hard to see if her pubic hair caused any impression on the fabric. He wasn't sure that it did.

Janus Brian continued to eat. He ate more than was merely necessary to avoid dying, he ate enough to lay down some fatty deposits, the first few subcutaneous cells were beginning to fill in a tentative reinstatement of his long-lost bulk. Almost daily his appetite increased, passing through the safety of dairy products to carbohydrates and even some protein. Half way through the second week of their three week (so long as the money lasted) holiday, Janus Brian was onto red meat. He even tried a small fillet steak in The Black Bear one evening, cooked rare. He managed half of it before sitting back and downing a double gin and tonic, gasping, with a look on his face of one who'd just come up from a long spell underwater, red eyed and breathless. Once, in Sam's Café, in a moment of utter gastronomic recklessness, he went for the London Grill, a platter of chops, rashers and offal rounded off with baked beans and tinned tomatoes in the midst of which Janus Brian was soon floundering.

His body, having closed down in order to make the best of the diet of alcohol and reconstituted savouries it had been fed for the last few years, was having trouble adapting to this new iron and protein and fat-rich diet. His digestive system generated great quantities of gas, so that Janus Brian was continually bubbling and burping, like a kettle coming to the boil. He was soon passing wind without a second thought; sitting in Sam's Café eating a buck rabbit, he would lean sideways slightly and let rip an anal eructation of table-shaking, floor-vibrating intensity, three or four times during a single meal. These solecisms, originally followed by a murmured apology, now passed without remark. Colette welcomed them, like the mythical sheikhs who considered the breaking of wind after a meal to be the highest possible compliment, they were signs of the reawakening of his body's metabolism.

'I'm really happy, dear,' he said to her one evening at the tent as he pawed his way through a packet of fish and chips, 'I never thought I'd be happy in this funny little town, but I am. You've made me happy.'

The evening was one of predictable tranquillity. In a summer of constantly reiterated weather when each day was a carbon copy of the one before, with a cloudless sky and a high, naked sun, the evenings likewise followed an identical pattern – long shadows, still air, dust, an uncomplicated sunset, the sun withdrawing with as little fuss as possible, shortly to return in the morning before the world had barely had a chance to cool down. Aldous had retreated to the tranquillity of the B & B. Julian was listening to the conversation from the comfort of the back seat of the car.

'I think that when we die,' Janus Brian went on, 'we return to that point in our lives when we were happiest, and we relive it for ever.' He paused while he worked on digesting a piece of fish, then he licked his shining fingers. 'In which case, I think that when I die, I will spend eternity eating fish and chips in Tewkesbury.'

Colette laughed.

'Either that,' he went on, 'or I will be watching Arnold Palmer on the eighteenth tee at Valderrama, with a jug of sangria and Mary . . .'

'I'm glad you're happy,' said Colette, 'perhaps you could look on this holiday as a fresh start.'

'No,' said Janus Brian flatly, 'I'm afraid that when all this is over and I'm back in that God-forsaken bungalow in that God-forsaken town, I know that within a couple of days I'll be back to where I was. I wish it wasn't true but there it is. This is nothing more than a respite, dear, it's not a new direction. It doesn't lead anywhere. I wish this holiday could go on for ever, but it won't. All things come to an end.'

'You mustn't talk like that, Janus,' said Colette, 'you can come away with us again next year, or before then . . .'

Julian, invisible in the car, winced.

'Next year? I doubt I'll be alive, dear. I'm rather astonished to find that I'm alive now, to be honest. When I'm in High Wycombe, alone in that bungalow, I sometimes sit there thinking, *if I'm dead, how would I actually know?* It's not like now. I'm definitely alive now. The fish and chips are telling me I'm alive. The chiming of the Abbey. You. But in that bungalow, there's nothing.'

'You need to move back to London,' Colette urged, while Janus Brian farted loudly, shifting position in the camping chair to ease the expulsion of gases, 'sell the bungalow and move back to London . . .'

Janus replied immediately and emphatically.

'No. I can't move back to London. That would be moving backwards. I have to go forwards, I can't go backwards.'

They'd been through all this before. Colette hoped that the happiness he was now experiencing would contrast so sharply with the loneliness of High Wycombe, that he would see sense and move back to London. She would have to wait and see.

'I think tomorrow I may go for a walk round the Abbey,' Janus went on. 'I'm not going to go back to religion or anything like that. I just really feel like walking round the building, looking at all the old tombs, all the old stuff that's in there . . .'

They were distracted by the arrival of a motorbike on the camp site, a rather loud, old motorbike that was driving slowly round and round the driveways.

'That's an old Vincent,' said Janus Brian, 'my word. Haven't seen one of those for years.'

'A what?'

'A Vincent motorbike. Don't make them any more. Not since the Japs came along. Reg had one years ago.'

Janus Brian was having to shout because the motorbike had slowed to a halt on the drive not far from their tent. The driver seemed to be looking at them. He was wearing an old-fashioned crash helmet with goggles and had black leather gauntlets on his hands.

'It's a bloody noisy one,' replied Colette, 'no wonder they stopped making them.'

The motorbike gave a sudden noisy rev, then steered towards Janus and Colette as they sat in the doorway of the tent.

'Hallo,' said Janus Brian, 'he's coming over.'

The motorcyclist slowly drove his machine right up to the tent, until his front wheel was almost touching Colette's foot. She was mildly amused. The motorcyclist killed his engine and dismounted. As he stood, goggled, beneath the silver dome of his crash helmet, he burst into a cackle of laughter and whooped.

'Janus?' said Colette, breathless with disbelief.

The motorcyclist unbuckled his helmet and lifted his goggles, then lifted the whole lot as one from his head.

'It *is* you,' said Colette, seeing her son standing before her. The helmet that had formerly contained his head was now under his arm, and he slowly pulled off his gauntlets. It took Colette a few moments to be sure it was Janus, because he looked very different. The beard and long hair that had enveloped his face for several years was gone. As a result his face looked small and raw, almost embryonic. The short hair Janus had cut himself, Colette could tell by the ridged, patchy quality of the cut.

'Where the hell did you get that?' she indicated with her eyes that she meant the motorbike.

'This? Just a bloke I know. He wanted to get rid of it. Threw in the helmet and gloves and goggles for nothing. She's my little darling. What do you think of her, Janus Brian, I'll take you out for a ride on her later.'

'No thanks,' Janus Brian laughed weakly, not stirring from his chair, nor hardly looking up from the mess of his fish and chips, unsurprised by his nephew's arrival, as he was unsurprised by everything.

'You're not staying here, surely.' Colette said to her son.

'Why not? I've brought the small tent with me.'

'You can't stay here.'

'But you said on your card, woman. "Come and visit".'

'No I didn't. I didn't. Not now. Not this minute. I didn't mean that.'

'Oh,' said Janus, 'In that case my feelings are rather hurt. Why shouldn't I come on holiday with my family? I've got every right.'

'But Aldous . . . daddy – he would be so upset to see you here. He would be devastated, to be frank. It would ruin the holiday for him, just as he's starting to relax . . .'

'Where is he anyway?'

'He's at a bed and breakfast in the town.'

'What? So Janus Brian . . . you don't mean Janus Brian is sleeping here in the tent.'

'Yes. And Julian in the car.'

Janus gave a sigh of disbelief.

'I told you he was up to something didn't I? He's finally got you into bed with him.'

'Don't be so filthy-minded, Janus,' said Colette.

'You're the one who's filthy . . .'

'Don't make smutty remarks, boy,' said Janus Brian through a mouth full of batter.

'What's it got to do with you?'

'Everything.'

'Don't talk to your uncle like that.'

'I'll talk to him how I like.'

'Oh Christ.'

'What's the matter with you?'

'I can't believe it. Just as things were starting to work out. Just as Janus Brian was starting to feel better and daddy was starting to look cheerful, you have to come along out of the blue and louse everything up.'

'I haven't done anything . . .'

'You haven't been here five minutes and we're already rowing. I think you should turn that machine around and drive straight back to London, straight back to where you came from.'

'Too late,' said Janus brightly, 'I've already paid for a night from that nice old gentleman in the office. He said I had the pick of the site. I can camp anywhere I like. And, looking around, I chance to see that there is an ideal spot for a tent just there,' he pointed to an area of empty grass next to the car.

'No, Janus,' said Colette, pleading, as though against an act of wilful cruelty, 'you can't stay here. I won't have it.'

Janus teased his mother for a little while longer until finally he agreed to go. After all, he'd only come over to the tent once he was certain his father wasn't around, and now he quickly mounted his motorbike, kick-started it, and trundled off, his mother recanting, 'You don't have to go this minute,' she called, 'I didn't mean . . .'

She watched her son as he returned to the crunchy drive, and then slowly trundled around the camp site. It soon became evident that he wasn't heading for the exit. Slowly the awfulness of what Janus was doing dawned on her, as he passed out of sight behind distant caravans, emerging on the far side from behind the toilet block, he drew up on an empty patch of grass and began assembling his tent.

'The cheeky swine,' said Colette, 'he's putting his tent up over there so he can spy on us. He's in full view. What'll Aldous say?'

'Shall I go over and tell him to shift his butt?' said Janus Brian.

'It wouldn't do any good. He'd just laugh. Oh God. When Aldous comes over in the morning, what'll happen then?'

What happened was nothing. Janus spent the morning sitting on the grass outside his tent, no bigger, from Colette's perspective, than a cat, and Aldous came over at about half past nine, bright and cheerful as he always was since moving into the bed and breakfast. He made no secret of the fact that he was really enjoying himself there, especially those meticulous little breakfasts Mrs Brown served him. A night of pure silence and solitude, then the descent to a table of white linen, toast in a silver toast rack, fried eggs and bacon on white porcelain, tea in a china pot, jars of marmalade. It was civilised and solitary, and Aldous had experienced these conditions rarely in his life.

And Janus remained at his tent, invisible to Aldous who would not, from that range, have picked him out from the dozens of other nondescript tents and caravans that populated the distant areas of the camp site. As Aldous merrily chatted, Colette was conscious of her son watching, and became aware, instantly, that this was to become part of a larger strategy of torment by observation. Janus watched his family continually, becoming a voyeur, almost, of his own life.

Colette, observed, felt continually intruded upon and yet was powerless to do anything about it. She felt guilty for not telling Aldous that his son was so close by and watching his every move. She felt almost as if she'd been adulterous, and felt a strong urge to confess, but resisted, because if her husband had caught wind of his son's presence, the holiday would have been ruined entirely.

She stole glances at distant Janus whenever Aldous wasn't looking, and noticed something odd about him, something she couldn't quite define at first, but it looked as though her son was wearing a mask. Sitting at his tent, staring in their direction, holding a mask to his face. Of all the odd things Janus had done in his life, had he done anything odder? What sort of mask was it? But she realized it was not a mask but a pair of binoculars. He was watching them through binoculars.

Colette felt furious. Whenever Aldous's back was turned she gestured frantically at Janus for him to put the binoculars away. She made a rejection gesture of two hands sweeping away invisible nonsense, and the gesture drew an immediate response from Janus, a friendly wave, a thumbs-up sign that showed not only how alert he was to Colette's movements, but how much he seemed to be enjoying himself.

He was enjoying the blindness he had instilled in his father, a quality he intensified over the coming days by approaching ever closer to Aldous's lines of sight, while remaining unseen. When the family traipsed off into the town, Janus would follow, sometimes only a few feet behind, resplendently invisible to

Aldous. Daringly he would sometimes sidestep through alleyways and shops to emerge in front of the party, and Colette's heart would jump into her mouth as Janus passed before them, one amongst a crowd, a ghost, sniggering, as his father gazed indifferently into shop windows. Once he went on ahead, waited in a bakery for the family to approach, emerging so suddenly and close to Aldous that he could have knocked him over, and then passing swiftly. Colette could hardly believe that Aldous had not seen him, and looked at him carefully, looking for any sign that her husband had been disturbed by a subliminally caught glimpse of his son. But there was nothing in her husband's face but that sunburnt, lazy, relaxed countenance he'd borne for the last week and a half.

In the evenings Janus would come over to the tent after his father had gone to the bed and breakfast.

'You'll be going home tomorrow, won't you Janus,' said Colette.

'Actually', Janus said, 'I was thinking of staying here for some time. I could live here through to September. I like it here. I really do like it here. I think I'll live here for ever.'

'Janus, you're going back tomorrow. Just go away. We don't want you here.'

'Who doesn't want me here?'

'No one wants you here.'

'Janus Brian?' said Janus, 'Do you want me here?'

Janus Brian looked as though he was about to say he would be delighted if Janus stayed, but then, remembering Colette's predicament, thought better of it.

'If it's bothering your mother, I think you should go.'

'Julian?'

Julian, sitting in the car, pretended not to hear. Janus repeated. 'Julian!'

'Don't ask Julian, it's not fair,' said Colette, 'just tell me why you're here. Is it just to torment us or what?'

Janus gave one of his incredulous laughs.

'I'm on holiday. Like you. I'm enjoying the charms of this little Tudor town. I'm enjoying the Abbey and the Avon. My only criticism is that we are in a place so far from the sea. We could hardly be further from the sea here.'

'The sea's for kids,' said Janus Brian, somewhat despondently.

'A human being needs water. Eight pints of it every day. Anything less and we're little more than caskets of dust. Booze doesn't count.'

'I like water,' said Colette. 'Doctors say we're ninety per cent water don't they?'

'Yes, except in Janus Brian's case they say he's ninety per cent gin.'

'Don't be rude to your uncle.'

'Why not?'

'Because he's your uncle.'

Janus gave a cackly laugh and patted Janus Brian's pate.

'Sorry your grace,' he said.

When Janus had returned to his tent, Janus Brian said, 'You worship that kid don't you.'

'I do not,' said Colette immediately, 'why do you say that?'

'Just the way you talk to him. It's your manner. You worship him and he knows it. He knows he can make you do or say anything. He works you like a puppet.'

'Don't talk such rubbish,' said Colette, 'he's my son. For all his faults – and he's got plenty, I'll be the first to admit, he's still my son.'

'You've got other children.'

'I had noticed.'

'You don't worship Julian,' he lowered his voice in case Julian should hear.

'I do worship Julian,' said Colette, realizing, as she said it, it was no longer true. She worshipped Julian as a child, as she'd worshipped all her children. But he was no longer a child. Colette could never understand where children went when they became adults.

'I worship all my children,' the sentence hung in the air for a while, both parties examining it closely to see if there was any truth in it.

'All your children,' said Janus Brian, 'have a sort of arrogance about them. I don't know what it is. Janus, of course, is arrogant beyond compare, but the others, too; James, Juliette, Julian as well, in his way. It must be something to do with how you've always told them they are better than other people.'

'But Janus is better than most other people. How many people can play the piano like he can? Perhaps a handful in the whole world – that is, if he'd kept it up, if he'd developed properly instead of throwing it all away, he could have been the greatest pianist of his generation. It's true . . .' Colette raised her voice to cover Janus Brian's mocking laughter, 'I heard it from one of his own tutors, years after he left the Academy . . . And what does he do now? Boozes his life away and plays plink-plonk jazz in pubs. That is why Aldous won't have anything to do with him . . .'

'I'll grant you that Janus has a special talent,' said Janus Brian, 'I'll certainly grant you that. There are, as you say, very few people around who can play like he does. But to play the piano truly well you have to know something about life, and I think that Janus does not yet know enough about life. He knows he doesn't know it, and that's why he drinks and why he's so arrogant, to cover up that profound ignorance of his.'

'You're going to say he needs a wife, aren't you?'

'He needs to have found someone, and to have lost someone, that's all. He's done neither.'

Julian's observations of the Birmingham family opposite were becoming obsessive. Some days the daughter of the tent, still oblivious to Julian's existence, played Swingball with her little brother, and once, the whole family gathered on the dead grass for a game of badminton doubles. Briefly their territorial range expanded right up to the skirts of Julian's own tent, the shuttlecock claiming new ground each time a wayward shot sent it toppling to earth out of reach of the players. Julian withdrew cautiously into the mouth of the tent in case that feathered ball should somehow hook him into a relationship with the family. The thought of friendship with the daughter was too terrifying to contemplate, the little brother also, with his fashionable gear, was menacingly confident. But Julian loved to watch them, the girl especially, even though he felt no desire for her, but her bodily presence was something he felt impelled to constantly monitor.

It was something of a relief when the fishermen arrived. They'd been deposited there by their father in a swish car, a

Jaguar XJ6. Two loutish-looking youths with fair hair and red skin, permanently unbuttoned shirts revealing shallow chests, voluminous trousers. They were a source of mild, localized disturbance in that corner of the camp site, laughing loudly late at night, leaving empty beer cans outside their tent door. They were, it gradually transpired, keen anglers who spent their nights on the banks of the Avon hoping to hook wild salmon, trout, or whatever breeds of fish swam in those waters. They would usually return in the small hours of the morning, belching and farting, sniggering and stuttering, talking in loud whispers. By day their tent was a sealed prism of nylon in which they slept deeply, emerging in the late afternoon, bleary and phlegm-filled.

One evening adult presence was absent from that corner of the camp site. The two Birmingham kids were chuckling in the porch of their frame tent, the night-anglers were smoking and drinking Harp in the mouth of their little bivouac, and Julian was writing his novel next to the car. About fifty feet of dead grass separated the Birmingham children from the night-anglers. How brave of that little boy then, to strut over to them, puffing out his little tank-topped chest, brandishing his green flares and saying

'Would you like to play cards with us?'

Suicide, Julian thought. To go over to those angling toughs, a snivelling little kid, and invite them to play cards. Pure suicide. And yet these large fair-haired boys did not smack the little one in the chops, stamp on his face, or kick him in the bottom. They didn't even tweak his nose and jeer at him. What they said was

'Yeah, alright.'

And they popped their smouldering dog ends into the open mouths of their beer cans and sauntered over to the Birmingham children's tent. And they played cards. They played cards inside the tent. Julian could hear them. It all began with restrained formality. Quite soon, however, the laughter came. Giggling from the girl. Eager, excited yelps from the little boy. Manly, gruff guffaws from the anglers. They got on so well. Julian was amazed.

From that time on the anglers and the Birmingham children went everywhere together. The anglers lost interest in fishing and instead became keen on Swingball and Badminton. A frisbee was produced, which extended even further the territorial claim of these people, a new outpost added to their empire every time the frisbee floated into uncharted regions. The anglers were introduced to the Birmingham parents, who seemed to like them. Julian could rarely make out the words of their conversations. Instead he got a sense of their flavour, which was nervously jocular. And he was fascinated to see where this friendship would lead. Was the girl a virgin? Almost certainly yes. Was she about to lose her virginity? It was a possibility. It amazed Julian how these fishing yobs, having hooked not a salmon but a sweet young girl, had become gentlemanly in an almost old-fashioned way. But surely the taking of this young girl must have been high on these youths minds. The problem was to escape both the parents and the little brother, and then to sort it out between themselves which one was to have her. A mountain of obstacles. But one evening they seemed to have managed it. To Julian's intense astonishment, though he couldn't be sure, the girl and just one of the fishermen were alone together in the tent. He saw the rest of the family go off in the car, and he saw one of the fishermen saunter off alone into the town. The girl was alone in her tent, and just one of the fishermen was alone in his. And then, after perhaps half an hour of silence from each tent, the girl emerged from hers and skipped, ever so self-consciously, in her bikini bottoms and a yellow pullover, to the fisherman's tent, and entered.

Julian's heart faltered. He could not believe what he had just seen. This demure young virgin had entered the narrow space of the fisherman's tent, skimpily clad. Surely she wasn't going to give herself to such a boorish lout. Julian almost felt like marching over and ordering her back to her own tent. He felt like telling his mother and Janus Brian what he had just seen. He felt like sneaking over to the fisherman's tent and listening at the wall.

But at that moment he was distracted by the arrival of his older brother, who'd come over on his motorbike.

Colette had observed that evening, with relief, that Janus was packing away his tent and was loading up his motorbike. She was glad because she didn't think she could continue to deceive Aldous for much longer, and that the cruel trick they had been forced to play on him would soon be over. She assumed that he'd come to say his goodbyes. Janus Brian was dozing in the tent. He'd taken recently to wearing only his underpants while at the tent, the heat was so intense. To protect his scalp he wore a small, perky trilby hat with a feather in it. Though shading Janus Brian's scalp, the heavy tweed of this garment caused the sweat to pour down his face. Janus Brian also continually wore sun shades that clipped onto his normal spectacles, and which could be raised and lowered according to the prevailing light conditions. When raised these twin dark lenses sat above and beyond his face, like a pair of cartoon eyebrows. And this was how he reposed. Socks, underpants, glasses with raised shades, tweed trilby. Exhausted.

When Janus came over to the tent, however, it was not to say his goodbye, but to announce that he was about to relocate his tent, and pitch it next door to their own.

'I'd like to be here to welcome my father when he arrives in the morning.'

He settled his motorbike on its stand, and began pulling at the straps of his bundled-up tent.

'I completely forbid it, Janus,' said Colette, 'if you put your tent here I'll call the office and get them to throw you out.'

'But I've paid. I want to live here for ever.'

Colette could see that, for the first time since his arrival in the town, Janus had been drinking.

'Don't be ridiculous.'

'I'm not being ridiculous.'

Janus had unstrapped a part of the tent. Colette got up and replaced the strap. Janus laughed.

'I'm begging you, Janus, go away from us. Go back to London. Why don't you go and see Bill?'

Janus gave a loud, single-syllable laugh of derision.

'Bill? Why should I want to see that bastard?'

'He and Juliette have split up. Didn't you know? I should think he's lonely.'

Stupid of Colette to suggest that, she realized shortly afterwards. Estrangement from Bill had been responsible, at least in part, for the relatively even keel Janus had managed to keep for the time of his suspended sentence. But she was desperate. She would have suggested anything. It did not occur to her that there had been a falling out.

'I do know,' said Janus, 'the bastard blames me for breaking up the marriage. I tried to kill him last week, but I chickened out at the last minute.'

'But he's your friend . . .'

'Bill? My friend? Don't make me laugh. That cardboard cut-out jumped-up Marxist? That two-bit artist, supermarket butcher, scribbler, dauber, talentless prick, that rambling, asthmatic shit-head? That pseudoLeninist mock-Stalinist, sham-Trotskyite, fungus-faced, fungus-backed, fungus-bollocked, cack-handed, simple-brained, colour-blind, pox-ridden block-and-cleaver merchant? That spineless, spleenless, mindless, skinless, boneless, brainless, prickless, pithless, bloodless, eyeless, fingerless, so-called artist? I wouldn't be seen dead with him. I'd like to chop his head off. I'd like to gut him and feed his liver to the Scipplecat. I'd like to crush his bones into powder. I'd like to roll his skin up into a ball and throw it out of the window. That's what I'd like to do to my so-called friend. Friend? He doesn't know the meaning of the word. Do you know what he does now? He sucks up to footballers in The Quiet Woman. He's never watched a bloody football match in his life before now and he goes every week to the Spurs to watch his friends playing. He drools all over them. Gets driven around in their Ford BMWs. He doesn't know the meaning of the word friendship. Blames me for the breakup of his marriage. Did I drag him to the pub every night? No, he used to come round and collect me. You saw him didn't you? He'd sneak away from Juliette and come round to Fernlight Avenue. It was he who wrote me letters nearly every week saying 'when are we going to get pissed? When are we going to get pissed?' If I ever went round to Polperro Gardens I wasn't allowed in. I slept there on the roses the other night. His precious fucking marriage. He punched me in the face. If that's what friendship means I'm through with it. I'm finished with it. It's all just putrid back-scratching. So vile. So false. Falseness. People are false. They're not real. They never

247

let you know what they are thinking. They won't let you know who they really are. You're all just puppets. You're all clockwork. Everyone. You, you're a dummy aren't you. You're a fucking waxwork . . .'

Janus went on like this, frightening his mother with an increasingly disturbed stream of invective (all through his speech she'd been saying, quietly 'no, Janus, stop, stop') and Janus didn't stop until Janus Brian emerged from the tent, naked but for his socks, pants and his tweed, feathered trilby, his spectacles with their Groucho Marx eyebrows. He tottered confidently from the tent straight over to the motorbike where this conversation had taken place, almost tripping on the guy ropes, and said 'Scram, sunbeam.'

'I beg your pardon?' said Janus, halted in his diatribe, all indignation.

'You heard. Buzz off. Vamoose. Skedaddle.'

Janus Brian's body was creamy white, with red at the extremities and a scarlet V at the neck, marking the ghost of a shirt. His absurd appearance somehow outranked his nephew's ranting, trumped his drunkenness.

'What's it got to do with you?'

'You heard the lady, if you don't beat it I'll give you a smack in the mush.'

Janus, collecting himself, laughed sarcastically. Janus Brian went on 'I'll give you such a wallop in the cake-hole you'll be shitting your teeth, I'll give you such a smack in the gearbox you'll turn inside out.'

'You're an old man,' said Janus, patronizingly, 'and I don't want to hurt you, so you just toddle off back to the tent, have some more gin, and let me talk with my mother . . .'

'You need to show her some more respect, buster,' Janus Brian said, 'you think you can pull these cockamamie stunts on your mother – I'm not having it. The game's up. You think you're a big shot but I can remember you before you'd learnt to piss in the pot . . .'

That hat. Now Colette remembered where she'd seen it before. It was almost the same as the hat Kojak wore on television.

'Janus,' she said, meaning her brother, 'don't be silly.'

There was an awkward pause, where no one seemed to know

what to do next. The younger Janus was waiting, it appeared, for his uncle's next move, but his uncle didn't seem to have thought that far ahead.

Suddenly, struck by an idea, Janus Brian crept swiftly over to his nephew's motorbike, his Vincent HRD, which stood, leaning slightly on its rest, a few paces away. He put both his hands on the machine and leant his weight against it.

'Scram,' he said, 'or this goes over.'

Janus seemed simultaneously amused and outraged by this act. Sensing the sincerity of his uncle's threat, he went over to the other side of the motorbike, and braced himself against it, ready for his uncle's push.

'Who the hell do you think you are?' Janus kept saying, increasingly indignant that someone should stand so firmly against him. Janus Brian seemed to be concentrating, feeling up and down the length of the motorbike, perusing it, stroking it. Then suddenly he pushed.

'Hey,' said Janus, in an admonishing, now-let's-not-be-silly voice, though he hardly needed to push against Janus Brian, whose slight body was barely able to stir the motorbike at all. Janus and Janus faced each other across the motorbike, the elder leaning steeply into the machine, finding at last a rush of strength enough to send the bike lurching towards his nephew, who then had to lean in opposition to stop the bike from falling. It shocked the younger Janus that his uncle had found that strength and had the will to carry out his threat. He was silently furious.

Janus Brian felt that he'd made his point and retired to one of the camping chairs, where Colette had also seated herself. He had a glow of satisfaction about him, as he picked up that day's newspaper that had been folded next to the chair, and began reading it, pointedly oblivious of his nephew's existence.

'No one's ever stood up to him before, that's his trouble,' he said to his sister, 'if you ask me all he needs is a bloody good whipping.'

Meanwhile younger Janus mounted his motorbike and spurred her into life. It was twilight. He flicked on the head-light, illuminating Janus Brian and Colette in its beam. They continued to talk quietly, ignoring him. Janus, meanwhile, caught sight of Julian, who'd been watching the whole incident from a safe distance. Janus winked at his little brother and said, 'I'm going to run that bastard over,' in a way that seemed to invite Julian's approval. Julian, however, was thinking about the telephone by the site office. He was thinking about another emergency call.

The motorbike gave a shrill scream, and shot forward at such a pace its front wheel rose into the air, tipping Janus off its seat and onto his bottom. The motorbike continued, riderless, missing Janus Brian and the tent by several feet, and headed off on its own swiftly snaking course across the grass towards the angler's small tent, which it crashed into. Caught in the tangle of guy ropes and poles the bike somersaulted and fell on its side. The tent was writhing as though it contained frantic escapologists. A man was screaming.

When eventually the fisherman emerged, red faced and tangle-haired, he looked about the camp site with incomprehension, as though his tent, having been picked up by a tornado, had landed in another country. He looked at the fallen motorbike. Then he saw Janus, who by now was standing. Then he looked back inside the tent.

'Look what you've done,' the fisherman said, his voice almost a whisper, shaking with fright, not the voice of gruff admonishment they were expecting at all, 'look what you've done. Look what you've done.'

Julian was already on his way to the phone box.

The fisherman carefully drew back the flaccid material of the tent further to reveal the reclining, unconscious head of the young girl. She was bare shouldered, and the fisherman, rather guiltily, revealed as little of this fact as he could. But her face was enough information. It was cut badly. The lips were as thick as plums. Blood was trickling from her nose. Then she gave a moan and ejected a spray of blood. The first sign that she was alive.

'You'd better go now,' said Colette to Janus, 'Go now, quickly.'

Without a further word Janus ran to his motorbike, lifted it with difficulty, and rode off.

The fisherman was too concerned, too frightened, about the girl, to notice.

'I told you,' Janus Brian said to Colette, joining her at the fisherman's tent, where the girl was now sitting up and crying through a mouthful of blood, 'I told you ages ago that you should have left him to me. I could have sorted him out.'

Graham's Flat
Don't know.

in a time of drought

Dear Janus

So, who saved who? Do you remember? I thought I'd better write and thank you, in case it was you that saved me. If it was me that saved you, I expect a letter in return, thanking me, plus a postal order for £10.

Will you believe me now when I say my drinking days are over? It is not as I would wish it, but you can see what happens. It's the booze that's causing the asthma, which means one drink and I'm short of breath. In effect, if I drink, I drown!! Thought I'd better set things straight, because I had the impression that you were expecting a revival of our great drinking sessions in the near future. Alas, it cannot be. If my condition is permanent I do not know. As you can imagine, the prospect of a lifetime on the shores of sobriety, while the great ocean of drunkenness lies before me, is one I can barely tolerate. In fact, I can't tolerate it at all. Even writing about it now is causing me to weep. I'm sorry to say I'm missing the bottle far more than I'm missing your sister (don't tell her that). Still, we are all prisoners of our bodies, when we are sober, at least.

As you can see I am no longer resident at Polperro Gardens. Had to move out sharpish once Juliette had left. Left most of my stuff there, which the landlady will no doubt flog in lieu of rent.

Don't really think it would be a good idea for us to meet, Janus, old friend, life-saver though thou art. At least, not for a while. I've moved into Graham's flat. I know you hate him, but he had space, and he's an old square who'll make sure I steer clear of the hard stuff.

So, so long, old buddy. No doubt our paths shall cross one

day in the future, until then, adios. By the way, I don't suppose you'll take much notice of this, you old boozer, but you could think about going on the wagon yourself eh? What do you think?

Yours sincerely

Bill

39 Cedar Way
High Wycombe
Bucks

27th October 1976

Dear Colette,

I am writing to thank you for the sensitivity and graciousness with which you handled the events of last Saturday. Since our relationship has become somewhat unsavoury over the last few years, I was anticipating that the experience might have been rather less agreeable than it was. In fact, you will not be surprised to learn, I had doubts about coming, and it was really only at the insistence of Lesley that I made the journey to Fernlight Avenue at all. But I needn't have worried. You made me feel welcome, and I am grateful for that.

It took the events of the funeral to make me realise how much Janus Brian must have meant to you. Lesley, in fact, has been too upset since the funeral to talk about it, which is why he is presently unable to write to you. You will remember that it was Lesley who discovered your brother's body. An awful shock. Sadly it has taken Janus's death to make Lesley realize how much his little brother meant to him.

We are both praying for him.

I hope now that you and I, Colette, can start afresh. We have little time on this Earth. Let us not spend it in petty dispute or trivial altercation.

Yours affectionately

Madeleine

Part Four

14

'I think you're very brave, Juliette, to have the party here,' said Veronica as she peeled the layers of crumpled foil from a clutch of cocktail sausages, 'considering everything.'

Veronica was wearing a maxi-dress fastened down the front by a long line of pea-sized buttons, the whole thing patterned with myriad forget-me-nots. Veronica's tall, full figure was somewhat lost within this column of fabric, though a square neckline revealed the beginnings of a smooth, unblemished cleavage.

'Brave?' said Juliette, 'Oh, you mean Bill. Him and Boris have met before.'

'And?'

'They're not exactly best friends, but they tolerate each other.'

'I still think it's a funny thing to do,' said Rita, who was busy with another foil-wrapped object, the loaf-shape of which puzzled Juliette and Veronica, 'having your twenty-first birthday party at your ex-husband's flat.'

The phrase 'ex-husband' still sounded odd to Juliette, even though Bill had been thus for nearly a year. But then she'd always felt odd referring to Bill as her husband anyway. She'd never felt properly married, being so young, and after that perfunctory ceremony in the Civic Centre with cheese sandwiches and sweet Spanish wine at Fernlight Avenue afterwards, then residence in a rented upstairs flat at Polperro Gardens, which had never seemed really theirs. Looking back on it now, on the evening of her twenty-first birthday, her marriage had seemed as ephemeral and as trivial as a passing teenage obsession with a pop group might seem – all-absorbing at the time, the reason for life itself, yet in hindsight a baffling, bewilderingly pointless act of misdirected devotion.

'It was Graham's idea,' said Juliette, 'Boris's place is too small and the walls are too thin.'

'Did he ask Bill first, we wonder,' said Veronica, with a half wink to Rita.

Graham's flat was over a lingerie shop on Windhover Hill Parade. It had one large living room which overlooked the High Street through two tall sash windows, the view partially obscured at the moment by roofers' scaffolding. Being adjacent to the zebra crossing the room was lit by the endlessly repeated glow of a Belisha beacon, which in the evening cast the shadow of a cheeseplant huge on the back wall. 'Free disco lighting,' Graham had bragged when persuading Juliette to use the flat. Bill now lived there as a sort of sub-tenant, occupying a child-sized bedroom down one of the narrow, twisting passageways. He and Graham seemed to fit in well together, and with the flat. There was a loose, scuffed, bohemian atmosphere to the place. A grotesque work of art hung on one wall, halfway between a painting and a sculpture, in which a figure that could have been a First World War soldier in helmet and gas mask, rendered as a bas-relief in white plaster, loomed phantom-like from a black background. On another wall hung a gallery of Russian icons, Bill's work. Juliette recognized some of the images that had hung on the walls at Polperro Gardens. Against the longest wall there was a long, soft, ripped couch. A record player with stereo speakers as big as fridges, which Graham never played above talking level, filled a corner. By the windows was an extended dining table, and it was on this that Juliette, Veronica Price and Rita Michaelangeli were arranging food and drinks for the party to come.

'Have they gone to the same pub?' said Veronica.

'Who?'

'Bill and Boris.'

'Bill is in The Quiet Woman, naturally,' said Juliette, 'and Boris said he was going to The Red Lion with Scott and some others. They won't meet until they're here, by which time the party will be in full swing and they won't even notice each other.'

Rita had unwrapped the mysterious object by this time, the result of a long and careful process, peeling away layer upon layer of foil, to reveal a rectangular cube of something that looked like not-quite-set plaster, with piped decorations along the edges, a row of sliced, stuffed olives along the top and whole hazelnuts at the corners.

'Is that something you can eat?' said Veronica, with genuine puzzlement.

'Of course it's something you can eat,' Rita snapped, though her face remained serene.

'What is it?' said Juliette who, with Veronica, was now bending down and peering closely at the object, as archaeologists examining a recently unearthed ivory casket.

'It's a sandwich gateau, and I spent all afternoon making it, so don't take the piss.'

'How did you make it?' said Juliette.

'You take a wholemeal loaf,' Rita began, with the eagerness of someone who'd been waiting all day for this moment, 'and then you slice it up. Then you make a white sauce and divide it into three. To one third you add salmon and cucumber, to another third you add cheese and chives and to the third third you add a dollop of Marmite. You spread these mixtures on alternating slices of the loaf, then you reassemble the whole thing, chill it, then coat it with a mixture of curd cheese and milk.

'Really,' said Veronica doubtfully, 'that sounds absolutely . . .'

'Disgusting,' Juliette finished with a laugh.

'It's one of my mother's recipes,' said Rita, bewildered by her friends' lack of gateau-enthusiasm, 'we have it every time someone has a birthday . . .'

'Talking of ex-husbands,' said Juliette, who, having noticed a tremor in Rita's lower lip, was anxious to draw the conversation away from the gateau, 'Yours, Veronica, is in The Quiet Woman with mine. I could say you were equally brave . . .'

Veronica gave one of her head-back, open-mouthed, shimmering laughs.

'Why on Earth should I be afraid of meeting Hugo?'

'I've heard that he'll be bringing his latest dolly bird with him.'

'Has she got her parents' permission?' said Rita.

'My dears,' said Veronica, her voice still rich with laughter, 'there is no person on Earth I could care less about meeting than that oafish, pot-bellied, strumpet-screwing lout of an ex-husband of mine, nor the latest sixth-form Lolita he's bamboozled into bed.'

'I think you should care,' said Rita, 'he needs taking down a peg or two, the way he treats women . . .'

Juliette caught the look that passed between Veronica and Rita, the intimate look of one-time adversaries now reconciled. The women who had once been rivals for the same man, and who now both despised him. Juliette felt momentarily envious. Was there a special closeness in friendships that form between former enemies?

'I wouldn't blame you Veronica,' said Juliette, 'if you wanted to attack him or anything. Do feel free, it's my twenty-first after all.'

'Do you think my tits show too much,' said Rita whose top was a diaphanous, black satin blouse decorated with stars. It was tied at the back and kept in place by a single bow knot. The neckline was deep, the sleeves high and frilly.

'If I was you I'd make sure I didn't lift my elbows too high,' said Veronica, peering in through the capacious sleeve.

'And that knot looks a bit tempting,' said Juliette, 'I can just imagine someone pulling one of the strings as you walk past.'

'Would it just undo?'

'Yes,' said Rita, who hadn't considered the possibility before, 'and if the knot undoes the whole top just collapses. I knew I should have put a bra on.'

'Haven't you got one on?' said Veronica in wonder.

'No,' said Rita, proudly.

'Very impressive, Rita. Neither have I, but you wouldn't think I had, would you?' She looked down at herself, then pulled her neckline forward and peeped in, giving a disappointed shrug.

'How can you say that, Veronica,' said Juliette, 'you look like Mae West from here.'

'Kind of you to say so, darling, kind of you to say so.'

'I feel stupid being the only one wearing a bra. Shall I take it off?'

The others murmured negatives while Rita, suddenly self-conscious, began redoing the knot at the back of her blouse, double tying it, asking for safety pins, requesting that the other two tug at her redone knot to see if it would hold, then deciding that it was too tight and restricting her breathing. When finally the blouse seemed secure Juliette said 'I'll just go and see how my sausage goulash is doing,' and skipped towards the kitchen.

'I think I'll get my Stilton mousse out of the fridge,' said Veronica, following Juliette.

After some stirring of pots and adjusting of gas rings, the trio returned to the living room. Rita suggested it might be time to open a bottle of wine.

'I suppose we could have some,' said Veronica, 'I hope everyone brings a bottle. Where did all these come from?'

'Graham gets a discount at Angad's,' said Juliette, 'him and Bill clubbed together and bought all this.'

'Won't last long,' said Rita in a tone of grim prophecy, 'not once Bill and that lot are back.'

'They won't get here for ages,' said Juliette, selecting a bottle and applying a corkscrew, 'they'll be the last. We'll have drunk it all by then . . .'

'I'm not so sure, Juliette,' said Veronica in a playful tone, 'I think I see what's going on here . . .'

'What's going on?' The cork came out with a creak and a pop.

'Graham persuading you to use the flat, then buying in all this booze, what does it look like to you, Rita?'

'What?' said Rita, who hadn't been following the conversation.

'It looks to me like Graham, sweet old thing, is trying to engineer some sort of reconciliation.'

'Me and Bill?' said Juliette, almost with disgust, 'No, not a chance. Anyway, Boris will be here soon. Perhaps Graham's trying to do something for you?'

'With Hugo? You must be joking.'

There was general laughter.

'Oh what a summer that was. What a silly, sultry summer,' said Veronica.

She meant the summer of the year before, the drought summer, during which the two marriages, hers and Juliette's, had effectively ended.

Thinking about such things inevitably led Veronica to her next question.

'I'm presuming Janus will not be here.'

'I hope not,' said Juliette.

'Does he know about it?'

'No.' Juliette said this with immediate certainty. Over the years she had become skilled at keeping things secret from Janus, 'Anyway, he's on permanent nightshift at the hospital . . .'

'Hospital?'

'Didn't you know? He's got a job at the East Edmonton Hospital, where we were all born . . .'

'I was born in Oxford, if you don't mind,' said Veronica.

'He must have been there for about a year now . . .'

'He's not still living at home is he, not with your poor old mother and father?'

Juliette gave one of her despairing, eyes-to-heaven looks.

'He is. Mum can't bring herself to throw him out for some reason, you'd think after last summer – you heard what happened when they were on holiday?'

The two women nodded.

'Mum says he's turned over a new leaf since then, and he's got this job at the hospital wheeling people around. He put himself on permanent nightshift, she says, so that he doesn't have any opportunities to go out drinking. Mum says he's got a girlfriend now, a nurse or something, though she's never met her.'

'So that's why we never see him in the pub any more, I thought it was because he fell out with Bill.'

'That as well. He doesn't go out at all now, he sleeps all day at home, gets up in the evening, goes to work, comes home in the morning, goes to bed around midday, or early afternoon, and then wakes up to go to work at night, I think his shift starts at ten.'

'Permanently?'

'Permanently, for the last few months anyway.'

'How can he stand it? I couldn't stand it, could you Rita?'

'No,' said Rita.

'At least it's keeping him on the straight and narrow,' said Juliette, 'he only just escaped a spell in prison after that incident in Tewkesbury.'

'Did the police never catch up with him?'

'No. Luckily he'd given a false name at the camp site office – John Speke, mum said, and the police could never trace the motorbike, as far as they knew it was registered to a man in Cornwall who'd been dead for five years. We never did find out where that motorbike came from, or where it went for that matter.'

'He has the luck of the devil, your brother, doesn't he,' said Veronica, 'he just does what he wants and gets away with it . . .'

'No one can get away with it for ever,' said Rita, still the grim prophetess.

'But if he really has turned over a new leaf . . .' began Veronica.

'And got a girlfriend,' said Rita, 'that would be a novelty . . .'

'. . . things must be easier for your mum and dad,' Veronica concluded.

'It just worries me,' said Juliette, 'if he has to put himself on permanent nights to keep himself off the booze . . . it's not the same thing as giving up drink is it? It's more like building a dam to hold back a river. The water builds up and up behind the ramparts, then eventually it spills over. As for the girlfriend, I'll believe it when I see it. More likely he's off on one of his infatuations with someone who's not interested in him. It'll be Angelica all over again. And I've heard stories from people connected with the hospital, that he drinks on the job . . .'

'No . . .' came the amazed negatives from the two women.

'. . . think what it must be like portering for a hospital through the night. There can't be that much work. He spends hours sitting in the porters' mess taking swigs of rum from his locker when no one's looking. That's what I've heard anyway. And I'm worried because now that he's got a steady job, if he doesn't get himself a place of his own now, he never will, and we're all just waiting for his next drunken bust-up, whenever it comes, then it'll be another night in the police cells, forgiven and forgotten the next day, and the cycle will start up all over again. Then they'll have to evict him, but they won't do it on their own, it'll be down to me to push them through the courts and sort it out . . .'

'Have you met Juliette's mum and dad, Veronica?' said Rita.

'Of course I have,' said Veronica.

'They're lovely aren't they?'

'They're on a spending spree at the moment,' said Juliette,

'dad's just retired and been given a huge lump sum, and mum's come into an inheritance from one of my uncles who died last year. I can't remember how much – several thousand. Anyway, they're rich for the first time in their lives, and every day they go out shopping. They bought their first ever fridge last week. They're having a new bathroom put in, and the house is just full of new stuff. Mum bought a fur coat, jewellery, they've bought statues, expensive cookware, tools, furniture, books . . .'

The two women laughed, then the three were quiet for a few moments.

'This wine tastes like grass,' said Juliette, putting her nose in the glass, then holding the glass against the light of a candle.

'It just tastes like wine to me,' said Rita.

They both waited for Veronica's opinion of the wine, since she claimed to be knowledgeable on the subject, but it didn't come.

Then there came a wheezy rattling noise from the landing.

'The door,' said Juliette.

'Guests,' said Veronica, with a trace of disappointment in her voice.

'I'll answer it,' said Rita, her voice full of eagerness to be helpful. She left the room.

Juliette experienced an unusual surge of nervousness as she listened for the voices, and stood up to refill her glass.

'That's two bottles gone already,' she said after refilling Veronica's glass.

'I'll probably slow down after this one,' Veronica said, 'I'm already feeling giggly,' and she gave a giggle, as if to prove it.

'I expect you to get more than giggly tonight Veronica.'

'I don't think it would be a good idea. I feel this urge coming on to fling myself at people . . .'

'All the more reason', said Juliette, applying the corkscrew to another bottle.

'But there's no point, there won't be anyone worth flinging myself at, they'll be either partnered already or they'll be hopeless old drunks from The Quiet Woman and The Carpenters Arms, Bill and Hugo's cronies, God what a dreary lot . . .'

'You never know.'

Veronica shrugged, then knocked back the full glass of wine

in her hand, holding it out to Juliette for a refill. They both chuckled.

It wasn't unusual that the arrival of Boris in the room should have been so quiet – he was a quiet man, with the face of a blond, slightly thick-set Jesus and a mildness of manner that sometimes did work miracles in pacifying the volatile confrontations that sometimes erupted in the pubs where he drank. His dress sense and hairstyle was that of a beatnik or hippy, or more accurately something in between, a style he had developed in the mid 1960s, and had felt so comfortable with that he'd clung to it ever since – shoulder-length hair, a beard, emerald green woolly pullover, jeans, suede ankle boots, with no variation whatsoever. The stubborn sameness, the Belisha beacon repetitiveness of his dress sense was often remarked upon. He would answer that it meant a complete freedom from thinking about clothes. He had worn them to Rita's birthday do at Chez Francoise and he had worn them to the Royal Opera House when he'd seen *Don Giovanni* with Juliette's mum and dad. The only time he wore anything else was at work when he donned the green overalls of a GPO engineer (the same shade of green as his pullovers), to scale the telegraph poles, or descend the inspection pits of Windhover Hill's telephone network.

'Is it just you?' said Juliette.

'Aren't I enough?'

'Isn't Boris good enough?' sniggered Veronica.

'I thought you'd be bringing people from The Red Lion.'

'I've brought Scott,' said Boris, turning and holding out a beckoning, stage-compere's hand as Scott entered the room.

Scott was wearing a white suit over a pale blue roll-neck sweater. He had recently grown his hair almost to shoulder length, swept back so that it seemed to follow him around. In combination with his steel-rimmed glasses and square jaw-line it gave him a distinguished air. He could have been a visiting American academic, or film critic for the *New York Times*, rather than the dole office clerk he was, processing applicants for Supplementary Benefit at the Windhover Hill branch of the DHSS. In his spare time, however, he played a slightly out of tune clarinet with a trad jazz ensemble called The Blind Stompers at various pubs in the area.

'What have you brought?'

'Brought?'

'I didn't see any bottles in your hands.'

'That's because there weren't any in them.'

'I like those pretty candles,' said Scott, grinning, 'They're really . . .' he searched for the word, '. . . twinkly.'

The doorbell rattled again. Rita went to answer it.

'Were we meant to bring anything?'

'I'm just worried there won't be enough drink.'

'Christ those candles look bloody good,' said Scott, 'they knock me out. This is fantastic. Christ! . . .' (he'd just noticed the bas-relief of the First World War soldier on the far wall) 'this place is just spectacular.' He gave Juliette a kiss on the cheek.

Rita re-entered the room with a new guest. It was a solitary woman, in her late forties. Her dark hair was bunched up as though she'd been lying on it. She was wearing jeans so loose they seemed about to fall down, a too large blue shirt clumsily buttoned.

She explained that she was from next door ('above the butchers") and that she was looking for her husband, though she failed to explain why she thought he might be here.

'Have a drink darling,' said Scott, offering her a glass. She took it eagerly and spoke with a smoker's deep rasp.

'You're a saint. I'd sooner have you for my husband, darling, than that old sod I married . . .'

As she spoke her story kept changing. She was not looking for her husband, she was trying to escape her husband. Then she said she'd come to the party by mistake, thinking she was in her own flat ('it's almost identical'), and that her husband was at home, 'Straight through that bloody wall, darling.'

After two glasses of wine the woman, already drunk, slipped into incoherence and was ignored thereafter, a situation she seemed at ease with.

'I saw your brother in The Red Lion,' said Boris.

'Janus?'

'No, the little one. Julian.'

'Julian was in The Red Lion?'

'And he was with three grotesques.'

'Who?'

'I don't know. Schoolfriends, I suppose.'

'Did you speak to him?'

'Didn't get a chance, they were thrown out for being under age. I got the impression they were trying to get themselves drunk enough for a party, which shouldn't take them long.'

'Why didn't you go over and rescue them?' said Veronica, 'the poor little angels. You just abandoned them when you could have used your influence to save them.'

'They're not so little, unfortunately,' said Juliette, genuinely perturbed by the fact of being outgrown by a much younger sibling.

'Have you ever met Julian?'

'Of course I have,' said Veronica. 'Such a sweet little pixie, a little leprechaun with curly hair and freckles and knobbly little knees, such a sweet little pixie . . .'

'Not quite how I'd describe him,' said Boris.

'With a lovely little gap in his teeth . . .'

'When did you meet him?'

'At Juliette's wedding.'

'That was five years ago. He would have been ten.'

'Well he can't have changed all that much.'

'Veronica, you've spent too long working in primary schools. You actually think children stop growing at the age of ten, when they leave your school, don't you.'

'Of course not.'

'Because they change even more rapidly in the years immediately afterwards . . .'

'I know, but I don't believe Julian can have changed as much as you think.'

By now the doorbell was ringing every few minutes and the flat slowly filling with guests – Ryan and Ewan, two regulars from The Carpenters Arms, Mimi, fashion student at Ponders' End Polytechnic, Callan and Rick, members of the Socialist Workers Party, Tipi, a tarot card reader from the Lee Valley, Bernadette and Geraldine, old schoolfriends of Juliette's . . . There were many people Juliette didn't recognize, or recognized only as faces that usually bobbed around in the background at

The Quiet Woman or The Carpenters Arms. Juliette slowly gathered from overhearing the conversations of these people, that many had come to the party on the strength of a rumour that there was to be a confrontation between Bill and Boris, on the one hand, and Veronica and Hugo on the other. Some, it seemed, had even been press-ganged by Bill and Hugo as support should any such confrontation erupt.

The stock of alcohol accumulated. Bottles multiplied on the table, while the food remained mostly untouched. A keg of beer had appeared from somewhere, and a permanent queue was formed to fill plastic beakers at its tap. Juliette learned from Boris during a clumsy tango that the keg had been supplied by Bill, who'd rolled it all the way down Chapel Street from The Quiet Woman.

Bill was quiet, however, so subdued that Juliette didn't notice him until late into the evening. She passed him on the way to the toilet. He was in the passageway talking with friends she didn't recognize. He gave her a rather hangdog glance of acknowledgement as she passed by. His hair was shorter and he'd shaved off his beard, though the moustache survived. She noticed his shoes, low rise platforms in black. They looked expensive. Juliette could never feel respect for a man in platform shoes. Her infatuation with Michael Barratt, presenter of *Nationwide,* had ended the day a full-length camera angle revealed the height of his footwear.

Hugo was sprawled on the couch. The couch was so low that Hugo's crossed knees seemed above the level of his own head. Beside him was a blotchy-skinned girl with a glossy mane of ginger hair. She was nestling into him, a plumpish hand fondly stroking his tightly T-shirted belly. Veronica, standing beside the food table with Rita, grappled with an urge to empty a glass of wine over the couple. Rita advised her that it was far better to ignore him completely, to appear happy in his absence, than to allow him the value of her attention.

'But I just hate the way he's sitting there. He's always had that way of sitting. He spreads himself out. He oozes into furniture, not caring how much space he takes up. I really want to throw wine over him, Rita . . .'

'Dance!' shouted Rita. The music volume had increased as the party progressed – David Bowie, Billy Ocean, The Stylistics. Veronica only glimpsed Hugo through a thicket of dancers. Shouting had become the normal mode of conversation.

'No, I want to throw wine over him.'

'I think you should dance.'

'I don't want to dance while he's in the room.'

'Dance with me,' said Rita, who was quite drunk by now, taking Veronica's hands and pulling her into the centre of the room.

'No,' said Veronica, pulling her fingers out of Rita's hands. 'Look at him, he's so bound up in his own little life – he's pretending he hasn't even noticed me.'

'Just dance with me. Let's dance together in front of him. Let's do a sexy dance together, then he'll have to notice you.'

'I don't think he's pretending. I think he really has forgotten. The bastard. The fat bastard.'

Rita was dancing now, a squirmy, chest and hip-thrusting dance that Veronica had never seen her perform before, and found rather impressive.

'Come on,' said Rita to static Veronica, again taking her hands, 'remind him what you're made of.'

Again Rita produced the most startling undulations and gyrations, her bangles and beads jumping.

'Rita, where did you learn . . .' Veronica began, 'No. I just haven't got the right body to do things like that . . .'

'Of course you have . . .'

'He's not even looking, Rita. And I'd be careful your tits don't fall out . . .'

As if to show she didn't care, Rita bent forward and shook her chest, offering Hugo, had he been looking, a long glimpse of barely controlled, swinging cleavage. The ginger-haired girl noticed, however, and responded by pushing her face into Hugo's, eclipsing him with her bright hair, kissing him deeply. Now all that was visible of Hugo was his stomach, his legs, and his bristly hands, which rested flatly on his thighs.

'The fat shit,' said Veronica, 'I would like to smash him up with a bottle.'

'Why don't we snog?' said Rita, offering her mouth to Veronica, who declined bending to meet it.

'Don't be stupid, Rita. I think we'd be debasing ourselves to do something like that. Why should we have to flaunt ourselves just to gain the attention of a clapped-out old berk like Hugo?'

'Because it would be fun?' said Rita, still pouting hopefully.

'The only fun for me would be in ending his life. Hand me a bottle, Rita, I'm going to brain the sod.'

Rita was about to hunt for an empty wine bottle, intrigued to see whether Veronica was serious, when she was distracted by faces at the window.

'There's someone at the window,' she said.

'But we're on the first floor.'

The figures outside were knocking on the glass, pressing their faces up against the pane.

'Who is it?'

'I don't know. Does this window open?'

The figures were gesturing at the window catches, miming the lifting of the sash.

'Do you think we should let them in, Rita?' Veronica said as she tried opening the window. She had to clear away books, lighted candles and bottles to make enough space. 'They might be gate-crashers wanting to cause trouble. Do you recognize them? It's difficult to tell, the way they're pressing their faces against the glass.'

The two women had to pull together to open the window. A blast of cold night air came into the room, then the giggly, youthful voices of those outside, then the people themselves. They seemed to float into the room as though they had been hovering, weightless, outside, but once in the room they became heavy and cumbersome, falling to their knees and rolling about, as though unused to the effects of gravity.

'There's so many of them,' laughed Veronica, as each successive body floated in and fell on the floor.

'There's scaffolding outside,' said Rita, 'they've climbed up the scaffolding.'

'That explains the levitation,' said Veronica thoughtfully.

'You're Julian, aren't you,' said Rita, bending down to speak to the giggling brother of Juliette, who was still on the floor.

'Yeah,' said Julian, sitting up and quietening.

'Julian?' said Veronica, amazed, 'it can't be, he's too long.'

'Who are these people?' said Veronica, indicating the three others who also, after initially raucous bursts of giggling, had become disappointingly quiet.

'This is O'Flaherty,' said Julian, suddenly rather formal, indicating the first boy who was holding a half-bottle of whisky, three-quarters full, 'and this is O'Hogarty and this is O'Malley.'

The three looked uncomfortable and awkward, shifting from foot to foot, wiping their noses with their hands, scratching their ears. They were dressed in clumsy attempts at adult garb, jackets and shirts obviously borrowed from their fathers and older brothers, and which fitted them badly. O'Hogarty was wearing his father's golf-club blazer and cravat. Their hair was combed and greased into side or centre partings, again in a bizarre parody of grown-up styles.

'Have they got first names?' said Rita. Julian seemed surprised that she should be interested.

'Yeah, er, Kieran, Seamus and Marcus.'

'Which is which?'

'The one with braces on his teeth is Marcus. The one with big teeth but no braces is called Kieran, and the one with green teeth and spots is called Seamus.'

'You've all got spots,' said Rita.

'Not on our teeth,' said Marcus.

'Show me your teeth,' said Veronica to O'Flaherty, who seemed to be shaking, a constant tremor enlivening an otherwise pasty and static face. Veronica, sensing fear as she approached, did something no one was expecting, she put her arms around his neck and kissed him, a little jab at first, then a single, longer, open-mouthed kiss. O'Flaherty's big white hands wavered in shock for a moment, then looked as if they would dare to settle on Veronica's rump, but instead came to rest on her waist.

'Would you like something to eat?' Rita said to Julian.

'Yeah,' said Julian, unable to take his eyes off Veronica and O'Flaherty's clinch, only half-hearing Rita's invitation.

'I think you should have something to eat, you look like a boy who needs to eat.'

'I do,' said Julian, perplexed and fascinated by what was happening before his eyes, 'desperately.'

Veronica had now moved on to O'Hogarty, who met Veronica's lips with a ridiculous and grotesque pouting of his own. It was clear Veronica was working her way through the boys in turn, bestowing deep, adventurous kisses on each, and Julian was worried, being last in line, that he would miss his turn if he followed Rita to the food.

All evening they had been eyeing girls from a safe distance, daring occasionally to approach, only to be sent away with withering sneers and disdainful titters. And all the time the best chance of female contact had been here, at his sister's party, with her older friends.

'There's some sandwich gateau left,' said Rita, tugging at Julian's sleeve, pointing to a solid, white slab on the table, untouched. 'Come and have some of my sandwich gateau, please.'

But Julian held his ground. Thankfully Veronica hadn't spent long in O'Malley's arms, and was now making her way towards him. But when she arrived, he felt a sudden pang of distaste for that mouth that had so recently been in contact with those of his friends, for the tongue that had dwelt amongst the cavities and corrective apparatus of O'Malley's teeth, that had steered past the protruding incisors of O'Hogarty, that had probed between the downy, encrusted lips of O'Flaherty, and he was amazed to find that when that tongue arrived in his own mouth, it tasted as pure and as clean and as sweet as a piece of scrubbed fruit.

Veronica kissed Julian longer than the other three, mainly because Julian yielded to her more, whereas the others had bitten back their desires out of strong, catholic fears. But when his own tongue, having waltzed in the cosy ballroom of their joined mouths long enough, broke free to explore Veronica's mouth, those hard, complicated teeth against which his own softly scraped, the tough, polished satin of her gums, he sensed a shift in the balance of their embrace, and after a few minutes Veronica produced a series of politely pleading whimpers to indicate she was having difficulty breathing. Julian withdrew.

Veronica's face filled his vision.

'Did you bring any drink with you?'

'O'Flaherty's got a half-bottle of whisky,' said Julian.

Veronica glimpsed at O'Flaherty, who was being pulled by Rita towards her sandwich gateau.

'It's half-empty,' said Veronica.

'It's a cold night,' said Julian.

Veronica laughed, throwing back her head, revealing a plump, white oesophagus. Julian took his chance and bit it, softly. He felt the vibration of her laughter, the little hive of her voicebox against his lips. He moved further down her neck, licked her clavicles, her shoulders. Was she really allowing him this? Was she very drunk? Had she not noticed what he was doing?

'You can't come in without a bottle,' Veronica said, then blurted out laughter. She collapsed in a mock swoon on a nearby chair bringing Julian down with her, their embrace remained unbroken.

Their kissing had been a cause for amusement amongst the other guests, and for a while they'd been the party's centre of attention, those who knew Veronica barely able to believe her footlooseness. But after a while interest dwindled and their continued contact was soon only under the observation of Juliette, who cast concerned glances in their direction every now and then.

Veronica had adopted the role of adored empress reclining on a burnished throne, eyes closed, head tilted back, the expression on her face betokening tiredness rather than ecstasy, Julian a besotted page kneeling beside her, his head rooting about in her neck and upper shoulders, daring, every now and then, to dip to the square décolletage of her dress, as though testing the waters of a pool. If he went too far in this direction Veronica would gently pull him away, though not to a distance which would discourage Julian from trying again, going a little further each time, millimetre by millimetre further into her skin.

There was a black, crocheted shawl draped on the back of the chair. Julian took this and folded it around Veronica's shoulders. It acted as a hide to conceal his activity from Juliette and anyone else. He folded himself into it. Caught himself in it. He had the sense of being engulfed. The party seemed to evaporate around him, to be replaced by Veronica, who had somehow taken on the proportions of the room they inhabited, so that instead of hearing Billy Ocean he heard Veronica's blood dancing through her heart, he heard the air coming and going from her nostrils, he heard the buzzing in her neck when she laughed, and instead of furnishings there were shoulders, a neck, ears, collar bones, all now damp with his slowly evaporating spittle. Now and then he managed to reach with fingertips inside her dress, a fascinating softness that seemed to go on for ever.

If he caught glimpses of anything beyond Veronica they were shadows. A cheese plant coming and going in the light of a Belisha beacon, a soldier from the trenches fossilised on a wall. Suddenly Veronica seemed to wake and gasp, 'My God. I haven't given Juliette her present.'

'Where is it?' said Julian, taking his face from her cleavage.

'I've hidden it in Bill's bedroom. I'd better get it now before I forget . . .'

She stirred from her chair, and Julian stirred from her. He looked round and saw his friends, O'Malley, O'Flaherty and O'Hogarty over by the food table. They were tucking enthusiastically into Rita's sandwich gateau. Rita was serving it up for them, on white paper plates. Julian had the impression of witnessing something underhand, the way the boys were so enthusiastically chomping on the food, the way some of the curd cheese was smeared around their lips, the way Julian caught glimpses of their open mouths, the cud of marmite and tinned salmon within, the sediments of chewed bread caught on O'Malley's braces, and Rita in the middle, the knife in her hand, waiting for the empty plates to refill.

O'Hogarty suddenly glanced in Julian's direction, gestured to him to come over.

'It's lovely stuff,' he said, a shrapnel of unswallowed gateau jumping from his mouth, 'come and have some . . .'

Julian nodded, but was following Veronica by now, entangling himself as best he could in her spidery shawl, taking a moment to consider the ridiculousness of O'Hogarty's invitation. Hadn't he noticed that he'd spent the best part of the last hour snogging a twenty-seven-year-old divorcee, that he was closer to having sex than he'd ever been in his life, far closer than those three were ever likely to come in the next half decade? Did he really think he should disengage himself for the sake of an ugly concoction of curd cheese and marmite? 'He had made the wrong friends,' Julian thought to himself, as he trailed after Veronica, out of the room and down the passageway. 'They were holding him back . . .'

Round the corner from the kitchen, the passage led directly to the lavatory at the far end. The door to the lavatory was open and the light was on. Spotlit in tungsten yellow was a middle-aged woman, standing awkwardly with her trousers round her ankles. It was the husband-seeking woman from next door. Her loose blue shirt was not long enough to conceal her dark, hispid loins, nor did she seem bothered by the fact, glancing lazily at the couple as she wiped herself.

Julian wasn't quite sure if Veronica was aware that he was following her, even though he had a hand entangled in her shawl, and was trailing behind her like a reluctant lapdog all the way down the corridor, but he convinced himself that he was being led on, and so he followed her into Bill's bedroom. She turned the light on. It was strangely like a temple inside, there was a sense that the space was composed of countless tiny objects, little pots full of pens, Egyptian anubi, statuettes of indecipherable provenance, small booklets on ancient pottery, miniatures of spirit, a bottle of Tia Maria, trinkets, baubles. There was a three-foot high Airfix model of a Saturn V on the floor, a mobile from the ceiling composed of intrarotating suns. A violin was propped on a chair.

Bill's bed was a single bed, an arabesque counterpane was filled with peacock eye cushions. Veronica was bending down to get something from under the bed. When she straightened up Julian began tickling her ribs so that she fell on to the bed in a sea of giggles, and he rolled on top of her, kissing her now with a more desperate sense of urgency, which soon dampened Veronica's laughter.

'No, Julian,' she said quietly and without emphasis, as Julian began working at the pea-sized buttons on the front of her dress. There was a button every centimetre it seemed, 'I really don't think we should, not here . . .'

'Where then?'

'Nowhere, Julian. You're forgetting yourself. I'm forgetting myself.'

Another button yielded, another centimetre of skin revealed.

The door opened. Veronica sat up, pushing Julian aside. She put her hand to her breast, concealing what was no more than a little dip in the straight cut of her dress.

Bill entered the room. He looked serious, a little worried. He was not alone. Hugo followed, then Juliette.

'Checking up on me are you darling?' said Veronica to Hugo.

Hugo was silent. Bill answered.

'I was going to show Hugo some drawings . . .'

'What are you doing in here Veronica?' called Juliette from behind the two men.

'You're all checking up on me, I only came in here to get you your present, sweetheart,' said Veronica. She was still having trouble with the buttons on her dress. Then she bent down to pick up the parcel she'd hidden under the bed.

Suddenly Julian lurched forward, taking Veronica by the shoulders and smothering them with drooling kisses.

'Get off me you twit,' said Veronica, elbowing Julian as she lifted the enormous parcel, 'I mean "twit" in a nice way – Juliette, this is for you . . .'

Julian bawled something incoherently and fell on the floor, at the feet of Bill. He then began dragging himself up Bill's legs as though he was climbing a rope.

'It isn't right,' said Bill, still serious, 'it's just not right . . .'

'What's not?' said Veronica.

Juliette was unwrapping the present, it was about as big as a suitcase and very light.

'A suitcase,' said Juliette, having unwrapped the present, 'how . . . nice.'

'It's not right Julian being drunk like this, it's just not right,' said Bill again. Julian was burbling and warbling incoherently, having fallen back on the floor.

'Do you know you could be arrested for corrupting a minor?' said Hugo.

'Dearest, there isn't a miner within two hundred miles of this room.'

The silence following this remark changed Veronica's tone.

'You're looking at these buttons – there are only three undone, how long have we been in here – Juliette, you saw us going out of the room, we've been in here about thirty seconds . . .'

'Julian,' his sister called from behind the men, 'I'll get Boris to take you home.'

'Is he going to be sick?' a more distant voice said.

'Veronica has agreed to be my wife,' Julian called from the floor, where he was writhing gently.

'This is utterly ridiculous,' said Veronica standing up, having finished fastening her buttons, 'Juliette, you're being stupid, the boy's just drunk. And as for you,' she turned to Hugo, 'I don't know how you can dare take that stern moral attitude with me when you sit on that couch with a schoolgirl oozing all over your big fat belly.'

'Michelle is thirty-three,' said Hugo quietly.

Boris entered, hoisted the now barely conscious Julian onto his shoulders in a fireman's lift and carried him out of the room.

'Goodbye my darling sweet gorgeous wife-to-be,' said Julian, his head dangling upside down, 'I look forward to our many happy years of marriage together. Our children will play cellos and feed us raspberries when we're old . . .'

15

Aldous opened his eyes.

Close to his ear the knuckles of a policeman were rapping at the car window. Aldous had fallen asleep in the driver's seat of the parked Hillman, his head resting against the window. He'd been having a long, complicated dream in which he'd been playing Lear at the Aldwych. Enjoyable at first, the dream had turned into a nightmare of anxiety when he'd become lost during the interval and couldn't find his way back to the stage. He'd been climbing a rickety mountain of chairs when the policeman's knock woke him.

Aldous felt a momentary panic, as he always did when waking from a car-bound sleep, fearing that the vehicle was in motion, that he had fallen asleep while driving and that he was waking in time to witness the last few yards of his life before it expired against the trunk of a tree, the pier of a bridge, or an oncoming family of four. When the peace of motionlessness fell upon Aldous, the realization that he was parked by the side of the road in Windhover Hill Parade, Aldous wondered what had aroused the interest of a policeman.

Colette, in the passenger seat beside him, was also asleep. Before her, the glove compartment door had been lowered to form a little shelf. On this shelf was an ashtray cut from a single piece of slate (an old souvenir from the mines at Corris), and a glass of whisky. Colette had abandoned the barley wines, believing they were responsible for her obesity. She began drinking whisky when Janus Brian died. Her weight had dropped considerably. She had regained the charming slimness of her youth. Her whisky figure, she called it. It had even improved her skin. Wrinkles had fallen from her face, bags from under her eyes, fatty tendrils from her neck. She had lost the double chin that had swollen her face for so many years. Aldous was pleased with his new wife. His whisky wife. She was much better than the unpredictable and gaunt, glue-sniffing Romac wife he'd known, and more attractive than the bloated barley wine wife of the last few years.

This may have been the cause of the policeman's presence. Perhaps he suspected that the whisky was for Aldous. Perhaps it was illegal even for passengers to drink. After all, a drunkard in the passenger seat might easily loll and lurch across the steering wheel, though Colette never had. Perhaps he was facing a driving ban.

Aldous didn't like the thought of being banned from driving. He relied on the car now. He'd stopped cycling to school a couple of years ago. The car was his only transport. He would miss their afternoon trips to the Chilterns for a whisky picnic in a bluebell wood, or a bottle of Corrida amongst the rabbit droppings on the cropped nub of some chalky hill, or even a crazy meander through the residential tributaries of north London which, to Aldous, were becoming as interesting and as strangely beautiful as countryside – as hedge-rich, grassy and flower-filled as any of the lanes they drove along in Herts and Bucks, probably more so.

Why was the policeman knocking? Was it a crime to be asleep in charge of a parked car? Aldous had become quite the car park rêveur, nodding off at the wheel while Colette did the shopping. This time though, as Aldous slowly remembered, he was on the open highway, parked by the side of Windhover Hill Parade, a few doors down from Angad's, the Indian grocery store where they did most of their shopping. Nearby was the lingerie shop above which Bill Brothers now lived.

Perhaps it was the booty in the back that had interested the policeman. There was quite a stash of things. They had spent most of the day shopping. It gave them an excuse to be out of the house while the plumber was doing the new bathroom and toilet. They'd spent the morning in Enfield, and Colette had finally bought a record player to replace the one Janus had smashed. It was the sight of Julian one evening, playing a Beatles 45 ('Strawberry Fields'?) with a darning needle on the still-working turntable of the old radiogram that had finally persuaded her it was time for a new record player. The poor boy had even made a little amplifying trumpet out of paper and had Sellotaped it to the needle, holding the whole thing carefully in position over the spinning disc.

Now the record player, or at least the box that contained it, filled the back seat of their car. Colette had been attracted by a table lamp as well, a pottery thing with bubbly, running glazes in blues and greens and a tall, swirly shade. In the afternoon they'd driven down to Wood Green to wander among the fridges and cookers of the domestic showrooms. Colette was wondering about more things for the kitchen. A washing machine? A food processor? A deep freeze? Such items were taking things a little too far – not in terms of money, they could have afforded them easily – but in terms of technology. Neither would have felt comfortable with so much machinery in the house, so much science. They opted instead for a little blender, principally so that they could make milk shakes.

That was on the back seat in its box as well. It could have looked odd, Aldous supposed, that stack of brand new goods. It was not Christmas, they could hardly be taken for newly-weds furnishing a starter home. But they had a perfectly good excuse for such lavish expenditure – Aldous and Colette were rich.

Years with repeated numbers always seemed to be lucky for Aldous – 1933 was the year he finally made it into art school, 1944 was the year he got married, 1955 was the year he discovered the farm at Llanygwynfa – now 1977 was the year he retired and came into his fortune – his retirement lump sum which had coincided with Colette's inheritance of her share of Janus Brian's estate. They had thousands in the bank. Colette had an account of her own for the first time in her life. The bank staff knew them by name, the bank manager would come over and greet them personally when they made their twice weekly visits to withdraw cash, to put money in their purse.

Strange then, that at a time like this, Colette should have taken to shoplifting. Aldous suddenly shivered as the policeman knocked again (all these thoughts had taken place in a moment) – there *were* stolen goods in the car, in the shopping bag on the floor at the back. Perhaps the staff at Angad's had finally cottoned-on and had sent the police after them. If a policeman went through the receipt he would find that a third of the items in the shopping bags had not been paid for.

Aldous didn't quite understand it. His wife had begun stealing from their local grocer's, at the same time as developing an amicably chatty relationship with the different generations of the Indian family that owned it; the mother who dressed like a princess in jewels and dazzling make-up, the father under his slightly tatty turban, the sweet daughter in her golden sari. With them Colette would exchange stories about their relations, their holidays, events in the news, the weather. Sometimes behind the strip curtain at the back of the shop she would catch glimpses of an older generation who never came out into the shop – an old man in a stiff-backed chair, handsomely white-bearded – and sometimes a crop of children in flowing clothes and sandals, who would peep out from doorways and cubby-holes, tittering and chanting.

It surprised Colette herself that she had made such a habit of placing items – tins of corned beef, pots of shrimp paste, sardines, jars of Marmite into her shopping bag instead of her basket. At home she would spread the stolen goods out on the kitchen table and total up their value, she and Aldous doing the sums together with pencil and paper, comparing the totals with their shopping of previous days and weeks. If the daily total was higher than ever before Colette would feel a sense of triumph, elation, pride. She had done something useful for her family. She had made up for her deficiencies as a mother, for the money she had wasted over the years on booze and fags.

Aldous suspected it was the essential thrill of stealing that motivated his wife into these petty crimes, and Aldous himself, who tried not to see Colette's legerdemain with packets of Uncle Ben's and tins of meatballs, felt that his wife's activities made shopping a more adventurous, even dangerous operation than could normally be expected, and he felt a vicarious sense of excitement as they – the ageing Bonnie and Clyde of Windhover Hill, looted their way through Angad's every other day.

Aldous didn't know quite what to do about the policeman, and was half-hoping he might go away if he ignored him, but the policeman was making a circling gesture with his hand, indicating that he wanted Aldous to wind the window down.

The glass fallen from his face, the policeman could speak.

'Are you aware that you are parked on zigzag lines?' he said, not seeming to see the whisky, and thankfully uninformed on the matter of Colette's shoplifting.

Aldous was only vaguely aware of what zigzag lines were, and it was true that they were parked close to a zebra crossing. Aldous apologized, the policeman smiled and walked away, while Aldous hurriedly reversed, then found that he was stuck in reverse. He had to drive backwards, slowly and carefully, all the way home.

Although Colette woke up during this journey, taking a sip of whisky then sitting up, straightening her clothes and her hair, she made no remark on the fact that they were travelling backwards. She looked dreamily out of the window, watching the houses and hedges and lime trees in their back-to-front procession as though nothing unusual was happening.

She looked over her shoulder at the approaching house and admired the lusciousness of its front garden.

The undergrowth of the front garden had grown very thick. Pyracantha, holly, sumac, orange blossom. Several unidentified flowering shrubs, some ferns, exotic grasses. Now, laid crookedly across some bushes which it flattened, was a bath. The old bath brought down from the bathroom. A white enamel tub filled with grime and dust, the streaked stain of verdigris just below the taps from the decades-old copper pipes that Janus had cut out. Blood stains from some of the birds that had died in it. It sat in the garden listing like the wreck of a lifeboat that had cast off from the house.

The front door was ajar so that Butcher, their plumber, could get in and out from his van which was parked outside.

Butcher had been their plumber ever since they'd moved into Fernlight Avenue. It was he who'd replumbed the kitchen sink, who'd repaired the storage tank in the loft when it froze one winter, who'd even reflashed the leaking chimney stack over the back bedroom. Colette liked him. She admired him, as she admired anyone who could work with their hands. Butcher was a model-maker in his spare time and had constructed a fully working model steam engine, big enough to seat him and his grandchildren as they chugged around his back garden. Once, when the kids were small, she'd met him by chance near to where he lived, and he'd invited them in and they'd spent an afternoon on the trains. He was a dog lover also, owner of two Dobermans, Minnehaha and Hiawatha, shark-like beasts Colette sometimes saw Butcher walking on the ends of two leather leashes.

Despite his tinkering with toy trains, however, Butcher professed to despise children.

'Children are cruel,' he frequently said, 'I've seen what children can do to animals.' He would then give an example, recounted from his own childhood, which usually featured the extended torturing of a cat by some backstreet kids.

'Not all children are like that,' said Colette, who couldn't recall her own children ever harming animals, except out of an innocent curiosity. James, it was true, used to like drowning wood lice in treacle, and she remembered Julian eating a caterpillar, but never had they been wilfully cruel. Juliette had wept, once, when she saw her mother annihilating bluebottles with a newspaper, and Janus had devoted himself to the care of sick Scipio.

'Children are born cruel. We all are. We have to learn to be civilized. Most of us don't manage it.'

There was such bitterness in Butcher, but a sort of resignation as well, a grudging acceptance of humanity's essential badness as something one had to live with. His children, Colette understood, were all outstanding successes. One had read law at Oxford, another was a journalist on a serious paper, another was a doctor, yet Butcher seemed to take no parental satisfaction from their achievements, putting them down entirely to the re-emergence of some long suppressed genetic trait. Butcher himself could barely read.

Now Butcher had his biggest commission at Fernlight Avenue – the installation of a new bathroom suite, a new lavatory, the fitting of an immersion heater on the landing to replace the long defunct heating system that had once been powered by the boiler in the kitchen, which Butcher was also to remove. This was Butcher's third day at the house. The lavatory had been the first to go. That old, white porcelain Howie unit, with its high cistern that only worked once out of every four or five pulls, had given Butcher such problems that in the end he had to take a sledgehammer to it. From downstairs it sounded like a cook had gone mad in his kitchen. Its replacement was a green enamel suite with a low-level cistern. Butcher was very proud of it. 'Hasn't it got a lovely flush?' he kept saying, turning the handle repeatedly, watching the water crowd into the bowl where it formed a tongue of froth, 'Perfect.'

Colette entered the kitchen and plonked her shopping bags on the table, relieved greatly to be unburdened. Aldous followed with the hi-fi in its box, leaning backwards slightly to take the weight, nudging his way into the music room. Butcher was on his knees before the boiler, poking at it with a spanner. Without looking up he said 'Bathroom's all done now my sweetheart. I think I'll have to leave this little lot until tomorrow, though. One of the bolts has snapped off at the back and the rear panel's rusted solid. Looks like another sledgehammer job.' He briefly put his arms around the cold, brown iron of the stove, as though hugging it, and gave it a token pull. 'Stuck fast. Thought I'd have been done today. Never mind.'

'So there's hot water?'

'There is. I'll show you how it all works,' and Butcher stood up, slowly and with difficulty. He was a big man, bull-shaped, and had back pain, which made him wince whenever he bent over. Husband and wife followed their plumber upstairs. He opened the cupboard on the landing. It was filled almost entirely by the tank which now was wearing what looked like a big red anorak. Butcher reached in with his hand behind the corner, 'there's a little switch here, it's on at the moment, and so there's a red light here . . .' He pointed, and Colette bent to see. 'It'll take an hour or so from switching on to get warm, another half an hour to be piping hot. Should last the good part of an evening, if you switch it on at, say, four o'clock, you'll have hot water up until bedtime.'

'Lovely,' said Colette.

'Feel it,' said Butcher, pressing his hand into the lagging. Colette felt. It was warm.

'Could we all speak a little quieter,' said Aldous in a loud whisper, 'we don't want to wake Janus.'

'Don't be silly,' said Colette, 'It's nearly time for him to wake up anyway . . .'

'I'm afraid I've been hammering and drilling up here all day,' said Butcher loudly, 'I even had to go in Janus's room a few times to get at the pipe run. He didn't stir once. I clean forgot there was anyone in there.'

They were just about to proceed to the bathroom when Butcher made a detour through to the back bedroom.

'I had to pop in here to get at the wiring behind the tank, and then I saw it . . .'

'Saw what?'

'That amazing thing. That thing on the table. What is it? Is it something you made Mr Jones?'

On the table near the window was Aldous's model of the fountain he'd designed for Brother Head.

'It's a fountain,' said Colette.

The piece did look impressive. A rising helix of doves, roughly cut from clay and speckled with viridian and white glazes, turning around a central stem where a pipe took the water to the top. Aldous claimed it was designed so that every dove would have water falling from its wing tips, the overall effect would have been magical in the full size version, a cascade of birds and water.

'This is scaled down is it? A model?'

'Yes,' said Aldous, 'it's one sixth of the size. So the actual fountain would be about eight feet high, and bronze.'

'Clever bloke aren't you,' said Butcher, fingering the sculpture delicately with filthy hands, 'to look at you you wouldn't think you had it in you, if you don't mind my saying. But this is really lovely. I can admire something like this, I don't go so much for your paintings, but something like this that's solid and full of lovely shapes – it's really beautiful. Where's it going to be built?'

'Nowhere,' said Colette, 'it doesn't look like it anyway. It was designed for a monastery up north but the bishop of Durham wouldn't come up with the money, and the monks don't answer our letters.'

'Should go somewhere though,' said Butcher, thoughtfully. Then he laughed. 'I've got a small foundry in my back garden. I use it to mould parts for my model railways, usually in cast iron – nothing on a big scale – just things like couplings and name plates. I'll have to look into doing something like this in bronze . . .'

A technical conversation followed between Aldous and Butcher, concerning the feasibility of casting the fountain in bronze in a small, backyard foundry. Butcher seemed very keen on the idea of casting the piece for a feature in his extensive back garden railway.

'Your back garden's enormous,' said Colette, remembering.

'I was very lucky,' said Butcher, 'bought the place thirty years ago for one thousand five hundred pounds. Tiny house but a garden the size of a park. I built a small lake in it for the railway to go round. This would look very nice in that lake. Very nice indeed.'

Aldous and Colette exchanged silent giggles as they followed Butcher to the bathroom.

The bathroom was Butcher's masterpiece. A triumph of sanitary engineering. Matching the colour of the lavatory, a sea-green bath with silver taps, streamlined and smooth as though cut from a slab of unveined marble. A pedestal washbasin, a little font on a pillar of onyx. It stunned Colette, the sheer newness of it, the perfection of it, even though there was still the detritus of Butcher's work, a litter of screwed-up tape, offcuts of moulding, a hacksaw lying on the floor.

Butcher stood in the middle of the room, gathered a few of the tools that were still in there. It amazed Colette that someone so filthy could have produced something so coruscatingly clean.

'I'll be off now then, my loves,' said Butcher, 'back in the morning to finish off the boiler.'

And after a slow gathering of his things and a general noise of his great weight moving around the house, he left.

There was a tankful of hot water, jacketed, in the cupboard.

'I think I'll have a bath,' said Colette, as though she'd only just grasped the purpose of these newly installed objects.

'Okay,' said Aldous, whispering, 'but be careful not to wake Janus. Remember, he's only through that wall.'

'Will you shut up about waking Janus?'

'I'll go and get the rest of the things from the car.'

Colette was alone in the bathroom. She turned on the hot tap. In a matter of seconds the water was painfully hot. The bath filled. Steam rose and fogged the windows. Colette undressed while the water thundered, echoing off the empty walls, a wild yet contained noise, as though the room had been built around a waterfall.

Colette had no bath salts, bubble bath or anything like that to add to the water, so the water remained perfectly clear. Entering it was like stepping into a window. She sank up to her neck and looked down at her body, bent and shortened by the distorting water, so that it looked like something preserved in a bottle.

'An average glass of water will almost certainly contain a molecule that has passed through the lips of Aristotle, such is the distribution and multitude of water molecules in the world.'

Janus Brian had said that, in one of his many water eulogies. Odd then, that his death had brought about this bathroom.

'What about Jesus?' Colette had replied.

'Jesus as well. Anyone, really.'

'Every glass of water you drink will contain a drop that was used in the miracle at Cana?'

'True,' Janus Brian had chuckled, 'that is very true, dear.'

Colette felt she was bathing in miraculous wine.

Money. She'd never had so much of it, not in her entire life, and it had never occurred to her that Janus Brian should leave her any, but then, who else was there? Expectations among her children in the weeks following his death had become silly. Perhaps she would be sole heir to her dead brother's estate. That bungalow was worth quite a bit, and he still had heaps left over from the sale of Leicester Avenue. Supposing she had got the whole lot? Forty thousand or more? In the end her brother's will, a very carefully considered document, divided his estate between a large number of inheritors. There was some for Agatha, some for Lesley, some for Reg and some for Reg's sons. Colette's was the biggest share, however. Eight thousand pounds, or just over. Money she had never dared hope for.

Janus Brian's death shouldn't have come as such a shock, but it did. Barely two months after they got back from Tewkesbury he'd died. It was always what she'd feared, and what he himself seemed to predict. The trouble with lifting someone like that onto a high is that afterwards they plummet deeper than before. The higher you lift them, the deeper they fall. In the autumn Janus Brian had fallen into a chasm of despair and died in a pathetic heap on its floor.

The doctor said he'd barely any working liver left, just a wedge of dead matter where it had been. He had drunk himself to death. Just as he had intended, right from the start.

What Colette likes about the bath is its depth. She can stretch right out in it. She could almost float in it. It's like having your own private ocean. She likes sinking into the water up to her eyes, and looking along the flatness of the water and seeing what degree of stillness she can bring it to. If she holds her breath there isn't a ripple at all. Or almost. Just her heartbeat causing a tremor on the surface of the water.

But then a larger ripple comes from somewhere, sending water into her eyes. It is Janus getting out of bed in the next room.

16

When Aldous and Colette first became rich, they celebrated by going out for a drink at The Goat and Compasses. They took Julian with them, and invited Juliette and her boyfriend Boris as well. Juliette and Boris had in turn invited some of their friends. This gathering at The Goat and Compasses had been so successful that it became a regular event on Saturday nights, and the number of people gathered slowly increased over the weeks.

James had moved back into Fernlight Avenue, having taken up postgraduate studies at the School of Oriental and African Studies in Bloomsbury. Though he was often out late, or spending the nights somewhere else, he usually came to the pub on Saturday nights, often with a girlfriend in tow. Julian would usually bring two or three of his friends – O'Hogarty, O'Malley and O'Flaherty. The gatherings could sometimes number over a dozen people, taking up three tables and a third of the saloon space of The Goat and Compasses, Aldous and Colette at its centre, stately, monarchical, rarely leaving their seats.

Towards the end of the evenings, when the maximum number of people had gathered, Colette would take a bunch of money out of her purse and offer it to whoever was nearest, asking them to get the next round in.

Colette and Aldous had not enjoyed a social life as rich as this since before the war. In those days they'd been part of a circle as large, if not larger, whose core was Colette and Lesley. It disappointed her to think of it, how that life had so abruptly ended thanks partly to the war, but mainly to the production of children. Their children came in such a chronological sprawl that it was, from the birth of Janus, more than thirty years before their youngest, Julian, was of an age to go in pubs. The old friendships in that time had long since evaporated. Their friends now were their children, and their children's friends. Once the cause of their isolation and solitude, their children now placed them at the hub of a bubbling, lively community.

At first they felt at home in the small bar of The Goat and Compasses. They got to know its clientele – Harry the Dust, the ex-con who'd made a model of the pub out of matchsticks while he'd been in prison, and which was now proudly displayed on the shelf behind the bar – Old Tom, the thick-spectacled gent with a club foot who never removed his cap, and whose slow journey along Hoopers Lane with the aid of crutches and sticks seemed to take most of the afternoon – Miss Steed, the old dear in the overcoat who drank two halves of shandy every evening, finding the cost of the beer less than the cost of the electricity she would have used if she'd stayed at home, especially since she always got a nearby stranger to buy her the second half, offering an inadequate few new pence as payment ('I can never understand this new money').

At about ten o'clock the shellfish woman would arrive, distributing tubs of cockles, mussels and jellied eels from a large wicker basket. Colette would always buy a tub of something, mostly to the disgust of the others. One evening she bought two tubs of jellied eels, one for herself, and one for Julian, who seemed keen to try them. Colette and her youngest son were sitting at opposite ends of the table, and later in the evening they began flicking little particles of jelly at each other, using the plastic spoons that came with the tubs, whose elasticity was such that the jelly could be propelled at quite a speed, and if clumsily aimed could shoot across the pub. As the two were quite drunk by this time, they began flicking jelly indiscriminately around the pub so that it landed in peoples' hair, their clothes, in their drinks. Or else it stuck to the ceiling where it hung for a while before dropping, at random intervals, on whoever was below.

This was the beginning of their falling out of favour at The Goat and Compasses. Harry the Dust grumbled under his tousled, boyish hair, in which bright particles glittered, that such things shouldn't be allowed. Miss Steed complained that her lemon shandy had 'gone queer'. Old Tom's cap glistened. Such a small thing, Colette lamented, the harmless scattering of congealed eel juice. Over the weeks she had taken a particular dislike to the moustachioed Irish barmaid that had admonished her and her son for their jelly-flicking that evening. She hadn't liked the tone the woman used. She hadn't liked her cheap make-up and jewellery, her cedar-red dyed hair, her Silvikrin bouffant hairdo. She began mocking and teasing this woman quietly behind her back as she came round to collect the glasses. The woman in her turn remained stoically tight-lipped, occasionally taking away glasses that were not quite empty, becoming stricter with the closing time routine, insisting that glasses were drained in good time for the closing of the pub.

'It's because she can't have children,' Colette said to the others one evening at closing time.

'How do you know she can't have children?' said Aldous.

'How else do you account for her behaviour?' said Colette.

The woman, who'd several times asked Colette to finish her drink, finally took Colette's quarter-full glass. Colette grabbed at it. An undignified tug-of-war ensued between the two women, which Colette won. As a sort of victory cry she blew a raspberry at the retreating barmaid, and this raspberry seemed to act as a final straw. The woman turned, snatched the glass away. Her lips were quivering with anger, but she couldn't find any words other than 'you . . . you . . .'

A few minutes later the barmaid returned with the landlord Gordon, a mild, quiet man in his sixties, his grey hair stylishly parted in the style of Edward VIII.

In the row that followed, the two women accused each other of having had too much to drink, an accusation that infuriated the sober barmaid, coming from Colette's slurred mouth. They may have come to blows had not Gordon intervened. Colette and her circle still felt a sense of betrayal, however, when Gordon quietly and politely told them not to drink in his pub again.

The following Saturday they took up residence in The Coach and Horses at the bottom of Owl Lane, a large, gloomy pub with a slightly rougher clientele – some bearded men with leather jackets always occupied one corner, Colette understood that they were called Hell's Angels, a youth cult of which she'd vaguely heard. Elsewhere there were sour looking old men in stained overcoats, or wan youths in shiny shirts and luminous socks. They didn't drink at The Coach and Horses for long. Although its space and noise meant that their presence didn't cause the disturbance it had at The Goat and Compasses, things became too noisy with the advent of live music. At nine o'clock every Saturday a lonesome cowboy would whoop and yodel through a wall of feedback while twanging a badly tuned electric guitar.

Colette and Aldous, after a few weeks, moved north with their entourage along Owl Lane to The Owl itself, a quieter pub. Its customers were the well-to-dos of Windhover Hill, the squires who owned the mansions of Parsons Lane. But its smallness and quietness meant their presence was soon causing an unwelcome disturbance. Colette for the first time became conscious of people looking at Julian in an odd way. She wondered if this was because some nights he brought his school homework to the pub and would sip halves of cider while solving problems of trigonometry, or discussing certain issues arising from the Russian Revolution, or whether it was because they recognized Janus in Julian. He was, as his adolescence progressed, bearing a stronger and stronger resemblance to his older brother.

'Put that homework away Julian, for Christ's sake,' said Colette one evening, feeling an unusual sense of shame at seeing Julian with his six inch ruler, his protractor, drawing circles with his compass, measuring angles, all the while munching dry-roasted peanuts and drinking Woodpecker.

Veronica Price was also made uncomfortable when Julian did his homework, especially when Julian would ask her for help, which he usually did, having manoeuvred himself into position beside her, so that he could show her the translation from French he was working on, or the plotted co-ordinates on a Cartesian graph.

'I really don't think it's a good idea for you to be doing your homework in a pub, Julian,' she said, 'what would your teachers say?'

'But you're a teacher, and you don't mind.'

'But I do mind. And I'm not *your* teacher.'

'I wish you were. Can I kiss you?'

'No.'

Julian kissed her anyway and giggled. Veronica feigned indignation.

'Anyway, how would my teachers know?'

'Well, they might . . .' Veronica paused, trying to think the problem through, '. . . they might smell cider on your homework.'

'I don't think so,' said Julian, sniffing his graphs.

Scott joined in.

'You might spill some on it, get your quadratic equations smudged.'

'Yes, and then what would your teachers say if they saw beer stains on your homework?'

'I'd say my girlfriend spilt it, and she's a teacher . . .'

'I'm not your girlfriend, Julian,' said Veronica, turning to the schoolboy and trying to speak with firmness. Seeing that her words had no effect she repeated them, but they were distracted by the intervention of Colette.

'Why do you have to do it now?' she said, 'when you've had all Saturday to do it – why do you have to leave it till we're in the pub?'

Julian didn't answer.

'Just so that you can embarrass me, isn't it?'

'Mother,' intervened Juliette, 'when it comes to embarrassment . . .'

Things came to a head one weekend when Colette had made a special plea to Julian not to bring his homework to the pub, and he had promised. But when they got to The Owl he sat there properly, drinking the pint of Stella she had bought him (Colette always got the first round in), and he'd waited until the others arrived – Veronica, Rita, Scott, Juliette, Boris, James – and had as usual managed to sit close to Veronica and quickly became engaged in some sort of intimate whispering and giggling that Colette wasn't sure that she approved of. When she saw Julian take out a school exercise book, a pencil with an eraser at its tip, and a ruler and begin measuring and drawing something in the book, having cleared a space amongst the empties, crumpled crisp packets and flecks of cigarette ash, Colette felt a blinding rush of anger that caused her to eject a half-finished glass of barley wine over the opened book, splashing generously across the open pages and beyond, into

Julian's lap, which caused Julian to jump and squirm in his seat as though he'd been electrocuted.

'There, explain that to your teachers . . .' said Colette, scowling. The drenched book, half a term's mathematics, smelling of fermented barley, a soggy mess on the table.

They stopped going to The Owl shortly after that, and migrated west along Taunton Drive to The Lemon Tree in Windhover Hill's leafiest quarter where, across a stretch of preserved lawns, the cemetery lay, and it was this fact that made The Lemon Tree only a brief interlude in the history of their Saturday nights, because whenever Colette left the pub she found herself in the vicinity of her dead loved ones, which at first she thought might be a comfort to her, but which turned out to be a source of intense pain which had her crying herself to sleep afterwards, and a sad Sunday to follow.

They moved back to the heart of Windhover Hill, to The Marquis of Granby on Hoopers Lane, a red brick, red tiled building with dormer windows, which had become the favourite drinking spot of young people on the make, whose Ford Capris were always parked outside like a regiment of streamlined infantry. The interior had been modernized, the furniture was bamboo and wickerwork, there was foliage everywhere. Here, at last, was a pub where Colette and her party didn't attract attention. Their various follies passed unnoticed by the self-absorbed, nouveau riche braggadocios that filled the bar – young men in T-shirts with tinted hair and neat moustaches, their girlfriends in leather jackets with short skirts and ice-cream hairdos. In one corner an older generation of drinkers gathered, who'd been drinking there since before the pub's refurbishment in favour of a younger clientele, but who remained and regarded their surroundings with the wide-eyed wonder and fear of someone witnessing visions of the future.

Aldous was a little worried at first about drinking in The Marquis of Granby. He had a feeling that Janus had been a regular in the past. But then he'd been a regular of every pub in the past.

'They wouldn't serve him in here,' said Colette with confidence, 'and anyway, he doesn't drink now.'

'Doesn't he?' said Aldous. 'That's what you think, is it?'

'I know it for a fact, and anyway, he's at work.'

But he didn't work every night. Even Janus had days off now and then. Usually they were midweek days. He was never off long enough to break his sleep pattern. On his days off he slept all day and was awake all night. Colette wondered what he did all night. Didn't he get lonely? *I love it,* Janus had declared. *It's like having everything to myself.*

'I don't think it can be a good thing to be on nights for so long. It's been over a year now. Or is it two years? He's been working nights all that time. It must do something to your mind after that long, it's not natural.'

'Can we stop talking about Janus?' said Aldous.

Colette did stop talking. So did Aldous. They would often sit silently like this, enjoying nothing more than watching their family and their family's friends enjoying themselves. They settled into a long spell as regulars of this pub. They spent a bleary Christmas Eve there. They drank out the old year and drank in the new. Their circle of friends continued to evolve. Every week someone new was brought along. James would present his latest girlfriend.

'She's a specialist in kinship systems,' he would say, introducing a serious-looking girl with no make-up and dark hair that hung in straight sorceress-like curtains around her face.

'Oh really, so she knows all about uncles and aunts, does she?' said Aldous

'Brothers and sisters have I none, but that man's father is my father's son,' said Colette.

'Actually, I'm investigating the incest taboo,' said the student.

'She's doing fieldwork in the Amazon next year,' said James, proudly.

Aldous and Colette were rather disappointed when the kinship specialist became a regular.

Colette found herself increasingly bothered by the flirtations that were continuing between Julian and Veronica. After observing them one evening, how Julian kept pawing at the woman, and how the woman failed to protest convincingly, she said to Aldous, 'Do you think Julian is sleeping with Veronica?'

'No,' he said with an immediacy, suggesting he'd already pondered the question himself, 'of course not.'

'Why "of course not"? Haven't you noticed how tall he's become? And he's started washing. He never used to wash . . .'

'Because we didn't have a bath.'

'Besides, I heard him and his pimply friends talking in The Lemon Tree, and they were talking as though he had slept with her.'

'Were they? How do you mean?'

'I caught phrases like *what was it like, what sort of noises did she make,* and more obscene remarks concerning anatomical details that I don't want to repeat. In short, O'Malley, or one of those three, I can never tell them apart, was asking him about the experience, and he was supplying rich, lurid detail.'

'Perhaps you misheard. They were probably talking about a film or something. Or else he was just pretending he'd slept with her.'

'Would it matter if he was sleeping with her, do you think?'

'I'm not sure. How old is he?'

'How old is Julian?'

'Yes.'

'You don't know how old your own son is?'

'I've forgotten. Can you remember?'

Colette thought for a moment.

'Well he's still at school isn't he? He must be too young. They'd be committing a crime.'

'To be honest,' said Aldous, 'if I thought that Julian was sleeping with Veronica I would find it a cause for celebration, even if it meant they both had to go to prison. I would light a box of Catherine wheels. I would hang flags from the acacia to celebrate the fact that I have a normal son.'

'Unlike Janus, you mean?'

'Yes, exactly.'

Colette sighed.

'I suppose you're right. In that case, perhaps we should be encouraging it. Perhaps I should have a word with Veronica . . .'

When she could, Colette did her best to eavesdrop on Julian's conversations with his friends and further became convinced that Julian was having an affair with Veronica.

One Saturday Julian didn't come to the pub, having gone

instead to a party at O'Malley's house in Dorset Street. Colette managed to seat herself next to Veronica, and while Boris entertained the company by performing tortoise races with the rest of the group (this consisted of balancing two cigarette papers on top of two glasses, the competitors then racing each other, each doing an impersonation of a tortoise eating a lettuce leaf, the slowest winning), Colette quizzed Veronica.

'I understand you're sleeping with my son.'

'What?'

'You're sleeping with Julian.'

'I'm not . . .'

'I don't mind if you are . . .'

'But I'm not – don't be ridiculous, he's a boy.'

'Yes, but he's very tall.'

'I'm sorry Colette. We're just friendly, that's all. We're not even that friendly.'

'I just want to make it plain that you have my blessing, that's all – and Aldous's. We've discussed it a lot . . .'

'Colette, please – the thought is too terrible for me to contemplate.'

Colette retreated for a while. Later in the evening she talked to Veronica again. By now a different game was taking place on the table. Boris had stretched a piece of tissue paper across a beer glass and balanced a coin on the paper. People took it in turns to burn a hole in the paper with the end of a cigarette. When the paper was eventually honeycombed with charred holes, whoever made the hole that finally allowed the coin to fall into the beer had to get the next round in.

'I have another son, you know . . .' said Colette.

'I know. He's sitting over there.'

'Apart from James, I mean. He seems to have a different girlfriend each week. I mean my son Janus. Do you know Janus?'

'Yes, I know Janus.'

'He's also very tall. And very good looking. He plays the piano . . .'

Veronica was holding up a hand.

'I know Janus very well, Colette, and I know what he's like. Please . . .'

Colette, crestfallen, retreated once more. She had done what she could. Janus claimed to be in a relationship with a nurse at the hospital. He had been claiming such for over a year, but he had never presented her at Fernlight Avenue, or any evidence at all that this nurse existed as anything other than a fantasy. Veronica would have been a good girlfriend for Janus. They were almost the same age (Veronica was a little younger), Veronica was intelligent, quite pretty in a Julie Andrews sort of way, musical, well read, she would have been an ideal match for Janus.

But Veronica didn't come to the pub the following week. Julian was back and looking wide-eyed and lost.

'Where's Veronica?' he said.

'She couldn't make it this week,' said Juliette, through whom Veronica made her arrangements for the Saturday evenings.

Veronica didn't come the following week either. Or the week after that. Each week of her absence caused an increasing level of anxiety visible in Julian's tetchiness and increasing drunkenness.

'I don't think she'll be coming back,' said Colette one evening.

'What do you know about it?' said Julian.

'Nothing, I just don't think she will.'

'You've said something to her haven't you. What have you said to her?'

'I haven't said anything to her. Anyway, you've been drinking too much. You must remember you're still a little boy.'

'But you bought me my drinks. You always buy my drinks.'

'Well I'm not buying you any more tonight, not when you talk to me like that, and stop leaning over the table, you'll spill Boris's drink.'

Julian began interrogating the others. No one knew anything, which was true, since the conversations between Colette and Veronica had passed unnoticed.

'Take it easy, Julian,' said Boris quietly as he filled his pipe.

'I'm going,' said Julian putting on the leather jacket he'd found one night in The Goat and Compasses and had worn almost permanently ever since.

'Where are you going?'

Julian didn't answer but left the pub.

His three friends, O'Malley, O'Flaherty and O'Hogarty, looked rather bewildered in his absence. Not having formed friendships with any others in the group, they seemed at a loss without him.

'You, you spotty twits,' said Colette, 'why don't you go after him, he might do something stupid.'

The three looked at each other, mumbled incomprehensibly and giggled.

'I'll go after him,' said Boris.

The group became a little subdued while Boris went in search of Julian. He was gone for over two hours. During that time James had amused himself by running a dampened finger round the rim of a wine glass to produce a high pitched wailing noise. The others, fascinated by this phenomenon, joined in with other glasses, producing a spontaneous orchestra of glassy wailing, until someone from another table, a young blond-haired man with a tight-fitting T-shirt leant across.

'Please', he said, 'it's frightfully annoying.'

James, Boris and Scott, quite drunk by this time, were taken aback by this intervention to the extent that they were silent for about ten minutes. Then feeling affronted by the request, revived their wine-glass wailing, at the same time as loudly ridiculing the well-spoken voice of the man in the T-shirt.

'Oh it's frightfully dreadful isn't it?'

'Yes it's most dreadfully frightful isn't it darling?'

'Yes its most dreadully awfully annoying darling . . .'

It seemed as though things might have turned unpleasant, as the T-shirted man was looking increasingly perturbed, and seemed to be discussing the situation with his T-shirted colleagues, when Boris returned with Julian. Julian looked bedraggled. It was raining outside.

'I found him outside Veronica's house,' Boris told Colette, 'sitting in the front garden in the rain.'

Julian didn't speak to his mother, or anyone else, for the rest of the evening, but remained silent, scowling from under a mop of damp, matted hair.

It was the arrival of Janus in the pub one evening that ended their nights at The Marquis of Granby. He came into the pub carrying Scipio under his arm. He quietly bought a drink for himself and sat at their table, the cat purring contentedly in his arms. Janus did not acknowledge the presence of anyone else in the pub. He didn't even make eye contact with anyone, he just sat there, Scipio washing himself in his lap, dabbing a paw at a crisp packet that moved in the breeze.

The group melted away quickly. Rita and Scott, James and his girlfriend. O'Malley, O'Hogarty and O'Flaherty remained, since they knew nothing about Janus. Eventually it was just them, Julian, and his parents left at the table, while Janus went on sitting there, as though he believed himself alone.

How old he looks now, thought Colette, who felt as though she hadn't seen him for years. The moustache made him look old, the long sideburns as well. But he was putting on weight. His neck had thickened. He had the beginnings of a double chin and a beer belly. The drink had taken its toll. And the long nights. He was getting bags under his eyes.

Janus remained silent. It was Julian who spoke. The first time he had spoken directly to his mother for several weeks.

'I'm leaving school this summer,' he said.

Colette was shocked.

'Are you allowed to yet? You're too young, surely.'

'I'm old enough,' he said, still sulky.

'What are you going to do?'

'I'm going to join the merchant navy.'

Colette didn't know what to say. Aldous was silent, although he smiled. Before she could discuss it Julian was gone, out of the pub with his three friends. Aldous and Colette were alone with Janus.

'He's running away to sea,' she said to her husband quietly.

'He didn't mean it,' said Aldous, reassuringly, 'can you imagine it, Julian a sailor? It's ridiculous.'

'I think he meant it,' said Colette, 'he *did* mean it. He's running away to sea. We've driven him – I've driven him – away . . .'

Janus continued stroking Scipio. He had not looked at his parents since entering the pub, instead he had looked at Scipio, intently. Petting him, stroking his ears, nuzzling his brows where the velvety, silver fur lay, stroking his nose, fondling his paws, his tail, his tummy.

Colette suddenly said, 'That cat looks different.' Then, 'He's got no whiskers!'

Janus looked up.

'I've cut them off,' he said.

Looking closely she could see. Scipio's white whiskers ended abruptly a quarter of an inch from his face.

'Why?' said Colette.

Janus looked at her. She could see that the redness in his eyes was not due to the sleeplessness of so long on nights, but to crying. Janus had been crying.

'Scipio is dying,' he said.

17

Scipio *was* dying. He died the next day, a Sunday.

At Janus's insistence, they had a proper funeral.

It was funeral weather that day in the back garden, clouds of varying shades of grey hurrying in the sky – a late spring chill. The garden was still in recovery from a severe winter, the hummocky lawn had a dirty, greasy complexion from several weeks under snow. The previous autumn's leaves rotted in the flowerbeds. Janus had dug a small grave beneath the pershore tree. It was a problem to know where to bury animals without disturbing the bones of previously interred pets. Janus had been about to dig beneath the lilac before Colette reminded him there were at least two cats buried beneath the tree.

The coffin was a brown cardboard box hand-decorated by Janus in a vaguely Egyptian design (Anubi and the eye of Horus were a prominent feature), and Scipio lay inside shrouded in fabric cut from one of Colette's old dresses – a crimson material embroidered in gold thread with horses, though this was visible to none of the mourners as Janus lay the coffin in the grave.

A reluctant Aldous was present at the insistence of Janus. Julian was there less reluctantly. Everyone looked down into the grave with solemnity while Janus provided an oration which began with a recital of Scipio's pedigree.

'Scipio, of the family Silver, of the line of Silverseal and Silverleaf, son of Sylvia Clairedelune and Silverseal Edward, whose grandparents were Silverseal Maurice, Hillcross Silver Petal, Silverseal Reginald Bosanquet, Silverleaf Tiffany, of the line of Bellever Calchas d'Acheaux, Silverseal Alouette, Jezreel Jake, Csardas Silhouette, Silver Lute of Blagdon, Silverleaf Leineven, Hillcross Silver Flute, Marguerite of Silverleigh, Lady Jane, Demon Lover, Silverseal Black Lion. O Friends, No more these sounds! Let us sing more cheerful songs, more full of Joy! Joy, bright spark of divinity, Daughter of Elysium, fire-inspired we tread thy sanctuary. Thy magic powers re-unite all that custom has divided, all men become brothers under the sway of thy gentle wings.'

Janus tipped earth onto Scipio's coffin. Colette was glad to see that he seemed to be coping well with the emotion of the day, particularly by the optimistic recital of Schiller to close the oration. She had worried a little about how the death of the cat would affect her son, who had been so unnaturally fond of the animal, especially since its injury. The first effect Colette noticed was that Janus had begun talking about death. It occurred to her that he had never talked much about death before, at least not since his childhood.

'Why doesn't it drive you mad?' he said to her one morning after coming home from work.

'Why doesn't what drive me mad?' said Colette.

'The thought of dying.'

'Why doesn't it drive *you* mad?' Colette returned.

'But you're so much closer to it. You're getting on for sixty now – and if you look at yourself in the mirror and think how you've treated your body over the years, you can't be expecting to get much further – so how do you cope with it? I suppose you just close your mind – but how do you do it?'

Then another morning, he would claim to have the answer.

'I know – you just get tired of worrying about it don't you? It's not that you ingore it, but that your mind just gets tired of it. Bored of it, I suppose. That's what happened when I went to the dentist yesterday. For three weeks I had been putting it off and letting the pain get worse and worse, and worrying about what the dentist would do, and I thought – how am I actually going to get myself through the door of the dentist's surgery without running away? But the day before I just stopped worrying – I'd used all my worry up and I just walked into the surgery as though I was doing nothing more frightening than buying a pint of milk. That must be what happens with old people like you – you just get tired of worrying about it and in the end you don't care about dying at all.'

'I wish you would stop talking like this,' said Colette, 'it must be the nights. You must stop working nights like this, Janus, you must come back to the daylight with the rest of us, you're getting too morbid.'

She felt it was true. He didn't sleep well during the day. There was an annoying motorcyclist who'd rented one of the garages next door and who spent whole afternoons tinkering noisily with his machines and wouldn't stop no matter how many times Colette complained. Sleep deprivation can kill people, so she'd read, slowly and unnoticeably, like a poison. And Janus's morbidity seemed to reach a new level when he came home one morning shortly afterwards.

He had brought home with him a large leather bag which, after making himself a cup of tea, he placed on the table. He unzipped it and lifted something carefully from within – a bundle of newspaper wrapping something that had, evidently, to be handled carefully.

'What have you got there?' said Colette with idle curiosity, taking a sip of whisky from the tumbler on the bookshelf.

'A brain,' Janus replied, quietly and flatly.

'What?'

Janus had lowered the wrapped object onto a cleared space on the table. He was carefully lifting the folded corners of the newspaper. He didn't speak.

'Did you say "a brain"?'

Colette was amused, thinking it some sort of joke.

'It's a brain,' said Janus, as though having confirmed something for himself now that the paper was open. From Colette's sitting position she could see nothing but folded newsprint.

'A real one? You don't mean a real, human one?'

'Yes,' said Janus, 'come and see.'

Colette stood up, but a weakness came to her legs as her line of sight approached the centre of the big open flower of newsprint on the table. She felt a powerful shyness come over her, an unexpected sense of dread and horror, of nausea. She could stand but wouldn't approach.

'I don't want to see it Janus. Just tell me you're joking.'

'I'm not joking.' Janus seemed amused by Colette's alarm.

'Where did you get it?'

'From work. I was helping out at the mortuary last night.'

'Mortuary? You don't work in the mortuary . . .'

'Someone has to wheel the dead bodies over. How do you think they get there? Stan, the mortician, is a good friend. He lets me watch some of the post-mortems. He even let me hold one of the circular saws once . . .'

'And he let you walk out with someone's brain?'

'They were only going to throw it away.'

'Throw someone's brain away?'

'They always throw the brain away. Come and have a look, mother. It's a wonderful thing. Look how big it is. When I first saw a human brain I was amazed at how big it was. I thought how could that possibly fit in someone's head? But they expand in the open air. In the head they're all tightly packed, but when they're outside they sort of flop out . . .'

Colette inched forward, her eyes fixed on the bundle of paper as though expecting something to leap out of it. Suddenly she caught a glimpse of something – organic matter, yellowy grey, shiny, convoluted . . .'

'Oh Christ,' she said, 'Oh Christ.'

'What's the matter with you?'

'I can't believe you've done this Janus.'

'Done what? They were only going to throw it in the bin like I said . . .'

'They wouldn't throw a brain away, not at the hospital.'

'You've no idea have you mother? In some post-mortems the brain is sliced up like a salami. It disintegrates like junket, they can't put it back in the head. They usually put the heart in the head wrapped up in a copy of the *Sun*. Then they throw the brain away. It was my job to dispose of this brain, but I saw that for once it was a relatively undamaged one. They'd only poked at it a couple of times because they knew what the cause of death was, and it wasn't anything to do with the brain. So I thought I'd keep it. It was very easy to sneak it back to my locker, where I kept it until I found this bag. Now I'm going to find a way of preserving it before it starts going off. I need to get some embalming fluid from somewhere, or some formaldehyde. I would have got some from the hospital stores but it might have attracted suspicion. Can I keep it in your nice new fridge for now?'

'No you can't. You're not even going to keep it in this

kitchen, or in this house. I want it out of this house now.'

Janus looked a little disappointed.

'But it's such a good fridge,' he said. 'Do you really want this brain to rot?'

'I don't want the brain at all,' then Colette added, in a quieter tone, 'whose is it?'

'It's mine.'

'You know what I mean. Whose is it?'

'It belonged to Mrs Ritchie. She died of cancer a couple of days ago. I was always wheeling her here and there. She knew she didn't have long to go. She used to give me her fags. I sometimes used to nip out and get a Chinese takeaway for her. She only ever ate the rice. She would ask for chicken curries and sweet and sour porks but she only ever ate the rice. Where's your egg-fried rice now, eh?'

Janus addressed the brain.

'Funny to think this object once desired sweet and sour pork isn't it? But Mrs Ritchie always used to say to me, "Janus, whenever I eat Chinese I always feel that there is a food I like more than this, but I don't know what it is. Can you tell me?" And I would say "Indian? Spanish? French? Italian?" and she would shake her head disgustedly at each one. We never did find out what that food was, did we, dear?'

Janus was looking down on the brain. Colette took another peep, glimpsed blood vessels, felt sick again.

'When people die in hospital they are never spoken about afterwards. The staff pretend they never existed. When I went in yesterday and asked what had happened to Mrs Ritchie the staff nurse looked really shocked and didn't know how to answer me at first. She behaved as though no member of staff had ever asked her a question like that before. You'd think in a hospital people would be more open about death, but the opposite is the case. It's more taboo than ever. There are no signs to the mortuary. There are signs to every other place, but none to the mortuary.'

'Well how would you like it if you were seriously ill and you didn't know what was wrong with you and someone was wheeling you down a corridor and you saw a sign saying "To the mortuary"?'

'I'd feel happy,' said Janus, 'to know that I was in a place where they take care of the dead.'

'And is that what you call taking care of the dead? Stealing someone's brain and wrapping it up in newspaper to take home and gawp at?'

'I went to the mortuary afterwards to look for Mrs Ritchie. I found her in one of the fridges, middle shelf, still in her nightie, just dumped there like a sack of potatoes. There was frost in her hair . . .'

'Shut up Janus. I don't want to know. Just take this thing away from here, I don't care what you do with it, just take it away from here . . .'

Janus was silent. He looked at the brain, folded the papers over it protectively.

'You want me to throw it away?'

'Yes.'

'In the dustbin?'

'Yes – no. Not this dustbin. I don't know . . .'

'Shall I bury it in the garden?'

'No. It's a person. I'm not having a person buried in my garden. You can't throw it in the bin, it wouldn't be right . . .' Colette was desperately confused. She didn't know what Janus had done. Somehow it seemed to her akin to murder, but perhaps it was only theft, but what order of theft? What magnitude? Kidnapping? And yet at the same time it was only a piece of organic tissue. She had to call for Aldous, who was unhappy to be drawn from his haven in the front room, where he spent the mornings until Janus went to bed. He was unusually decisive.

'Take that brain away or I'll call the police.'

'And what do you propose I do with it?'

'That's your problem. And you're not disposing of it here. It needs to be treated properly.'

'I keep telling you, at the hospital they were only going to throw it away.'

'Throw it away where?' said Colette, 'Tell us exactly what they do with them.'

'They go in a big bag that gets taken to the incinerator along with all the other hospital rubbish.'

'But they probably have a special incinerator for body parts,' said Colette.

'I don't think so.'

'Have you actually seen it, though?'

'No.'

'Well it's probably a special incinerator that's been blessed by the local bishops and rabbis and all the other religious people.'

'I doubt it mother. The hospital regards things like this as waste, nothing more, there's nothing special about it. A hand is not a person, just as a person is not a hand. This brain is no one. Saying this brain is someone is like saying the television is Tommy Cooper or Des O'Connor, or whoever happens to be on at the time. This is merely the atrophied machinery that was once operated by a conscious force.'

'Then why is it so important to you? You associate this thing with the living woman it once belonged to. This Mrs Ritchie, if you were thinking of keeping it as some sort of memento you can see yourself that it is a special thing, it is a part of a human body.'

'So is a toenail clipping. Should we bury those in consecrated ground?'

'This is getting us nowhere, Janus,' said his father.

'It's interesting though isn't it?'

'No, Janus, it's sick. You have only one option. Take this brain back to the hospital where it can be disposed of properly, or I'll call the police this minute.'

It seemed, after a little more discussion, that Janus was seeing sense.

'I'll take it back when I go to work tonight.'

'No, Janus, take it back now. Immediately.'

Reluctantly Janus left the house with the brain in his bag. He'd first complained that it would be difficult to smuggle the brain back into the hospital system if he went there outside his shift, but his parents persuaded him that a suitable excuse for his presence could be found.

'I can't take any more of this,' said Aldous once they were alone, 'worrying about the next thing Janus does. We've been worrying like this for more than ten years, worrying about what we'll find when we get home, worrying about what Janus will be like when we get home, worrying about what he'll bring home with him. A brain! What'll it be next time, a whole corpse? How long before he kills someone . . .'

'Don't be so melodramatic Aldous. The boy just has a natural curiosity about things. He's been obsessed with death since Scipio died . . .'

'You always find some way of justifying his behaviour don't you? You always have done. If you could be made to see sense about that boy he could have been living in his own place by now like a relatively normal human being instead of wasting his life wheeling dying people down corridors . . .'

'Oh don't come all that wasting his life muck with me, Aldous, we all know you're just jealous of the boy . . .'

'Jealous?'

'. . . yes, jealous, jealous of his gifts, jealous of the fact that he's a true artist while you're just an art teacher . . .'

Colette bit her lip. Aldous retired hurt to the front room. They rarely argued along these lines and rarely discussed Janus together. But Colette was disturbed by Janus's behaviour to an unusual degree, not just by his morbid curiosity, but by the presence of human organic matter in the house, as though a stranger had intervened in their affairs, and that was what had made her snap at her husband. She apologized later, but Aldous had affected a vague indifference, as he always did in situations like that.

They waited for Janus to come home from having returned the brain. But he didn't come home, and that concerned them. Janus had not been on a bender for over a year, more like two. Colette had begun to think that those days were over. *They can never be over*, Aldous had said. *No matter how long Janus stays off the bottle, he will always be in between drinks. Not until he drops dead without taking a sip can you say he has truly quit drink.*

'Something's gone wrong,' said Colette to her husband that night. 'Should I phone the hospital to see if he's turned up for work?'

'No,' said Aldous.

'I've got this horrible feeling that he's in trouble for stealing that brain. Supposing he was found out. Suppose someone saw him with it. Would it be a serious crime, do you think?'

'I don't know,' said Aldous.

Janus didn't come home the following morning, and was absent the entire day. Colette's imagination raced.

'I think he tried to put that brain back where he found it. I think he tried to put it back in Mrs Ritchie.'

'Don't be absurd.'

'She might still have been in the fridge, he might have cut her open . . .'

Janus didn't return home the morning after that either. He was gone, in all, for three days. And then, one evening, Aldous and Colette sitting alone in the kitchen, heard an odd noise. It was a little bell ringing. A little tinkling bell, like those the little altar boys ring during the celebration of mass. Tinkle-tinkle-tinkle, distant at first, then it came nearer. At one point it was so close that it sounded as though it was in the alleyway beside the house.

'Go and see what it is,' said Colette, 'there's someone in the alley.'

Aldous hesitated. It was dark outside. Then the tinkling receded, and eventually faded into the distance.

But it came back. Tinkle-tinkle-tinkle, distant at first, coming nearer. Again it came as close as the alley. The noise rose and fell as the bell went back and forth along the alley.

'See who it is, Aldous,' said Colette.

'It'll be Janus,' said Aldous, standing up, 'who else would do something so ridiculous as walk around ringing a bell?'

'Go and have a look all the same. I'd ask Julian but he's out tonight.'

Aldous went to the back door and opened it. The house lights lit up the nearby leaves of the fruit trees, but beyond that was blackness. To the left the gate that led to the alley. He leant across and peeped over it. He could see that the alley was empty. The ringing had stopped as soon as he'd opened the door. Aldous came back into the kitchen.

'Nothing,' he said, 'Just Janus mucking around. He must have run off.'

'There it is again,' said Colette, 'over there this time. It's on the other side.'

'Just ignore it,' said Aldous.

They tried to ignore it. The ringing continued for half an hour or more, receding into the distance, returning, receding, returning. Sometimes it sounded as though it was in the streets beyond the garden-ends, in Hoopers Lane or Woodberry Road. Sometimes, when near, it was as though it was in the garden itself. Then, just as they were beginning to think that the sound had stopped, there came a new sound, shockingly loud, as though inside the house, not a bell this time but a peculiar sound, like the chopping of wood, but with a ringing undertone to it.

'The piano,' said Aldous, and went to the music room. Colette followed. In the music room they found Janus, who had broken in through the French windows. He had a stone in his hand, a large white chunk of quartzy rock, probably picked from a front garden rockery. With this he was knocking splinters of black wood out of the body of the piano.

Aldous and Colette took a moment to react, because Janus looked so different. He was wearing a long, brown, suede trench coat with the collar turned up, and a white panama hat. To the belt of the coat, whose strap was hanging down, he had tied a small brass handbell. Bending down to take another blow at the piano with the rock his face was invisible. When he lifted himself and they could see his face, they saw that it looked very calm and pale, but cold. It was not the sort of face he had when drunk, which was red and floppy.

Aldous was immediately firm in his schoolmasterly way, marched towards Janus demanding that he stop.

'This instrument's worth thousands of pounds, you fool.'

He was unprepared for the way Janus pounced on him. Perhaps he was sober after all, because he could never have managed such a manoeuvre in the slurred states of his drunkenness. He grappled his father, twisting his arms behind his back so that he was helpless. Aldous yelped. It had been some years since he had had to use force on Janus, and during that time he'd become an old man, while sober Janus had a newfound strength built up over the two years he'd spent pushing and lifting patients of all sizes and weights.

'No, Janus,' shouted Colette, bashing Janus with her fists as he passed, pushing her husband before him, rather like one of the trolleys or stretchers at the hospital. Her blows went unnoticed. Janus was talking matter-of-factly.

'Let's see how you like it now, dear father. Think of all those times you've had me thrown out of the house. Now it's your turn. How would you like to be thrown out on the streets like a dog, eh? But at least you'll have shoes on.'

Janus was pushing Aldous through the hall towards the front door.

'What's the matter, Janus, what's wrong?' called Colette, following behind, trying to pull Janus back.

Janus paused and turned to her.

'You've got me the sack from my job, so I'm going to throw you out of the house . . .'

'What do you mean, the sack? You haven't been sacked have you?'

'I think that's what you call it when they say you can't work there any more. I was trying to put the brain back like you told me to, and they thought I was taking it, so there we are. The sack. Now you're getting the sack.'

'Janus, just think for a moment,' said Aldous, as Janus opened the front door.

'I've been thinking for days, father, thinking for days of all the ways you've tried to spoil my life, of all the times you've had me thrown out of the house, of the times you've punched me in the face. You are a very violent man, father. I've thought of all the times you've tried to stop me working in the jobs I love, and all the times you've separated me from the women I've loved. Gwen, Christine, Angelica, Mary, you frightened them all away didn't you, and now you've separated me from my true love . . .'

'What's he talking about?' Aldous called to his wife as he was pushed through the front door. Janus let go of his arms and gave him a shove that nearly knocked Aldous over, but he managed to keep his balance and instead jogged calmly along the path to the pavement. He made no attempt to retaliate, but waited on the pavement, his hands in his pockets.

'What do you mean your true love, Janus?'

'Your turn now, mother,' said Janus, taking his mother by the arms as he had done Aldous, and pushing her out of the door. He slammed the front door shut and turned the hall light out.

Aldous and Colette, alone on the pavement, noticed how chilly it was, and silent.

'We'll have to call on the Milliners,' said Colette, after a moment's thought.

'They're not in,' said Aldous, 'I heard them going out this evening.'

'We'll have to go to the police then. We can't . . .'

'Oh sod the police!' Aldous suddenly snapped, 'it'll be the same old story, *Sorry guv, nothing we can do, domestic.* The police never do anything, they just leave it to us, he's our son, its our house, what can they do . . .'

'Well we can't stay here all night. We have to face it, we can't handle Janus any more, he's too much for us . . .'

'I'm glad to hear you say that at last. How long has it taken you to realize that?'

Colette paused. The two of them let their frosty breaths fight instead.

'Have you got your keys?' said Colette.

'Yes.'

'Let's just go back in then.'

'Later, when he's calmed down. We could go to the pub in the meantime . . .'

And so they went to The Red Lion and drank there until closing time. They said very little to each other, and only when they'd left the pub did Aldous crumble.

'I'm not going back home,' he said, as they walked along the orange-lit Green Lanes, 'I can't face it. I just can't . . .'

'But it's our home.'

'Not tonight it isn't. Let's go to a hotel or something. I'm not going home . . .'

Colette was about to remonstrate – *are you going to let your own son drive you out of your own home,* but she realized it would have been no use. Then she had an idea.

'Let's go to Juliette's flat. It's not far from here.'

It was only a fifteen minute walk from The Red Lion, across the little Venice of the New River, through winding, leafy back streets until they came to the quaint little Grange where Juliette now lived with Boris. The Grange was an old pre-suburban mansion converted into flats. The main entrance was flanked by twin greyhounds in recumbent pose, the building itself a restrained fantasy of Victorian gothic, packing turrets, spires, domes and buttresses into a small area between a car park and the North Circular Road.

Colette was struck, as she always was, by the cosiness of her daughter's abode. They only had three rooms on the first floor of a crowded block, and yet the space seemed far more secure than Colette's, whose house stood almost in its own grounds. The Grange was a safe, secure little haven that Boris had fitted out with all the accoutrements most people thought appropriate to a dwelling of the late twentieth century – wall-to-wall carpets, central heating, a colour television, a hi-fi. On first visiting the flat Colette had been gently condescending – 'Wall-to-wall carpets always seem so bland, there's no variety in floor surface' or 'Central heating always seems so bland, there's no variety in temperature from room to room' or 'Colour television always seems so bland, there's no variety in tone or contrast . . .' But now she felt disinclined to criticize. Wall-to-wall carpets now seemed a welcoming thing to her, they meant that wherever you fell in the house you would always have a soft landing.

She was surprised how forcefully Boris reacted to the news of what Janus had done. Juliette had warned her mother that this mild telephone engineer had a ferocious temper when roused. And now she saw evidence of it. He was about to drive round to Fernlight Avenue to confront Janus himself, and would have, they believed, had they not restrained him. It was too late now, they said, leave it until the morning.

'You've got no choice now, mother,' said Juliette once the four of them had settled down on the brown, fluffy three-piece suite, 'You will have to get him legally evicted.'

Colette looked sulkily into her coffee, she felt like someone who had lost a long-running argument. Her defence came in a weak, apologetic voice.

'He's just a bit mixed up about death at the moment, ever since Scipio died, and he's suffering from sleep deprivation, I know it . . .'

Her comments were met with a barrage of derision from the other three, that made her instantly recant.

'All right. He needs slinging out. I agree . . .'

'And something else,' said Boris, 'You need a telephone.'

'But Aldous hates telephones, don't you darling?'

The three turned towards Aldous, who was unable to say anything.

'I insist you get a telephone,' said Juliette, 'I'll have it put in myself.'

'But they take ages, you have to wait months, even years for a telephone,' Colette began, but Boris knew about telephones.

'You can plead special circumstances,' he said, 'If you can convince them that your life's in danger they'll put a phone in for you tomorrow.'

'I'll convince them,' said Juliette, 'they shouldn't take much convincing.'

Aldous had closed his eyes dreamily, by this time, and was waving his hand gently, as if to say he no longer cared what anyone did about anything.

And so Colette and Aldous slept on the floor of their daughter's living room.

18

Boris took the morning off work and Juliette missed her morning lectures to take Aldous and Colette home the next day.

Juliette had geared herself up for a confrontation with Janus, but as they drove towards Fernlight Avenue they saw him walking along the street in the opposite direction. He was still wearing the suede trench coat and the panama hat, and still came the tinkling noise from the bell tied to his waist.

Julian was at home when they arrived.

'Why aren't you at school?' said Colette.

'Why weren't you at home last night?' her son retorted.

The house seemed more or less in order. The sink was a mess of unwashed crockery. The piano had taken no further injuries, though records and music manuscripts were scattered on the music room floor. According to Julian there had been no incidents the night before. He had come home late from a friend's house and had gone straight to bed. He'd seen Janus in the morning, and reported that he'd seemed in very good spirits.

'He kept saying how happy he was, how good his life was. Then he tried to borrow money off me. I didn't have any. Is he out of work again?'

'Let's go and find a solicitor now,' said Juliette.

'Now?' said Colette, 'We've only just got in. Can't we have a cup of tea?'

Aldous had already crept away to the front room to read the paper.

'We've got to act now,' said Juliette, 'don't you remember what you said last night?'

'I was upset last night. I'd just been thrown out of my own home.'

'And now everything's fine again, is that what you're saying?'

'I'm just saying I'd like to have a cup of tea and a sit down before we go rushing into anything.'

Julian sloped off to his bedroom.

'If you don't do something now, you'll never do anything. You'll have Janus living here for the rest of your life.'

'Of course I won't. He'll sort himself out eventually. He needs time. He's a very sensitive man. Disturbance upsets him, changes to routine. Losing his job was a big blow for him. You don't know what it's like to lose your job, do you? I can remember how I felt when I left the buses. You don't just lose a job, you lose your friends, you lose your skills, you lose your reason to live, almost. And Janus was in love with one of the nurses there, so he's lost the woman he loves. That is bound to make you act strangely, surely.'

'Mother, you must stop deluding yourself about Janus. He's not going to sort himself out, ever, while he lives here . . .'

Juliette and her mother continued to argue. Juliette couldn't quite believe that her mother was prevaricating yet again.

She asked Boris.

'Boris, go and get daddy, he's disappeared again. He needs to help me persuade mummy to go to a solicitor.'

Boris returned from the front room to announce that Aldous was refusing to come out.

'He's drinking a bottle of whisky.'

'Daddy? Drinking?'

'Neat whisky,' added Boris.

'So that's where it's gone,' said Colette brightly, 'I thought Janus must have found it. Boris, would you go and get the whisky for me?'

'How can you even think about drinking after what's been going on here for these last couple of days?' said Juliette.

'My nerves are shattered, Juliette, I need a drink . . .'

There then followed further discussion during which the subject of Aldous drinking in the next room was forgotten, until they heard a groan.

'What was that noise?'

'It sounded like someone in pain.'

Boris went to investigate, and returned to announce that Aldous had drunk almost a whole bottle of whisky.

317

Then Aldous appeared, flinging the door open so it banged loudly against Juliette's hair. His face was a deep purple which made his white hair seem stupidly bright. He was grinning in rather a menacing way.

'Have you drunk all my whisky?' said Colette indignantly as Aldous swayed uncertainly across the kitchen towards the sink. Thoughts of Janus Brian came to Colette's mind. That careful stagger he used to have. Aldous picked up a saucepan and a small dining knife with a loose, yellow-boned handle.

'Come on sirrah,' he said, brandishing the knife as a sword, the saucepan as a shield, 'I'll stab you up, I'll stab you up you wench, you harlot. You do me wrong to take me out of my grave. You are a soul in bliss and I am bound upon a wheel of fire!'

He lunged with apparent playfulness at Colette with the knife, who managed to get out of her chair in time. Juliette laughed. She had not yet fully understood her father's state and took his behaviour for welcome tomfoolery. Boris, uncertain as to how to handle the patriarch of his girlfriend's house, moved as if to grapple the knife from him, but hesitated. Aldous swung the knife randomly.

'You see me here, you gods, a poor old man, as full of grief as age . . .'

'Get the knife off him Boris,' said Colette, sheltering behind her daughter. Aldous was so drunk he seemed unable to see anything, and continued to take swipes at the empty chair where Colette had been. Boris was still nervous about manhandling Aldous, and made only tentative efforts to take the knife.

'Spit, fire, spout rain, I never gave you kingdom, called you children . . .'

Aldous was at the sink again, swishing his knife clumsily at the broken crockery. He turned the tap on full, splish-splashed in the dirty water, sent spray everywhere. Boris again made an effort to grapple with Aldous, but he was a small man against Aldous's lumbering bulk, and he took a knock from the base of a saucepan that felled him briefly.

'The art of our necessities is strange that can make vile things precious . . .'

The words were barely intelligible amid the slurred growling of Aldous's drunken locution. Plates fell to the floor and broke.

The stacked dishes in the sink fell with a clatter. Aldous's flailing saucepan hit a light bulb and shattered it. He stumbled forward, fell against the cooker on which a pan of water for Colette's tea was boiling. Bubbles were just beginning to form. He picked the steaming saucepan up.

The others gave little screams, and felt terror at seeing boiling water in the hands of a drunk. The pot tipped back and forth, and some scalding water spilt. Bubbling water splashed onto Aldous's wrists but he seemed not to feel it. Colette and Juliette ran for shelter, ducking down beneath the kitchen table as Aldous wildly threw the water across the room. It landed on the table, and dripped to the floor on all sides, surrounding Colette and her daughter.

Then a pause in the activity. Colette and her daughter emerged from under the table to see Aldous standing in the middle of the room. He was frowning, his head lowered, as though concentrating deeply. A hand felt blindly for the chair behind him, Colette's chair by the boiler space, and Aldous sank slowly backwards into it, still frowning, his eyes closed, a hand to his brow, concentrating deeply. Finally he said 'oh dear' and slumped forwards, then sideways, a loose arm flopping out.

'I have never seen my father drunk in my entire life,' said Juliette, thoughtfully. Colette went over to her husband and slapped his cheeks. There was no response other than a deep groan, confirming that he was alive.

'You can see what you've done to him,' said Juliette.

'What *I've* done to him?'

'What you and Janus in combination have done to him. You've driven him to drink. You've driven him to the depths. Can't you see? You've driven him over the edge.'

Colette was shocked into contrition by Aldous's behaviour. She had not seen Aldous drunk before.

'Alright,' she said finally, sitting down, 'we'll go to a solicitor, but not today.'

'Let me go, mother,' said Juliette, 'You and daddy won't have to do anything except sign some papers. We'll sort it all out for you. Me and Boris can sort it out this morning.'

'Do what you must,' said Colette, 'just leave us in peace for a while.'

So Juliette and Boris left the house, Colette sitting in the armchair opposite her unconscious husband. She watched him for a long time. She pondered for a while how rarely she had had the opportunity of observing Aldous asleep. Not since she'd begun taking sleeping pills had she been conscious while Aldous dozed. But now she was awake and he was asleep. How he frowned in his sleep. Did he always frown like that when asleep, she wondered. He must be having terribly serious dreams. He must be dreaming he was a high court judge with a complex and difficult case to sum up. He must be dreaming he was a scientist pondering a new theory of gravity. Or a composer wrangling with the development section of the third movement of his fifth symphony. That was it. With his furrowed brow and sternly set mouth, and his wild coif of white hair, he looked like Beethoven. But only when he slept.

After a while he stirred. And then he said something.

'What was that?' said Colette, bending near, 'what did you say?'

'Let me not be like Janus Brian,' Aldous gasped, his eyes still closed, still asleep, 'Not Janus Brian. I don't want to be like Janus Brian. I don't want to see the golf courses of Spain.'

Part Five

19

Robin F. Queen & Co
1867 Green Lanes
Windhover Hill
London

26th April 1978

Dear Mr and Mrs Jones

I have been contacted by your daughter, Mrs Juliette Brothers, regarding the matter of access to your property – 89 Fernlight Avenue.

Mrs Brothers informs me that she has explained the situation to you, and that you are satisfied with the arrangements so far undertaken. However, before we can proceed further, I will need to see you both in person. This is in order that I can satisfy myself that you are both in agreement on this matter. I also require your signature on the relevant documentation.

Would you be kind enough to attend my office on Tuesday 30th April at 11am? Please telephone if this is not convenient.

Yours sincerely

Robin F. Queen

Colette wondered if she'd done the right thing in getting a telephone. Its bell seemed rather quiet. From the kitchen they had trouble hearing it. It gave out a ringing sound with the feebleness of an old lady rattling her jewellery. Then when she picked up the receiver she would usually be told off by the caller (who was nearly always Juliette), for taking so long to answer. She supposed she would get used to it, though it would take time. She was still putting her milk in the cupboard when they'd had a fridge for more than a year.

But these things now seemed to be out of her hands. As her daughter had arranged the telephone, so she had also set in motion a process that would lead to the legal banishment of her eldest son from the house.

Juliette drove them to the solicitor's office.

The solicitor was a man slightly younger than Janus, though as tall. He had dark hair, dark little eyes and a big, beefy face, shiny with sweat. He had a beautiful, soft, melodious voice.

He told Aldous and Colette that they had a very strong case for evicting their son. His age, for one thing, worked against him, as did his criminal record. There were plenty of police officers willing to testify, which would in itself provide sufficient evidence for the judge to find in their favour.

At Colette's request the solicitor provided an outline of the impending legal process.

'Once the wheels are set in motion I, or one of my clerks, will serve a court summons on your son. By this we mean that the document has to be physically placed in your son's possession. At a future date we will discuss when and where would be the best time for this to take place. Failure to serve the summons correctly could jeopardize the whole case. Once that is done we can go to court. If we can plead urgent circumstances . . .' here the solicitor cast a fleeting glance in Aldous's direction, 'then that could happen in a matter of days, though more likely weeks. Altogether your son could be legally evicted within about three weeks if things go smoothly, though more likely four to five weeks.'

'And once he's evicted? How does that happen?'

'If the case is successful the judge will set an eviction date. Your son's solicitor will of course plead that this will be as far in the future as possible, particularly if your son is out of work and doesn't have means to support himself. It's all down to the judge and the various pleas we make. However, once a date is agreed upon, your son will have to leave your premises by that date and time. If not, the police will have the right to forcibly remove him, and if he repeatedly breaks the eviction order he will be liable to a prison sentence. The eviction will not be simply from your home, Mrs Jones, but from a specified area surrounding your home. Again, that is up to the judge. They sometimes set absurdly precise limits, such as five hundred and eighty-four yards, but more usually a quarter, or half a mile.'

'You mean, he could be banned from the area altogether?'

'Yes, Mrs Jones. It could be the case that if your son comes within half a mile of your house, he could be arrested.'

Aldous didn't say anything. He said very little these days. Not since he'd started drinking. The whisky binge of the previous week was not, as it turned out, a one-off act of desperation. Aldous drank whisky regularly now. Though he didn't get blindly drunk, as he had done that day, he drank enough to deaden himself. He spent long hours in the red armchair in the front room. Where once he'd read Shakespeare in that chair, now he just watched television. He watched the racing on ITV. He watched *Watch With Mother, Pebble Mill at One, General Hospital, Crown Court*. Sometimes he dozed off.

He came alive only in the late evening, when it was time to go over to Juliette's. They had decided to spend the nights at Juliette's permanently until Janus was evicted, sleeping on the floor. Juliette and Boris's flat was out of bounds for Janus. They were fairly certain he didn't even know where it was, and that he would have no means of finding out. Juliette and Boris had been careful to keep their address secret from him. Their friends and acquaintances knew enough about Janus to know that he wasn't the sort of person to whom one could casually divulge an address. It was not safe to let him know such things. So Aldous and Colette felt that The Grange was a true haven from their son. They spent pleasant evenings there chatting, listening to music, watching television, secure in the knowledge of an uninterrupted night's sleep before them.

Janus's behaviour, on the other hand, had not settled down.

'He seems drunk now, even when I know he's not,' said Colette, one evening at Juliette's, 'it's as though his personality has changed. He's neither drunk nor sober, but somewhere in-between.'

'Do you think he's gone mad?' said Boris.

'Not mad,' said Aldous. 'He appears mad, but it's because he can't be bothered to behave conventionally. He knows he doesn't need to in order to survive, because we've always looked after him. If he had to survive on his own, he'd soon find the energy to behave normally. His madness derives from laziness. It's a kind of voluntary madness.'

'I do agree that it takes a lot of energy to be normal,' said Colette, 'but I think his madness stems from deeper causes than mere laziness . . .'

'Like what?' said Aldous.

Colette hesitated, knowing she was following an all too familiar argument that would have the others groaning at its predictability.

'Please don't use the word "genius" in your next sentence,' said Juliette, 'or talent, or gift, or any of those words . . .'

'I wasn't going to.'

She was beginning to understand that defending Janus was a hopeless cause. The machinery was in motion. Aldous was drinking himself deeper and deeper into depression. If she stopped the machinery, or even hinted at slowing it down, Aldous would sink deeper. Already he was getting a yellowy, glazed look to his eyes.

It troubled Colette that Janus appeared so happy. In the week following her visit to the solicitor, he seemed to have gained a new-found joy in life. He also, to her surprise, had taken a new job. He was a roadsweeper. This was news that delighted Juliette and the solicitor. Because he could support himself financially, the eviction was likely to be sooner rather than later. She had seen him from the car sweeping the gutters in Windhover Hill Road. He was still wearing his suede greatcoat and white panama, working a big bristly broom in the dust by the side of the road.

When he was at home he played loud, vivacious jazz on the piano, and walked noisily about the house whistling and singing

'I'm a hap-hap-happy guy . . .'

Aldous and Colette were surprised at how much money Janus seemed to be earning. He spent large quantities on clothes, nearly every day displaying some new, expensively made garment or other. He'd never shown much interest in clothes before. In the past his clothes had been secondhand, and worn until they were rags. Now he'd become a regular customer at Houseman's, the gentleman's outfitters on the Parade.

'Look at my trousers,' he would say to his mother, having come home from a day's sweeping, 'look at the quality of them. Look at the lining.' He would take his trousers down and show her the quality of the lining. Other times it was all-wool pullovers, silk shirts, suede waistcoats, brogues, insulated socks. *Look at the stitching on this. Feel the quality of that.* It confused Colette further. On the one hand a wanton disregard for his future, on the other a sudden interest in sensible clothing.

'You can't beat a good pair of trousers,' he would say, 'look at people in the street and at the terrible synthetic fabrics they're wearing – polyester, crimplene, nylon. Let's face it, if clothes aren't made out of one hundred per cent organic materials they're not worth putting on your body. What would you rather wear – a cashmere shawl or some sludge from the bottom of an oil refinery, because that's what nylon is. I would rather wear trousers made of burlap or hessian than nylon. I would wear a shirt of sackcloth or gunny rather than polyester. I saw a leather coat in a shop once made of polyvinyl chloride, which I think is what they use to insulate electric cables. About as comfortable to wear as a suit of concrete. One day we'll all be poisoned by our own clothes and the Russians won't have to do anything unless we fight them in the nude.'

But mostly he didn't say anything. He carried on as though he lived in the house alone. He nearly knocked Julian over in a doorway by walking through him. He could not be engaged in conversation. If Colette tried talking to him, he would give little twitches of irritation, as though brushing away an annoying insect. If Colette persisted, the twitches would grow until they were almost convulsions, kicking his legs into the air, flicking his head back in one whole-body spasm of annoyance that was powerful in its effect.

'What the hell's the matter with you?' Colette would say, almost disgusted, while Janus would only smile to himself.

She felt she was giving him one last chance. One last opportunity to account for his behaviour. To explain himself. She was silently pleading with him to give her a good reason to cancel all this eviction business. But his manner only strengthened her resolve. While he slammed and sang about the house, and while her husband sank deeper and deeper into his red armchair, she felt a new resoluteness. Janus had had his last chance.

'He doesn't see us any more,' Julian said, 'he thinks he's the only person here. He thinks he's beaten us.'

Janus had driven them all out of the house and lived there like some tyrannical, usurping duke, the giant in his castle scoffing the rations. He seemed to think it was a permanent arrangement, and had no inkling, as far as Colette could see, of the crisis that was about to erupt.

The night of the delivery of the summons had been carefully arranged. Janus now usually stayed at home in the evenings. The solicitor's clerk had arranged to call at the house on a Wednesday evening. Aldous would be out at his evening class, where he had continued teaching after his retirement. Julian would be at home, and it was his job to answer the door, and let the clerk know whereabouts in the house Janus was. Colette imagined that Janus might cotton-on and take fright when the clerk appeared and she wanted to keep him in the kitchen, whose back door she could lock. If he was playing the piano in the music room he could escape through the French windows. In the event, it all went smoothly. Janus was lounging in the kitchen, spread out on the armchair with his hands in his pockets staring into space while Colette pottered about at the sink. There was a knock at the door. Julian went and answered. A few moments later and the clerk appeared in the room. Rather a scruffy man, Colette thought, for a solicitor's clerk. In contrast to the shiny neatness of the solicitor himself, the clerk was a bedraggled young man with long, lank hair and a crumpled mouth. Around his neck a kipper tie was loosely fastened.

'Are you Janus Jones?' the clerk said to Janus, unable to conceal the nervousness in his voice.

'Yes. Who the hell are you?' Janus replied.

'I just need to give you this,' the clerk said, and landed a folded document of white paper on Janus's spread tummy.

Janus really didn't understand what was happening. He looked down at the paper quizzically for a few moments.

The clerk gave a brief nervous nod to Colette, and then left.

Colette had for days been dreading Janus's reaction to this incident. Julian had also, as he was Colette's only protection that night. But in the event there was little reaction from Janus. Without altering his slumped posture in the chair he took the summons, unfolded it and read. Colette watched him carefully from the sink. He read carefully. He made a thoughtful, clicking noise with his teeth. He didn't say anything.

He stared at the document for a long time. He seemed to be in a trance. Colette felt impelled to break the silence.

'There's still time, Janus,' she said, 'if you find a place on your own we won't need to go through all this – and then you'll still be allowed to visit us . . .'

'Allowed to visit you?' he said, as though the phrase was barely comprehensible.

'Yes. If you're evicted you won't even be allowed to be within a half a mile of the house . . . It's terrible, Janus, but it's what you've driven us to.'

'Allowed to visit you?' Janus repeated.

'Yes.'

'What the hell makes you think that I would want to visit you?'

20

How far was half a mile? Colette found herself pondering this question a great deal. She'd never had a very good sense of distance. She asked Aldous. He told her that it was about a mile to the Triangle. A mile to Southgate tube. A mile to The Grange. Half a mile, therefore, to the Parade. Half a mile to the solicitor's office where Janus's exile was being planned. Half a mile to The Green. Half a mile, or perhaps a little more, to The Owl.

'How will they measure it?' Colette said to her husband in the car a few days later. 'Will the police have to get a map out and tell Janus if he takes another step in a certain direction they will have to arrest him? How precise will they have to be?'

'The solicitor said they might make it a mile, or even two miles. He said in rural areas they can impose limits of up to ten miles. If you're in a little village and you have to go shopping in the big town ten miles away every other day, a half mile exclusion zone won't be much good.'

'Ten miles is ridiculous,' said Colette, 'he couldn't have a ten mile ban, he'd have to leave London altogether, or go south of the Thames, which is the same thing isn't it?'

They were heading for the Thames. Julian was in the back of the car. Aldous and Colette were driving him into London for his interview with the merchant navy. Every now and then Colette would turn and give her son a long look that was meant to be comforting and supportive, but which seemed to Julian more quizzical, as though she could not believe, quite, that he was her son.

'Are you really leaving school this summer?' she would say, incredulously, to which Julian would only raise his eyes to heaven, 'I can't believe this boy's childhood has passed so quickly. It seems only last week that I was taking him up to St Nicola's and he was making me come with him into the cloakroom because he was frightened of that teacher who used to dance the flamenco – what was her name?'

'Mrs Buckley,' said Aldous, whose memory of the woman was vivid.

Colette turned again to face Julian as Aldous managed the heavy traffic.

'Wouldn't you rather stay on at school, do your A Levels? Don't you want to follow in your brother's footsteps?'

'Which one?'

Colette laughed as though she'd been tricked. *Not Janus, of course I don't mean Janus*, she thought, but couldn't say.

'You're very bright aren't you?' Julian detected doubt in her voice. 'You could go to university and do something clever, like James. You could do anything you wanted, couldn't he Aldous? He could do anything.'

Colette was finding it hard to disguise the shock she was feeling, not merely at her son's choice of vocation, but that his schooling seemed to have passed without her noticing. And now he was about to embark on a career that could take him to the other side of the world for months, years at a time.

Then, out of the blue it seemed, Colette turned to Julian and said 'You know Veronica Price would have been far too old for you.'

'What's that got to do with anything?' Julian snapped.

'Well that's why you're doing this isn't it? Just to get back at me for splitting you up, as you see it, though in fact I was trying to get you together. I think it would have been a perfect match, you and Veronica . . .'

'You just said she was too old for me.'

'Too old now, but age differences dissipate as one gets older . . .'

Colette turned away and her thoughts returned to Janus's eviction.

'I still don't understand how they will do it. If on the appointed day he hasn't found anywhere to live, what happens then?'

'That would be Janus's problem.'

'But what would the police do, just take him to a spot half a mile away from the house and dump him there?'

'I'm trying to concentrate,' said Aldous, who'd just been honked at.

The journey into London had been a journey back in time for Colette. They were heading for somewhere called the Mercantile Marine Office, which Aldous said was in Whitechapel, and he had intended to drive from Tottenham straight down through Stoke Newington and Dalston to Shoreditch and then Whitechapel, a perfectly starightforward route following the ancient Roman thoroughfare of Ermine Street, but Colette had insisted on a number of detours. First, to see her birthplace off St Anne's Road, to see if the sycamore tree (that she had planted) still grew in the backyard (it did), and then to deviate along Clapton Common Road to see where she'd walked her Airedales before the war, and where the Man Who Thought He Was Jesus had failed to turn the water into wine. Then Aldous became lost trying to regain the original route, and an unexpected one-way system near the Royal Mint meant that they were almost late for Julian's interview.

The Mercantile Marine Office was a dingy, rather sinister looking building in a narrow cobbled street surrounded by empty, decaying warehouses. Now it was Aldous's turn to be nostalgic. He had had a job round here somewhere, for a few months after he left school and before Lesley got him into the Hornsey. An office job in the accounts department of a firm that manufactured confectionery, he couldn't remember the name of it now. He peered down side roads looking for familiar buildings while looking for the narrow street that was the gateway to Julian's future.

'Shall we come in with you?' said Colette as Aldous parked the car.

'No,' said Julian, getting out. 'Meet me afterwards. They said I'll be out by lunchtime.'

'We'll come in and see where we can wait,' said Aldous, and so the three of them made their way towards the building. There was little on the outside to indicate what this building housed. Eventually they found a small, modern doorway in the edifice of Victorian brickwork, to the side was a plaque which incorporated a red ensign as a logo.

They entered. Julian, seemingly embarrassed by the presence

of his parents, hurried to a reception window and presented his appointment letter. The three of them were directed to a shabby, wooden lift which took them up three floors to a waiting area. Some other boys were sitting on chairs. There were no other parents.

'Just leave me,' Julian hissed before they became within earshot of the other interviewees, 'I'll meet you here or outside in a couple of hours.'

Colette looked closely at the other boys. Crop-haired and in ill-fitting, uncomfortably smart clothes, Colette could see instantly that these were rough, uneducated kids. Toughs from the bottom class of their derelict comprehensives. Julian would stick out like a sore thumb among recruits like those. Colette took some comfort from the sight of them. Julian wouldn't be the sort of person these retired, deskbound officers would be looking for. Or if they did take him, he would soon realize the mistake he'd made, and leave.

'I don't understand why you're so against him joining the merchant navy,' said Aldous as they made their way out of the building, passing a man in naval uniform, another in shirtsleeves but with epaulettes on his shoulders, 'Can't you just be thankful he's found something he wants to do?'

'Haven't you read these leaflets? In the first year of training he could be at sea for up to six months.'

'What's wrong with that?'

'But he's my son. My youngest. That little boy on the high seas? At his age?'

'I seem to remember you were the one who suggested it?'

'Me? When?'

'When he was younger. When he was very young. You were always saying to him "why don't you become a sailor like your great grandfather, you've got salt water in your veins, none of my other children have become sailors, you're my last hope," and countless other things like that.'

'Did I? I don't remember. It must have been when I was sniffing.'

'The funny thing was Julian always said no, that he didn't want to be a sailor, that he would never be a sailor, and that used to really upset you.'

The pubs were open by now. After some wandering among the Dickensian ruins of the old Docklands, Colette and Aldous found an Edwardian pub called The Flag, where they stayed for two hours.

They read through a brochure they had picked up at the offices, and which summarized the course Julian would be undertaking

> *. . . entry as a deck rating onto a three year sandwich course leading to a Class Five Certificate and qualification as a deck officer up to a limit of 5,000 tons in home and western European waters, then a further three years before qualifying to take command of ships trading world-wide . . .*

> *. . . boat handling, rigging and maintaining cargo gear, steering, lookout and watch duties, engine room layouts, instruments, signalling, basic navigation, chartwork and meteorology, possible promotion to Petty Officer at end of course . . .*

'Does he realize this, do you think?' said Colette. 'Six years before he can take command of ships trading world-wide? I think he has this idea he'll be captaining sloops up the Congo this time next year.'

'I think Julian was more interested in the other career route,' said Aldous, 'I don't think he wants to be an officer. He wants to be a junior deck rating progressing to ordinary seaman, then able seaman . . .'

Colette laughed

'Can you really imagine Julian as an able anything? *Able seaman?*'

'It says here an able seaman could be working on ships trading world-wide in three years.'

'Even so, three years. You could do a degree in that time. It sounds like nothing more than a glorified portering job. Loading cargo, untying ropes . . . My grandfather was a captain . . .'

'Perhaps Julian will be a captain one day.'

Again Colette laughed.

'I wish he would just stick to writing unpublishable books. Do you realize, if Julian gets through this interview, his course will start in September. He could have left home by the end of the summer. I'm not sure I could cope with the loss of two sons in one summer.'

'We're kidding ourselves if we think we can get rid of Janus so easily . . .' Aldous began.

'Easily? You call this easy? Going to solicitors and serving summonses and going to court, you call that easy? If it was so easy we would have done it years ago. You're only calling it easy because Juliette has organized it all. You've had to do nothing. We've just had to carry you into the solicitor's office so you can sign some papers, sign our son's life away . . .'

Colette's voice trailed away. They spent a long time in silence. After a while Aldous noticed that his wife was crying. If crying was the right word, because her face had barely moved in the ten minutes she'd been staring blankly into space. It was rather as though her eyes were leaking. Tears were forming, then spilling.

'I feel as though I'm never going to see him again,' she said, quietly.

'Who?' said Aldous, 'Janus or Julian?'

'Both of them.'

Julian did not hear from the British Shipping Careers Service for over two weeks. Finally a letter came with a red ensign on the envelope. Julian had been accepted. In September he would go to the National Sea Training College in Gravesend. He was to be sponsored by Sealink.

The letter came the day before Aldous and Colette were due to attend court, which meant that Julian's news barely registered with them.

Janus had changed since the serving of the summons. He was quiet, polite, friendly, charming. Aldous and Colette still stayed at Juliette's flat every night, however. They intended to do so until Janus was gone.

Most evenings at Juliette's, Colette would gently try to argue Janus's case for him.

'He's very different now, Juliette. You wouldn't believe how different he is. He hasn't touched a drop of alcohol for weeks. It's daddy who's the alcoholic now. He drinks himself silly every afternoon and falls asleep in the red chair, while Janus and I have lovely conversations, once he's home from work. He's stopped wearing those daft clothes and he's really very normal.'

'Very sly, isn't he,' said Boris. 'He's trying to make you feel guilty about evicting him. He thinks that if he behaves himself you won't have the heart to go through with it . . .'

'You've got to go through with it,' said Juliette, 'there is no turning back now.'

'I know,' said Colette.

Inside she was angry with Janus. At first she thought he would have gone into wild rages, gone on drinking benders wrecking the house and terrorizing the neighbourhood. But that would have been easier to cope with than the mild, happy, sweet Janus that had emerged in the last few weeks.

'Have you got yourself a solicitor yet?' she asked him one evening.

'Why would I want a solicitor?'

'To plead your case for you in court.'

'Against whom?'

'Against us?'

'Why do you want me to plead against you?'

'To give you a chance. Are you just going to let us throw you out? You will need time to find somewhere to live.'

'That's not my problem. It's the problem of the people evicting me. I haven't asked to be thrown out on the street.'

At other times he seemed to be welcoming the prospect of eviction.

'I'm really glad you've decided to evict me, mother. I will plead in court that the exclusion zone be as wide as possible. I will ask for a twenty mile exclusion zone. Or thirty miles. I wonder if I can get myself evicted from the whole country. I will go and live in Africa. That's where I'd like to live. The jungle.'

As the date of the court hearing approached he softened even further. One evening he even apologized.

'I'm sorry I threw you and dad out of the house that night. I was just a bit upset because I'd been sacked, and I took it out on you. I was very deeply in love with a nurse who worked on one of the geriatric wards, and now I can never see her again, at least not until I get very old.'

The evening before the hearing he shocked Colette by begging forgiveness.

'Don't throw me out on the streets, mummy, I love you, I love this house, I love my piano, I love the garden, I love my father, I love my brothers and sisters, I couldn't live without all that . . .'

It reduced Colette to tears instantly. 'Please don't say that, Janus, you're breaking my heart.'

At which point Janus instantly revived and looked at his mother with quizzical amusement.

'I'm only joking mother. Can't you tell yet, when I'm joking? I can't wait to be evicted. I'm really looking forward to it.'

When the time came, however, there was no need for Janus to appear in court, because on the morning of the hearing he was arrested and taken into police custody.

His arrest had nothing to do with the eviction, nor did it affect the eviction process. Aldous and Colette did not hear about his arrest until they were in court, since they went there straight from Juliette and Boris's flat. Their solicitor beamed at them as they arrived, 'We've just been told that your son has been arrested and is being questioned by the police, and won't be appearing in court today.'

'Arrested?' said Colette, 'what for?'

'We don't know yet, but this really is wonderful news. There's nothing that could make our case stronger than to have your son in police custody at the actual time of the hearing, I can't believe our luck . . .' He clenched his fist in triumph.

The hearing was a drab, tedious, unglamorous event. The judge barely acknowledged the presence of Aldous and Colette, all business conducted was between the legal people. Eventually, after going through papers in a bored sort of way, the judge pronounced that an eviction order be served upon Janus Jones with immediate effect, and that the area of exclusion should be set at a radius of one half mile from the property.

Aldous and Colette that afternoon returned home in a state of bewilderment. They had been expecting Janus to be at home for at least a couple more weeks. The solicitor, during the course

337

of the morning, had managed to find out more about the situation with Janus. He had been arrested and charged with *threats to kill*. He was being held in police custody until his magistrates court appearance, where an appeal for bail, in view of his eviction, was unlikely to be granted. The solicitor thought it was likely that he would go to prison on remand.

Threats to kill, they were told, was a serious offence, and could mean a prison sentence.

The eviction order would be served on Janus while he was on remand. When he came to leave prison, he would not be able to return to Fernlight Avenue.

'He's gone,' said Colette, once they were home, taking in the oddly different atmosphere of the empty house, 'just like that, disappeared. For good.'

'Yes,' said Aldous.

They didn't know what to do with themselves in the house. They realized, for the first time, how deeply their lives had revolved around Janus and where he was. Aldous would normally have retired to his red armchair in the front room, his haven from Janus, who'd always felt the room out of bounds, while Colette kept him talking in the kitchen. Now there was no need for Aldous to retreat to his corner. Janus was locked up. He was likely to be on remand for at least a month, and then a possible prison sentence. There was no chance of him breaking his eviction order. The house was safe.

It took Aldous and Colette a long time to absorb everything that had happened. They spent the afternoon silently exploring the house. Aldous ventured nervously into the music room, which had been his son's territory. They realized that they would no longer have to sleep at Juliette's flat.

'We've done it,' said Colette, in a voice of mocking triumph, 'we've finally got rid of him.'

She looked at Aldous with a look that said *I hope you're pleased with what you've done*.

'He got rid of himself, in the end,' Aldous replied, aware that Colette was trying to pass the burden of evicting Janus onto him. She was reasoning that Aldous, through drinking heavily, had put pressure on her to evict her son. 'We didn't have him arrested.'

'No,' said Colette, 'I wonder who did.'

Julian, when he came home from school, could throw no light on the subject, though he described how the arrest happened, since it had happened in the early morning, before Julian was out of bed.

Loud knocks on the door. Janus had answered. Julian had listened at the top of the stairs. It had all happened very calmly and politely. Two detectives were on the doorstep. They asked Janus who he was. They explained that they would like to ask him some questions at the police station. Janus had politely agreed, had spent a moment putting on a jacket and some shoes, and then was gone.

Aldous and Colette learnt more over the next few days. Janus had been conducting a hate campaign against his former boss at the East Middlesex Hospital, the man who had sacked him. He had been writing him letters, anonymously, promising, in meticulous detail, a slow and painful death for the man. He drew coffins and skulls on the envelopes.

In his defence Janus claimed that he had been unfairly sacked. This complicated the matter, as the reasons for his sacking had to be taken into account, which raised the matter of the stealing of Mrs Ritchie's brain. For a while it seemed that this might create a more serious offence, but the matter of the brain was dropped after a while, and Janus was charged solely with threats to kill.

Colette did not visit her son while he was on remand. The trial, a month later, made the local newspapers. Colette read the reports with horror.

Lovesick Porter Threatens to Kill Boss
Head Porter – 'I was afraid for my family'
Lovesick Porter Sent Skulls through Post
Lovesick Porter blames his family
Lovesick Porter – 'My Parents Don't Understand Me'
Lovesick Porter Was Served Eviction Order While in Prison

'It's outrageous,' said Colette to her husband, who had refused even to look at the papers, 'in all these reports, they haven't once mentioned that Janus is a pianist. And what's happened about that brain? Why has no one mentioned the brain? The hospital's embarrassed about it, that's why. They don't want their dubious practices exposed to public scrutiny. But it makes a big difference doesn't it? Why were they letting him work in a mortuary in the first place, a sensitive boy like that? He told me they even let him hold the circular saw, the one they use to open the skull – that could account for a lot of his subsequent behaviour. If they mentioned the fact that he was a pianist who'd been allowed to run loose in a morgue, that could explain a hell of a lot. And their sloppy post-mortem practices – if it hadn't been for that insensitive handling of a brain, Janus would never have been sacked . . .'

Colette may as well have been talking to herself. Janus received an eight month prison sentence.

21

A summer came and went while Janus was in prison. Colette and Aldous received several letters from him. The first was chirpy and full of bravado.

HM Prison Brixton
24th June 1978

Dear Mum and Dad

I'm having a really super time here. I'm sharing a cell with two Scottish burglars called Jim and Mick. Very nice blokes. They have taught me a lot about the routines here. The thing is, could you send me a parcel containing some pants and socks, some chocolate and some fags? It's the only way to get things in here, see you soon, hope you aren't missing me too much. Don't worry, I'm having a great time.

Love to you all

Janus
xxx

There were a number of other letters in this vein, to which Colette had always dutifully responded, sending parcels of fags and chocolate, and any other luxuries she thought he might be permitted. He never asked for books, or any music manuscripts, which rather surprised her.

Then came a longer, more serious letter, which covered six pages of the small, thickly lined prison notepaper.

Dear Mum and Dad

I've been in here for over two months now, and I've had a lot of time to think about things. There is nothing to do in a place like this apart from think, and I thought it would be a good idea if I set down some of the thoughts I've had in the time I've been here.

Principally, I want to provide an account of my behaviour over the last few years. I'm not intending to excuse that behaviour, or to [words crossed out], I just want to set things straight.

I believe that my problems stem from my childhood. I believe I had one of the happiest childhoods any child could ever have. I remember so fondly that big old house in Edmonton with its great cherry tree and the wonderful rambling garden full of flowers, and then those exquisite holidays at the farm that were like summers spent in paradise. I honestly thought that things would carry on like this for ever, but unfortunately childhood ends, and the adult world is much less attractive. In fact it is rather ugly. In my imagination I feel that I blamed my father for my childhood ending. My mother gave me my childhood, but my father took it away. He didn't, of course, that's just how my subconscious mind saw it. I saw my father as the one impelling me into the adult world of work and responsibility. I have never felt comfortable in this world, and I turned to drink in order to avoid it. I'm afraid that my temperament will not allow me to earn a living through music, either through teaching or performance. I am much happier with the menial jobs I've had over the years, in fact some of my happiest times were spent as a roadsweeper, the job I had when I was arrested. I like these jobs because of their simplicity, and because of the honesty and integrity of the people one works with. It is the same reason I enjoy the company of my fellow inmates here.

But of course I know I was a deep disappointment to you both because of this, but especially to my father. That is another reason for my turning to drink. I know I can never live up to your expectations of me.

This may all sound rather trite and clichéd to you, but I will remind you that expressions only become clichés through over use, and they *are only overused because of their truth value. The truth, in the end, is often trite.*

Yours Sincerely

Your Son (Janus)

Aldous at first refused to read this letter, just as he had refused to read all the others, or to read the newspaper articles about Janus, or even to talk about him. But Colette felt that this letter was important. She felt that it was sincere, and nagged Aldous into reading it, which he eventually did, with great reluctance.

To Colette's disappointment, he was dismissive.

'It's as though he's written an essay for the approval of the parole board,' he said. 'How can you take it seriously, nonsense like this, when you know how devious he can be?'

'I think he means it,' said Colette, 'I think he's being honest about himself.'

'But look at how it's written – so impersonal, he talks about "my father", and "my mother", as though we were just abstractions. This isn't sincere, it's not heartfelt, it's just pseudo-psychological claptrap.'

'Well what would he have to do to convince you?'

'Frankly, nothing. Explanations for his behaviour are point-less. The point is he's done what he's done, and there's nothing that can excuse it. At least he got that right in the letter. This is just the first step in his campaign to worm his way back into your affections, and into our house . . .'

Colette no longer had the will to stand up for her son. The problem was that her life had improved since Janus had been in prison. Both their lives had. There was no denying it. Janus going to prison was the best thing that had happened to them in years. She didn't even worry about how he was coping any more. She had at first, especially when that first letter came, with its stark information – *sharing a cell with two Scottish burglars.* She imag-ined these two bruised, scabby men bullying her sensitive son, bending his fingers back, stamping on his toes (she could only imagine bullying in the most childish terms), but subsequent letters convinced her that he was coping well, and that he was popular among his fellow inmates, as his last letter had suggested. She even cherished a hope that the whole experience might shock him out of his old behaviour patterns, and that he might steer his life back onto a normal course. It was his last chance. She realized that when he came out he had a hard choice to make. He could either stop drinking and begin to lead a useful life, or he could go back to his old ways, which would surely mean a swift return to prison, and then a life in and out of jail.

It was odd, but Colette had never known anyone who'd been to prison before, not even the remotest friend of a friend, or distant fifth cousin. No one she knew had even been in trouble with the police before, not among any of her relations as far as she knew had any of them ever been on the wrong side of the law. And now she had a son in prison. It had taken some getting used to, but by now, after three months, she had.

Colette had not visited Janus. She had thought about it, but had decided against it. Brixton seemed to her a long way away, somewhere south of the river, in territory she'd never visited before. She had no intention of making the journey by herself on public transport, and Aldous refused point-blank to take her, so she had no choice. She explained all this in her letters to Janus, but he had never asked for a visit anyway.

The most noticeable change, however, was in Aldous. He had rediscovered his enthusiasm for life. His skin, which had faded to white, was now colouring. He had stopped drinking whisky, during the daytime, at least. He'd become interested in the garden, opening up a section of the lawn to grow vegetables. He had started painting again. He took Colette to the theatre, catching the Green Line bus down to the West End to see plays at the Aldwych, or concerts at the Wigmore Hall. They went for long, meandering drives in the country in a new car.

The Hillman Superminx's useful life finally ended in July with a trip to Cambridge, where the car's gearbox once more seized up while in reverse. Aldous had at first contemplated making the journey all the way home backwards, but soon found it too tiring on his neck, and so the car was abandoned to a Fenland garage, who kindly pointed out that the repairs would cost more than the car was worth.

By chance Juliette knew of a friend at the newspaper office where she was now working as a trainee journalist, who had a nearly new Hillman Hunter he was selling for a bargain price. The Hunter was white with red upholstery, which made it seem like the old car turned inside out. It gave a smoother, faster ride than the Superminx. The quality of the ride encouraged them to use it more. They discovered areas of Hertfordshire they'd never known before, lanes twisting through mazes of purple willowherb, byways trimmed with lacy cuffs of cow-parsley alongside harvested fields. Sometimes their meanderings would take them to the edge of the Chilterns, or the clay-bound foothills of mounds remotely related to the Chilterns, which they came to think of as a new boundary to their known world, beyond which the plains of the midlands began – Bedfordshire, that odd, unknown county, its rectangular fields of cabbages and sprouts. From the cowslip slopes of the hills above Barton Le Clay they would gaze out upon this plain like stout Cortés, and never venture into it, preferring instead to return to the known nooks and folds of their local hills.

One day, shortly before Julian was due to begin his course, Aldous and Colette took him and his new girlfriend, Myra, for a drive in the white Hunter to a village they had become fond of visiting, Little Wessingham, a hilltop settlement with a spike church and a view across the valley of the Lee towards the Shredded Wheat factory at Welwyn Garden City.

Colette had been very keen to meet Myra. Until now she'd only known her as a softly sweet but insistent voice on the telephone asking for her son. After much pestering and teasing Julian was finally persuaded to produce her. She'd arrived that morning and Colette had opened the front door to her. A tall, pretty, porcelain-faced creature with oval lips and oval eyes, the sweetness offset rather alarmingly by the Tutankhamun eye make-up she was wearing, and what appeared to be a grimy, silver-studded dog-collar around her neck.

'Myra is in mourning for the death of Sid Vicious,' Julian had explained.

Colette could only think that Sid Vicious was a pet dog.

There was a pub on the edge of the village that overlooked this valley. After a walk in the nearby woods they went to the pub and sat in the garden, where a heap of leaves was smouldering.

'I hope you'll talk Julian out of this stupid idea he's got of running away to sea,' Colette said to Myra while Julian was in the toilet.

'I don't know,' she said, unhelpfully.

'He has told you he's running away to sea next week, hasn't he?'

'He said he'll only be away during the week. He'll come back every weekend. Or I might go down there . . .'

'Oh might you?' said Colette sarcastically, a little shocked to discover that plans had been formed without her knowledge. 'And I suppose he's told you all sorts of secrets and horrible things about me.'

'No,' Myra said, repositioning her dog–collar and scratching at the red rash it had produced, 'he hasn't told me anything.'

Colette wasn't sure whether to feel glad or disappointed about this.

'Tell me where you met Julian.'

Colette was keen to get as much information out of the girl as she could while Julian was absent.

'At a school disco. My best friend's brother goes to St Francis Xavier's. I go to St Bernadette's.'

'So you're a good Catholic girl?'

'Not "good".'

'How odd that he should choose from within his religion.'

'Why's it odd?' said Aldous.

'Not odd. Encouraging,' said Colette, 'it's become part of his identity when I never thought it mattered to him . . .'

'It's just coincidence,' said Myra. 'My school is the female version of Julian's. Lots of the girls have brothers at St Frank's, we're always going to each other's discos . . .'

'So where does Julian take you?'

'To the pictures sometimes. We saw *The China Syndrome* last week. *Porridge* the week before. *The Bitch* the week before that. Or we go out with O'Malley, or O'Hogarty . . .'

Colette moaned at the familiar names denoting the unfamiliar characters. They had stopped coming to The Volunteer recently, as had Julian.

'Do they ever speak, those boys?'

'Not much. O'Hogarty has fallen out with O'Malley. O'Hogarty wanted to go out with O'Malley's sister, but O'Malley wasn't keen because O'Hogarty's a half-caste with epilepsy, and O'Malley's a racist who plays rugby. I've told Julian to get rid of his friends, they're too boring. He prefers mine anyway.'

Julian was back by this time. Colette's interrogation of Myra continued.

'And what do your parents do?'

'My mum's just a housewife . . .'

'*Just* a housewife?'

'Yes. My father – he left when I was little. I'm not sure what he does. I see him every now and then. My mum's living with a bloke, he's got a blotchy face – we don't like him much . . .'

Colette was pleased to detect promising signs of dysfunction in Myra's family. She always felt relieved to hear about unstable families, broken marriages, step-parents, absent fathers – it cast her own family in a better light. She may have a son in prison but at least she and Aldous were still together and the rest of their children thriving.

'Does your mother take you to church?'

'Once in a blue moon.'

'You're asking a lot of questions,' said Julian.

'I'm only interested. Did you go to church as a child?'

'Nearly every week.'

'Same as us,' said Julian.

'Tony, that's mum's boyfriend, he's more strict. He goes every Sunday and tries to make us go too, but mum won't go any more, though she still believes in God and all that . . .'

'Can't we just look at the Shredded Wheat factory?' said Julian, 'Myra hasn't seen it yet,' he began directing her gaze, 'can you see that white strip between the yellow fields, just behind that forest? I once came here with binoculars and I could see that it was the Shredded Wheat factory . . .'

'I can't see anything . . . Do you come here a lot?'

'We have this last few weeks. It's what we like about the suburbs. In half an hour you can drive to beautiful countryside like this, or half an hour in the other direction and you can be at the door of St Paul's.'

'We never come out here,' said Myra, 'but then we haven't got a car.'

Aldous suddenly held forth –

> *As one who long in populous city pent*
> *Where houses thick and sewers annoy the air,*
> *Forth issuing on a summer's morn to breathe*
> *Among the pleasant villages and farms*
> *Adjoined, from each thing met conceives delight*
> *The smell of grain, of tedded grass, or kine,*
> *Or dairy, or Shredded Wheat, each rural sound . . .*

'Be quiet, darling,' Colette said to her husband as he'd gigglingly recited, then, to Myra. 'Forgive my husband, he's prone to these outbursts.'

'But I've never realized before what a paradise Hertfordshire is. We've always felt the need to go beyond – to Bucks or Berks for their hills and woods, or out the other way into Suffolk for its shingles and churches. I'd always thought of Hertfordshire as a bit boring, but it just takes longer to appreciate . . .'

Later, when Aldous had driven them all back to London, Myra and Julian went off on their own to The Bamboo Palace for a meal. As usual, they were the only customers. A red-tasselled, frosted panelled Chinese lampshade rotated solemnly above their heads, almost identical to the one that had sat on a bookcase in Janus's bedroom for several years. The Bamboo Palace had been Windhover Hill's first Chinese restaurant. Before then Chinese food couldn't be obtained outside Soho. Its opening, therefore, had caused a stir. The whole family had pored over a takeaway menu James had brought home one evening, and lively discussions followed as to the meaning of *Sweet and Sour*, or what exactly *Spring Rolls* were. It must have been around that time that Janus had stolen the lampshade. By now The Bamboo Palace was just one amongst many exotic restaurants, and the crowds had gone elsewhere, leaving the waiters and chefs looking forlorn and lonely.

A waiter in white shirt and bow tie, a permanent look of shock and disgust on his face, observed Julian and Myra from a safe distance, and occasionally delivered food to their table.

'Always the same, always the same,' said Myra pityingly as Julian poured orange sauce over his battered pork, 'why do you never try anything different?'

'Because I know I'll like this.'

'But you might like something you haven't tried before even more.'

'But I might hate it, and then I'll have wasted all that money . . .'

'But you've got to take the chance.'

'Are you saying I'm unadventurous?'

Myra's food arrived, an indecipherable mêlée of things looped together in a bowl, and something else sizzling dangerously on a hot plate.

'Yes, I think you are.'

'You can't say that. I'm just about to join the navy. I'm going to be off around the world soon . . .'

'So what will you do if you land in Shanghai or Bangkok and you need to get something to eat?'

'They'll do sweet and sour pork out there won't they?'

'Not like that they won't. Not with chips.'

They laughed and were silent for a while as they ate.

'Your mother seemed very interested in me today, she kept asking me all these things.'

'I know.'

'All the way home she was asking me. Her sharp little elbows were digging into me. Why's she so interested?'

'Just being nosy.'

'What did she mean when she said she hoped you hadn't told me all your secrets?'

'Oh,' Julian thought carefully, chewing pork, what *had* she meant? 'Probably . . . I've got a brother who's in prison. We slept in his bed last night.'

'Prison?' Myra's eyes rounded, 'that's fantastic. You've really got a brother in prison?'

Julian nodded cautiously, not quite sure of how to read Myra's response.

'That's just so brilliant. You live in that big house in that posh street and you've got a brother in prison, while I live in a broken home on a council estate in Enfield Highway, and my brother's training to be an accountant. What's he in prison for?'

Previously unaware that Janus's incarceration might be something with which to impress young women, Julian exaggerated his brother's crime.

'Attempted murder,' he said, quietly and casually.

'Christ,' said Myra, twiddling her silver earring, then giggling, 'fantastic.'

'Before he went inside I couldn't have taken you round to my house. It would have been too dangerous. He was very violent, and very unpredictable. He used to drink . . . If he was around now I would be worried all the time that he would know we were here and would come and find us and cause trouble, we'd have had to have taken steps to make sure he didn't know where we were going . . .'

Julian spent the rest of the meal offering more details of Janus's career, exaggerating the violence once he'd learnt it brought low whistles and 'wows' of wonder from Myra.

'But your house seems so calm. Your mum and dad are so calm. And it's such an interesting house. It's so full of things. All those paintings. And that mural of a waterfall in the hall. That piano. Do you play the piano?'

'No. My brother was the pianist.'

'The one in prison? He was a pianist?'

Julian nodded.

'Quite a famous one, or he could have been . . .' Julian added the second part of the sentence below the level of Myra's hearing.

'Does anyone else play it?'

'Mum and dad play a little bit, although they seem to have stopped now. It never gets used.'

'Why don't you start learning it? It's such a waste of a piano.'

'Me?'

'Let me look at your hands . . .'

She grabbed hold of Julian's hands and spread the fingers out.

350

'You've got piano-playing hands. You should learn. Did you know I could read palms?'

She turned Julian's hands over, and read through the lines with her fingertips as though tracing text. Suddenly she discarded the hands and returned to the remains of the meal.

'Aren't you going to tell me what they said?'

'They said you're going to drown in the South China Sea.'

22

It had not crossed Colette's mind that she should do anything with Janus's bedroom. She had hardly been in there since his eviction from the house, and perhaps might never have gone in there again had her daughter not said to her one day, 'Did I tell you the lease is expiring on Boris's flat soon?'

'No.'

'Well, it is. I wanted to ask you if you'd mind if we moved in here. Just for a short while. A temporary thing while we look for somewhere else to live. Boris is on the waiting list for a council flat and he thinks he could get one in a few months.'

'But which room will you have?'

'The front bedroom of course. That's the only one available isn't it?'

'Janus's room?'

'Yes. His old room. Why are you looking so shocked? He's not going to be using it any more is he? Or were you and Dad going to move back into it?'

'No. I just wish you hadn't asked me, that's all. Not yet.'

But Janus had been in prison for three months. Her daughter's suggestion was not unreasonable, and Juliette felt justified in feeling a little cross that her mother should not have been delighted by the proposal.

Aldous was more keen.

'It sounds like a good idea to me.'

'Don't you think it's a bit disrespectful? It's as though we're dancing on his grave. It's almost as if she made us go through all this just so she could have his room . . .'

But even Colette could see that these protestations were rather weak. A large empty room was going to waste. Juliette and Boris would fill a painful, ugly gap in the house.

At first Colette had intended to clear the front bedroom herself, but when she saw the quantities of junk stockpiled in there she had to enlist the help of Aldous who in turn enlisted the help of Julian and James. They had to abandon the first attempt because of the cat fleas that pounced on them, hungry after their long, patient wait. Not really knowing what to do about them, Colette and her family made a second attempt, this time wearing trousers tucked into socks. If they bent down too close to floor level, the fleas would jump onto their faces. 'They can sense the warmth,' Boris said, who seemed to know about fleas.

Most of the junk could be disposed of immediately. There was a crumpled bicycle, rusting drain covers, hurricane-lamps, dented car doors, fenders, fire-place ironwork, dustbin lids – all things Janus thought he could sell for scrap if he ran out of money. Then there were the clothes, the books, music manu-scripts, piles of shoes and boots, slithering heaps of pornographic magazines. Colette tried to sort out what should be thrown away and what should be saved. She continually had to restrain the others who seemed determined to put everything in the skip Juliette and Boris had hired.

'He's not dead, you know,' she shouted to Boris, who was dragging a bag full of clothes out to the skip, 'he might still want some of these things when he comes out . . .'

Colette took some things downstairs and stored them under the piano in the music room. Bulging bin-liners full of clothes, stacks of books, notebooks, maps, box files filled with letters and assorted paperwork. The space under the piano became a sort of temporary abode for Janus's belongings, although the clutter soon began to spread and take up space in the room.

With the floorspace clear in Janus's bedroom the little single bed suddenly seemed disproportionately small. The bare floor-boards gave the room an echoey, chapel-like atmosphere, enhanced by the mural that still covered the main wall – Janus as Adam, Angelica Sweetman as Eve.

Colette hadn't expected Juliette to move in so soon, but a day later she and Boris arrived with a car full of boxes. Janus's last few belongings were removed from the bedroom and dumped in the music room with the rest of his things and

Boris set to work installing a latch-key lock on the door.

'Why are you putting a lock on the door?' Colette asked her daughter.

'Daddy said we could . . .'

'But no one's going to come in without knocking, no one's going to steal anything while you're out . . .'

'Aren't they? Look, we're entitled to some privacy.'

Aldous stood up for Juliette, putting her side to Colette later.

'She's been living as a married woman in her own place for five years. She wants to preserve her independence. Without the lock she's just our daughter living back home again. With the lock she's an independent woman renting a room in a house that happens to belong to her parents.'

'I still don't like it. That room used to be ours. It was where Julian slept as a baby. It's like a bit of the house has been taken away.'

'Don't worry,' said Aldous, rummaging in his pocket and producing a little brass Yale key, as shiny as new money, 'I made it a condition that I have a spare key, in case there's a fire or something.'

Colette had only just got used to passing the door with the little round lock fitted, when she noticed Juliette and Boris staggering in the front door with huge cans of Dulux non-drip emulsion in their hands.

'You're not going to decorate the room are you?'

'Of course I am, mother.'

'But you haven't even been there a week. Why do you have to do everything so fast?'

'Do you think I can sleep easily when I'm being stared at by a picture of Janus nearly naked, painted by my ex-husband?'

'She's decorating Janus's room,' she said to Aldous a little while later.

'Good. That'll save us the trouble.'

'But – shouldn't we have a say in it? It's our room.'

'She's paying rent for it. Where's the beef?'

When Julian, egged on by Myra, decided to play the piano and walked into the music room, he felt like Howard Carter breaking the final seal that opened onto treasures. But these were junk treasures. Crumbling old books, crusty pairs of shoes, hillwalking boots still caked in mud. Janus hadn't walked over hills in ten years. The room was given a faintly rank odour by the presence of these things. Pornographic magazines were clumsily stacked beneath the piano.

'Why doesn't your Mum throw these away?' said Myra.

'In case they come in useful,' said Julian, sitting nervously at the piano. He hadn't sat here for many years. The last time had been for one of Janus's drunken tutorials, which he gave occasionally, mainly to express his disgust at the lack of musical knowledge in his young sibling. There was a piece open on the music rest. It was Mussorgsky's Pictures at an Exhibition. Julian knew the names of the notes on the musical stave, and, after some thought, could remember where middle C was on the keyboard. In theory it seemed a simple task. Merely put one's fingers onto the notes described by the notation, and hit them in the right order. The opening Promenade was teasingly inviting, a single line of melody, one note at a time. It took Julian only a few minutes to play those opening bars, and he was delighted by the fact that he recognized the music. The next bar consisted of chords, however, and proved more difficult, though Julian managed it, at a hundredth, perhaps, of the required speed. He made a diagram on paper of the notes on the keyboard so that he could stop going through the alphabet every time he wanted to find a note. After a day's practice he felt he could give an almost passable performance of those opening bars, the chords as well.

In the kitchen, the sound of the piano disturbed Colette. Its hesitant, clumsy slowness, the way Julian had to try two or three times to get a single chord right. In her memory Janus had never played like that, even in the earliest days of his learning. He had begun with the simplest pieces, of course, but they had always been confidently played, right from the beginning. Even when he played wrong notes one almost didn't notice them. Julian's playing was a parody of that. It was as though the old piano had been lobotomized, and was reduced to a stuttering, slurring fool.

For a week Julian hammered away at the first Promenade and then, having mastered it to his satisfaction, moved on to

Gnomus. The night before he left for Gravesend, he said to his mother, 'Mum. I've decided I want to be a musician. I don't want to be a sailor any more. I want to be a pianist.'

Had Julian said this a few months before, Colette would have been delighted. Instead she now found herself irritated by her youngest's fickleness.

'Believe me, Julian, you will make a much better sailor than you will a pianist.'

She had come up to his room while he was packing. She was surprised by the tidiness of the room, which she rarely visited. Aldous had redecorated it a few years previously, giving Julian the choice of colours. At first he'd enthusiastically insisted on black. He'd wanted black everything – walls, ceiling, floor, bedclothes . . . Aldous had refused, to Julian's disappointment, who seemed to expect his father to share his vision. Aldous had to patiently explain that in an entirely black room, light would never get much beyond its own bulb. It would sink into the walls never to return. This didn't seem to put Julian off, but eventually they reached a compromise. Julian had his room papered with dark purple wallpaper in rigid, geometrical designs. A dark blue carpet on the floor. Purple curtains. The hovel, apparently, of a manic-depressive, though Julian had never seemed happier.

'Aren't you sad that you're leaving home?' Colette asked her son.

'No,' said Julian. He had his framed rucksack on the bed and was loading it with books.

'That's a bit hurtful, Julian . . .'

'You want me to be sad? You want me to be unhappy?'

'No . . .' Colette felt unable to explain her feelings. Julian wouldn't have understood.

'Do you really think you should take all those books? What have you got in there?' She peered into the rucksack. 'You seem to have the complete works of Joseph Conrad. It'll weigh a ton . . .'

'I don't have to carry it far . . .'

'And what's all that scrap paper? You won't have to do much writing will you . . .'

'That's my novel,' said Julian, quickly covering up the wad of paper that was leaking from the rucksack.

'Novel? Is it a new one? You haven't given me anything to read for ages. What's it about?'

'I don't know,' said Julian, as though the question had been a stupid one.

'Do you think it's safe to take it, I mean it might get lost, it looks like a lot of work there . . .'

'Conrad lost his first novel. He had to rewrite it from memory. This is coming with me to China . . .'

Colette was surprised at how tearful she felt when Aldous drove Julian to the station the next day, though she didn't actually weep. But the house was changing too fast for his absence to be noticeable for long.

That evening she and Aldous were invited to Juliette's room for a meal. An elaborate piece of theatre, because the meal had to be cooked in the kitchen, and Aldous and Colette were confined to the lounge so as not to spoil the surprise. At eight o'clock they went upstairs and knocked on Juliette's door with a bottle of wine in their hands. Boris answered and allowed them into the house within a house that was Janus's old room. Colette was disorientated. She recognized nothing of Janus's room. Even the structure of walls, ceiling and floor seemed to have altered. His single bed had gone, replaced by the pale grey sofa bed from Boris's flat, on which Aldous and Colette had slept during their weeks of exile from Fernlight Avenue.

The walls had changed from blue to green and were covered in framed pictures. The bare bulb was now dressed in an enormous spherical lamp shade that looked as though it was made of paper. The furniture had been painted. A floor level lamp created a warm, homely glow and soaring shadows. A piece of vegetation Juliette called a rubber plant grew lusciously from a pot on the bureau. The oddest difference was in the floor. Previously it had echoed, but now it was silent, gagged by a thick, light brown carpet.

Colette realized that her daughter had not got rid of Janus in order to take his room, but rather had moved into his room in order that he should not try to move back.

'You'll have to decide what to do with the music room next,' said Juliette, once they'd sat down in front of the lasagne that Juliette had made.

'What do you mean?' said Colette.

'You can hardly get in there at the moment it's so full up with stuff. It could be such a lovely room. The trouble is with the piano in there, and all Janus's things, there isn't room for much else.'

'I'm not getting rid of the piano,' said Colette.

'But with nobody to play it . . .'

'Me and daddy play it, thank you . . . And Julian has started learning it.'

'But you could get yourselves a little upright,' said Boris, trying to be helpful.

'A little upright?' said Colette in disgust, 'that's like asking the owner of a borzoi to swap it for a poodle . . .'

The changes kept coming. One morning Colette was going through her booty from Angad's, the goods she still felt impelled to take. She spread them out on the kitchen table, as was her habit, and then was totting-up on a sheet of paper the total cost of the things she'd stolen – shrimp paste thirty-five pence, Sparkling Spring fifty-two pence, a roll of Sellotape fifteen pence – when she was aware that the dark-haired female anthropologist, James's girlfriend, had passed by her into the room and was making tea at the stove.

James had always been very secretive about his girlfriend, and had tended to smuggle her in and out of the house, which made Colette feel she was the proprietor of a sleazy seaside guest-house. The girl, whom Colette called 'The Anthropologist', but who was in fact called Marilyn, was making herself a cup of tea using leaves from her own packet. She sat at the table where Colette's stolen goods were displayed, and drank.

Colette was interested in her tea, which seemed to be purple.

'You're not studying us, are you?' said Colette, after several minutes of awkward silence.

'Studying you?'

'Yes. You're an anthropologist, aren't you? Don't they study people?'

'Yes.'

'I should warn you, James's girlfriends tend to come unstuck when they start trying to delve. He was going out with a psychology student once. She tried psychoanalyzing us all. She didn't say as much, but that was what she was up to. James should have warned her. I humoured her, but then she tried it on Janus, that's James's older brother, and the poor girl ran from the house. We never saw her again.'

'Are you trying to frighten me?'

'Frighten you? No, why, is that the effect?'

'James has told me all about Janus,' she said, 'I think it's a very sad story. Someone so gifted failing so badly. I admire your bravery, not many mothers could do that to their own children.'

'Do what?'

'Have them sent to prison.'

'Is that what James told you, that I had him put in prison?'

For the first time the anthropologist's calm, assured demeanour slipped. Colette had paused in her work of putting her stolen goods in the larder, rearranging the already over-stocked shelves to make room for them, and it was perhaps this sudden bearing down of her attention on the seated anthro-pologist that caused her unease.

'No, he didn't say that, but that's all part . . . I mean, he's in prison anyway, but you would have – if he'd broken his evic-tion rules – wouldn't you?'

Colette gave the woman, whose face was hidden partly by hair and partly by the mug of tea she was holding protectively to her lips, a long glare, which did its job of tightening even further the knots of her faux pas.

'Do anthropologists ever study their own countries?' she asked sternly.

'A bit.'

'Do anthropologists brought up in the African bush ever come and study life in somewhere like London?'

'Not much. Anthropologists raised in the African bush will tend to study the African bush.'

'Isn't that a bit stupid?'

'Not really. Anthropology has always been about the West looking towards other cultures. If someone raised in the African bush has studied anthropology, they've become westernized to a degree, which means they're part of this Western discourse of self and other . . .'

'I don't understand,' said Colette, 'so you make everyone see the world from your point of view. Is that the idea?'

'No, on the contrary.' The anthropologist, having reached securer ground, lowered her tea, revealing three-quarters of her face, which Colette could see was pretty, despite a certain puffiness around the eyes, which had the slow, moist blink of a tortoise. 'We're trying to make the West see the world from other points of view. That's why we're not really interested in places like this . . . I mean this country. This place. We're only interested in other places . . .'

A month after his departure, Julian returned for a weekend at Fernlight Avenue. Colette was astounded by the change such a brief time away had wrought. She hardly recognized her son. It was partly to do with the uniform he was wearing, the dark black trousers and light blue shirt with silver epaulettes.

It took her a long time to get used to his voice, which seemed to have deepened and become louder. He'd been so quietly spoken before. Now he seemed to be bellowing around the house.

'Why are you shouting all the time?' Colette asked after their early conversation in which Julian had filled everyone in on his activities. He'd spent most of the last four weeks bobbing up and down the lower reaches of the Thames playing at captaining little boats. In the last week he'd had experience of handling a small pilot ship.

'Ships are noisy places,' Julian yelled at his mother across the kitchen, 'you have to talk like this just to make yourself heard, sometimes you have to use a megaphone . . .'

'I shouldn't think you'd need to,' said Colette, her hands over her ears.

That evening Julian spent a long time at the piano, his fingers staggering through the first Promenade. He said that there was a grand piano, a Steinway, at the college, and that he'd been practising there.

Myra arrived in the evening and everyone went to The Volunteer to celebrate Julian's first month away from home.

Julian visited nearly every other weekend after that. A quiet, rich Christmas followed, the most peaceful Colette could remember. Suddenly everyone in the house was moneyed. Julian had money from his Sealink sponsorship, Juliette was now getting a grown-up wage from the *Finchley Mercury* where she'd quickly progressed to reporter, even James was getting money from somewhere or other. It meant that the presents round the Christmas tree nearly filled the room, heaped like a coastal defence. Their unwrapping took the whole afternoon, and the paper that had sat so smartly around the cubes and cylinders of the presents flooded the room in its torn, unwrapped dishevelment. Aldous, who spent the afternoon in his red armchair, did, at one point, actually vanish beneath wrapping paper, his hand rising feebly, Canute-like, against its tide.

'Just what I wanted,' said Julian the sailor, unwrapping *The 1979 Beano Book*, while drinking a glass of Madeira.

That Christmas afternoon Colette felt was the happiest of her entire life. Myra came over from Enfield Highway to spend the rest of the day at Fernlight Avenue, Juliette and Boris were around for the whole day, even the anthropologist joined in the occasion, and although she might, on the quiet, have been analyzing the day in terms of kinship and ritual, it didn't stop her pulling a cracker with Colette, and a wishbone with James, and even wearing a paper crown. They all wore crowns that afternoon. There wasn't enough space at the table for them all, not even with both its leaves extended. The drunkenness of the evening was pleasant and sociable. They played games in the front room, mainly charades. Colette couldn't remember playing games like this before (it had been Boris's idea), even when the children had been little. Nor could she remember laughing quite so much. Aldous trying to mime *Monsieur Hulot's Holiday*. ('*The French Connection*?' Marilyn had said).

Only once or twice did Colette allow herself to remember Janus, and how he might be spending his Christmas. During the dinner she considered proposing a toast in his honour. She just wanted everyone to think about him, for a moment. But, looking at the happy faces around the table, she couldn't bring herself even to mention his name. She might have felt saddened that he seemed to have been forgotten so thoroughly, but the sensation was lost in the warm tide of laughter that filled the house that day. Everyone was laughing. She hadn't known laughter like it before. Laughter that hurt. That deafened.

23

In January Colette sent a birthday card to Brixton Prison. But Janus had already been released. He phoned her a few days later. Colette didn't recognize the voice at first.

'Hallo, how are you?'

'Who is it?'

'Janus.'

She felt terrible for having had to ask, but she had never heard Janus on a telephone before.

'Janus. How are you?'

'I'm okay,' he said.

There was a flatness to the voice, a coldness.

'Where are you? Are you out of prison?'

'I was released last week.'

'Where are you staying?'

'I've been put in a probationer's hostel in Hackney.'

'Janus, are you okay?'

'Yes, I've said.'

'Are you sure?'

'Yes.'

'What are you doing?'

'Doing?'

'Yes, have you got a job? Are you looking for a job?'

'Yes, I've got a job . . .'

'What sort of job?'

'It's just a job. Listen, can't we talk properly? I can't really tell you all this over the phone. Can we meet somewhere?' Filling a pause left by Colette, Janus went on quickly, 'Don't worry. I'm not coming round. My probation officer has made it all very clear to me. I can't go within half a mile of the house and I'm not going to. But I don't want you to come down here, it's not really very nice, so can we meet somewhere on neutral ground?'

'Yes, of course, Janus. Where . . . ?'

'How about the café in Brimstone Park? I can meet you there on Saturday. I work the rest of the week. Can I meet you there on Saturday at one o'clock?'

'Yes, okay Janus. Do you want me to bring you anything? Anything from the house?'

'No, just yourself.'

Colette managed to add, 'Are you sure Brimstone Park's more than half a mile away?'

'Yes, I've checked on the A to Z.'

'You don't have to look so miserable,' she said to Aldous, having recounted the conversation, 'He's got no intention of coming round here. He's fully aware of the terms of his eviction.'

'It's just the thought that he's out there, roaming free. I can't relax any more.'

'But he won't be coming round.'

'That's what he says now. What happens when he gets drunk? He won't care about his eviction order then. He could do anything. Well, it was nice while it lasted, this time of peace. It was a wonderful Christmas, but now it's all over.'

'You can't have your son in prison for ever. And I'm sure he's changed. His voice, it was so different. So sensible sounding. Efficient. I've never heard him talk like that before.'

But Aldous wouldn't drive her to Brimstone Park. She had to take a bus.

The café in Brimstone Park was at the back of the odd little Tudor mansion that housed the art gallery and museum. On weekdays it was used only by mums and au pairs, who chatted dolefully over cups of strong tea while their swaddled charges slept or sucked at teated bottles of milk. As Colette entered, stooping first beneath the low bower of dead wisteria, then through the little, white, glass-panelled door with a brass handle, she immediately saw Janus sitting uncomfortably between prams, hunched over a cup of tea.

He was wearing unfamiliar clothes. A black duffel coat with

the hood down, a pair of jeans. Expensive-looking walking boots. It was the first time she'd ever seen him in jeans. She found herself rushing over to him, bending down to hug him before he'd even had time to realize she was there.

It was an unusual sensation. She couldn't recall ever having hugged Janus, even as a child. If she ever tried he pushed her away, telling her not to be ridiculous. But this time he yielded, and even ventured to return the gesture, reaching up to pat his mother comfortingly on the back. Her face buried in the depths of his duffel coat, Colette felt she was looking at her son down a long dark tunnel. It must have been the months in prison that had introduced these new, alien layers of odour. The scent she recognized as her son was somewhere underneath it all, remote and fragile.

The embrace lasted longer than she sensed Janus felt comfortable with, and she sat down on the seat opposite him. She wiped the tears from her eyes with a piece of tissue paper she took from her cuff.

Janus was thinner. His face had sunken a little and he had a dull white pallor. His hair was longer than when she last saw him, but unkempt and greasy. He still had a moustache.

They didn't know what to say for a few minutes, muttering stupid pleasantries. Colette told Janus how well he looked. He returned with his usual gauche honesty by saying she looked awful.

'You're so thin,' he said.

'So are you.'

'But you're abnormally thin. You look ill.'

'I've grown thin worrying about you.' She made a sudden attempt to change the subject, 'What was it like in prison?'

Colette felt immediately the question had been silly. How could he be expected to sum up the extraordinary experience of prison life in a chat over tea? She sensed a shyness in him, amongst the young mothers, an embarrassment. She didn't probe further. He'd survived. But then she suddenly snapped.

'Janus, this is all wrong. This is terrible.'

'What is?'

'This situation. Me having to meet you like this, like we're spies passing secret documents. We might as well be in Berlin.'

Janus shrugged, as though the situation was nothing to do with him. Then he asked, 'Will I never be allowed home?'

The voice came from the little child she remembered from thirty years ago.

'I don't know, Janus. I wouldn't say "never". But not now, and not for a long time.'

'I know *not now*,' the familiar, sardonic voice had returned, 'But how long will I have to wait?'

'Don't ask, Janus. It's far too early to think about that. You've got a hell of a long way to go before you can even think about coming home. Daddy didn't even want me to see you today. I had to get the bus, he wouldn't give me a lift. Do you think we went through all this just so that you could come home again? This is serious, Janus. You've got no choice but to pull yourself together. Now tell me about where you're living.'

Janus passed a scrap of paper across the table.

'I've written the address down. It's quite a nice place. It's a hostel for people who come out of prison and haven't got anywhere to live. A big old Victorian house. Hackney's nice. I've never really been there before . . .'

'And what have you got, just a room?'

'Yes. A room. I share a kitchen and a bathroom with about four other people . . .'

'And they're all ex-prisoners?'

'Yes. There's Jim, he's a burglar. Keith, a pickpocket. Maurice, I think he murdered someone about thirty years ago. It's funny, he was wondering what had happened to all the trams, he's been inside so long. He's got no idea about prices. He thought a loaf of bread should cost about half a shilling. When he got his first dole cheque he thought there had been a mistake there was so much money in it, he came over and said *Janus, they've given me twenty-three pounds* . . . he was going to take us all out for a slap up meal at the Savoy.'

Janus looked disappointed when his mother failed to laugh at this.

'Janus, why couldn't you just be a normal child, a normal man, why did you have to turn out like this?'

'How could I be normal with a mother like you?'

'What do you mean? You're trying to blame me? But Juliette

and James and Julian have all had the same mother, and they're fairly normal . . .'

Janus shook his head.

'But I knew you as a young woman. How old were you when you had me?'

Colette had to think, but Janus answered before she could do the calculation.

'You were twenty-four. A sweet young woman. A girl, almost. That's how you were when we first met. How old were you when you had Julian? Forty-two. He has only ever known you as an alcoholic, drug-addicted old bag. He hasn't witnessed the decline that I have. He hasn't seen the way you fell from grace like I have. You're a fallen angel, mother, and I've had to witness not only your physical decay but your psychological disintegration and moral self-neglect as well, all in one package . . .'

'The others have had it much worse than you. You were nearly a man by the time I went off the rails. The others were still children, they hadn't formed their shells yet. You should have been stronger, it should have had less effect on you . . .'

Janus didn't answer, but looked hurtfully at his empty cup of tea. Colette felt inclined to accept his argument.

'Okay Janus. I don't care if you want to blame me. Everyone else does, I'm sure. But that doesn't alter anything. We're still stuck here, in this little café, and you've let your life drift away from you. You need to think how you are going to get it back. You could start by admitting that everything you've done to make us throw you out was your own fault in the end, and if you apologized that would help . . .'

Still Janus managed to find his tea interesting.

'What about if we both apologize? I'll say sorry for being a lousy mother if you say sorry for being a lousy son.'

Janus gave a hopeless laugh, though still looking into his cup.

'You are sorry, aren't you, Janus?'

'Of course I am. I said all that in my letters didn't I? Or didn't you read them?'

'Of course I read them.'

'And did daddy read them?'

'Yes.' This was only partly true. Aldous had read only the first of Janus's explicatory letters.

'And what did he think?'

'Not much, to be honest Janus. Daddy will need a lot more time. It's hard to convince him of your sincerity.'

'But are you convinced?'

'Of what?' Colette felt cautious.

'Of my sincerity.'

'Yes, of course Janus.'

'Then why the hell do you keep me away from my own home?' Janus suddenly cried, banging the table with his fist. The mothers behind him turned their heads. A baby that had been asleep throughout opened its eyes. Janus, as though taken aback by his own outburst, continued in a loud whisper, 'I come out of prison and find that I'm still in prison. That's what it's like. I'd just love to see my room again, to be able to look at my things, to play the piano . . .'

Janus broke off as Colette began weeping.

'All right,' he went on, irritably, 'I don't mean . . . look, I am sorry. Very sorry for everything I've done. I just want to know how long you're going to go on punishing me.'

'I've told you. You can't come home yet. Not for a long time. I don't know how long,' Colette lifted her spectacles and wiped the tears that were gathered on her lower eyelids, 'as long as it takes for you to convince me and daddy that you aren't going to carry on the way you have been for the last ten years or so . . .'

'But what do I need to do? Give up drink? I've given up drink. I haven't had a drop since I went inside.'

'There are other things you need to do as well,' Colette said, but was thankful when this line of conversation gradually petered out, and Janus stopped making her feel guilty about his exile.

They passed another hour chatting over tea. Janus told her more about his time in prison, which he managed to make sound like fun. He told her about his job, which was in a shoe factory. That was where the new walking boots had come from, unsaleable due to scratches on the leather. And then Colette declared it was time she got back.

They walked together through the chilly, flowerless park. Janus wrapped a scarf around his neck so that it covered his mouth, and put on a pair of woollen gloves. Colette could not recall her son ever wearing these items before – a scarf and gloves. That was clothing too thoughtful, too cautious for the old Janus. This was the new Janus, she hoped, who now worried about catching a chill. Who could feel the cold.

'Don't worry,' said Janus when they reached the main road at the Triangle, 'this is as far as I can come. I've measured it very carefully on a map. If I walk another hundred yards or so up that road,' he nodded in the direction of Green Lanes as it headed towards Palmers Green Cathedral, 'I could be arrested.'

So they stopped and faced each other. Janus then did another thing Colette couldn't remember him ever having done. He kissed her on the cheek, the abrasive bristles of his moustache scraping her skin.

'Could you do me a favour?' he said.

'What is it?'

'I need some things from the house. There's a pair of shoes I left there, and some books I'd like. I suppose you could post them to me,' he added quietly.

'Don't be ridiculous. We'll meet again. I'll bring them with me. Write down what you want me to bring.'

Janus produced a pencil and notepad from the pocket of his duffel coat.

'Shall we meet next Saturday?' he said, handing her the list.

'Perhaps not that soon. Give it a couple of weeks. You mustn't start getting reliant on me. Let's say two weeks . . .'

'But not in that café. I didn't like that café. There's a café just over there,' he pointed across the traffic lights to The Bread Basket, a little bakery that had a café at the back. 'We could meet there.'

At home Aldous seemed only to half-listen to Colette's account of her meeting, refusing to lower his newspaper as they talked.

'It's a trick,' he said.

'What's a trick?'

'Asking for those things. If he needed them why didn't he ask you for them when he phoned?'

Juliette thought it was a trick as well. Colette had hoped to keep her meeting with Janus secret from her daughter, but Aldous had told her. She was disgusted.

'But you can't expect me never to see him again . . .'

'And now he's already trapped you into meeting him again,' her daughter snapped, 'you've fallen for it straight away. Soon you'll be meeting every week and then, before you know it . . .' She made a walking gesture with her fingers that struck Colette as oddly uncharacteristic.

'You're so suspicious, both of you, so cynical. I think this time he's really changed. He said he hasn't had a drink since he's come out of prison, and I believe him. And he's got a job, and he's wearing normal clothes, I think he's really changed . . .'

She looked at the pencilled list her son had given her.

> *Bach B Minor Mass score – should be by my bed.*
> *Pair of brown shoes somewhere in my room*

And that was all.

Colette had never been to The Bread Basket before. It wasn't very nice. A long, narrow, windowless space behind a bakery. Janus was early again, sitting at one of the small, beige Formica tables. The customers this time were mainly old men in caps sitting alone over cups of tea and shrunken little cakes.

'Do you have any other clothes?' she said to Janus, who was wearing exactly the same garments as two weeks before. He still had his gloves on.

'Did you bring the things?' he asked.

Colette handed him a plastic carrier bag.

Janus looked at it eagerly, brought out the shoes, a brown suede pair with elasticated slip-ons, and examined them all over carefully. He smelt them, knocked them against each other and laid them on the table. Then he took out the music score and treated it in a similar way, opening the book, putting his nose in and sniffing, shutting the book loudly. He was behaving like someone who'd not seen many books recently.

Then he said he was hungry.

The only hot food available was things in pastry, sausage rolls, meat pies, Cornish pasties, and chips. Colette bought Janus a

Cornish pasty and chips, which he ate in the same way as he'd examined his shoes – thoroughly.

They spent a little while laughing quietly at the other customers, the old man whose toothlessness was giving him problems with a sausage roll, another old man who was drinking his boiling-hot tea with such a relishingly loud slurp.

Colette witnessed, at another table, an odd act of involuntary ventriloquism. A sour-faced, dour-looking couple, she in a purple overcoat and green turban, he in a shabby suit with a tattered combover, were deep in conversation, yet their talk was so lively and bubbly, so full of humour and intrigue, much of it concerning the sexual machinations of certain third parties (Colette could only catch the odd word), that she felt curiously heartened that such lively minds could inhabit such spent, forsaken bodies. But when the couple got up to leave, the true owners of the voices were revealed. At the table beyond, completely hidden from Colette's view by the old couple, were two teenagers, a boy and a girl, deep in a gossipy conversation. The familiar disappointment in people and their predictable ways returned.

'I've been going to Wigmore Street,' said Janus, who'd been silent throughout his swift devouring of the Cornish pasty, 'to play the pianos.'

'They have pianos in Wigmore Street?'

'The Steinway showrooms. You can go in and wander around, play the best pianos in the world. I spent all last Saturday afternoon in there. They're such exquisite instruments. Such lightness of touch. You just have to drop a finger onto a key and this wonderful sound reverberates round the whole showroom. It's like paradise.'

Colette pondered the thought of heaven as an endless vista of pianos.

'Anyway,' Janus went on, 'the manager was so smitten by my playing he said I could come in any day I liked and play the pianos. He said he'd pay me.'

'Janus, that's wonderful – perhaps you could get a proper job there, it could lead to all sorts of things . . .'

Janus made a restraining gesture with his hands, as if to say 'one step at a time'.

371

'It has to be better than working in a shoe factory,' said Colette.

'Cobblers,' said Janus, 'I'm quite enjoying it there actually. I've progressed from sandals to brogues. I'm learning how to operate the stitching machine. I was on the conveyor belt before, and I can have all the free shoes I want.'

'Then why did you want these shoes I brought you from home?'

Janus seemed not to know for a moment.

'Because they're from home,' he said, eventually, 'They remind me of it. And I can remember all the good times I had in these shoes, all the places I walked, all the steps I danced. By the way, could you bring my green corduroy jacket with you next time?'

And so Colette committed herself to another meeting soon.

It became a regular part of her life, Colette's meetings, roughly once a fortnight, with her son in The Bread Basket. Colette hated the café with its windowlessness and its aged clientele, but Janus seemed to like it. She realized it was the nearest café to home. Even Aldous and Juliette began to accept their assignations. Once the weeks and months built up and Janus had shown no sign of breaking his eviction order, they began to think that the situation might work out. Just as in the house there had been invisible boundaries across which Janus usually never strayed, now these had been established in their surrounding neighbourhood.

Colette enjoyed seeing Janus. Once their routine was established their meetings lost the nervous edginess they'd had at first. Janus stopped asking about home, he stopped pressurizing her into making a decision as to when he could return. He seemed to accept that if he ever returned, it would only be as a visitor, that he could never live there again. Then one day he said, 'Mum. The man at Steinways has offered me a full-time job starting from next week – demonstrator and sales person.'

'That is wonderful, Janus.' Colette was genuinely overjoyed.

'It's good pay,' he went on.

'I'm so pleased, Janus.'

'The only trouble is I have to work all day Saturday.'

'Why's that a problem?'

'We won't be able to meet any more.'

'What about Sunday?'

'This place doesn't open on a Sunday.'

'Oh. Well, we can meet somewhere else.'

'Where though? I don't want to meet in Brimstone Park. I don't like that café.'

Colette thought. The district wasn't rich in cafés. She couldn't actually think of another one.

'The only other thing would be to meet in a pub,' said Janus, casually.

Colette spoke as if she hadn't heard. 'Isn't there a Wimpy Bar down by The North Circular?'

'You wouldn't want to meet there, it's full of noisy teenagers. We could meet for a quick lunchtime drink in a pub. I wouldn't drink any alcohol, I promise. I've told you, I've given it up.'

'I don't think it would be good to meet in a pub, Janus.'

'Okay. That's okay. You're probably right, it wouldn't look good if anyone saw us. I suppose we'll have to leave it then. We might as well say goodbye for good, then. Will you write to me?'

Colette was thinking.

'Don't be stupid, Janus, there must be a way round this . . .'

'If you can think of somewhere to meet that's convivial and easy for you to get to . . .'

Colette thought it over silently for a while, conscious of Janus's expectant face bearing down on her lowered head.

'If you promise,' she said, 'not to drink any alcohol. Not a drop. If you drink a drop I'm going straight home.'

'I promise.' He bent forward to kiss her again. The touch of the kiss, the pleasure on his face, this was enough in itself to make her decision worthwhile. 'Shall we meet in The Coach and Horses? It's the only pub I'm not banned from.'

'Yes, okay, hang on though . . .'

'What?'

'Isn't that within half a mile of the house?'

Janus shrugged dismissively.

'Perhaps an inch. It's borderline. Don't worry, no one's going to get out a tape measure. Anyway, I've got to rush. See you in a fortnight.'

And he was gone.

Colette looked at the map that evening at home. It was very difficult to work out exactly how far The Coach and Horses was from Fernlight Avenue, there were several corners and changes of direction that had to be taken into account. Then she wondered if half a mile was meant 'as the crow flies' or actual distance travelled. Surely it must mean 'as the crow flies'. In which case it was definitely within the boundary, probably by an eighth of a mile. Though by road it was more like, as Janus had said, on the boundary. If something went wrong, if they were spotted, she could at least plead ignorance, say she thought it meant distance by road, and not as the crow flies. That bloody crow. That stupid crow.

She didn't tell Aldous that she was meeting Janus in a pub. She didn't tell anyone. She said she was going to Brimstone Park. To her horror Aldous came with her some of the way. On the days she met Janus, Aldous had taken to going on his own into London to visit the galleries. It was as if he couldn't bear to be in the same neighbourhood as his son. Usually he made his own way there, but this time he took the bus with Colette, staying on for the tube at Wood Green while Colette got off at the Triangle, as if she had been going to Brimstone Park. In fact she had to walk back quite a way to The Coach and Horses, where she found Janus sitting in the saloon bar, early as usual, a glass of orange juice in front of him, a copy of the *Sunday Times*.

He had undergone another transformation of dress. The duffel coat and jeans had been discarded. He was wearing a tweed jacket, a white shirt, a green tweed tie, beige corduroy trousers. He had the sensible, professional air of a teacher, or a doctor. As she approached he noticed her gazing at the orange juice.

'Do you want to test it?' He offered her the glass, smiling. 'Just orange juice, like I promised.'

Wordlessly Colette took a sip from the glass. It was just orange juice.

'You just sit and watch me,' Janus said, when he came back from the bar with an identical glass for his mother, 'I'll drink soft drinks all afternoon and enjoy it. Now would you like to hear my good news?'

'Yes,' said Colette, looking around her in case there was anyone she recognized among the customers. There wasn't as far as she could see, though the pub soon filled and she couldn't keep up with monitoring the new faces.

'Well, someone came into the shop last week, heard me playing, and has booked me to play at a private do in a big house in Chiswick. His wife's fortieth birthday party, she's a big Chopin fan, and was a child in Auschwitz. And he's going to pay me five hundred pounds. Aren't you happy for me?'

'I am,' said Colette, as though in a daze, 'though the news is somewhat overshadowed by what you said about Auschwitz. The poor woman . . .'

'The poor woman is now married to a millionaire piano collector . . .'

'But she probably lost her whole family . . .'

'Anyway,' Janus said, evidently wishing he hadn't mentioned Auschwitz, 'I've made other contacts as well. It's amazing who comes in the shop. Vladimir Ashkenazy was in last week, I didn't get a chance to speak to him. Artur Rubenstein is a regular customer, apparently. These people just get through pianos like trousers. The company loans pianos to people like Rubenstein just for the publicity. The only problem is I keep meeting people from college . . .'

'Why's that a problem?'

'Because they're so bloody happy. And they had jobs like mine when they'd left college and have moved on. Working there is a bit like a champion racing driver working in a petrol station.'

Janus kept to his promise, and drank nothing but orange juice until the pub closed at two o'clock.

The second time they met he did the same.

When he offered to buy Colette her second orange juice of the day she felt she couldn't take any more.

'This orange juice is playing havoc with my insides. After the last time I had terrible heartburn for the rest of the day.'

'What do you want then, lemonade? Tomato juice? Barley wine?'

Colette looked sheepishly pleading. Janus was encouraging.

'It's okay for you to drink, you know. You don't have to abstain in solidarity. They do Gold Labels here. Shall I get you one?'

Colette gave a tiny, frightened nod.

24

There was a knock at the front door.

'It'll be canvassers,' said Colette, 'you answer it Aldous, you're so good with them.'

'Can't someone else answer it?'

He looked around at the company in the crowded kitchen. There were many who could have answered it. James and Marilyn were over for lunch. Julian was back for one of his weekends at home, and Myra had come round to visit. It was a warm Saturday in May 1979, a week before the general election, but no one was talking about politics. They were talking instead about Julian and Myra's plans to hitch-hike around Europe.

'I'm not sure if I really should allow you,' had been Colette's instant response once the two had unveiled their plan. Julian didn't seem to take this remark seriously, as though her permission had been the least of their problems. Aldous had been keen.

'The boy's nearly a captain, he's been on boats out in the North Sea for goodness' sake . . .'

'It's not Julian I'm worried about, it's this girl. Do you think we should leave her in the charge of this *Beano*-reading sailor, in all these desperado countries – where did you say you were going?'

Julian reiterated a well-rehearsed list.

'France, West Germany, East Germany, Poland, Czechoslovakia, Hungary, Romania, Yugoslavia, Italy and then France again.'

'And where have you got all the money for a trip like this?'

Aldous, having delayed answering the door for as long as seemed acceptable, was beginning to hope whoever it was might have gone away, when a second, louder knock came, dragging him reluctantly out of his chair. No one else seemed to have heard it, apart from Colette.

On the doorstep he met a tall, thin man with pouting, feminine lips. A blue rosette was attached to his lapel.

'Good afternoon sir, I'm calling on behalf of the Conservative Party.'

'Oh. Are you?'

'I was wondering whether we could count on your vote in the forthcoming election.'

Aldous hesitated for a moment.

'Of course,' he said. 'I've always voted for your party, actually.'

The man gave a beam of satisfaction that Aldous found rather rewarding.

'That's splendid sir. Thank you. Goodbye.'

Aldous returned to the kitchen feeling flushed.

Julian was explaining how cheaply they could live in Eastern Europe.

'It would cost us practically nothing. Myra's saved some money from her Saturday job, and I've got some saved . . .'

'Surely you're having enough adventures at sea without having to gallivant over dry land as well . . .' Colette protested. But she suspected Julian was suffering some mild disillusion with his chosen career. He seemed to come home more and more, almost every weekend. He was gradually coming to understand that his Sealink sponsorship meant he had little prospect of working on anything other than cross-channel ferries for the foreseeable future. There was a chance of more exciting routes, such as Felixstowe to Copenhagen, or Hull to Bergen and other Scandinavian ports, but there were several years of cadetship to endure before that prospect. After the summer he was due to spend six months on the ferry from Dover to Calais, mainly on bridge-watch duties. He didn't seem to be looking forward to it much.

'You'll need visas,' said James, who was also in the kitchen, with Marilyn, 'Half these countries might not let you in.'

'I went to the Polish embassy yesterday, I've got all the forms . . .'

'Who was at the door, darling?' Colette called across the room to her husband.

'Someone from the Conservative Party.'

'I hope you told them to get lost,' said James.

'I certainly did.'

'Because I'm leaving the country if they let that woman in.'

'You'll be leaving the country anyway,' said Marilyn.

'Why, where are you going?' said Colette.

'He's my new research assistant,' said Marilyn, laying a protective hand on James's shoulder. 'He's coming with me to Venezuela in the summer.'

'Only for a few weeks,' said James.

'What has happened to my family?' moaned Colette, 'Why are you all leaving the country? Juliette's said she's going to France in the summer . . .'

'Everyone goes abroad these days,' said Julian, 'it's not a big thing . . .'

There was another knock at the door. To everyone's surprise Aldous went to answer it without a fuss.

There was a stocky, whiskery man on the doorstep with a Bobby Charlton combover. He had a red rosette on his lapel.

'Good afternoon sir, I'm wondering if the Labour Party can rely on your vote this coming election.'

'Of course,' said Aldous, 'I've always voted Labour actually.'

The man checked himself, as though he'd been prepared for an argument, then beamed, giving Aldous an even stronger sense of satisfaction than before. He'd found a foolproof way of dealing with political canvassers – express support and they simply disappear. He returned to the kitchen feeling slightly giddy.

'I hope you told him I've got five pounds riding on this election,' said James.

He went on to explain that he'd placed a bet with William Hill, at odds of six to one, on a Labour victory. Easy money, he said. He should have put more on, now he'd come to think about it.

'Five pounds?' said Marilyn, 'I heard the Tories were ten points ahead.'

'Yes, but if you compare the personal ratings of the leaders, Callaghan's miles in front. When it comes to the crunch the British public would never let that stuck-up woman run the country.'

'I don't know why everyone's getting so worked up about this election,' said Colette, 'nothing's going to change.'

'I suppose you'll be voting for her,' James then said to his mother. But Colette pulled a face of disgust at the idea, which delighted her children. For once mother and sons had found common political ground.

When a third knock was heard, Aldous thought he was entitled to delegate the answering to someone else. James agreed, and shortly returned.

'There's an enormous Irishwoman at the door asking for Myra,' he said.

Myra went white.

'Oh no. It's my mum. Don't tell her I'm here, please don't.'

Colette went to the front door.

'I've come for my daughter,' the woman said. Colette saw Myra's prettiness hidden somewhere in the puffy, worn features of the woman on the doorstep.

It turned out that Myra had been lying to her mother, saying that she was sleeping at a friend's house. Her mother had discovered the deceit, so here she was.

'She's not here.'

Brown eyes stared at Colette, mother to mother.

'You must understand, I can't allow this to go on . . .'

A man in a city coat with a blotchy face was standing in the background, at the end of the path, looking with disdain at the tangled, rotting mess of the front garden.

'Allow what to go on?'

'I know you have different standards from us . . .'

Colette was suddenly absorbed by the woman's clothes. A navy blue dress that ballooned around her enormous bosom, to which a red carnation was pinned. She had a sort of neckerchief affair around her neck – blue dots on white. It was as though she was en route to a wedding. She had dressed in her Sunday best to come here. How odd, thought Colette, that these council estate dwellers from the marshes of the Lee basin should feel such a frisson of feudal inferiority, that they should need to dress up to visit the avenues of Windhover Hill. Did they think they would be laughed at otherwise, would have the dogs set on them? It annoyed Colette deeply.

A small row ensued, sparked by the sense that she had of being criticized by this woman for being a drunk, a lapsed Catholic, for having her hair too long, for not keeping her front garden tidy, for the peeling paint on her front door. Seeing that Colette was about to slam it on her, the woman appealed again to their shared burden of motherhood.

'Myra told me she preferred your house to her own home. How do you think that makes a mother feel? We've never seen eye to eye I'm afraid. She's a very wilful girl . . .'

I wish I could trust you, thought Colette. I wish you were a real friend, and that I could talk to you about Janus, and we could share our sorrows about children slipping away from us. I wish that you weren't the bloated, varicosed, uneducated, God-fearing, narrow-minded fool that you evidently are.

'Myra is a nice girl. She's a good girl,' said Colette, 'she is very sensible.'

Colette wished that Janus was here. He could have given this woman such a fright she would never have come back. As it was she bore the woman's words, spoken, as they were, in a rough, southern Irish brogue, until the woman had said all she had to say, and then closed the door on her, promising to pass her message on to Myra if she saw her.

'What's all this about you two spending nights together without Myra's mum's permission?' said Colette, half-laughing. Myra's trembling face had become something she now treasured, in the light of what her mother had said. That she preferred this house to her own. Myra had said that to her own mother.

'The woman's mad,' Julian said. 'Since Myra spent a weekend at Gravesend she's refused to talk to me. If I call for Myra at her house, her mother gives me hand-written notes instead. Look – I've still got one on me.' He took a crumpled scrap of paper from his pocket.

Myra don't want to see you

'She doesn't know I'm spending some weekends here. But now it's the only way we can meet up.'

'So that's why you've been coming back so much. I thought it was because you were fed up with Gravesend.'

'No,' said Julian, surprised, 'I love Gravesend.'

No one in the room was sure if he was serious.

'So what does your mother think about you hitch-hiking around Europe with Julian?' said Colette, turning her attention to Myra, who had now changed colour to lobster-red, deeply embarrassed at hearing her mother's voice at the front door. 'But I don't suppose you've told her yet have you? What if she says no?'

'Then Myra will make a rope of bed sheets . . .' said Julian.

Colette thought about Myra's mother a lot after that. She toyed with the possibility that the woman was right, that the two should be kept apart, not allowed to sleep with each other. But at the same time the thought was ridiculous. Myra was leaving school this summer. Julian was a sailor-to-be, living half away from home. And young people had different expectations these days.

'There's no point in trying to impose the standards of our generation on our own children,' Aldous had said when she'd raised the matter with him. She thought it was true. There had been such sweeping changes since they were young, those pre-war childhoods they'd spent seemed to belong to a remote past which today's schoolchildren now studied in their history classes. But Colette didn't really like it. She didn't like the way children were growing up so fast.

'Soon there won't be any children. There will be babies, and then there will be small adults. That can't be right, can it? We should be doing the opposite. Childhood should be made to last for as long as possible.'

And it did make her feel uncomfortable when her children would suddenly talk openly about sex.

'I have just realized that music and sex are the same thing.'

Julian said this one Friday evening, having come downstairs after spending an hour in his bedroom with Myra, during which time a quiet, rhythmic underbeat had filled the house. When she'd first heard this noise Colette had thought there was something wrong with the pipes, or that there was someone up on the roof mending tiles. It was only when she'd discerned an accompanying squeaking noise, a human vocalization of ecstasy, that she realised what it was. Then she heard it everywhere. From James's bedroom where he often spent the weekends, the witch-haired anthropologist giving similar mouse-like noises. Even from Juliette's room once, though thankfully Juliette was silent. Instead it was Boris who provided the voice part, a series of deep groans, a noise she hadn't heard since Janus had had toothache.

'I'm going to write an essay on it,' Julian went on, 'all that music, it's just sex. Rhythms building up, slowing down, building up, pausing, getting diverted, wandering, then the rhythms building up again, falling away, then a great climax at the end. That's all it is.'

Colette had still not told anyone that she met Janus once a fortnight in The Coach and Horses. Everyone assumed they were meeting in Brimstone Park, and for this reason kept clear of the area on Sundays. Each time they met Janus seemed to have more good news to tell her. Another private concert booking. Promotion at the Steinway Showrooms. Meetings with old friends and colleagues from his college days.

'But why are you still living in a probationer's hostel?'

'I've got it rent-free till the summer. What's the point of paying for a flat until I have to? Anyway, I'm saving up a big deposit so I can get a nice place. A friend of mine has promised me a place in this big house in Holland Park. I've got over a thousand pounds saved thanks to these concerts I've been giving.'

'Perhaps you'll do a public recital soon?'

'Yes, perhaps.'

When Janus went to the bar for another round of drinks, Colette froze at the sight of a face she recognized at another table. It was the solicitor's clerk, the one who delivered the summons to Fernlight Avenue. He was sitting there in his casual clothes, a rough-looking leather jacket and ripped jeans, the antithesis of his legal self. He'd caught Colette's eye and was giving her a wry, pitying smile, as if to say, *after all we did for you, now you've gone and blown it.*

But she hadn't. The Coach and Horses was borderline. On

the boundary of the legal and the illegal. And there was no stipulation that she could never see her son again. When he returned he was carrying the usual barley wine for his mother, but this time for himself he'd bought a half pint glass of something that looked like beer.

'It's only shandy,' said Janus. 'Less than half of it is beer. You can't expect me to sit here for all these weeks watching you get tipsy on barley wines and not feel a desire for a little tipple myself. Anyway, the orange juice was getting to me, like it was with you. I was pissing orange juice last time.'

'That man over there – don't look!'

But Janus had already swung round to stare in the direction Colette had indicated. Luckily the clerk wasn't looking.

'What man?'

Colette suddenly became aware of the foolishness of drawing her son's attention to the man whom he could reasonably hold responsible for ruining his life, albeit in the role of a functionary.

'It doesn't matter.' Luckily Janus hadn't recognized him. 'I thought I knew him. He's gone now.'

Janus eyed his mother suspiciously, while he swallowed his shandy. Colette noticed a shiver pass through his body as the alcohol took up its residence.

'Just one shandy,' said Colette.

'Two,' said Janus as he returned to the bar.

Colette wondered if she should make a dash for it. It had been a mistake to meet in the pub like this, but they had been carrying on for so long without Janus succumbing to the temptation of all-surrounding booze, that she'd thought everything was going to be all right. But now it looked as though he was going to get drunk speed-drinking shandies.

He returned with a pint this time.

'No, Janus. This is going to far.'

'Too far? It's a soft drink, virtually.'

'If that's half beer you'll have had three-quarters of a pint by the time you've finished it . . .'

'What's three-quarters of a pint? I used to have to have four special brews just to feel relaxed enough for proper drinking. This is no more potent than a bag of wine gums . . .'

'I'm going,' said Colette, picking up her bag and lifting her coat from the seat beside her, 'I'll see you in a fortnight, but I'm not staying here while you get drunk.'

Janus said nothing, but sat back and took another pull on his drink while Colette made her way out of the pub.

In the busy, bright air of Green Lanes, Colette walked quickly towards home, aware, soon after she left the pub, of footsteps hurrying behind her.

'I'm sorry,' he said, pulling on her shoulder to make her stop. She turned and saw that his mouth was shining, and there were dark, splashy stains on his shirt. He had rapidly finished his pint before coming after her. 'I promise I won't do it again. You can't blame me, I have to sit there, like I said, with you drinking, how could I not be tempted? How do you think it makes me feel, sitting here on the margin of my own neighbourhood, knowing I can never see my home again?'

Colette turned and walked on. Janus followed.

'I feel like I'm stranded on a lonely island. That's what the Romans did with people they didn't like but couldn't kill. They'd cast them away on a tiny, barren island until they died of loneliness. That's what you've done to me, I've got nothing but seagulls for company . . .'

'Janus, stop following me, you're straying into forbidden territory. If you come any further you could be in trouble.'

'I'm already in forbidden territory. That pub's an eighth of a mile inside the exclusion zone. I'm deep inside forbidden territory. I have been every fortnight.'

'Then we'll have to stop using that pub. Janus, will you stop?'

Colette halted, but Janus went on. He walked a few yards further and then stopped. Turning, he beckoned to his mother to follow.

By now they were almost at Palmers Green Cathedral.

'Just let me walk you a little way home,' he said, 'it won't matter if anyone sees us. They wouldn't recognize me anyway would they? I've walked round here loads of times. I've even walked past the house a couple of times.'

'You've walked past the house? When?'

'A few nights ago. I saw a pretty little girl go in. She had hair a bit like a pineapple. Who was that?'

'Oh, you mean Myra. Julian's girlfriend.'

'You didn't tell me Julian had a girlfriend.'

'I didn't think you'd be interested. You've never asked how Julian is, not once in all the meetings we've had.'

'And you've never talked about him either . . .'

'That's because I've been waiting for you to ask about him . . .'

Colette stopped again.

'Janus, there's a bus stop over there. You go and wait there for the bus. You are not coming any nearer to Fernlight Avenue. I'll see you in a fortnight, but if you come any closer to the house I'm going to go over to that phone box on the corner and call the police.'

Janus looked incredulously at his mother.

'I'm only trying to have a conversation with you. You wouldn't . . .'

Colette made towards the phone box.

'All right,' Janus laughed, 'you've won your little game. Very well done. I'll catch the bus,' he was holding his hands up, palms out, in a surrendering gesture. 'Say hallo to Julian for me,' he called as he crossed the road, 'and to Myra . . .'

Two weeks was a long time. Longer for Janus, Colette supposed, but long for her as well. It was long enough to have lost the thread of what had happened a fortnight before. When they met again in The Coach and Horses it was almost as if the differences of the previous meeting had been wiped from the slate, though both mother and son were back on the orange juice. By the meeting after that, Colette had forgotten about Janus's drinking of shandies. She drank barley wines again. When Janus bought a shandy she thought little of it. Shandy, after a difficult introduction, had become acceptable in their lives.

By the summer it had become acceptable for Janus to drink two pints of weak lager and escort his mother up as far as the traffic lights at the cathedral. About half way home from the pub. He would give her a hug as green turned to red above them, and then cross the road to the bus stop.

One Sunday in late June, making the excuse that he needed some cigarettes, he walked with his mother past the cathedral and round the corner to the shop on Dorset Street. Inch by inch. Then this too became a routine. All through July he walked her to the corner of Dorset Street. It was only a ten-minute walk from here along Hoopers Lane to the house itself. Deep inside forbidden territory. Three-quarters of the way in. He was illegal.

He made his final push on a Sunday in mid August.

'What are you doing?' said Colette, finding that Janus, instead of departing along Dorset Street, as he usually did after buying his cigarettes, was walking with her down Hoopers Lane.

Janus just smiled. There was no excuse he could use. There was no shop he could pretend to visit, it was just houses all the way to Fernlight Avenue.

'Just thought I'd like to see the old house . . .'

'No.'

'But you said everyone's away. Julian's in Hungary with Myra, you showed me his postcard. James is in Venezuela. Juliette and Boris are in Brittany, and dad's in the middle of London somewhere.'

It was true. The house was empty, and would be until Aldous came home in the evening.

Colette walked on. Janus walked beside her.

'This is madness, Janus. It's madness.'

'I agree,' said Janus. 'Don't worry. I'll just walk as far as the corner, and then I'll go. It just makes me feel so safe being here, in these familiar surroundings, these familiar streets and houses. Hackney's so bleak and desolate, the people are so gloomy looking.'

They reached the corner of Fernlight Avenue.

'They lopped the limes,' said Janus, noticing the mutilated trees that lined the road. 'I wish they wouldn't do that. Why can't they just let the trees grow and grow?'

'They do look funny,' said Colette. The trees had lost all their lower branches leaving only narrow, vertical trunks above a crown of arthritically swollen stumps.

'Can I just have a look at the piano?' said Janus, having followed his mother to the front door itself.

'If you promise me you'll go straight away and never come back, then just this once,' said Colette, who would rather get her son quickly inside than remonstrate with him publicly on the garden path.

'Oh that old, familiar smell,' said Janus once they were inside and the door had been closed, 'that pleasing mixture of sweetness and decay, like overripe fruit. I'd forgotten that smell.'

'You do promise, don't you, that you'll be gone in an hour?' The thought of Aldous coming home while Janus was in the house terrified Colette. Aldous was very regular in his habits these days, however. He was never home on Sunday before six, and was usually later.

'Of course. I just want to have a look at the old piano. Why don't you make us a cup of tea?'

They walked into the music room. It was still stuffed with Janus's belongings. Colette had told him about Juliette and Boris moving into his old room. He showed little interest in the junk, his attention being drawn solely towards the piano. Colette watched him. She was moved by the slow reverence with which he approached it, the cautiousness, as one might approach the hospital bed of a loved one. He reached out and rested his hand on the lowered lid, caressed it, stroking his hand all the way along the curved body of the instrument.

'It looks terrible,' he said, after a pause. It was the way in which the piano was surrounded by junk, by heaps of old clothes and piles of books, bin bags full of rubbish, that made it seem as though it was actually on a scrap heap. But it was also the injuries it had sustained over the years, the brutal treatment it had received at Janus's own hands, when in times of rage and frustration he had attacked the piano. The deep scratches in its black finish, the broken music rest, the cracked and lost ivories. Then Janus looked at the keyboard and saw that someone had gummed the names of the notes to the keys.

'Someone's learning it,' he said to himself, almost incredulously. 'Who's learning the piano?'

'Julian is teaching himself,' said Colette. 'He's doing quite well, considering.'

Colette left Janus at the piano and went to the kitchen to make some tea. As she was filling the kettle the music started, the wandering chromatic scales of the second étude, Opus 12. It was one of the first serious pieces he'd learnt as a child. The swiftness with which he'd learnt the Chopin studies had been one of the first signs that Janus's abilities at the piano were exceptional. She may have been suffering from the exaggeration of nostalgia, but as far as she could recall he had just seemed to play these pieces straight off. Hearing the music again, the sweetness of it, the fluency, the expressiveness, after having so long endured the naive blunderings and hesitations of Julian's playing, made her heart feel full and warm.

'You have to cross your middle and marriage fingers until they hurt,' said Janus as Colette re-entered the music room, where Janus was playing the piece for the third time. 'This piano's had it, I'm afraid. I'm so used to playing the Steinways in Wigmore Street that this old Bechstein feels like playing a barrel organ in comparison. The sound's not too bad but the touch is very sticky.'

'You could make any piano sound wonderful, Janus. Play that other study, the one I love, I can't remember the number, it's the shivery one.'

'No. 7' said Janus, 'more fluttery than shivery, I'd say.' He swept through the piece, 'butterflies on the meadow.'

They spent almost an hour like this, Janus playing any pieces his mother requested, and explicating the complicated structure of this piece or the subtle impressionism of that piece. Colette didn't think they'd ever talked like that before. There was no condescension in Janus's voice, no lecturing, or sarcasm, or disdain. He was talking as a musician, passionate about his work, to an interested, intelligent audience, equally passionate.

After he finished playing, Janus spent a little while rummaging through his possessions. He found a box file, an old wooden one that was stuffed with scrappy documents.

'I think I'll take this,' he said. 'It's some old letters and things. You can throw everything else away.'

Janus then left. He'd been in the house for exactly one hour.

25

Throughout the summer postcards kept arriving at Fernlight Avenue, from James in Caracas, Julian and Myra as they travelled through Europe, from Juliette and Boris in France.

James's postcards became letters once he'd travelled into the interior of Venezuela. They arrived, crumpled and smudged, as though they had spent a week in the sack on the back of a mule.

> . . . We have spent two days in a small aluminium row boat on the Orinoco River. Then two days trekking. My face and hands are puffy with gnat venom. I am writing this while sitting cross-legged on the edge of the compound while tribesmen dance all around me, long spears in their hands. They have been dancing like this for about six hours. They have been taking ebene, a sort of hallucinogenic snuff that makes them think they are birds, and which dribbles out of their nostrils and down their chests in long, green strands.

> Marilyn sends her love . . .

The postcards from Juliette and Boris expressed an equal degree of fascination with a far more proximate version of otherness. Their first card came from Paris.

> . . . it's so foreign here. The policemen have real guns, and everyone is talking French.

The cards from Julian and Myra were intermittent and traced the shape of a coiled snake around Europe – Paris, Freiburg, Innsbruck, Vienna, Budapest, Belgrade . . . They had missed out Poland and Czechoslovakia due to a failure to obtain visas.

The postcards had become so frequent that Colette was almost surprised if there wasn't one on the mat every morning. Towards the end of August, however, she was surprised when there arrived a postcard from Janus. It showed a view of Edinburgh, and had been posted in that city the day before.

Dear Happy Family, I've journeyed ticketless by British Rail to the Athens of the North. Thinking of you in your house, See you soon. Love, Janus

The postcard deeply disturbed Aldous and Colette. This wasn't the sane, balanced voice Colette had come to know over the months since his release, the voice she'd reported on so enthusiastically to Aldous.

Three days later another card came, this time from Bath.

Dear All, Have travelled here by high-speed toilet. Intend having yet another fascinating day. Love, Janus

The following day there was a knock at the door. They recognized the knock. Only Janus ever knocked with such brisk, rhythmic assuredness. They were in the kitchen at the time. They wondered what to do. The knock came again. Aldous peeped through the kitchen door, which gave him a view of the hallway to the front door at the end. Even from this distance, through the distorting frets of the front door's glass, Janus's shape was unmistakable. With a sudden decisiveness, after some hesitation, Aldous strode to the front door and opened it. Janus looked surprised, as if he'd been expecting his mother to answer.

'Hallo,' Janus began, in an affectedly polite tone, 'long time no see . . .'

'Go away Janus,' said Aldous, quietly but firmly.

'I just wanted to drop by and say hallo.'

'Okay, well you've said it now. You should go away now.'

Aldous closed the door. He could see through the glass that Janus had remained on the door step. As he retreated down the hall, the figure remained. By the kitchen door Aldous stopped. Here Colette was also watching. Aware that they were too far into the house for Janus to be able to make them out, they watched Janus's sliced-up shape as it stood on the doorstep, shifting uncomfortably from left to right before it finally receded, then vanished.

'What's he playing at?' said Aldous.

'Had he been drinking?' said his wife.

'Hard to tell. He looked very different. But then I haven't seen him for a year.'

'What was he wearing?'

'He looked smart, like you've described him. Jacket, shirt, tie . . .'

'I don't like this, Aldous. What'll we do if he comes back?'

'We'll call the police. It's simple.'

'And have him put in prison for years? Supposing he is just being friendly, supposing all he wants to do is say hallo? Could you really put him in prison for that?'

'He knows the rules, darling. If he's sensible he won't come back, or if he does, he'll simply go away, like he did just now. If he tries anything else, if he tries breaking in, then it's straight to the phone for the police.'

'He wouldn't do that. He's not so stupid.'

The next day there was a telephone call from the police. The Cornish Police.

'Yes, this is Penzance Police Station. We have a Mr Janus Jones here. He was caught on the train from London without a ticket. He has no money on him and says he has no means of getting home . . .'

What the hell, thought Aldous, did they want him to do about it? The policeman went on to point out the legal situation. Janus was liable for a fifty pound fine. They seemed to want Aldous to deal with it. The policeman seemed to suggest that Aldous should come down to collect his son, or make arrangements for him to travel back. Did they really think he was going to wire money to some Cornish branch of the Midland Bank so that Janus could stay in a hotel, pay his fine and travel back first-class on The Cornishman?

'I'm sorry, he is not my responsibility,' said Aldous, and put down the phone.

'But if they find he's got a criminal record, that he's on probation, he could go back to prison.'

'So the hell what?' said Aldous. 'If he wants to start playing the fool again while he's on probation, what can he expect? He obviously hasn't learnt his lesson has he? He's not the changed man you so frequently claimed after all your little tea shop liaisons. The whole exercise has been a waste of time. He may have changed for a while, but the shock of prison is starting to wear off. He's starting to forget all his resolutions and he's reverting to his old ways. Phone calls from the police. It's happening all over again.'

Aldous drained a glass of whisky.

There was that knock again the next day. The sharp, perky, rat–a–tat.

The cold comfort they'd derived from the knowledge that at least Janus was stranded three hundred miles away in Cornwall where he couldn't bother them, was dispelled.

Colette answered the door this time.

'We had a phone call from the police yesterday,' she said, in her severest voice.

'The Cornish police are the stupidest in the country,' said Janus. 'I've outwitted them all, just as I outwitted the Edinburgh police and the Somerset police.'

'And did they know that you were just out of prison?'

'No. They didn't know anything.'

'Don't you think they might find out, eventually. These Cornish police will pass your name around, word will get back to your probation officer. You can't fool people like that, Janus. They may appear stupid, but they have method. They have systems. Eventually they will catch up with you, and you'll go to prison for not buying a train ticket.'

'I couldn't give two hoots mate,' said Janus.

'No, I didn't think you could. In that case we'll call the police if you come here again.'

'You didn't say that the other Saturday.' Janus repeated this loudly for the benefit of his father, whom he could see standing halfway down the hall, 'I said she didn't say that the other Saturday! I don't suppose you've told him have you. She let me in for the afternoon to play the piano! Now she's toying with my emotions, like she's always done. She lets me near then she pushes me away . . .'

Colette closed the door at this point. Janus's speech continued at a third the volume, only partly discernible.

'What's he talking about?' said Aldous.

'Nothing,' said Colette, 'he's just raving.'

'I'm going to call the police,' said Aldous, walking into the front room where the telephone was.

Colette hurried after him.

'Wait a minute darling, I think he's going now.' She could see the tall figure of her son through the front room window, half-obscured by front garden foliage, as he strode away from the house. Aldous had lifted the receiver half way to his ear. He watched Janus as well. When he had gone he put the receiver down.

'Next time,' he said, 'just one more chance.'

They both remained in the front room for a while, watching out of the window for their son's return. Because of the thickness of the vegetation they couldn't see far. They decided to go upstairs, Aldous using his spare key to gain access to Juliette's room, which offered the only clear view from the front of the house. They suspected that Janus might be just lingering at the corner of the road, but from here they could see no sign of him in either direction. Colette went downstairs, sat in her chair and tried to read a book. Aldous remained in the front bedroom for a while, watching out of the window.

'He's probably on a train to some remote part of the country,' said Colette when Aldous finally came downstairs. He made no comment but sat gloomily in a chair opposite his wife, picked a local paper from the heap on the table next to him and leafed through it.

'I hate August,' he said after a while. 'Now that we don't go on holiday with the kids, what's the point of it?'

'Perhaps we should have gone away somewhere,' said Colette.

At first they'd been happy to stay at home for the summer while their family went their disparate ways. They'd enjoyed the peace and calm, the quietness of their usually crowded house. But now it had been going on for too long. James and Marilyn had been away for nearly two months. Julian and Myra had been away almost six weeks. Boris and Juliette had been gone a fortnight. Their isolation made them feel how alone they were in the world without their family. They had no friends.

Janus returned late, just as Aldous and Colette were beginning to feel sure that there would be no more disturbances that day. The familiar rat-a-tat came at twilight, when the long August day had finally, with great reluctance, begun to wane.

'Don't answer,' said Colette. They were still in the kitchen. They remained still for a while.

The knock came again.

'It's no good,' said Aldous, 'if we pretend not to be in, he might try breaking in, or come round the back and see us sitting here through the window.'

Another sharp knock, much louder than before.

Aldous finally got out of his chair and went to the front door. 'Just clear off,' Aldous said after opening the door.

'I want to play my piano,' said Janus. This time his voice clearly registered that he was drunk.

'Just clear off. I'll call the police.'

Aldous shut the door but Janus put a foot in it. Aldous pushed harder. Janus yelped as his foot was squashed, then put his shoulder to the door. Aldous did likewise, but found himself sliding slowly backwards, inch by inch.

'Colette! Help!'

Colette came out, saw her husband almost horizontal in his effort to keep Janus out, and she ran to add her little strength to the task. They could hear Janus grunting and sighing with the exertion. No words were exchanged. It seemed now that everything came down to muscular toil. Two against one. It only needed one party to flinch for a second and the door would either lock shut or swing open. Aldous found a breathy voice.

'Just go Janus. Please.' He had to breathe between each word, 'We won't call the police now if you just go.'

It was a pleading voice. A frightened voice. A voice he'd never used before.

Finally, just as Aldous and Colette felt themselves being pushed irredeemably back, Janus paused to reposition himself, and in that instant the door clicked shut. Aldous and Colette collapsed on the doormat, Colette face down on the floor, grimacing with exhaustion. Aldous was on his back propped against the door, taking deep breaths. Then the door shuddered as something exploded against it. There was a dripping noise. Then another tremendous crash.

'What's he doing?'

'The milk bottles,' said Colette.

There were three full milk bottles on the step. They still hadn't got round to lowering their order, and they were taking in far more milk than they needed. Sometimes they forgot it, and the milk stayed there all day. Now Janus was hurling the bottles, one by one, at the front door. They heard leonine roars before each one landed. Aldous and Colette crawled on their hands and knees down the hall to escape the showers of glass that would come if one broke the window. When they got far enough to see clearly, they saw that one had actually hit the window, but miraculously it had withstood the impact. There was milk dripping all the way down it.

Then came a different type of impact. Quick footsteps, a yell, then a powerful, house-shaking crash, accompanied by a groaning sort of cry. Then again, and again. From the front room window they could see what was happening. Janus was simply hurling himself at the front door. He was walking calmly and methodically to the far end of the path, then running and leaping, like a long jumper, launching himself like a missile at the front door.

Aldous picked up the phone. He was beginning to dial when Colette gave a cry. Aldous turned and she beckoned him to look out of the window. Janus was lying in a heap on the path, near the doorstep.

'He slipped,' said Colette, 'on the pyracantha berries. He bashed his face on the step.'

'Leave him,' called Aldous, as Colette ran to the front door and opened it. Aldous followed, intending to pull his wife back into the house. By the time she reached him, Janus was slowly lifting himself up. Blood was streaming down his face from a deep cut above his left eye.

'I'll tell them you did this,' he said, smiling at Colette through a web of blood. He turned and walked swiftly away.

There was a smeared pool of pink blood on the path. Neighbours were watching from lit porches and windows. A few minutes later a police car arrived, having been called by one of these neighbours. Aldous was sweeping away the shards of broken glass from the front path.

'We can't really arrest him unless we actually find him within the prohibited area,' said the policeman after he'd heard and taken note of all the details, 'so if he does come back you need to contact us straight away. In the meantime we'll keep a patrol car on the lookout in the surrounding streets.'

'He was so close,' said Colette through her tears afterwards, 'so close to getting it right. He was just inches away from a normal, useful life. Now he'll almost certainly be going back to prison, and for how long this time? He could get three or four years. He'll be nearly forty.'

'Forget him,' said Aldous as they made their bed in the front room settee, 'we've lost him. We lost him a long time ago.'

It was one of those rare occasions when Aldous referred to Janus as their joint offspring, and not just Colette's son.

Colette didn't sleep that night. She decided not to take any sleeping pills. She wanted to be conscious and alert in case Janus returned. If she took her usual handful of Nembutals she would doze through any commotion, no matter what the volume. So instead she lay awake. At first she tried reading *Bleak House*, the book she'd never finished reading to Janus Brian, but her mind couldn't cope with the long sentences. She couldn't get to the end of one without her concentration drifting off towards her son. Instead she closed the book and lay back, watching the twitches in the tree shadows that filled the room – the acacia, the pyracantha, the holly. The nearby street lamp created this theatre of shadows, branch upon branch bisecting, forking, diverging, ramifying. At night the front room looked like an anatomical diagram – the arteries and veins of the heart, its capillaries and valves all mapped out in black on the walls.

The knock came late, about two o'clock in the morning. It wasn't Janus's knock. Instead it was a single thud of metal, guillotining the endless thread of Aldous's snoring.

They listened for the confirming second knock. It came soon, and louder.

'It's not Janus,' said Colette, as Aldous stirred.

'How do you know?'

'It's not his knock.'

Aldous knew this as well.

He crept out of bed and walked over to the window.

'There's a police car outside.'

Suddenly the two were animated by a panicky urgency. They struggled to find clothes and half-dress, stumbling in the semi-darkness before, after further loud knocks, making it to the front door.

'It's about your son.'

There were two policemen on the doorstep, both young, both rather nervous looking.

'What's he done now?' said Aldous, wearily.

'Do you mind if we come in?' one of the policemen asked.

'He's dead isn't he?' said Colette in a toneless voice.

'Don't be silly,' said Aldous.

The policeman refused to answer Colette directly. It was as though he didn't want to deviate from a script he'd carefully rehearsed to himself.

'I'm afraid your son has been involved in an accident.'

'Accident?' said Aldous, 'What sort . . . Is he all right?'

The policeman looked at Colette with an expression she wasn't able to decipher until much later. It was a look of fear.

'I'm afraid . . .' he hesitated once more, then let it out, 'I'm afraid he *is* dead, Mrs Jones.'

'I told you,' said Colette, almost satisfied. Her face was clenched, tight as a fist. She moved about the hall uncertainly, as though looking for a hidden exit.

'Dead,' said Aldous, reproducing exactly the policeman's grim intonation of the word.

'What sort of accident?' said Colette.

'His body has been found on the railway line, just outside Windhover Hill Station. We believe he was struck by a train at approximately half past twelve this morning. The driver tried to stop but he didn't have time. It took us quite a long time to find the body, it was thrown so far . . .' He paused, wondering if he was offering more information than was wanted. Aldous's wince told him that perhaps he was, ' . . . and in the dark, with all the bushes . . . you understand, otherwise we would have been here sooner . . .'

'Are you sure it's him?' said Aldous.

The policeman nodded.

'There was documentation on the body giving his name and address. We contacted this address . . .' the policeman showed Aldous the typed address of the probationers' hostel, 'but he hasn't been there for several days. The warden there was able to give us your address. Would you like my colleague to make you some tea?'

This question passed unheard. The other policeman having looked hopefully expectant of having something useful to do, now looked deflated.

'There is still the question of formal identification,' the policeman continued. 'Although we don't believe that there is any doubt that it was your son that was killed this morning, a formal identification has to be carried out for legal reasons . . .'

'I want to do it,' said Colette, 'I want to see him.'

How cold the house was. Bitterly, wintry coldness filling the house. Was it really summer. There must be ice on the windows.

'Sometimes we think it is best to spare parents this duty – it can be very distressing. Is there anyone else, a family friend or other relative?'

'No, there isn't anyone else,' said Colette.

'In view of the circumstances of your son's death, and the particular injuries he's suffered, we can use a family doctor to carry out the formal identification . . .'

'No. I want to do it . . .'

'Because in some cases, a visual identification can't be relied upon.'

'You think I wouldn't recognize my own son?'

'In cases of severe injury, only medical or dental records can provide accurate identification . . .'

Colette understood. She reconsidered.

'Perhaps it would be best not to,' said Aldous, as Colette slowly and gently put her face to rest in her hands.

Janus was later identified by his teeth.

26

Aldous and Colette spent a day and a night alone. For much of the time they sat in the kitchen, huddled together, Colette crying into Aldous's body as he encircled her. Their isolation became palpable. It was as though Janus had died to reveal this one fact – they were utterly alone in the world.

By chance, however, Julian and Myra returned to Fernlight Avenue the next day. They'd run out of money and energy and had spent the night before sleeping on the platforms of the *Gare du Nord*. Their arrival – dirty, hungry, happy, brimming with stories to tell of their six weeks away, brought an end to this most intense period of loneliness. Colette stopped crying for the first time in a day, and was a little perturbed when Julian reacted so oddly to the news of his brother's death. He didn't quite dance a celebratory jig, but there was no trace of sorrow in his face either. Rather, there was excitement. Awe. It was as though he'd been told of some unimaginable political event – the re-unification of Germany, or the collapse of the Soviet Union.

Twelve hours later Juliette and Boris were back from France. They showed more sensitivity to the news. Juliette even managed a few sobs. By sheer chance James arrived back two days later. It was as though Janus's death had broadcast homing waves from the epicentre of the railway. James had found the rigours of anthropological fieldwork harsher than he'd expected and had quarrelled with Marilyn. So the house was soon full, when only a few days before it had been hideously empty.

Janus was alive for the week until his funeral. Dumb, motionless, deaf. Colette found herself silently screaming at a figure on the doorstep who dissolved into a puddle of milk. She found herself running down the street to catch up with a dark figure walking quickly, and she was never able, quite, to reach him. She found herself touching the piano, then withdrawing her hand in shock at a feeling of warmth.

The funeral itself attracted a larger gathering than Colette and Aldous had expected. Fearing an almost empty church, they had phoned all the numbers in the back of a little pocket diary that had been found on Janus's body. This resulted in a church full of strangers. Many of them Colette supposed were recent acquaintances from her son's time in prison – burglars, fences, blackmailers. She could tell by their shuffling awkwardness, the hastily combed hair, the badly ironed shirts. There were some vulgarly dressed young women as well, barmaids, perhaps, who'd once leant Janus a sympathetic ear.

Bill Brothers knew some of these people. He was exchanging nods and smiles with them as Colette and Aldous arrived. Colette found herself seated next to Bill during the service, and clung to him as one of the few people she knew in the church. There were Lesley and Madeleine on the other side of the aisle, and Colette was delighted to see Christine as well, all dressed in black. Some other cousins had also managed the journey.

The service itself Colette found embarrassing. How Janus would have scorned the sentiments that were expressed by the obsequious young vicar who'd replaced that kindly, shambling old German. She was also embarrassed because after all the ritual of the Sacrament and Transubstantiation, not one member of the congregation came forward for Communion. Not even devout Lesley and Madeleine. Was the priest really going to let all those consecrated wafers go to waste?

She turned to Aldous.

'I've eaten,' he whispered to her.

In the end Colette felt impelled to take Communion. Just as the priest, after a moment's embarrassed silence, was about to return and dispose of the hosts in whatever way they do, she went up alone to the altar and knelt for the Communion.

At the graveside, an hour later, the embarrassment continued. When it came to the sprinkling of holy water onto the coffin, they found that this liquid was to be dispensed from a plastic squeezy bottle, when for previous funerals it had been contained in a silver chalice. When it came to Bill Brothers's turn, he took the bottle, looked at it in a quizzical way, then pressed it so that a long squirt of holy water splashed onto the coffin below them. Colette, whose arm was through his, did the same when the bottle was passed to her.

'Give him plenty, he needs it,' she said as she passed the bottle on. Her voice was distinct in the silence. The priest felt impelled to comment.

'It doesn't actually do anything,' he called from his breezy position at the head of the grave, the opened prayer book flickering in his hands, 'it's just a sign that we show, a symbol, it's not a sort of special magic medicine . . .'

Colette wasn't listening. Her head was fixed in downward contemplation of her son's coffin.

At Fernlight Avenue the atmosphere lightened a little. The cousins did their best to cheer people up by relating amusing anecdotes that had nothing to do with Janus whatsoever.

Colette drank Bloody Marys with Bill Brothers. He looked very different. His beard had gone and so had the tweedy clothes of the Marxist intellectual. Instead he was wearing jeans and a cheesecloth shirt that seemed too tight, a brown leather jacket with coarse stitching and wide lapels.

He was accompanied by a friend whom Colette vaguely recognized – a tallish man with gold, curly hair who was dressed in black – like the Milk Tray man but with dark glasses and black leather gloves as well.

'Steve has just finished filming with Roger Moore for the next Bond film. I'm his personal assistant stroke bodyguard.'

'*Moonraker*,' said Steve, pointing a leather clad finger at Colette, pulling an imaginary trigger.

'This man is going to be so famous. So famous and rich. He got fifty thousand dollars for just a week's work on the set with Roger. But Roger's a personal friend and got him a good deal with United Artists, he's got a contract to appear in the next three Bond films. Not even Roger's got that.'

'I play bowls with Roger at his house in Flushing. He's very good at bowls, you know. Very good.'

'I organize Steve's life. In turn he keeps me off the hard stuff. He's very strict, aren't you darling?'

'Your son was a very funny man,' said Steve, ignoring Bill and looking at Colette over the top of his dark glasses.

At one point Julian went up to his mother.

'Do you think it's a good idea to have all these people over here? I've just been talking to someone who said he shared a cell with Janus. He said he was a burglar. He said he still is . . .'

'They wouldn't steal from the house of their dead friend's mother, there's honour among thieves.'

Colette was aware that Janus was being talked about with a sort of awe. She was fascinated to find that, amongst the gathering there, there seemed to be a widely held belief that Janus's life had meant something.

'He wouldn't have any nonsense would he, not old Janus,' this came from the mouth of an ageing Teddy boy with a greasy grey DA.

'No, not old Janus. He wouldn't stand for any of this old rubbish.'

She gathered they were talking about the funeral, the rituals, the dressing up.

She caught another old lag talking about Madeleine in her extravagantly tailored dark suit.

'He wouldn't hold with any of this dressing up and showing off. He may have been educated but he was always for the working man.'

Colette almost felt like taking the Teddy boy by the lapels and interrogating him.

'What do you mean? Are you saying my son was a revolutionary, that he believed in something, that he understood anything about the world, that he had a purpose to his insanity, that what we took for random acts of aggression and destruction actually had some coherence to them?'

'Funniest bloke I ever knew!' said someone else.

'Always had time for you,' said another.

Were they just finding kind things to say about him at his funeral, or did they mean these things?

A tall, grey haired man with a white goatee spoke to her. He had been one of Janus's tutors at the Royal Academy, and had seen Janus recently in the piano shop.

'So he really worked there? I thought it might have all been a fantasy.'

'Oh yes, he certainly worked there. I'm a very good friend of the manager. He said he hadn't heard playing like Janus's anywhere. He said his rendering of the Opus 111 was reminiscent of Schnabel. Of course, I remember young Janus as a terribly good sight-reader. That was his special ability. He could understand a piece just by reading it, and he was always reading at least half a page ahead of his playing. But I really had no idea . . .' he paused, drawing his gaze across the motley assembly of vagabonds and barmaids that filled the front room, 'that it all went so wrong for him.'

'Could he have ever been a great pianist, do you think? Answer me truthfully,' said Colette.

'Oh, undoubtedly,' the professor of music said, 'it's always puzzled me why we never came across his name in the concert programmes or recording catalogues, or why he never kept in touch with the Academy. There would always have been a job for him there . . .'

Perhaps this was just another instance of exalting the deceased, an impromptu eulogy. She felt like saying, if he was so special why didn't you come and find out what he was doing, why didn't you support him, help him into a performing career, or offer him a post at the Academy?

She didn't of course. The man had come all this way to an obscure church in a remote suburb, then to a tangled, clumsy house full of crooks.

'Such a waste, such a waste, such a waste,' Madeleine intoned.

'People here are saying his life meant something for them.'

'Yes, I heard a car thief saying he had great respect for Janus.'

Perhaps it was the host she'd swallowed that morning, perhaps it was the sweet Spanish wine she'd been drinking, but Colette suddenly felt an overwhelming sensation of love, that the humblest, basest things were suddenly rich and beautiful. Directed towards Madeleine, in her bluebottle clothes, this sensation caused Colette to embrace her and plant a kiss on her plump, roseate cheek.

The experience of engaging with Madeleine's softness was so

rewarding, the sense of human contact so rich, that Colette maintained the embrace for several minutes. Madeleine seemed to take the gesture as a signal of mental collapse, that Colette had broken under the grievous pressure of bereavement, and she rubbed Colette's back consolingly, patted her shoulders, stroked her hair. When Colette finally withdrew her face from Madeleine's neck, Madeleine had expected to see it damp and puffy with tears, but instead Colette was laughing, her face bright and animated.

'I love you Madeleine,' she said, holding her sister-in-law's face between her hands, planting another stream of kisses on her cheeks, these jabbing little kisses more resembling the way a hawk will pick at carrion. She held Madeleine's face so tightly it was almost painful. Madeleine began to totter, and whimper softly, not knowing how to control grieving Colette. But Colette finally stopped just as Madeleine was about to cry for help.

'You're a sweet woman,' Colette said, giving great weight to the adjective, 'you are a sweet, sweet woman.'

Colette then found Lesley, who was drinking orange juice in the kitchen. She did the same to him, though this was a less rewarding experience. Lesley was hard and unyielding, and rather thin beneath his clothes. She may as well have hugged an apple tree.

'I'm sorry for all the horrible things I said to you and Madeleine,' Colette whispered urgently after having filled her brother's rough face with kisses.

'Let bygones be bygones,' said Lesley.

'Are you really teetotal now?' she said, having heard a rumour that he was.

'I haven't touched a drop since the day you came to High Wycombe,' he said.

Colette laughed.

'So I made you give up drink?'

'Madeleine, dear. I did it for her sake. I know you despise her, but she is an angel. A real one. There are such things in the world, dear, but you have to be able to see them.'

'I can,' said Colette, pausing momentarily, and glancing slowly around the room.

It was true. There were angels in abundance. She could see

their wings shyly fluttering, even on the shoulders of burglars and pickpockets, and the experience filled her with a sense of infinite delight which lasted for the rest of the day, even when the relatives had gone and only a core of hardened criminals remained, who, mildly drunk, talked and laughed with thunderous volume.

Janus safely stowed in the earth, Colette surprised herself by experiencing a sense of achievement. She remembered from before that odd, strangely satisfying feeling after a loved one dies. It didn't last for long. It stemmed from a sensation of completeness. Of a life having come to a conclusion, the knowledge that there was nothing Janus could now add to the narrative of his life.

She also had the sense of having survived a catastrophe. As though she'd been found by rescuers in a cupboard having endured an earthquake, or had hung on to a twig while the floodwaters surged beneath her. It was almost elation. And there was something else that was sustaining this mild euphoria; the access his death gave to a sense of the infinite, to the life beyond life.

The feelings were short-lived. It was the house itself that was the problem. It bore his traces everywhere. His things. Things he had touched, things he had broken. He was coming alive again, in that pathetic, useless way the dead have, lingering in all the rooms of the house, curled up in cupboards, asleep on bookshelves, tucked away in drawers. Colette quickly realized that she would have to do something about these objects if she was going to survive.

The music room was the hardest thing. The junk that sat there, under and around the piano, swollen bin bags lying beneath the piano as though that instrument had spawned a brood of blind pups, formed a solid, immovable complex of memories.

Colette had wanted to burn it all. She wanted to light a big bonfire at the end of the garden, like the bonfires they used to have every autumn, those rich conflagrations given an extra zest by the empty aerosols Janus and James would put in the fire, which exploded with a white flash as high as the oak tree and sent red sparks drifting across the neighbouring gardens. Aldous persuaded her against it, perhaps remembering the time the police were called when a neighbour's fir tree caught fire. Instead he persuaded her to let him take the things to the municipal dump.

Aldous filled the car with the bin bags and other obvious rubbish. The pornographic magazines, the drain covers, road-works signs, old bottles . . . However, they found it difficult to penetrate further into Janus's life. The music manuscripts couldn't be thrown away. Nor could the records or books. And the piano remained, a deadweight filling most of the room.

'We'll sort it out some time,' said Aldous. They consoled themselves with the thought that they'd preserved the good things about Janus. They had disposed of the offensive and the dirty. The music room was now a shrine to his achievements, his music and reading, his creativity. One day they would sort the room out properly. Redecorate it. Arrange the manuscripts properly, alphabetically, rebind the crumbling older books, put up some proper shelving.

'Perhaps we should do something about the piano . . .' said Aldous.

They were arm in arm contemplating the new spaciousness.

'No,' said Colette, 'not the piano. We have to keep it.'

'I didn't mean get rid of it. I meant restore it. Get it prop-erly tuned. Maybe even restrung and refelted. New ivories. Then there's all that broken woodwork. And the whole thing needs to be properly polished . . .'

'Yes,' said Colette, enthusiastically, 'we could make it as good as new.'

Somehow this only needed to be said. The desire, the inten-tion, was enough. It didn't have to be followed through with action. They both knew that a complete restoration of the piano would cost far more money than they'd got in their two dwin-dling bank accounts.

When Julian, fresh from Dover, played the piano one evening, as badly as ever, clumping through a Chopin waltz with all the grace of a cow doing ballet, Colette in the kitchen broke down in heavy sobs.

'I don't think your mum likes you playing the piano,' Myra said to him, having glimpsed through the kitchen door a scene that disturbed her, Colette and Aldous sitting opposite each other, clasping each others hands, Colette in uncontrollable weeping, while next door Julian hammered out the slow movement of a sonata. 'I just can't bear the thought of those beautiful hands smashed up . . .' she had heard Colette say.

Julian looked at Myra with puzzlement. As though it hadn't occurred to him that his mother could be sad about Janus.

'Why are you so insensitive?' Myra went on, 'can't you see how upset your mum is?'

'She only cries when she's been drinking,' Julian said, coldly.

Julian was still playing the piano, Myra was standing next to him. She was bored with Julian playing the piano, playing the same little phrase over and over again, with the same little mistakes, the same hesitations, repeated ad nauseam, the endless, mechanical reiteration of practice.

'I thought we were going to the pictures tonight,' she said, irritably.

'There's nothing on.'

Myra sighed.

'I might as well go home then.'

'Hang on,' said Julian, trying a phrase again, and repeating the mistake.

'I don't understand how you can play this piano yourself,' Myra went on, with sudden exasperation, 'doesn't it make you feel weird?'

'Why should it?'

'Being your brother's piano, and the fact he's just died.'

'I couldn't have played it while he was around.'

'But you're upsetting everyone. Don't you realize every time you touch a note you're reminding everyone in the house about Janus?'

Julian didn't reply.

'I'm going home,' said Myra. It was as though Julian didn't hear. Silently furious she left the music room, glimpsed again through the kitchen door the desolate figure of Colette, sobbing into her husband's hands, and made to leave the house.

Julian caught up with her at the front door.

'I've got a surprise for you,' Julian said, giggling and pulling her back.

'It had better be a good one.'

Julian took from his pocket two tickets.

'Two tickets for a concert tonight.'

Myra's face broke open with genuine delight.

'To see The Clash?'

'No. Radu Lupu playing the Debussy Preludes at The Queen Elizabeth Hall.'

The sight of Myra's face, round eyed with either bewilderment, or horror, or both, stayed with Julian for a long time.

It disappointed Colette a little when no cards arrived for Janus's birthday in January, but then he didn't get many when he was alive. In the following April, however, a parcel arrived at the house addressed to Janus. It bore a British Rail logo, and the name of Paddington Station.

'There are bound to be people who don't know he's dead,' said Aldous. The parcel was difficult to open, being thoroughly sealed with brown packing tape. In the end they had to use a bread knife to cut it open.

The first thing that Colette saw when she peered inside the parcel, was a pair of brown suede shoes.

'Oh no,' she said. It could hardly have disturbed her more had it contained her son's own head. She lifted them carefully out with one hand, examining them closely. Old slipons, the soles smooth with wear, the suede glazed at the toe caps. She put them to her face and sniffed deeply. He was there, his recognizable scent. She passed the shoes to Aldous, who quickly put them on the floor, while his wife extracted the next item.

'Why would someone send us his shoes?' Aldous said.

'There's a note here,' said Colette. It was from the station authorities advising that these items were unclaimed from locker number 342 at Paddington Station.

Colette lifted up a small, thick book. The Schirmer edition of the Bach B Minor Mass. Then a pewter tankard. The only other thing was an old crumbling box file stuffed with documents.

The box was wooden covered with a ripped veneer in imitation of seasoned leather. She recognized it vaguely as an object that had hung around the house in different rooms for years, never attracting much attention, one of those objects that becomes invisible with over-familiarity.

Inside the lid there was a small grey illustration depicting Christ holding open a Decalogue that was only numbers.

The box contained assorted documents. There were all the letters from Bill gathered together with a thick rubber band. Their scrolled italics and decoration made them seem like a wad of medieval charters. She didn't read the letters. They were almost impossible to decipher, the writing either so ornate or so clumsily written as to be illegible.

'We don't have to go through it all,' said Aldous, rather feebly, because he was as inexorably drawn to the matter in the box as she was, sitting down at the table next to his wife and picking through all the papers with her. The documents were so randomly assembled, old school reports mixed in with old wage slips, letters, official documents, photos, memos, that every layer contained a new and baffling surprise.

There was a copy of a booklet entitled 'Notes on Sickness or Industrial Injury Benefit'. A letter from Humphrey Burton, presenter of *Aquarius* on BBC2, telling him his contribution to their programme on Paganini wouldn't be needed. A school report book over which Janus had scribbled his own comments and amendments. An envelope addressed to the Senior Chief Supervisor (male) International exchange, Wren House, 15/23 Carter Lane, London EC4. A certificate of full-time education or part-time training. A till receipt from WG Peters (off-license) for fifty-two pence (7th May 1971). A negative of Janus and James standing on a grey dune before a black sea. A letter with dying lilies on it. A letter demanding £33.50 on settlement of a hire purchase agreement on a Vincent HRD motorbike. There were some drawings by Janus, on Basildon Bond notepaper, one of a corduroy jacket. A postcard of Moelfre on the back of which was written the names for organ stops

Choir
Swell
Cong
Diap
Congra
Octave

Wald
Fluto
Priest's Note
Dulcima

A sheet of blank notepaper on which was written the words

ICH BIEN DIE

A slate from the off-license

A letter written in pencil in clumsy handwriting

Dear Mr Jones
It may have slipped your memory but just before you resigned
you borrowed a pound from me. This may not be a large amount
but I would be grateful for its return.
Yours sincerely
Terry

There was a list of dialling codes

```
01  Advise Duration
02  Advise Duration and Charge
03  Try Again - answering machine
04  Attended call office
05  Coin box cancelled
06  Circuit cut off
07  Collect
08  Connect
09  Charge to Distant
010 Defer until
011 Delay
012 Deposit paid
013 Directory enquiry
014 Engaged
015 Engaged, do not interrupt
016 Engaged, refused call
017 Enquiry
018 Extension
019 Full rate
020 Fresh call booked
021 Further delay
022 Fixed time
023 Generals
024 How long holding?
025 Hasten report
026 Heard to finish
027 Incoming international subscriber dialling
028 Local
029 Local will advise
030 Looking for required person
031 Minutes
032 No lines
033 No reply
034 No tone
035 No trace of number
036 No trace of person
```

A Short History of the Parish Church of St Thomas of Canterbury at Northaw, Herts (illustrated).

A pocket diary that petered out after April.

A list of names in biro

> *Seamus*
> *Percy*
> *Wally*
> *Ron H*
> *Ron S*
> *Gordon*
> *Harold*
> *Jack*
> *Bert*
> *Fred*
> *(Sam)*
> *Martin*
> *George*
> *Harry*
> *Geoff*
> *Stan*

A vet's business card.

An advisory booklet on Enfield smoke control area.

A ticket to a recital by Paul Tortelier and Eric Heidsieck at The Queen Elizabeth Hall.

A list of books

> *Idle Days in Patagonia*
> *The Way of All Flesh*
> *The Poets' Pilgrimage, WH Davies*
> *Don Quixote*
> *Nietzsche, the Case of Richard Wagner*
> *Chopin, Man and Musician*

Chopin, The Man and his Music
Chopin

A list of books overdue from Windhover Hill library

```
Tank  Engine  Thomas                         2/6
Loxton,  Railways                           12/6
Crompton,  William  the  Rebel               5/-
Kipling,  Captain  Courageous               10/6
Blyton,  Five  go  Adventuring  Again       10/6
Virgil,  Works                              10/6
Burton,  True  Book  about  Deserts          5/-
Awdry,  Henry  the  Green  Engine            5/-
```

Your clock number has been changed to 1909

A ten pound fine from Tottenham magistrates court (Drunk and Disorderly).

A postcard of the Wolsey closet, Hampton Court Palace.

'A Day In Wales', by William Arthur Poucher

And the cherub stands before God.
All who can call at least one
Soul, Theirs join in our
Song of Praise; but any
Who cannot must creep
Tearfully away from our circle.
All creatures drink of
Joy at Nature's Breast
Just and Unjust alike
Taste of her
She gave us kisses and gifts
The fruit of the vine
A tried friend of the end
Even the worm can feel
Can feel contentment

J'aime les oeuvres de beaucup de compositeurs en effet de tous Les compositeurs mais l'un qui est Mon favouri s'apelle F. Chopin. Lependant a vrai dire, Je n'ai pas un compositeur favori, mais J'aime les ouvres do Chopin parce qu'ill composa de la musique pour le piano et le joue au piano.

Le premiere raison plus importante pourgoi Je M'amuse de jouer les ouevres de ce compositeur est parce qu'il est un compoisteur romantique, comme Robert Schuman et Francoise Liszt, et donc ses oeuvres satisfient mes sentiments romantiques.

Le piano est le moins sensitif de tous les intruments, mais ce fait aile seulemnt a clarifier le brilliance de Chopin, pour il pouvait fair chanter le piano et faire chuchoter cet instrument insensitif.

Cependant il ne avait pas ecrir de la musique pour l'otchestre et ce foublesse et le seul de Chopin. Combien de compositeurs on ecris des oeuvres commes les vingt-sept etudes de chopin. Les etudes son tres beauc et musiceaux et en mem temps ils sont tres utiles a un pianiste qui veut developer son technique

My Justices will Allow you Until the Eleventh
of January 1974 to pay your outstanding
fine in full. If not paid by that date
enforcement action will be taken.

Clerk to the Justices
L.A.C. Fish LLB (Lond)

Keep some Whitbread
in your house   31
but please return your empties

7 Gold.	8 7½
20 Berph's	24
	1- 1 ½

Dearest Scipio
I congratulate you on having attained your
fourthbirthday. I have not, as yet, arranged
to purchase a birthday gift for you, but
I would like to point out thatXXXXXXXX I
have not yet, asyet, decided on the kind
of gift I will get for you.

Love from your owner

Also in the box, near the bottom, almost the last thing they found,
was a photograph of Colette taken perhaps twenty or more years
before, a small black and white photograph of her sitting on the
beach at Llanygwynfa, perhaps that first holiday they'd spent there,
back in 1955. She was laughing in the picture, sunburnt and happy.
Colette could see that there was something written on the back
of this photograph, the writing had embossed itself in reverse on

the picture. She turned it over. There was a poem on the back

Ode to Colette (Eau de Colette)

Bless her, Whom I (Janus)
Love above all other people,
Things, Rocks, Mountains, Music,
The Blue Sky, drink, animals,
Life itself.
She is the sweetest thing
I have ever seen, felt,
Spoken to.
But she is not all that I could wish for.
But I love her with all my being.
A lovely creature.

27

'Drive me somewhere,' said Colette, after reading the poem. 'Drive me somewhere out of this city. Anywhere.'

So they got in the car and drove. They drove the usual way, a long, twisty crawl through suburban streets and shopping centres, until gradually the buildings depleted and green fields emerged. It was a pleasant spring day, a warm, low sun, a yellow sky.

Colette fell asleep in the car, so it was up to Aldous where they went. They ended up at Little Wessingham, the village they had visited many times the previous summer. Aldous parked in the small car park by the pub, two ponies staring at him over the fence, and beyond them the view across the meres to Welwyn Garden City and the Shredded Wheat factory.

Colette woke up shortly after Aldous switched the engine off. She looked around her, laughed at the ponies, then said 'Why don't we have a picnic? It's a beautiful day.'

Aldous hadn't expected his wife to be so full of energy, but she was soon out of the car and making her way towards the little village butcher's and the grocer's next door. There they bought food. There was a chicken pie in the butcher's, the last pie in the shop. When Colette asked for it she heard a mournful voice behind her say 'Well goodbye pie.'

They bought a bottle of wine in the grocer's, and some rolls, and a small fruitcake and some cheese.

Aldous assumed they were going to have the picnic in the car, but Colette wanted to walk into the woods. There was a footpath that began at a stile beside the pub. They crossed this and walked across a field of pasture, made muddy at the start by the trampling of cattle, who were by now lying down in the opposite corner of the field.

Colette walked purposefully, as though to an urgent appointment. Aldous had to rush to keep up.

It was a walk they'd done many times before. They crossed a stile on the other side of the field and followed a winding path through a wood that was vivid with bluebells. The footpath slowly descended, and eventually came out on a bank above a river. Primroses littered the slopes.

They sat on the grassy bank. The river was a thick, swiftly flowing current lush with watercress and trailing green plant life. The view beyond was of the fields rising on the other side of the valley, topped by another wood. In the nearby mulberry bush were several mossy Corrida wine bottles, left as memorials to previous picnics. It was a place they'd begun to think of as their own.

'Nothing has changed,' Aldous said, though secretly he was worried about the way the old wine bottles looked so old. In less than a year they had nearly vanished beneath dead leaves and plant stalks.

They talked about the food. They commented on how delicious the pie was, the rolls, the cheese. Interspersed with this would be comments on the beauty of their surroundings, the sprouting mallows and pennyworts by the river. Now and then Colette would suddenly say 'Look, a kingfisher!' or 'A water rat!' and point to an area of the riverbank. Aldous, however, would only catch the retreating tail disappearing into a hole, or a telltale ripple in the water. But for most of the time they were thoughtfully silent. Until Colette brought the photograph out of her pocket. Aldous was surprised to see it. He'd thought she'd left it in the box. She looked at the picture of her younger self and smiled. Then she turned it over and read again the poem on the back.

'He could have written it anytime.'

'Let me have another look,' said Aldous, reaching out a hand. Colette passed it to him.

'He could have written it years ago,' Colette went on, 'or he could have written it the day before he died.'

'We were so young then,' said Aldous. Then, 'I bet the farm's still the same. I bet nothing has changed. I bet Mr and Mrs Evans are still there, don't you think? The National Park authorities would never have given them permission to turn it into a caravan park . . .'

Colette ignored these remarks, which had been prompted by the location of the photograph – the beach at Llanygwynfa.

'It has his recent voice,' she said, 'there's something fresh about it.'

'Yes,' said Aldous, 'that's a good word. *Fresh*.'

After another period of silence, during which Colette continued to reread the poem, she gave a deep sigh and said, 'Shall we kill ourselves?'

Aldous thought carefully.

'How?'

'The river. Do you think I would make a good Ophelia?'

'Very,' said Aldous.

'We'd need something to weight our pockets with,' said Colette.

Husband and wife looked at each other. Colette was the first to weaken. She began sobbing.

'It *has* changed,' she sobbed, 'it's not pretty any more.' She folded her face into her arms, brought her knees up. 'It's not . . .'

'We'll find somewhere else,' said Aldous.

Colette dried her eyes, gasped a little, then took another swig of wine from the bottle.

Then she lay down.

'I'm going to sleep,' she said.

The sun was as high as it was ever going to be that April day. Colette went to sleep very quickly. Aldous remained awake, listening to the river, wishing he had a book with him, or something to sketch with. Looking at his wife as she reclined on the grassy bank, her long, painted hair trailing out towards the mulberries, he thought that it would make a very good subject for a drawing. The awkwardness of her pose, the way the thorny strands of the bush seemed to be reaching out for her, as if to consume her. He thought about the painting he would do. Then he lay down and tried to sleep.

But he couldn't. He didn't feel tired. He lay as if asleep, however, for perhaps an hour.

Then he felt hungry, and sat up to cut another slice of pie with his penknife. He shooed two flies off the fruitcake, then noticed that a wasp was drowning in the wine. He let it drown. They probably wouldn't drink any more wine that day.

Colette was in the same position. Aldous looked carefully to see if she was still breathing. There was a faintly discernible rise and fall to her breast. He looked at his watch. It was two o'clock. They still had most of the afternoon. Aldous ate his piece of pie, and watched some rabbits in the opposite field.

After another hour Aldous was beginning to feel uncomfortable on the grass. His back was beginning to ache. He stood up and walked around, peed beside a tree, then continued walking in and out of the trees. He clambered down to the river itself, tried to see if he could see any fish or frogs. He couldn't.

After another half an hour of this he really felt like going back to the car, but it seemed such a shame to wake Colette, she was sleeping so deeply, so peacefully. He decided to give her another half an hour. At four o'clock, if she hadn't already woken, he would wake her.

So, at ten past four, he began talking to his wife to rouse her. But talking wasn't enough. He had to shake her, gently at first, then more forcefully.

'Come on,' he said, repeatedly, 'come on. Wake up.'

She opened her eyes, smiled at him, then closed them again.

Aldous thought that his wife must have had more to drink that morning than he realized. She was blotto. Out cold. Dead to the world. It was odd, though. She'd had no more than her usual couple of tumblers of White Horse that morning, then a few swigs of wine, perhaps half a bottle. When further rousing proved useless, Aldous wondered if they should resign themselves to spending the whole afternoon on the riverbank, to allow Colette time to sleep it off.

Then it began raining. The clouds had been thickening steadily since Colette had fallen asleep. The temperature had dropped, and now little bursts of light rain were beginning to fall. Still Aldous couldn't wake his wife, or elicit from her anything more than a brief opening of the eyes, a murmured 'go away, let me sleep', or smile. The rain became heavier. Aldous had to pick his wife up (how light she was), and carry her over to the shelter of the trees. He put her down on a dry bed of golden moss, out of the rain, and looked back at the site of their picnic, a few yards away. The wine bottle was still there, and the remains of the pie in its foil dish, the bags and other paraphernalia. He was about to go and gather them up when he noticed large drips of water falling on Colette, and the volume of the rain increase from a mild hiss to a gravelly roar. He picked Colette up again and carried her through the woods.

He managed to carry her all the way back to the car, although he had to put her down and rest several times. She woke once, and laughed at him, before falling back asleep.

No one was around to see him carry his wife over the stile and across the lane to the car, or see the way she flopped and drooped when he propped her against the side of the car while he searched for the keys, though it was with great relief that he finally settled her in her seat. They were both sopping wet.

Colette didn't wake on the journey home, though by the time they pulled up outside the house, she was conscious, and looking dreamily about her.

'Are you alright now?' Aldous said, 'are you going to wake up?'

Colette nodded and she managed to walk into the house slowly, but once inside dropped into her armchair and, yawning deeply, fell asleep again.

Aldous unfolded the bed settee and made the bed for her. He carried her into the front room and laid her down to sleep there. She didn't wake up.

Colette didn't wake up the next day, not properly. She would wake enough to open her eyes, acknowledge her surroundings, drink some water, but she was asleep again within a few minutes. She said only odd words '*hallo*', '*thankyou*', '*what time is it?*'.

It wasn't until Juliette came round on the second day that Aldous was pursuaded to call a doctor.

Dr Low suggested Colette was suffering from anaemia, and prescribed iron tablets.

'I told you it was nothing to worry about,' said Aldous triumphantly to his daughter, 'just low energy. She'll soon be fine.'

Juliette wasn't convinced.

'She's not just tired,' she said, 'she looks to me like she's wasting away.'

They tried the iron tablets. They seemed to bring Colette

to consciousness for longer spells, though she wouldn't get out of bed.

Colette had trouble climbing the stairs to the toilet. She insisted that she take up residence of the front bedroom, recently vacated by Juliette and Boris, but still bearing their traces. The coordinated decoration, the screen by the old sink, the carpet.

She had been a little hurt when Juliette and Boris had announced their plan to leave, having taken out a mortgage on an upstairs flat near The Lemon Tree. After all the effort they'd spent on transforming Janus's old room it seemed rather a waste. But she was glad of the welcoming space they'd left.

'It's such a cosy room now,' said Colette sleepily, 'such a cosy room.'

When, after a week, Colette had shown no sign of improvement, Juliette called her own doctor. He recommended that she go into hospital.

So Colette spent a week in Hope Ward. The hospital took lots of blood from Colette, and conducted lots of tests. They tested so many things that they seemed to lose the thread of what they were looking for, it seemed to Aldous. Whenever he asked what was the matter with her, the doctors said they were waiting for the results of some tests, or if they'd had results, these results were dependent on other tests. After a week Aldous was no clearer on what was wrong with his wife.

In hospital she seemed to improve. She was sitting up and talking.

'They've been telling me off about my drinking,' she said, in an amused, almost pleased way. She seemed pleased that they were interested enough to notice.

Colette had stopped drinking. She had also stopped taking sleeping pills.

When she came home from hospital, she was back to her normal self for a few days, but the tiredness gradually came back. She had to retire to bed again and this time she seemed to fall into a deeper state of weakness than before.

She remained in bed for nearly a month. Because she had been in hospital, Aldous felt that the medical route had been followed to a dead end. They either had forgotten about her or had decided there was nothing that could be done.

Aldous, in the meantime, was taking on a full-time nursing role. He had to do everything in the house, the shopping, cooking, washing, cleaning as well as tending to his wife's needs. When he phoned the hospital again, they sent around a home help, a brisk woman full of unwanted advice, who offered to clean the house one afternoon a week. It was Myra who eventually persuaded Aldous to call an ambulance. She hadn't seen Colette for several weeks, and the physical changes in her appearance were more apparent to her.

'She looks as though she's turning into a reptile,' she said.

Further tests were conducted.

This time the results were more decisive. The doctors declared that Colette was suffering from cirrhosis of the liver. She was put in an intensive care unit where she was fed with drips and her body condition monitored by a little assembly of machines. One of the doctors explained that she had only ten per cent of working liver left.

'It's a funny thing about the liver,' the young doctor explained, 'it withers away bit by bit, and you don't notice because it can carry on functioning perfectly, even down to about twelve per cent. But less than that and it suddenly throws in the towel. So, in other words, you get no warning. Half your liver could be dead and you wouldn't know anything about it. I'm afraid your wife's down to the very limit of her functioning liver. Her recovery will depend on very careful control of her diet, and how she responds to treatment . . .'

After two days in hospital she suffered a stroke.

She lived for another five days.

During this time Aldous and the children visited frequently. Colette didn't appear to comprehend anything that was said to her. When she spoke it was to utter incomprehensible, or seemingly meaningless, phrases.

'Some terrible things have come out of the Matto Grosso,' she said, quietly, as she twisted and turned. She appeared restlessly energetic in her bed, which had bars around it to stop her falling out. She constantly writhed in her white sheets, and her red hair was large, glossy and ruffled. She didn't appear to be in any discomfort, just restless. Her hands had been bandaged to stop her scratching her face. She constantly bit at these bandages in an attempt to remove them. Over the days she talked more, though her words still contained no sense. She seemed to recognize Aldous, and would frequently hug him.

'Orpheus and his lute,' she said. They were the last words Aldous heard her say. She suffered a second stroke that night, and died.

When the phone call came, Aldous felt a curious sensation of strength. Of emboldenment. He insisted on viewing her body. The children went as well. He was glad they did because she looked beautiful, and in her motionlessness, peaceful. It was as though she was relishing stillness, in the way that athletes do when they've finished running, or a mountaineer when he reaches the summit and lays himself flat to bask in thin sunshine.

28

The very day after the funeral, Aldous had to drive James and Marilyn to Heathrow for the flight to Caracas that had been booked weeks before. Having recovered from the wounds of their earlier expedition they were to spend eighteen months doing fieldwork in the Venezuelan rainforest. The general feeling was that the timing was fortunate. It meant Colette's death could not be dwelt on too much. It meant that everybody had to be focused on continuing life. The whole family made it to the airport to see James and Marilyn off. They didn't have suitcases, they had rucksacks, one rucksack each, which contained all they needed for a year and a half. Aldous suddenly felt very envious of James, with his whole life contained in a rucksack, whereas he had a whole house to lug around for the rest of his life. The casualness with which young people travelled these days continued to astonish him. At his son's age Aldous would no more have thought of travelling into the South American jungle than he would have of camping on the moon. The only people who ever went there were either monocled missionaries or explorers in pith helmets. And yet James was wearing nothing more than a faded purple T-shirt and a floppy pair of jeans.

Later he watched the couple as they were consumed, first by the passport control, then by low cloud as their plane climbed. The cloud was of such density Aldous was almost expecting a *pluff* sound as the plane entered. And then they were gone. Juliette, Boris, Myra, Julian and Aldous stood in a line on top of a breezy multi-storey car park watching an empty patch of grey weather. Already another plane was lined up on the runway to follow it.

It was just Aldous and Myra who came to see Julian off at Victoria Coach Station, only a week later. He had taken a job as a deck cadet aboard the Sealink ferry *Vespasian* which plied the channel between Dover and Ostende. He would be based at Ostende. Aldous was surprised at how little Myra seemed affected by the occasion. He'd expected a tearful, *Brief Encounter*-style parting, but instead Myra seemed rather bored. Once Julian had boarded his Dover-bound National Express coach she stood alongside, and they mouthed things through the window at each other, failing completely in their lip-reading, and giving up. Then Julian vanished in a blue cloud of carbon monoxide.

At home, what had seemed fortuitous timing in these distracting departures, now appeared almost crass in their swift following-on from Colette's death. It made Aldous feel as though he had been ignored in the plans for a mass breakout, and was left pondering over the open trapdoor in the floor. He had a sense of being left behind, of being the only object in his house. He was now the only living thing it contained.

Aldous convinced himself that all his life he'd wanted nothing more than to be alone. That solitude was his preferred state, his ideal condition. How happy Adam should have been, he thought, to have been sole occupier of paradise, to have his own garden to wander in. For the first time in his life Aldous realized he could do anything he wanted without having to consider the ways and desires of other people. So, a week after Julian had left for Belgium, he decided to take a train to Oxford, for no other reason than the fact that he'd never really looked properly around the place, and that he'd always wanted to. The train took little more than half an hour and Aldous walked into the city with great enthusiasm. He bought a little guide book and wandered among the carved quadrangles. He felt a little like Jude Fawley in *Jude the Obscure*. The towering architecture began to take on something of the appearance of battlements and fortresses. In a museum he came across a blackboard that had been used by Einstein in one of his lectures. Someone had thought to frame it and protect the ephemeral chalk markings with glass. The marks on the board were little white worms dangling in empty space. Incomprehensible equations. Aldous read that the lecture had been concerned with the nature of time.

Afterwards Aldous sat in a small park of ornamental willows

and wept. He realized he now had more time than he knew what to do with. More time than he could ever want. He was healthy. He was sixty-seven. He had no job, no wife, no children, no mortgage, no pets, and perhaps a good ten years of active life left, perhaps fifteen, perhaps twenty. Those years spread before him with a vastness such as the early palaeontologists must have recognized when they first realized that the Earth was much older than the Bible had told them. Not a few thousand years old, but five billion years. What had the world been doing all that time, what species had risen and fallen, what ages had passed? And in the future, the pathway of time stretched further than the human race could ever walk. More time than humanity could ever fill. No matter how long the human race lasted, it would only ever be a flicker in the life of the universe, a twitch of an eyelid.

When he got home he found a letter for him on the mat. It was his new bus pass. A free bus pass. The GLC had recently announced free travel on London Transport for all old age pensioners.

At first Aldous used the bus pass as a means of escape. He could ride the red buses all day and not have to sit at home in an empty house. He could spend a whole day on the Circle Line going round and round and round. He descended the escalators and travelled the tunnels, he rode the red buses as far as they would take him, to all the termini, to all the depots. He wanted to feel, as he did so, a part of the metabolism of the living organism that was a great city, whose streets and museums and galleries, whose pubs and cafés and theatres and lights and colours and people were all waiting to be explored.

But it didn't work. Somehow the city would not yield itself to him. Like the parapets and battlements of Oxford, it seemed shut against him. Closed, withdrawn, impenetrable.

Janus Brian kept coming to Aldous's mind. He had watched a man go through the process of losing his wife, of becoming a widower. He had watched him crumble and disintegrate. But Aldous was determined he wasn't going to be like that. He wasn't going to go down that road. But at the same time Aldous found himself wandering down that very same road – Leicester

Avenue, where Janus Brian had lived before moving to High Wycombe, the cul-de-sac where no one ever walked unless they lived there, or knew someone who lived there. Aldous walked the gently sloping road, deepening between houses, the bright front gardens that became steeper and steeper, until the houses were high in the air, like castles on mounds, behind stepped front gardens brilliant with lavender.

Outside Janus Brian's old house he stopped. Structurally it was the same building, the same garden, yet in every other way it was different. The front garden had been turned over, the old honesty bush had gone, and the carefully constructed rockery had been dismantled. Rockeries were old fashioned now. The new garden was full of small pine trees. The window frames of the house had been replaced. There seemed to be a new roof, Aldous couldn't be sure. But there was a general sense of smartness about it. There were lavish-looking curtains in the window tied up in fussy bunches. Upstairs the small front bedroom displayed evidence of children. A mobile hanging, a teddy bear propped on a sill and watching crookedly through the glass. They were living properly, the new people in this house. They knew what they were supposed to do. They knew what to expect and what was expected of them.

And so did everyone else in Leicester Avenue. The road was a series of repeated statements, colourfully expressed in flowers and paintwork, in cars and stained glass, with only minor variations. Hardly variations at all. If he had any sense, Aldous thought, he should go home now and make the same statement, tear down that confusion in his front garden, fell the acacia, slaughter the pyracantha, plant a lavender bush and some ornamental pines.

He walked all afternoon through the streets that contained these gardens, more gardens than he could have dreamt of. Has no one realized it before, he thought, that if all the gardens of London could be fitted together and their fences removed we would have more garden than buildings. Roses and tulips and saxifrage and lobelias and spindthrift and monkey-puzzle trees, a whole county of them. More flowers than we have a right to enjoy. More trees. More lawns. Another street of gardens. Another avenue of lavender. All on display. All saying we are here and we are doing fine. Aldous's mind was drifting into an immense garden that was ranged before him in a hostile manner. He swung his fists at a laurel bush, he punched a camellia in its bright pink face. He kicked the heads off roses and fell into a tulip bed where he rolled in the flowers, kicking like a baby.

'It's Mr Jones isn't it?'

Aldous looked up and saw someone he vaguely recognized. A bulky, unshaven man wearing a sort of sailor's cap.

'That's not your garden is it?'

Looking around him, Aldous slowly became aware of his situation. He saw he was sitting in the flower-bed of a front garden. He looked at his hands, they were fists gripping bunches of tulips. Now he realized what that creaking, popping sound had been. The stretching and snapping of tulip stalks.

'Bit hungry are we?'

The fat man was looking faintly amused. Then Aldous noticed the taste in his mouth. A bitter, sharp taste. There was something in there. He dropped the tulips from one of his fists and brought the hand to his mouth. There was something long and floppy protruding. He gently extracted it, carefully, so as not to dislodge his palate which was slightly entangled with it. He saw the thing. A tulip with a long stalk. A shiny strand of Aldous's own saliva clung to it.

'Good job no one's in,' the fat man said. Aldous looked over his shoulder and saw a house he didn't recognize. One of the tall, older houses with a wooden front veranda that you found in older parts of the district. There was a grey stillness in the windows indicating the house was empty. Aldous could not remember how he had entered this garden.

'How's the bath? Holding up?'

Again Aldous looked around him, as if trying once and for all to get the hang of his situation, sitting squarely on his bottom, his legs stretched out straight before him, a havoc of torn and tangled flowers all around him, green tulip-stalk juice dribbling down his chin, the shreds of tulips in one fist. Yes, it was rather like having a bath. What a clever thing to think – that he was having a bath. Aldous looked closer at the man. He was a dirty man. Grimy, greasy, like a coal miner, which made the white paper bag he was holding in the crook of his arm seem all the whiter. Eventually Aldous placed him. It was Butcher, the plumber who had installed their new bathroom.

'Yes. The bath is very good. And the toilet as well.'

'They're very good toilets those ones. Very good toilets.' The plumber spoke as one who knew all the makes and models of toilets on the market. He made as if about to leave, then hesitated and said, 'My place is just around the corner. Do you want to come round for a cup of tea?'

'Yes,' said Aldous, clambering out of the flower-bed. His knees and bottom felt damp. He staggered a little after straightening up, and as he made his way out of the front garden back onto the pavement, he nearly fell over. The bulk of Butcher seemed all the greater up close, and being out of doors he was made even bulkier by the great black donkey jacket he was wearing, the collar turned up. When on the pavement Aldous could see that he had two Dobermans, their two leads bunched in his one fist. Minnehaha and Hiawatha. The dogs were sleek sharks, glossy and tapered, but somehow calm and respectful.

'I've been meaning to call round for ages,' Butcher said as they walked along side by side. Aldous had difficulty keeping a steady course, so that he kept crashing softly into Butcher, who absorbed these impacts easily. Such a solid man. 'It's been up and working for months now, but I only finished it properly the other week.'

Aldous had no idea where he was. He didn't recognize the street they were in, or the busy road they turned into at the end. Butcher lead Aldous over a zebra crossing, then down a side street, slightly shabbier.

'I'm retired now, like you. So I've had plenty of time. I've spent many happy hours . . .'

They were at the plumber's house. The building itself was one of the old houses that had survived the influx of suburban building, an elegant rural villa like many that had once dotted the pastoral countryside. Still Victorian, but going back deeper into the nineteenth century than any of the surrounding structures. It stood apart from the uniformity of the streets. The front garden was an undergrowth of brambles and shrubby sycamores.

'I cut the bastards back every now and then but they just keep coming up.'

Butcher rattled his keys and they entered the house.

'I bought this place because of the land. It used to be owned by the lord of the manor hereabouts, when this was all farms . . .'

They moved through the hall and then a room heaped with junk that stank of socks and urine, to a conservatory area at the back where a row of white enamel lavatories stood with an inverted row on top of them.

'There you are. What do you think?'

Butcher gestured at the view beyond the glass. The dogs pawed at the door to be let out. It was an enormous garden. Exceptionally huge. Not even the chief executives who lived in Parsons Lane had gardens this big, Aldous thought. To the left was a large shed with a chimney which looked remarkably like, and in fact was, an old blacksmith's workshop. Then there was a tangle of metalworking paraphernalia, heaps of glittering swarf in long curlicues, rusted bits of machinery, half-made wrought iron gates, fences, pergolas. The main part of the garden was an open space bordered by a high fence and a fringe of stately ash trees, and seemed to be landscaped for a miniature railway whose tracks cut a snaking course around the garden. Aldous remembered Butcher talking many times about his passion for model railways, though he had had no idea it had been on such a grand scale. There were tunnels, bridges, and an engine shed to the right. The whole arrangement was focused on a large pond in the centre of the garden, almost a lake, prettily decked with rushes and lily pads. There was so much in Butcher's garden that it was a while before his attention came to rest on the thing in the centre of the pond. A tall structure that Aldous had at first taken for a dead tree, until he saw that it was intricately made of bronze, and consisted of a flock of doves, interlinked and frozen in their moment of rising from the ground and soaring into the air.

'Doesn't look bad does it? Nearly three years' work there. A hundred and fifty separately moulded parts welded together. Just about the biggest thing I've ever made . . .'

Aldous had become a statue himself, open-mouthed.

'Wait till you see it in water,' said Butcher. He put down the white paper bag on the table and ambled back into the main part of the house. Aldous glanced down at the white bag, saw that it contained four iced finger buns. There was some distant rummaging from the back of the house, then a muffled cry of 'Here we go.' Aldous looked out of the window. For several seconds, nothing. Then, at the very top of the fountain eight feet in the air, a little wobbling bulge of water. It then broke and began sliding across the backs of the bronze doves, falling off the wing tips of one dove onto the backs of others, then onto others and so on as the water spread throughout the structure, weaving in and out of the wings, falling in daintily straight lines, just as Aldous had hoped it would, a great web of falling water through which the doves appeared to be soaring.

'That is what I call a decent fountain,' said Butcher as he unlocked the back door for the dogs. They shot into the garden like two fighter jets, snapping at the air and twisting, then peeing emphatically against one of the trees. 'Come on. Let's have a look.'

They passed through into the garden. The ground was barren, grassless. The fountain made a cooing noise.

'How did you . . .' Aldous began.

'Your wife,' said Butcher, 'just after I finished the bathroom, she came round and asked me if I wanted to have a go at doing your statue. I'd already said I'd like to, if you remember. So I thought I'd have a go. I came round to pick the model up one day when you were out. I think she told you she'd posted it off to Durham, or wherever those stingy monks were. She wanted it kept secret. A surprise for you . . .'

'She's . . .'

'I know,' Butcher said hastily, 'I read it in the paper. I'd say welcome to the club, but mine's still alive, though she ran off with an electrician ten years ago. Perhaps that's worse. It's a bad business whatever way you look at it. I read about Janus as well. Children are cruel, I've always said it. You've got to try and make them happy, though – I've learnt that from my railway. I made this for me, this railway, being a big kid myself, but once word got round that I'd got a railway in my back garden the kids were coming from miles around, hanging over the back fence to get a look. I tried telling them to piss off at first but they just kept coming back. I tried putting higher fences up, but they'd watch through the cracks. Then I thought – how can I sit on one of my trains, a grown man, riding round and round my garden, knowing that dozens of kids are watching me, wishing they could have a go? In the end I had to let them in and give them a turn. So now every Sunday this garden's full of screaming kids and me chugging around. It's the only way I can cope with them. They're not bad once you let them in. They're still cruel little bastards, but they're not that bad. When they saw the fountain working for the first time they were bloody amazed. They thought it was even better than the trains, for a while.'

Butcher turned to Aldous, as though struck by a sudden idea.

'Why don't I get them going for you?'

'What?'

'One of my trains. It only takes about half an hour to steam them up. I'll show you. You can only really appreciate your fountain when you see it from the train.'

Aldous wasn't left with any option as Butcher made his way over to the engine shed, although he did call over his shoulder, 'Not in a hurry are you?'

No. Aldous wasn't in a hurry. While one of the engines was firing up, Butcher made them tea. He brought out a little table and a pair of chairs, and he put his iced buns on a plate, and they ate iced buns and drank strong, sweet tea, while one of Butcher's home-built steam engines produced a gradually increasing hissing sound from inside its shed.

When the hissing had built to a crescendo and wisps of steam were coming from the shed, Butcher disappeared into it. There was a sound of metal levers shifting, a change in the volume of the hissing. It suddenly became muffled. Then there came a puff. Not the toy-train, pipsqueak puff Aldous had been expecting, but a real, deep-throated puff, a serious, grown-up puff as from a real steam engine. Then another, then another, and a cloud of white steam suddenly billowed out of the shed, and then from within this cloud emerged a steam engine, about the size and bulk of a large sheep, though longer, a beautifully made model, in red, of an express shielder of the sort that worked the railways in the last days of steam. And on the tender sat Butcher, his hat now suddenly making perfect sense, it was an engine driver's hat. Aldous was dumbfounded by the craftsmanship of the thing, the perfect rendering of its detail, the wheels, the pistons, the little brass whistle.

'You didn't make this all yourself,' he said as he walked up to the now stationary engine.

'My life's work,' said Butcher, proudly slapping the cabin roof, which resounded with a reassuringly solid noise of ringing metal. 'Climb aboard.'

Aldous climbed onto the seat behind Butcher. There was only just room, and behind him was a stack of coal.

And then they were off. Aldous felt the surge of machinery beneath him, the pull of steam power, boiling water, fossil smoke, that old familiar smell he hadn't smelt properly for years, and the vibration and click click click of the rails beneath. They journeyed the circuit of Butcher's garden, building up to a decent speed, a fast walking pace, then faster than walking, enough to conjure a breeze around Aldous's ears, as they journeyed around the lake, the dove fountain sparkling, then through a tunnel, over a bridge, through a cutting, past the lake again, the doves still trickling . . .

The noise was such that Aldous couldn't hear what Butcher was saying to him as he called over his shoulder, but he could see what he meant. He was pointing to a hanging lever in the cabin, gesturing that Aldous should pull it. So Aldous, knowing what it was, reached forward as far as he could. A triumphant shriek of steam burst into the air. Just like a real train whistle. Butcher laughed. Aldous laughed. They were coming up to the tunnel again. Butcher gestured that Aldous should give it another go, but Aldous didn't need asking. He pulled the lever again and again sending piercing shrieks echoing around the trees above them, and each shriek accompanied by a plume of white steam, as they rushed round the bend, whooooosh!

BY GERARD WOODWARD
ALSO AVAILABLE IN VINTAGE

☐ **August**   0099286920   £6.99